# A TOAST TO LOVE

Jeff poured another inch of champagne into Meg's glass. "Let's see if the moon is still up."

They strolled arm in arm to the porthole. The moon had disappeared behind a bank of dark clouds. The deck was semi-illuminated by the ship's lights streaming onto it from the lounge and dining room directly above. They could hear the waves rushing against the sides of the ship with powerful regularity. The darkness and the rocking somehow hinted of danger, and the effect on both of them was like a powerful aphrodisiac.

Jeff touched her glass lightly after he had poured out the final drops of champagne. "To my darling Meg," he said. "I love you. I will love you forever." They finished their drinks and spontaneously touched glasses again. Then he took the goblet from her hand and placed it on the dresser. "Come," he said simply.

He was even gentler and more tender than he had been the last time they had been together. Tonight he was determined that everything should be perfect. He sensed a difference in Meg as well. The passionate abandon he had glimpsed in her seemed close to the surface. She responded to his kiss eagerly, willingly. Meg felt that she was on an island where nothing existed except Jeff—an island where there was no horizon, no sky, no sea. Only Jeff was real.

We will send you a free catalog on request. Any titles not in your local bookstore can be purchased by mail. Send the price of the book plus 50¢ shipping charge to Tiara Books, P.O. Box 270, Norwalk, Conencticut 06852.

Titles currently in print are available for industrial and sales promotion at reduced rates. Address inquiries to Nordon Publications, Inc., Two Park Avenue, New York, New York 10016, Attention: Premium Sales Department.

*A Tiara Novel*

---

# LOVE WILL REMEMBER

*Bella Jarrett*

TIARA BOOKS     NEW YORK CITY

**For Joe Hourigan 1938-1980**

A TIARA Novel

Published by

Nordon Publications, Inc.
Two Park Avenue
New York, N.Y. 10016

Copyright © 1981, by Bella Jarrett

All rights reserved
Printed in the United States

# Chapter 1

Jeff McAllister winced as the girl, slipping through the classroom's cramped row of chairs, came down on his toe with the heel of her shoe. Damn these people who showed up late for the first class! She turned and began to whisper a profuse apology, the distress on her face almost equaling his own. He stared at her, discomfort forgotten. She had one of the most arresting faces he had ever seen. Long black hair pulled back severely with a slim black ribbon; face thin and narrow except for high, wide cheekbones; lips blooming into unexpected fullness; thick-lashed, liquid brown eyes, now startled into hugeness.

Meg Gardner, mumbling the apology, averted her eyes from the face of the young man she had offended. If she had dared look at him, she would have seen a sandy-haired man with pale brown freckles scattered over his nose, and quite compelling hazel eyes under thick straight brows. She was continuing down the row when one of the other students, rising to make room for her passage, inadvertently clipped the corner of her loose-leaf notebook, sending papers flying over that section of the room like errant birds set loose from a cage.

By now the class was in something of an uproar. Several students leapt to their feet to help retrieve the wafting papers, and others attempted to stifle clandestine laughter. The instructor, Dr. Laglen, who had little patience with disruption of any kind, pounded the flat of his hand on the desk.

"Please, ladies and gentlemen. Let's have order. This, after all, is not a kindergarten—it is an intermediate course in photography designed for adults. Please act your ages and I will attempt to go on with my lecture." He peered over his Benjamin Franklin half-glasses, unamused. "You are Miss—?"

"Gardner. Meg Gardner. I'm sorry I caused such a commotion. I had to work late, that's why I'm late to class. I'm sorry." Her voice was low and breathless.

As she spoke, Jeff examined her more closely. If she wore makeup, it was undiscernible. He got the impression by the manner in which she spoke, of quick intelligence masked by shyness. Her voice, he thought, was Southern, although perhaps he got that impression only from its softness.

She was very different from the other women in the room, whom he had been idly observing before the class began. Most seemed to be widows or retirées looking for a new hobby to fill their hours, or bored housewives hoping to make new social contacts, or overweight college girls eager to take an additional course to fill an inactive social life. Photography, he supposed, was one of those subjects almost everyone wanted to dabble in. A pursuit not meant to be studied (at least by most in the class) as a serious art, but more substantial than basket-weaving or numbers-painting.

The professor continued droning, first about the parts of a camera, then about the advantages of setting up one's own darkroom. Since Jeff was already using a part of his dressing room as a darkroom, he did not feel compelled to confine his attention to Dr. Laglen's words. He studied Meg Gardner's shoes and the hem of her skirt—the only scraps of her person visible to him at the moment.

The shoes were mid-heeled, black, functional. The legs were sheathed in opaque black stockings, which made it impossible to define their shape. The triangle of skirt was nondescript black-and-white wool, or a synthetic made to resemble wool. There was no hint of "New York chic" in her dress—no designer jeans, no signature scarf, no fifty-dollar sneakers. Her wardrobe seemed to have been chosen on a purely utilitarian basis.

When class was over, Jeff watched as she methodically assembled her papers, rearranged the sheaf of notes and replaced the colored pencils in her well-worn leather shoulder bag. He made a pretense of gathering his papers slowly, imitating her painstaking movements. She closed her notebook; a fraction of a second later he followed suit. The room was empty now except for a couple of middle-aged women who were strolling to the door, chatting amiably.

Meg made her way up the row toward him, then stopped in confusion as she realized who he was. "Oh! You know, I'm real sorry about mauling your foot. . . ."

He raised both hands in protest. "Don't worry about it—my lawyer will be in touch."

Her eyes widened; her expression reminded him of a startled bird poised for flight. He immediately regretted his attempt at a joke.

"Wait a minute!" He began to laugh. "You didn't take that remark seriously, did you? Only kidding. I'm Jeff McAllister."

"Meg—Meg Gardner." She looked into his eyes for only a fraction of a second, then quickly averted her gaze.

"Well, since you apparently need to be convinced you're not going to be slapped with a lawsuit, how about letting me do the convincing over a cup of coffee?"

Reluctantly, she brought her eyes to again meet his. His expression was so open, his eagerness for her to accept his invitation so transparent that she could not hide a faint smile. The movement of her head was so slight he could not even be sure it was acquiescence, but he decided to take it as such. "Well, shall we go before they lock us in for the night?"

Her smile broadened. "Yes, okay. Oh, wait a minute." She returned her camera to its case and carefully snapped it shut. "There. This snap has gotten very stubborn lately. Can't let anything happen to Petunia. She's the love of my life."

He was mildly surprised. The camera was at least seven or eight years old and appeared to have led a fast, hard life. Self-consciously he moved the strap of his expensive Hasselblad to the shoulder away from her.

As he held open the outside door, a gust of October wind sliced into the corridor. "Whoo! B-R-R!" He spelled the letters.

"What did you say?" she asked uncertainly.

"B-R-R. Somebody said it that way once on a television show or something. Instead of 'brrrr,' "—he rolled his lips—"they mistakenly read the letters: B-R-R."

She laughed belatedly, as if embarrassed he had had to explain the joke. Sensing this, Jeff said quickly, "Totally silly. I don't know why it stuck in my mind. But listen, it's damn cold. Why don't we make it Irish coffee?"

He took her hand, feeling the slim fingers with a sudden shock of pleasure, and led her running down the street to McBurney's, a narrow, smoky bar that had, many thought, the best Irish coffee and hamburgers in Greenwich Village.

As they entered, he raised one finger in greeting to his old friend, Louie, the bartender. Meg took off her coat and glanced around.

"Don't worry," he assured her. "It's mainly students and painters who come here. They're scruffy but harmless."

"No, no, it wasn't that. I was just looking at that beautiful leaded glass behind the bar."

"Yeah. This place got the glass and that mahogany bar when they tore down Charies Five a few years ago. It used to be a damn nice restaurant—the showplace of the Village. But when the old man died, they demolished it and auctioned off the fixtures. Sometime I'll have to take you to Bedford's—they got the Tiffany lamps."

"You live in the Village then?"

"No. Uptown. This is just my adopted neck of the woods."

The waiter brought glass mugs of steaming Irish coffee. After her first sip of the foamy brew, Meg asked, "What's in this delicious stuff?"

Was she serious? "Irish Whiskey, coffee and whipped cream. Maybe a shot of cinnamon, depending on where you have it. But I could have done without the whipped cream—Louie should have remembered my idiosyncrasy."

She looked at him unbelievingly. "You don't want it? Hand it over."

He ladled the snowy mound into her mug. "Laglen gives me the impression he's going to be a Teutonic prig. What do you think?"

She shrugged. "A little early to tell, I guess. I was so thrown when I came in late and caused all that confusion that I had trouble concentrating. Did I miss anything important?"

"Nuttin'," he answered, using the New York accent jokingly.

She smiled. The difference it made to her face was amazing. When her features were in repose, she seemed almost wistful, but her smile, revealing short, even, white teeth, lit her whole countenance and gave her a look of childish delight. He could not help but contrast her smile to Jessica's. Jessica's smile was brittle and fleeting.

Meg toyed speculatively with her spoon. "Did you notice that nervous tic Dr. Laglen has? I wonder if it's psychosomatic."

"Wait a minute. Are you one of those nuts who's going to try to analyze what I *really* mean everytime I say hello?"

She laughed outright, a surprisingly gutsy laugh. "No, no. Just trying to sharpen my powers of observation. After all, isn't that part of being a photographer?"

"Yep. You know, I saw something the other day that would have made a wonderful photograph. One of those shopping bag ladies was on a corner with a huge cart piled to the sky with rags and old newspapers and anything else she could lay her hands on—a terrible-looking mess. And hanging on the side of the cart was a grocery bag that read 'It pays to shop well.' "

"Did you get it?"

"Get what?"

"The picture."

"No, dammit. Didn't have my camera with me."

She slid one forefinger against the other in the traditional gesture of shame. "That's the first commandment. Don't be caught with your camera down."

The almost off-color remark surprised him again. "Your point is well taken, Madame. I consider myself chastised."

"What do you do? For a living, I mean?" Her voice was ingenuously curious.

"Me? Oh, I'm one of your button-down stockbroker

types, I'm afraid."

"Gee." She pillowed her chin in the palm of one hand and eyed him earnestly. "I'd never have guessed. I'd have thought you were the black sheep of a rich, overprotective family. Black sheep in their eyes, I mean." she added.

"No." A small sigh escaped his lips. "I've never had the courage to be a black sheep. My dad founded the firm I'm with and I guess I always knew he expected me to follow in his footsteps."

"Oh. Button-down on the outside, a rebel on the inside?"

He was again surprised. Not many people picked up on the sense of gnawing dissatisfaction and guilt that lay under his conventional exterior. He bit his lip, pushed his introspection aside and brought his attention back to Meg.

"And you?" he asked. "Tell me about you. First, you're from the South, right? That much I can guess."

"Yes. A tiny little town—hardly more than a wide place in the road. Martinsville, Georgia."

"Your parents still there?"

"No. I was brought up by two aunts." She answered his unspoken question. "My father died when I was five and my mother shortly after that."

"I'm sorry."

There was a pause before Jeff continued. "And how do you make your bread? I mean what sort of work do you do?" Anyone could see she was not the type who idled away her days in shopping and lunching.

"I'm a social worker."

"God, I admire you. That must be tough at times."

"Yes." Her answer was straightforward, but there was a definite period at the end of the word and he did not pursue it further. Her manner of speaking was quite different from that of the other women he knew. It was blunt, direct and unadorned by superficial adjectives. He could not imagine, for instance, Meg describing something as "smashing," "terrific," "chic," "in" or "wow." She made simple, declarative sentences and let them speak for themselves. He guessed instinctively that she was bedrock honest.

While they had a second drink she told him an anecdote about having witnessed a minor traffic accident. She played all the parts with skill and animation—the furious cab driver, the obtuse, paranoid motorist, the policeman trying to separate the "perpetrator" from the complainant." Jeff laughed heartily. He was not used to women with a sense of humor. Jessica and her Radcliffe friends were neither interested in nor capable of wit.

It was after midnight when they left the small saloon. "Let's get a cab," he said.

"Oh no, don't bother. I just live a few blocks east. I can easily walk it, as a matter of fact. That's one of the reasons I signed up at the New School—its location."

"Then I'll walk you home. Cabs seem to have become extinct anyway."

They started walking the long crosstown blocks. After three or four of them, the carefully tended, postagestamp lawns and neat, wrought-iron fences gave way to sidewalk garbage cans and abandoned cars. Jeff realized they were in the middle of the not-so-fashionable Lower East Side.

"You would have walked this alone?" he asked in amazement.

Her look was almost defiant. "I know everybody says it's dangerous, but it's like a small town to me. I know all the storekeepers around here."

He shook his head hopelessly. "You need a guardian. All these storekeepers you know—where do you think they are at one o'clock in the morning?" He wanted to continue the lecture, but stopped himself for fear of sounding like a paternal scold.

He entered the building with her; he stood facing her at the doorway to her apartment. She held her keys but made no move to use them.

"Go ahead, open the door, Meg. I'm not going to come in. Just want to be sure you're safe inside."

She nodded and without speaking opened the door. He saw a glimpse of a book-lined room with lots of plants and little furniture, but homey nonetheless—a room devoid of trendiness or pretence.

He couldn't imagine why he wasn't making a serious pass at her . . . she was an extremely beautiful and appealing young woman. Maybe her appeal was partly naif. Perhaps that accounted for the strange protectiveness he felt.

"Goodnight, Meg." He put his hands under her elbows and brushed her lips very lightly with his. He released her abruptly, for at the moment of contact, he had felt her body immediately stiffen.

## Chapter 2

On the way home to his place in the East Seventies, Jeff could not quite analyze the strange effect Meg had had on him. She had certainly put him in a peculiar mood. For an hour or more, in the coziness of the bar, she had been delightfully lighthearted and witty, dropping completely her earlier shyness and reserve.

Then, when he had taken her home, the curtain of aloofness had fallen again. Jeff McAllister was not used to being rejected. But no, it had not even been rejection —simply a certain mercurial elusiveness. He thought again of a wild bird in the instant before it takes wing— a quality of being warily poised for flight. He had the impression she had not been in New York long. Perhaps it was the tentativeness with which she had viewed the raffish bar, or her hesitancy when he invited her for coffee. She didn't seem to have yet absorbed the aggressiveness (perhaps necessary for survival) of most New York career women.

He heard his phone ringing as he opened the door. He did not want to answer. Meg was in his mind like a challenging puzzle. He wanted to stay with her mentally, to concentrate on the solution.

"Hello?"

"Jeff! Where have you been? I've been trying to reach you all evening."

Jeff tried to restrain his impatience. "Jessica, I told you I was starting photography class tonight."

"Oh. Yes. Well, it must have been exceedingly

engrossing to have lasted till two o'clock in the morning."

Jeff sighed. His father and everyone else had assumed he would one day marry Jessica, melding the fortunes of the two families, but Jeff had never been able to bring himself to make it official, in spite of Jessica's occasional broad hints. On the other hand, out of the guilt he felt toward his dead father, he hadn't broken it off either.

"Look, Jessica," he voice was weary. "Some of us in the class went out for a drink afterward, that's all."

She sensed his resentment and her voice softened at once. "I didn't mean to pry, darling. It's just that I remembered tonight was your first class and I was eager to know how it went."

He knew she remembered no such thing. But never mind. "It was . . . interesting."

"You don't sound very enthusiastic."

"No, I think it'll be very good—the first class is always concerned more or less with preliminaries. Look, Jessica, is there any particular reason you called? I don't mean to be rude but I have an early day tomorrow and—"

"If you have such an early day tomorrow," her voice was silken, "I should think you might have made it an early night tonight."

"Touché. Okay, I'll talk to you tomorrow."

"No, wait, Jeff. I wanted to remind you we're to go to the Benningtons' for dinner Thursday night."

He snapped his fingers, remembering the date had been made several weeks ago, long before he had signed up for the photography class. Now, the idea of spending the evening with a group of Jessica's Radcliffe friends and their husbands seemed particularly uninspiring.

"That's the night of the second class. I hate to cut so early in the game."

"But you know how long this dinner has been in the works, Jeff. Sandy will be really teed off if you're not there. And Frannie's husband—the executive vice-president or whatever at General Brands—you wanted to meet him, didn't you?"

More accurately, Jeff's boss wanted him to meet the man from General Brands. He thought a congenial social setting might induce Mr. General Brands to bring some business their way. Now the prospect seemed distasteful. Jeff did not like the idea of a social evening being colored with trying to make business points.

"I don't know, Jessica. Let me get back to you early tomorrow, how's that?"

"How's that?" She repeated the words disdainfully. "I thought a social commitment was a social commitment. But if you prefer not to go, I can easily find another escort. I'll make your apologies, so you needn't even bother to call Sandy. Goodnight, Jeff." She hung up the phone quietly, though he knew she was in a raging fury.

He sat down and picked up the latest *Forbes*. There was an article in it by a friend of his father's that he wanted to read. But the words made no sense to him. He found himself remembering instead the look in Meg's eyes as he tried to kiss her goodnight.

"Good God!" He threw the magazine across the room in disgust. He had not been haunted like this by a female since he was a high-school sophomore. It was ridiculous.

After Jeff left her at the door, Meg undressed absentmindedly and crawled into bed. Jeff McAllister was so attractive that he frightened her. Yet she sensed an odd vulnerability in him too. It was more than an hour before she fell asleep, and when she did, her rest was shattered by a dream that seemed endless. Meg moaned and tossed as she relived one of the most vivid and horrifying moments of her childhood.

Meg and her two aunts were visiting the Pittmans one Sunday afternoon when she was eight. The Pittmans had three sons of assorted ages, the oldest of whom, Frank, was a precocious and malicious twelve. Meg and the two younger sons spent a good part of the sultry August afternoon playing hopscotch on the sidewalk in front of the Pittman home. The adult Pittmans and their visitors were gathered on the porch in rockers and gliders, sipping iced tea and talking desultorily about the merciless heat, the peach crop, and the new family who had moved into the neighborhood the previous week.

Meg had to go to the bathroom, but since one did not discuss bodily functions with members of the opposite sex, she entered the house under the pretext of getting a glass of water. The screen door slammed hollowly behind her. The whole house was silent; it too seemed to be in the grip of the midsummer doldrums. Starting up the stairs, she thought she saw a shadow move on the landing, but perhaps coming into the dim interior from the white-hot sunlight made her eyes play tricks on her. She entered the bathroom and closed the door noiselessly. From outside the high, open bathroom window, she could hear the two younger boys still yelling at their game, and the deep, low humming of bumblebees or wasps, who must have built a nest under the eaves just outside.

She pulled down her white cotton underpants and sat down on the commode. A few seconds later, she heard a sudden rustle. Frank Pittman shoved aside the shower curtain, rods clattering. "I saw you pee! I saw your thing!" He intoned the phrases over and over in a low triumphant singsong. His face, angrily splotched with acne, creased into a malevolent grin. She could not move, but was instead held motionless in terror.

He quickly unzipped his trousers and proudly exhibited his small, limp penis. "I've got one of these, and you don't!" His voice dropped to a threatening whisper. "Did you ever see one before? I betcha didn't, did ya? Do you know what I could do to you with this? I could make you blow up like a balloon and burst!"

Meg stared, hypnotized at the strange, rosy protrusion. She could think only of the raw chicken necks Aunt Emma sometimes used to make stock. She had never seen anything so repellent in her life.

At last she found her voice. Her face was a deep, mortified scarlet as she gasped, "You get out of here!" She managed to stand up, and backed away from him as far as possible within the limited confines of the small room. The grin seemed plastered on his face as he waved the offensive organ before her. She could see the mossy, pale green substance between his teeth; he was famous throughout the school for never brushing them. He took a slow step toward her, but she managed to elude him and made for the door, scrambling to adjust her clothing as she fled.

Just as she reached it, the door opened and there stood her Aunt Emma, as stolid and immovable as a rock. Meg stopped dead in her tracks. Frank turned away and hastily zipped up his trousers, then turned back and stared at Aunt Emma with defiant insolence. The woman took in the situation at a glance and her own face colored with embarrassment and anger. She grabbed Meg's arm and pulled her down the stairs.

When they returned to the porch, Aunt Emma gave her sister Bess a tight-lipped, surrreptitious nod and began to gather her purse and sun hat from a small round metal table.

"We must be goin', Clara," she said to Mrs.

Pittman, still holding Meg's hand tightly. "You'll be wantin' to put supper on the table pretty soon." Her voice was steady and pleasant. She guided Meg to the car and opened the back door for her. Meg got inside without a word. She was shaking with fright and red-faced with shame. She felt as though she were choking.

When they got home, Aunt Emma took Meg silently to the gardening shed behind the house, stopping on her way to pick a switch from the hedge that bordered their lot. Inside the shed, she instructed Meg to take down her "undergarments" and lie on the workbench. She switched the small girl's backside thoroughly with the frail but stinging limb.

"The idea! Going into the bathroom with that wild Pittman boy! You must never do anything like that again, you hear me?"

Meg did not answer, nor try to defend herself. Better to be punished than to have to explain what had happened. She could not have related the horrifying incident to her aunt if her life had depended on it.

"You must stay away from boys like that and never get into such a situation again. They'll take advantage of you and get you into trouble like they did your mother. Now you hear me? You keep away from boys like that!"

Aunt Emma helped her back on with her panties, ignoring Meg's red contorted face and dry-eyed silence. They went back into the house together and Meg secluded herself in her room. The pleas of poor bewildered Aunt Bess to come down to supper went unanswered; she lay silently on the bed until, hours later, she fell into a stuporous, exhausted sleep.

The next morning Aunt Emma made her her favorite waffles for breakfast, but Meg did not touch them. It was nearly a week before she was able to speak normally to her aunts.

In the dream, the episode was even more frightening than it had been in reality. Frank Pittman was not the twelve-year-old Frank, but a giant of a man, with a long, unkempt, black beard from which protruded an enormous, blood-red penis. Only the acne, the mossy teeth and the evil grin were the same. He started toward her and came closer and closer until Meg woke herself with a series of shrill, rasping screams.

The next morning, Jeff called her before he got out of bed. Pulling the telephone from the night table onto the mattress, he dialed information and found her listing under new phones.

"Meg? Jeff McAllister."

"Jeff?" Her voice was groggy. "What time is it?" She felt as though she had just fallen asleep. That wasn't far from the truth, she suddenly remembered. With an effort, she pushed the grotesque images of the dream into the back of her mind. After she awoke screaming, she had lain and watched a pale sliver of dawn through the blinds before her eyes finally succumbed again to their heaviness.

"Did I wake you? I'm sorry—it's seven-thirty. I wanted to catch you before you left for work."

"No, that's all right. I should be up anyway."

"I was thinking—there's a photographic exhibit at the Museum of Modern Art I think you'd enjoy. I want to see it again. What time do you get off work?"

"You mean tonight?"

"Well, after work. The museum closes at six. We could have a bite of dinner some place afterwards."

For a moment she wavered. It sounded lovely. But was she capable of coping with someone like Jeff McAllister? With relief, she remembered she had a perfectly legitimate excuse. "Oh, Jeff, I'm sorry, I can't. There's a client of mine—Mrs. Gillespie—the textbooks would call her a battered wife, I suppose. Anyway, her husband works at night and that's the only time I can see her alone. I promised her I'd come by this evening."

There was a brief silence on the other end of the line. Then he recovered almost instantly and his voice assumed a bantering lightness. "I only hope Mrs. Gillespie deserves such devotion. Okay, in that case, I'll see you tomorrow night in class. And forgive me for waking you—it was just a sudden brainstorm. The photographs are really remarkable and I thought we could enjoy them together."

"No, that's all right. Thank you for calling."

"Have a good day."

While he dressed for work, Jeff felt a gnawing frustration at the back of his mind. He was not a conceited man, but as an attractive and eminently eligible bachelor, he had never had trouble finding girls who would change their plans for him. It was a fringe benefit of youth and wealth that he had unconsciously taken for granted.

He was forced to admire her conscientiousness. Or was it indifference rather than integrity that had caused her refusal? Perhaps Mrs. Gillespie was only a convenient excuse. Perhaps Meg simply found him unattractive. Wondering why someone had refused a date with him was, he realized, a new experience and a not altogether pleasant one. On the other hand, it intrigued him and piqued his curiosity. He sensed a finely honed stubbornness in Meg beneath the shy reserve.

During the morning at the offices of McAllister, Warren and Sloane, he found himself bemused. At noon, his friend Peter, who had been with him at Harvard, came by his desk and murmured *sotto voce*, "What the hell's the matter with you today, Jeff? Did Jessica finally get fed up with your on-again, off-again courtship?"

Jeff turned the question from his personal life to his professional one. "Did you ever think of getting out of Wall Street altogether, Peter?"

"Hell, no. I love it. Let's go to lunch—I'll cheer you up."

"No. I—I have to run a couple of errands." He did not feel like a convivial luncheon.

He took his camera from his desk drawer and walked out into the bright October sunlight. Near City Hall Park, he stopped at a sidewalk vendor's cart and picked up a large salted pretzel for the pigeons and a hot dog for himself. He sat down on a bench, closed his eyes and let the sun soak the fatigue from his body and mind. As the son of the former senior partner of McAllister, Warren and Sloane, he had to work twice as hard as anyone else in order to escape charges of nepotism. He tried to do his job well, but today was one of those days when devotion to duty gave him little satisfaction. Shuffling money around on paper—no matter how large the sums—seemed irrelevant.

He opened his eyes and laughed. The pigeon he had dubbed Gandhi, darker and smaller than the others, had lighted at his feet. While the rest of the flock swooped greedily down for the bits of pretzel Jeff threw them, Gandhi, following the policy of passive resistance, watched and waited. Then he would waddle up to Jeff with perfect assurance to claim a choice, salty crust. After pecking it triumphantly out of Jeff's hand, he too would take to the air with a throaty gurgle and disappear.

Jeff felt a sense of empathy with Gandhi; they were both part of a structured society and yet somehow loners. He felt especially disengaged today, disengaged and restless. He got up and sauntered down the concrete walkway. Autumn chrysanthemums transplanted from some hothouse glistened in the bronze and gold sunbursts along the borders. He adjusted the camera's microphoto lens and took a few closeups. The sky was that deep and brilliant blue seen only in October. He composed a shot through the trees, the sun glancing in obliquely. He hoped the camera had caught a falling leaf or two in midair.

He saw a girl approaching, a tall slender girl with flowing dark hair. She wore a black-and-white skirt. He lengthened his stride in elated disbelief, then saw that this girl's eyes were small and close, her thin lips a bold slash of red.

He ignored the sudden knot of disappointment in the pit of his stomach, slung the camera over his shoulder and headed resolutely back to the office.

## Chapter 3

On Thursday morning, Jeff was in his darkroom by seven. He wanted to develop the shots he had made the previous day. He took them from the solution and hung them to dry, then went into the sleek, modern kitchen, opened the refrigerator and extracted an English muffin. He tossed it jauntily into the toaster, buttered it carefully and grimaced as he tasted it. It must have been around for weeks—he would have to do better in giving Mrs. Paulsen his shopping lists. He looked again inside the fridge. A half-empty carton of milk, now soured; a container of grapefruit juice foaming evilly; two unopened tins of caviar someone had given him for Christmas.

He slammed the door shut in disgust. The contents of the refrigerator had literally made him lose his appetite. But he'd pick up a doughnut or something on the way in. He so seldom ate at home that it seemed a waste of time to buy groceries. Jessica consistently preferred to dine out: restaurants were one of her hobbies so long as they were sufficiently expensive. He enjoyed good food too, but some of his favorite eating places were the provincial little family-owned ones that he made a practice of seeking out all over the city. It never failed to amaze him that in New York, one could spend enormous amounts on mediocre food and yet dine regally at inexpensive little holes-in-the-wall, if one knew those which still concerned themselves with excellence. Little Italy and Chinatown were full of them. He wondered if Meg would enjoy Vincent's Clam Bar on Mott Street.

On Wednesday evening, Meg came away from her visit with Mrs. Gillespie exhausted and angry. Mr. Gillespie had somehow found out that afternoon about her impending visit and had knocked Mrs. Gillespie around more violently than usual to demonstrate his disapproval. The woman opened the door to Meg with visible bruises on her face and arms. Meg hid her alarm and kept her voice calm as she confronted the distraught woman. She would have advised her to leave her husband at once, except for two-year-old Ronnie and four-year-old Jane. Mrs. Gillespie had no job skills which would enable her to provide for them. Mr. Gillespie, an electrician, made a good salary and was generous in providing for his wife and children. He also did not drink, gamble or chase other women. His one flaw was his uncontrollable temper. It was a difficult and distressing case.

Reviewing it on the bus home, Meg sighed. Why must life be so damnably complicated? Mrs. Gillespie was not unintelligent, nor did she show signs of being a masochist who unconsciously invited physical violence. She had simply married a presentable, hardworking young man who proved to have a fierce, destructive temper. If only Mr. Gillespie would consent to meet with her, Meg thought she might get some insight into what made him strike out so irrationally. But so far, he had adamantly refused to see her.

She got off the bus at Eighth Street and started toward Ninth. A light drizzle had begun to fall, which surrounded the street lights with misty shrouds. She paused to focus her camera and try for a time exposure. When her footsteps stopped, she heard a step behind her also stop. She had not been conscious of the step until its absence registered retroactively. She looked behind her, but there was only a man in a dark windbreaker, window-shopping before one of the dingy clothing stores in the area. She accelerated her pace and turned in time to catch the man in her peripheral vision. He was sauntering slowly away from the window, hands in pockets. Then his steps seemed to gradually quicken.

On Ninth Street, she darted into a small delicatessen and leaned against the door, catching her breath. Mr. Lopez looked at her with concern. "What? You run home tonight? You are one of them joggers now?"

Meg laughed weakly. "No. I thought someone—"

She saw the man pass the window and continue down the street. She must be becoming paranoid. "Could I have a quart of milk, please, Mr. Lopez?"

"Sure you are okay?"

"Oh yes. Fine." She counted out the change and picked up the carton.

"*Hasta la vista*. Now you be careful. You know the old lady always walk that brown spot dog? She was mugged yesterday."

"My God! Was she hurt?"

"Not thees time. They took her bag, but she not have much in it."

"Oh, I'm glad she's all right. *Buenas noches*, Mr. Lopez."

She was going up the steps of her building when the man in the windbreaker appeared from behind a column at the top of them. He stood watching her ascent, his face expressionless. He could not be simply a mugger— he would have confronted her on the street. Her mind was racing, but she was otherwise quite calm. Slowly, he began walking down the steps toward her.

"What do you want?" Her voice was level.

He took her arm roughly and pulled her down the

steps to the sidewalk. "I want you to stay away from my wife."

"Your wife?" The truth burst in on her. "Mr. Gillespie?"

"That's right, Mac Gillespie. I took off work tonight to tell you to stay away from my wife."

"I'll stay away from her when you stop using her as a punching bag."

The man's eyes were sorrowful and gentle. He did not seem at all to be the type who would physically abuse his wife. But as she spoke, she saw a desperate cunning come into his face, the look of a trapped animal.

"That's between the two of us. There's no call for an outsider like you barging in and telling her what to do."

Megs' temper flared. "It's not between the two of you when you leave her black and blue. I just saw her—"

The man suddenly exploded in ugly anger. "Goddam it, I don't want to have to tell you again—leave her alone!" He took her by the shoulders and began to shake her. Meg's teeth rattled in her head; otherwise the man was not actually hurting her. But when he released her, she heard a sickening thud of breaking glass and, looking to the sidewalk, found that the camera had dislodged itself from its case and lay several feet away.

Meg bent over it and picked it up. The lens was shattered, she could see that at once. She examined it in wordless dismay. The shock of the camera crashing to the street seemed to have jolted Gillespie out of his anger. "I'm sorry I caused that, little lady. I didn't mean to bring no harm."

"Maybe it's only the lens—I guess I can get that replaced," she murmured. She suddenly decided to take advantage of Mac Gillespie's momentary lapse into humility. She might never have the chance again. "Mr. Gillespie, don't worry about the camera. Would you like to have some coffee and talk for a little while? Maybe I can be of some help."

He backed away, suspicion clouding his eyes. He muttered almost inaudibly, "No, I've got to be going. I'll be all right."

He thrust a hand into his back pocket and drew out a wallet. Quickly, he pulled out a twenty-dollar bill and tried to thrust it into Meg's hand. "To get that fixed," he muttered, pointing to the camera

Meg shook her head. "No, I'll take care of it. I tell you what—buy Sarah a present with that. Surprise her with something nice, okay?"

"Well. Maybe I will." Irresolutely, he pocketed the wallet and started to turn away. Then he wheeled and pointed a sturdy forefinger at her. She thought he was going to issue a final thrust. "You get inside now before somebody comes along and hurts you."

He walked away, back towards Second Avenue. Meg felt a wild urge to giggle at the irony of his parting remark, but once she let herself into her apartment and closed the door, she found she was shaking. She chided herself for being upset by a man who had proved (on this occasion, at least) to be a paper tiger, then realized the source of her agitation was probably more the damaged camera than fear of Mr. Gillespie.

She turned the radio to the classical music station she had become addicted to, and the joyful, liquid strains of *The Trout Symphony* gradually brought a degree of calm to her disordered mind. She wondered fleetingly if she should press charges against the man. Perhaps being hauled into court would impress him with the seriousness of his behavior. She dismissed the thought almost immediately. It would only make a bad situation worse for Sarah. And perhaps after tonight, he would consent to sit down with Meg and she could persuade him to seek professional help.

Her eye was caught by a sudden movement at the windowsill. Jody and Jacob, a neighbor's Siamese cats, were sitting in identical positions, peering intently into her apartment. It would make a superb shot! Automatically she reached for the Minolta and tried to capture the moment on film. But when she pressed the shutter, there was no click. So it was not the lens alone which had been damaged. She tried again, but the shutter remained immobile. She opened the camera case but was unable to find any reason for the malfunction. Disheartened, she laid it aside and tried to forget it. Tomorrow she'd try to find a repair shop somewhere.

She poured herself a glass of milk, still fretting over the broken camera. Though the instrument could very nearly have qualified as an antique, as cameras go, the pictures it produced were excellent. A camera shop owner had once explained to her that cameras are like automobiles or almost any other product: some function superbly for years and others are lemons from the beginning. Meg had been lucky enough to find one in the former category, which helped to explain her fanatical devotion to it.

She had been fascinated by photography since she was eleven, when Aunt Bess had given her an inexpensive pocket camera for Christmas. Expecting her to use it for conventional vacation snaps and family celebrations, her aunts were nonplussed when Meg started producing what they thought of as "arty" photographs of picturesquely dilapidated buildings and silhouetted winter-naked trees. They were equally startled when on her sixteenth birthday, she spurned the offer of a new party dress and chose instead the used Minolta from a pawn shop in Atlanta.

Meg tried to make candid portraits of her aunts as they went about their weekend chores, but she soon desisted out of sympathy for their acute embarrassment.

"Don't you dare click that thing around here this morning, Meggie! Look at me with this rag tied on my head—I look like the worst white trash in the county. If you want to take pictures, make them this afternoon after I've had a chance to bathe and get into something decent!" Meg smiled as she remembered their horror.

The following morning Meg took the camera to her office with her. When she went out for lunch, she stopped in at a neighborhood camera store someone had recommended and asked the gray-haired old gentleman behind the counter to look at it. He examined it with an expert's deliberation and after some minutes shook his head.

"Miss, to tell you the truth, I'm not sure it would be possible to get the parts for this camera. Not for some months—I'd have to track them down. The shutter I could fix, but these teeth are dislocated, you see here?" He pointed the parts out to her with a pencil as he talked. "This model is over ten years old, that's the problem. There are some places on Canal Street where you might get a good buy on a used camera. You can look them up in the Yellow Pages. One of the best is Bernie's—you might try there."

She left the shop in a daze. The fee for the photography class had flattened her bank account, and without a camera the course would be an exercise in futility. The afternoon was a long and dreary one. One of the cases on her caseload that she had thought was well on the way to a solution turned out to be much more involved than she had anticipated. She tried to concentrate but her mind kept going back to the problem of the camera.

She stayed in the office to complete the necessary paperwork until after seven. When she looked up from the intricate forms, she saw she would have to get the subway directly to class. Tired and discouraged, she boarded the screeching train, got off at Fourteenth Street and headed for the New School.

The classroom was filled. Laglen was standing impatiently at his desk. As she walked inside the door, she felt a light touch on her elbow. Turning, her eyes met those of Jeff McAllister. "I saved you a seat," he whispered and pulled her into it.

"Look at your cameras, everyone," Laglen said in his faint German accent. "Tonight we will concentrate briefly on how the camera lens works. Most of you have the single-lens reflex mechanism. Look through your lens and focus on—let's say on me, just for practice." He gave a small laugh, adjusting his tie self-consciously.

Reluctantly, Meg held up her camera and tried to focus through the shattered lens. Jeff glanced at her and did a startled doubletake. "What happened? Did you get hit by a truck on your way over?"

"It's a long story. I'll tell you later," she whispered back.

At that moment, Meg's lens caught the eye of Professor Laglen. "Miss Gardner, tell me, do you expect to take some kind of surreal masterpiece with that lens?" He beamed mischievously at the class to indicate he was making a joke and waited for the expected laughter. There ensued instead an embarrassed silence.

"Dr. Laglen, I hope to have my camera in working order before the next class." Her voice was even, but a slow line of red suffused her face. Jeff let his hand rest on hers supportively for a moment, then resumed his focusing.

When class was over, Meg began to gather her papers, not looking at Jeff or anyone else.

"Ready for an Irish coffee?" he asked.

"I—I don't think so. Not tonight. I'm beat."

"All the more reason to have one. It'll make you

sleep. Come on." Refusing to take her demurral seriously, he grabbed her arm and steered her through a small clutch of students in the doorway. "That stinking bastard Laglen. I had an idea he was a bully at heart."

"Oh, I think he was just trying to be humorous without quite knowing how." She did not have the strength to be angry.

"You're too charitable. He's a real Nazi, that man."

Once in the open air, Meg felt a hunger pang and was reminded she had had no dinner. "I think tonight I'd better eat rather than drink, Jeff. I'm sorry."

"Well, my culinary skills are limited, but I do whip up a mean omelet." He had heard the unmistakable fatigue in her voice. "Do you have any eggs?"

"Dozens, as a matter of fact. They had them on special this week. Oh, but I don't have anything to drink—" It was not until the words were out that she realized she had just invited him to her apartment.

"That situation can be immediately remedied," he said, tapping his forefinger brightly against his temple. "Watch Uncle Jeff walk. Watch Uncle Jeff walk into liquor store. Watch Uncle Jeff ask for bottle. Watch liquor store man sell Uncle Jeff bottle."

"You fool." Meg's shoulders shook with laughter. She suddenly felt completely giddy. Jeff watched her, noticing again how her face suddenly lit up like a thousand watts when she surrendered to her impish sense of humor.

The bottle of Scotch tucked under his arm, they headed for Ninth Street. Wind gusted around every corner, so that when they entered her small rooms, they were like a snug haven after a gale.

"If you'll make the drinks, I'll set out the eggs and stuff," she said.

"No sooner said." He took two glasses from the shelves and ice from the refrigerator, envying its neatly stocked order and abundance.

"Make mine very light, though," she warned.

"Oh, now," Jeff said in mock disappointment. "I was goin' to ply ye with liquor, me fair beauty." He twirled an imaginary mustache with a wicked leer.

"And I'm far too clever for ye," she replied smugly.

"So it seems. So it seems." Jeff handed her her drink and began breaking eggs into a bowl. Meg left him to his own devices. The kitchen was much too small to accommodate two cooks. While he bustled about, flaunting his capability like a chef's hat, Meg wandered into the living room and tucked her feet under her in the big wing chair. Soon she heard a furtive epithet, followed by the sound of toast being scraped. She concealed a knowing grin with difficulty.

"Sorry about the toast," Jeff handed her a plate. "Guess I'm a little rusty."

"S'okay," Meg mumbled gratefully, her mouth full. "Tastes wonderful."

"Thank God you're easy to please. Now, what the hell happened to your camera?"

Between bites, Meg told him the story of being accosted by Mr. Gillespie. Jeff listened, a frown knitting his forehead. At the end of her narration, he shook his head in wonder.

"I told you you needed a guardian. And you actually invited the man in for a nice chummy cup of coffee." He smiled wryly and shook his head again. "You're incorrigible, you know that?"

"Oh, Jeff, don't be silly. I'm a pretty good judge of character. I wouldn't have asked him in if—. But when he broke the camera, he was so apologetic—all the fight went out of him. I'd have been perfectly safe."

He gave up and reverted to the immediate problem. "What are you going to do—try to get it fixed?"

She averted her eyes. "The problem is that I don't

think I can. It's over ten years old now, and the parts for it are very difficult to find."

"Tough break." His tone was casual as he seemingly dismissed the subject, and veered to a happier topic. "Hey, got some snaps I want to show you."

From his briefcase he drew the photographs he had made the previous day in City Hall Park. Three of the photographs, they agreed, were worth enlargement and framing. She gazed at them with admiration. The colors caught were unbelievably subtle.

"You're really good," she said, not without envy.

"I don't know about that. I'd like to be someday. It's pretty difficult to find the shot-in-a-million during lunch hour."

"You'd like to give up Wall Street and work at photography fulltime someday?" Meg had not realized his interest was so serious; she had thought he viewed photography merely as a pleasant avocation.

"Oh yes. Hell yes." He began pacing itchily. "Yesterday in particular, the job really got to me. I deal in big chunks of money, but it seemed somehow pointless in the cosmic scheme of things." He broke off with a snort of derisive laughter. "Listen to me. I sound like a sophomoric jackass."

"No you don't. It isn't sophomoric if your job gives you no sense of satisfaction. You're obviously very, very talented, Jeff. Why not change careers? Go at photography hammer and tong!"

He smiled at the old-fashioned phrasing. "I'll think about it. Now—" He came to the sofa and moved in beside her. "You know, I've never seen any of your work."

She got up shyly but eagerly. "I'm afraid they're not in the same class with yours. But—" She shrugged and brought out a shoe box. The photographs were remarkably well composed, he saw at once. There were pictures of semicollapsed houses and barns, and another group of portraits of children.

"Who modeled for these?"

"When I was in college, the dean of women was a young widow. These were her children. I worked part of my way through school by taking care of them. They were darlin' little critters."

"It's odd," he mused.

"What?"

"The two subjects you seem to find most fascinating. In a way, they're diametrically opposed. I mean, crumbling buildings and budding children."

"I suppose. I'd never have thought of it that way."

"If you had to confine yourself to one group, which would you choose?"

She thought for a long time before answering. "Either one would be hard to give up completely. Buildings at the end of their usefulness have always fascinated me. Not because their time is over, I think, but because of the richness of what has happened in them during the time they were used. But of the two, I think I find people more interesting. I once read something that a famous portrait photographer said. He said that before he started photographing a subject, he always asked himself: 'What if this were the last person alive in the world? What would be most worth saying about him?' "

"I like that," Jeff said. "You could translate that to any subject really, 'What if this were the last garbage can left in the world? What would be most worth saying about it?' "

Meg laughed her paradoxically robust laugh. "Yes, crazy as it sounds, I think that's valid. But to go back to you, Jeff. I think you should give some serious thought to going in another direction with your life, if that's what you know you really want."

"The one thing that makes me hesitate is that I feel I'd be letting my father down. It was very important to him that I come into the firm and—oh, I don't know—maintain its continuity, I suppose."

Meg's voice was gentle. "But don't you think he'd want you to do whatever would make you happiest? I can't believe he'd want otherwise for you."

After a pause, Jeff's eyes met hers. "You're right, of course. You've got a hell of a lot of common sense for a little girl from Martinsville, Georgia."

A sudden gust of wind blew in through the open window behind her. She got up to close it, shivering. "B-R-R," she said, spelling the letters.

"You remember my feeble little joke?"

"I think it's kind of funny." She tugged at the window but the innumerable layers of paint had made it balky.

Jeff sprang up. "Here, let me do that. Move aside. This is a man's job." He pulled mightily at the frame, which refused to budge.

"A man's job, eh?" She stood aside and watched him struggle, not bothering to hide her amusement. At last she took pity and joined in, and together they managed to slam the thing shut. They looked at each other and grinned with satisfaction. He took a step forward and the room seemed suddenly and unnaturally warm.

No one could have said who instigated the move. They were in each other's arms, clinging together tightly. They stayed that way, not moving, hardly daring to breathe, for several seconds. The world outside was on another planet. She could feel his hand at her ear, caressing her hair, moving it away from her face. She found it difficult to breathe; she had a strange feeling that she was being reunited with a long-lost part of her own body. When Jeff kissed her, her response was almost violent in its eagerness. He took a step backward to look at her. Her gaze was wide-eyed but unflinching. He took her hand and led her into the bedroom.

# Chapter 4

The bed was only three-quarter size—a bed Meg had found in a used-furniture store on Bleecker Street. But as they lay down on it together, neither was conscious of its narrowness. They held each other close, their bodies plastered together. Jeff covered her face with kisses, his lips moving lightly from one closed eyelid to the other. He could see the fringe of her long lashes trembling in the half-light. Her mouth was slightly open. He could hear her short, shallow breathing.

A semi-transparent curtain separated the bedroom from the well lit living room, and gave an ethereal diffuseness to the bedroom light. He unbuttoned her blouse, lingering deliciously over his first glimpse of the deep cleft that separated her breasts. They were surprisingly full—the slender, elongated lines of her clothed body were deceptive. He reached behind her and unclasped her bra, then cupped his hands around her full breasts. He pushed the blouse off her shoulders, and holding her in a semi-sitting position, removed the blouse and bra. She was grateful for the gentleness of his touch. She did not want him to know the extent of her inexperience, and certainly not about the humiliating failure and incompleteness of the one experience she had had.

He kissed her breasts tenderly, moving his hand to the zipper of her skirt. His movements wre economical and expert, but in no way rough or hurried. The removal of each garment was a small ritual. The skirt slid down off her ankles, then her panties, and he looked at her still, naked body. Again it struck him how she was much more sensuous nude than clothed. He had seen women where the reverse was true. He decided that Meg simply did not dress to draw attention to her sex appeal. In fact, she seemed completely unconscious of the importance of clothes. But those half-formed thoughts lingered in the far region of his mind. His breath accelerated as he viewed the wondrous soft curves. He was strongly aroused, and yet he retained that special sense of protectiveness toward her.

He sensed an uncertainty in her that he had not encountered before in a woman. As her nudity was revealed, her body stiffened and she moved her legs together primly. Well, he thought, she was probably made self-conscious because she was nude while he was still fully clothed. He started to unbuckle his trousers but she lifted a pale hand to stop him. Fumbling, she undid the buckle and zipper and unbuttoned his shirt. He helped her off with the shirt and trousers and removed his shorts in one swift, eager motion. He stood before her unashamed. She glanced at him fleetingly and averted her eyes.

"You're beautiful," he whispered. "You're so beautiful."

"I want to be good for you," she whispered slowly, her voice half-muffled by the pillow.

He lay down beside her and cupped her chin, moving her head back to face him. "You're already good for me. Don't you know that?"

"You don't know me, Jeff." Her voice was all but inaudible, but curiously insistent. "You don't know how foolish and frightened—"

He stopped the words by turning her head toward him and covering her mouth with his lips. Gradually, his gentleness changed to urgency as the kiss became more searching. Though she still lay unmoving with her legs extended and close together, her mouth responded hungrily. Her tongue sought his and she bit his lips with tiny, kitteny nips that hinted the kitten might someday emerge a tigress.

He put his hand between her legs and felt a dewy dampness. He began to stroke her very lightly, and the lips opened like a blossom. His own hardness became an ache and he moved above her and began to penetrate the opening flower. At first she tried to resist him; her hands touched his chest in a half-hearted attempt to push him back. Then there was a sudden, harsh, surrendering moan as he entered her. With his deep, slow thrusts, she began to experience steadily rising pleasure. Then, without warning, a searing image burst into her brain. She saw again the wild, forest-thick beard and the raw, grotesquely huge penis. Pleasure was replaced by something akin to panic, as she struggled for control. The image faded somewhat and she became aware of Jeff's whisper: "Tell me what to do, darling. Tell me what you want."

"Nothing. I'm fine." The voice was terse, flat.

He knew she was lying; her body was motionless and apparently unaroused. He slowed his thrusts and separated himself from her and for a few moments stroked and kissed her body. She needed more time.

When he tried to reenter her, he found himself limp. "Make me hard," he whispered urgently.

"How?" Again the word was hesitant and barely audible.

He guided her hands with his and she followed willingly but inexpertly. After a few seconds, he realized it was impossible—he had become too clinical, too detached, analyzing her needs. He moved her hand away and put his arms around her. Since that first moan, she had made no other lover's sound. He raised his head slightly and kissed the tip of her nose. She still lay motionless, eyes closed.

"Meg? I'm sorry, darling."

"There's no need for you to be sorry. It's not your fault."

"Yes, it is. I wasn't patient enough."

"No, it's me. I think—I think there must be something missing."

He whistled softly. "You? Never. On a scale of one to ten, you're at least a twenty."

"No, I'm serious, Jeff. When I was in college I dated a boy for about six months. I finally let him make love to me—or tried to. But it was the same thing. Nothing happened to me. I think I must be frigid."

"Nonsense, Meg. We just need time to get used to each other."

"No." Her voice was impatient, almost angry. She went to the closet and pulled a terrycloth robe about her. She sat down on the side of the bed facing away from him. "I was raised by two maiden aunts. I don't think they meant to do it, but they had been brought up to believe that sex outside of marriage was dirty—was unthinkable. I guess I subconsciously inherited their attitude."

He put his hands behind his head and stared up at the plaster ceiling. He could make out, dimly, a faint crack in one of its corners. God! He wasn't at all sure he could cope with this. His own guilt was as much as he could handle at the moment. Now Meg seemed equally weighted. Never mind that Jessica sometimes annoyed him with her preoccupation with current fashion and chic restaurants. In bed at least, they were superb. Jessica was uninhibited and obliging . . . the exact opposite of this complex woman whose whole background seemed one of repression and denial.

He sat up and swung his legs over the side of the bed. After staring blankly at the wall for a time, he fumbled into his clothes, feeling like an A-Number-One bastard.

"Are you going?" It was really a statement rather than a question—an acceptance of abandonment.

"I have to, Meg. It's late."

She slowed her breath to keep her sigh inaudible, and turned on the lamp. One-thirty. "Yes, I guess it is," she said, and curled into a forlorn ball on the bed. He looked at the dark hair flowing against the pillow, and sat down gingerly on the bed's edge.

"Don't, Meg," he pleaded. "Don't brood about it. Please look at me."

She muttered something he couldn't understand and he leaned closer. "What did you say?"

"I said goodbye." Her voice was small and cold.

"Oh, God, Meg, I'm sorry. It was as much my fault as yours. Don't blame yourself."

"I *said* goodbye," she repeated dully.

He stood up once more, looked at her irresolutely for a second, then went into the living room, gathered his topcoat, notebook, and camera from the arm of the sofa and let himself out the door.


Meg lay silently for a time, fighting the threat of becoming physically ill. Then she crept out of bed and got into a flannel nightgown. The floor was icy against her bare feet, but she walked to the outside door, pushed the double bolt and latched the chain. She stood with her back pressed against the wall and began breathing deeply and rhythmically. It was a trick someone had once told her would ward off hysteria, a condition she felt pressed dangerously close at the moment.

Why had she thought this time would be different?

Of course, Bruce Quinlan had been rough and insensitive—and as inexperienced as she—but with Jeff it had been worse in a way. She had wanted so desperately to please him and she had spoiled it for him as well as for herself. She found it impossible to be angry with him for his abrupt departure. What man would want a psychic cripple for a bedmate? She might as well just admit that she would never be able to respond normally to a man. Her emotions were irreparably twisted.

She wanted to weep but the release of tears would not come. She had felt a quality in Jeff which had given her hope. For a fraction of time, she had believed he could, through some mysterious communion, heal her wounds and make her whole. Unlike the disenchantment she had suffered with Bruce, from Jeff she had received only tenderness and touching concern with her needs, her fulfillment. But she could not surrender to her body's instincts. She was hopeless.

She realized the apartment was frigid, or perhaps the chill was only in her bones. She took an extra blanket from the closet and tossed it crookedly over the bed. She crawled in under it and at last fell into an exhausted sleep.

At some point during the night, she bolted awake, her heart pounding. She had been in a deep, thick forest and had finally found her way into a clearing where there bloomed a circle of large shrubs with exotic red blossoms. She gasped at the lushness of their beauty, but as she drew closer, she saw that the stamen and petals of the flowers were perfect replicas of male genitals. Horrified and fascinated, she reached out to touch one, and found it unbearably hot. From the deep woods behind her, a cacophony of derisive, half-human, half-animal laughter floated out to her, then faded, leaving her surrounded by the circle of obscene bushes, which seemed to be moving closer and closer.

# Chapter 5

After leaving Meg that night, Jeff had his own disturbing dreams. At one point, he watched a girl drown, and laughed as her long, dark hair spread like a fan on the water, then slowly sank and disappeared. And there were other jumbled episodes which he could not clearly remember when he awoke—only amorphous impressions of letting terrible things happen while he stood by, a powerless and cowardly witness.

Throughout the morning, and for most of the afternoon, Jeff's mind was occupied with what he should do about Meg. It was true that she had affected him perhaps more deeply than any woman ever had before. But he did not feel prepared or patient enough to help her. Her problems seemed too deep-rooted for him to be her savior.

Aside from that, their backgrounds were totally different. She was like a superbly sculptured *objet d'art* or the most fragile crystal, which a dissonant sound could shatter. If his background had been without trauma, he might have felt strong enough to shelter and protect her. But he thought back to the deaths of his father and then his brother. Both of those incidents had proved that he was not the stalwart personality he sometimes liked to think himself. His own weaknesses had been pointed up not once but twice. He could not allow himself to become involved in another situation where he might again be found wanting.

Closing his mind on memories too painful and shameful to be entertained, he went back to his work. But Friday afternoons were always slow anyway, and concentration was almost impossible. He began to think of Jessica. Perhaps she was superficial, but in a way, it was relaxing to be with her precisely because of that superficiality. She had no psychological difficulties that required deep, probing analysis; the most taxing problem she encountered was whether to wear the Halston or the de la Renta to dinner. He needed her mindlessness for a while; he had not talked to her since the night before the dinner party he had failed to attend.

He pulled the desk phone closer to him and dialed.

"Jessica? Jeff."

"The prodigal lover returned to the fold? Edward Steichen taking a short vacation? Richard Avedon on a coffee break? Ansel Adams deserting the tripod long enough to call little old me?"

Damn her glib sarcasm. He ignored it. "Jessica, I'm sorry about the other night. From now on, we'll just have to build our social schedules without Tuesday or Thursday night engagements."

"I'm perfectly willing, Jeff, dear. Forgive my so-called wit. It's good to hear from you. Anything in particular in the air?"

"I'd like to see you tonight."

"Just a minute—I'll check my social calendar."

Jeff smiled to himself. Even if Jessica had another appointment, it had never stopped her before and he knew it wouldn't deter her this time. He waited, drumming his fingers on the glass top of the desk.

"All clear, darling. Aren't you the lucky one? What time and where are we going?"

He had not considered that an evening with Jessica inevitably involved an elaborate dinner. "I don't know—I hadn't thought about it. Oh, hey, maybe we could just order something sent in—"

"Jeffrey McAllister, you haven't called me in over a week. If you think I'm going to sit here in this dreary apartment and have dinner from foil containers, you're crazy. Now where are we going?"

Jeff sighed. He knew when he was beaten. "All right. How about Trinculo's?" Trinculo's food would never elicit rapture, but the place was sufficiently "in," with its clientele from the theatrical and literary worlds, to make it acceptable to Jessica, and at least it wasn't far from her apartment.

"Oh, all right. There's a new place I want to try but—okay, Trinculo's. See you—when? Sixish?"

He hesitated. An idea suddenly jelled in the back of his mind. "No, make it seven. I have an errand to run."

"*Muy bien, amigo. Buenos tardes.*" She hung up.

Jeff smiled wryly. Jessica had been to the Spanish resort of Marbella during the summer, had come back determined to conquer the Spanish language, and so had immediately signed up at Berlitz. Prodded on, Jeff had no doubt, by some handsome Spanish suitor. He had never inquired too closely into his competition for Jessica's affections.

On his way to Jessica's apartment, Jeff stopped at a Fifth Avenue store and made a purchase, giving the saleswoman meticulous instructions.

At Trinculo's, the food was as unremarkable as Jeff knew it would be, but Jessica was pleased because Woody Allen was dining two tables away. When they returned to her apartment, she went to the stereo and turned it on. "Listen to this, Jeff. I got it just this afternoon."

The goading, sensuous strains of a classical Spanish guitar filled the room. "Very nice," Jeff murmured. "Now come here." He crooked his forefinger roguishly.

Her lips were warm, familiar and compliant, as they sank onto the modular sofa, covered in oyster-white Haitian cotton. She was wearing a deep blue dress of silk crepe de chine with the narrowest of straps across her shoulders. One strap fell seductively off the shoulder, revealing the rise of her breast. She suddenly rose, pulled him off the sofa and instantly unzipped her dress, which fell to the floor, revealing her utter nudity. There was a sudden throb throughout Jeff's body as they fell to the floor together.

"Take off your clothes, for God's sake, Jeff." Her voice was a cracked and urgent whisper. Jeff threw his clothes onto one end of the sofa. Jessica began to plead in fragmented, incoherent phrases as Jeff entered her. She followed his rhythm effortlessly, expertly, to its soon-realized crescendo.

Jeff lay still for a moment, then got up and lay down on the sofa. His body was released, but his mind was spinning. He and Jessica were like two superb machines. From their very first encounter, it was as though they had been made for each other. There had never been a time when either was left unsatisfied. How simple it all was with her, he thought. Why, then, did he feel such an indefinable emptiness, as though once the physical act was done, nothing was left? Unsummoned, the vision of Meg's long supine body entered his mind, her legs rigid, her eyes wide and fearful. Dammit! What was he—a masochist?

He got up and dressed. Jessica, eyes closed, was lying on the plush carpet. When she heard him moving about, she opened one eye and looked at him archly.

"Where do you think you're going? Have a late date?"

"Sorry, Jessica. I really am. I have to go out to the beach place early tomorrow to see about getting the storm windows in."

She sprang to her feet with a sudden, feline motion. "Well, by God! What's happened to Slattery, or whatever his name is?" Slattery was the year-round overseer of the family estate on Long Island, who also took care of the small beach cottage.

"Slattery is having a well-earned vacation," Jeff lied. He did not plan a trip to the country. He simply knew he had to get away from Jessica and try to get his head on straight. He felt terribly confused.

"Goddammit! This is a pretty kettle of fish," she muttered in annoyance. "Wham bam, thank you ma'am, huh?"

He put his arm around her and kissed her lightly. "Sorry, Jessica, truly. I'm—well, we'll make up for it next time, okay? I'll take you to dinner at the Palace."

He moved to the door and let himself out. He knew he had behaved like a cad. He hated himself for it, but he could not rid himself of the image of Meg's dark, reproachful eyes.


Fortunately, Meg's job on Friday was so demanding that it brought her forcibly back to reality, and by the time the grinding workday ended, the hideous dream of the previous night had receded somewhat.

It was not until she went to bed that evening that it again became vivid and disturbing. She was unable to sleep. Finally, she got up and made a cup of hot tea, which seemed to soothe her. When she crawled back into bed, it was after four.

She was awakened by the insistent clamor of her doorbell on Saturday morning. Glancing groggily at the clock, she saw that it was only a quarter to ten. Who could be ringing her bell at this hour? She dragged herself out of bed and into the oversized man's shirt she used as a robe, trying vainly to locate her bedroom slippers. She opened the door into the hallway and looked out to find a uniformed figure on the building's front steps. Perhaps the mailman.

She buzzed to let him in and waited in the open doorway. As he entered the building, she saw that it was not the postman but a messenger with a box about a foot square in his hand.

"Miss Gardner?" Meg nodded.

"Sign here, please."

"Wait a minute. What is this?"

"I don't know, Miss. I was told to deliver it to you."

The label carried the name of a famous Fifth Avenue store. She signed and handed the paper back to the messenger. With the help of scissors and a kitchen knife, she managed to get inside the sturdy cardboard carton. Scattering the shreds of white packing material onto the floor, she dug inside and pulled out a brand-new Minolta camera in a soft leather case. There was also a leather carrying bag containing telephoto and zoom lenses, three varicolored filters, an electronic flash attachment and four rolls of film.

What in heaven did it mean? She could not imagine receiving a present of such extravagance out of the blue. Jeff! He must have done it. Who else would have bothered? But he must know she couldn't accept such a gift. Especially after the episode two nights ago. She must call him and get the matter straightened out at once. Was he trying to buy her off? Assuage his conscience by giving her something he knew it would be difficult for her to refuse?

She picked up the telephone angrily, then realized she did not have his number. When she called information, she was told the number was unlisted. She hung up the phone and sat fuming. How dare he humiliate her like this? Especially when he was leaving her with no recourse until she saw him at the Tuesday night class.

She had looked forward to having the whole day to herself, browsing through secondhand camera stores and pawnshops in the distant hope that she could find an inexpensive replacement for her old Minolta. Now it seemed futile and pointless. But she could not keep the new camera!

She made coffee and half-heartedly scrambled an egg. The food looked unappealing. Halfway through the breakfast, she couldn't resist examining the camera and doing some practice focusing. What a magnificent instrument it was. The shutter snapped easily with hardly a sound; the f-stops went all the way to 1/1000 second; her hand curved around it without effort. It was exquisitely designed and engineered. Suddenly impatient with her own weakness, she packed it back into the carton and got dressed.

"I'll forget I ever got it. I'll go out and try to find a camera as though I hadn't gotten it." She pulled on a pair of tan corduroy slacks and got into a cream-colored turtleneck sweater. She dabbed on lipstick and took her well-worn pea jacket from the closet. She went first to Bernie's on Canal Street, the discount store the gray-haired camera store man had recommended. The store was packed with customers, and when she finally caught a salesman's eye, she was told at once that Bernie's no longer carried used cameras. "Too much trouble, too little profit," the man pronounced curtly.

"Do you know where else I might try?"

The salesman was eager to get back to customers interested in more lucrative mechandise. "Lady, there are some pawnshops around the corner on the Bowery. You might try there." He turned away and approached a prosperous-looking middle-aged couple obsequiously.

Meg left the store and went from one pawnshop to another. There were plenty of used cameras for sale and a few seemed to be in good condition, but all the stores were cash-and-carry, and even the least expensive of the 35-millimeter cameras carried a price tag out of her range.

The sidewalks were strewn with wine bottles and human flotsam. Meg longed to have a working camera with her. The eyes of the men she passed were hauntingly empty; she could tell that a few of them had been very presentable—even handsome—before time and alcohol had taken its toll. She was struck by the names of the bars she passed. "Sunshine," "Liberty," Bluebird," "Happy Morning."

This was the milieu that intrigued her—the belly of the city. What intrigued her most of all was the unbelievable juxtaposition of luxury and squalor on some blocks. A new high-rise apartment house was going up, with sunny balconies and wide French doors. Next to it was a flophouse, with crumbling bricks and windows boarded up with plywood.

Her quest for the camera seemed hopeless. Where was it Jeff had told her the "Streets of New York" exhibition was showing? Oh, yes, the Museum of Modern Art. Well, until she could solve the problem of her own camera, she could learn something from what other photographers were doing with theirs. She caught a bus to 53rd Street. She had been to the Museum of Modern Art only once, at the behest of her aunts, to see one of Monet's "Water Lilies," which had proved to be a magnificent work of art indeed. She was glad for an excuse to go back, though she probably shouldn't spend even the modest price of admission. But it was Saturday and her soul felt bruised. She needed solace. She wanted to see "Water Lilies" again, but she would save it for last and leave the museum, she hoped, in a more tranquil state of mind. If anything could achieve that, it would be the serene panorama of Monet's exquisite flowers.

She went to the second floor and was immediately engrossed in the display of photographs. They were all in black and white, which was an initial disappointment. However, when she started examining them, she could see that they would have been much less effective in color. Stark contrasts added to their impact; there was a most effective shot of a long expanse of narrow, snowbound street taken either at dawn or dusk, with a lone man's figure bent against the wind. Then she found another that arrested her gaze—a geometric close-up of a playground fence, the children's figures behind it misty and only half-defined. She laughed aloud at a portrait of an ancient man and a very small child, sitting close together on a park bench, both sleeping the sleep of the innocent.

Her heart felt lighter—this had been a good idea. At least it had taken her out of herself temporarily. She moved on to another photograph. As she looked more closely to try to decipher the photographer's name—"James"? "Janis"?—she suddenly caught sight of a brown suede jacket and achingly familiar, red-brown hair. Jeff! Though he was at the far end of the room, she was certain that she was not mistaken. The shape of his head, the line of his shoulders. . . She ducked through the knots of people frantically. She must tell him she could not accept the camera.

He still had not seen her, as his attention was concentrated exclusively on one of the blow-ups in the exhibition.

"Jeff!"

He turned slowly, as if not quite sure whether the sound had been real or imagined. When he saw her, his eyes were at first wary. Then he turned to her and a small, crooked smile crossed his face.

"Hello, Meg."

"Jeff, I tried to call you this morning, but—I—"

Suddenly she had no idea what to say next. What if, by some remote chance, he had not sent the camera? He would think her a lunatic. But who else? It must have been Jeff.

"Jeff, you know you'll have to take it back. I can't keep a gift like that. I appreciate your—"

His eyes became cold. She felt suddenly shabby in the frayed pea-jacket and slacks. He, with his suede jacket, tweed trousers and Irish hunter's cap, looked very much the self-assured young man-about-town, out for a casual Saturday afternoon round of the museums before going on to a festive evening at an expensive watering-hole.

"I haven't the vaguest idea of what you're talking about, Meg." His expression was puzzled.

"Oh, but Jeff, you must! This morning someone delivered an expensive camera to my door. It had to be you—who else could have done it?"

"You've got me. But everybody in the class knew your camera was broken. Maybe you've got a secret admirer."

She frowned and looked at him in disbelief. "But I was so sure it was you. You're the only one who knows—who knew that it would be so difficult for me to get another one. Jeff, please admit it and take it back. I don't want charity. I'll manage to get a camera somehow."

He took her hand as one would calm an hysterical child. "I tell you, Meg, I didn't send you a camera. I don't know who did. But if they wanted to remain anonymous—as they obviously did—why don't you just accept it gracefully and enjoy it?"

"But I can't. I'd never stop trying to figure out—"

"When manna falls from heaven, don't look a gift horse in the mouth," he said. "To mix a few metaphors. But you get the point."

She pulled her hand slowly away from his. He made it seem so unimportant. If he really hadn't sent it, she must appear very foolish to him. If he had sent it, he was obviously not going to admit it. She supposed there was a remote possibility someone else in the class, some wealthy eccentric or, as he had said, a "secret admirer," might have done it out of a wish to play God, or a hope to score at a later date, or even conceivably out of sheer altruism.

She stood irresolutely, the afternoon sun streaming in on her lightly freckled face, the worried eyes, the long hair now loosened from its barrette and framing her face like a dark hood. Jeff looked at her and felt an irrational urge to take her in his arms and tell her everything would be all right—to murmur soothing nonsense sounds, like crooning to a baby.

"What do you think I should do?" Her eyes widened as if she were waiting for an answer from an oracle.

"I've already told you, Meg. Keep it, use it, enjoy it and don't worry about where it came from. There's nothing else you *can* do, is there? You can't interrogate every member of the class at gunpoint."

The vision conjured up by his final sentence brought a short burst of involuntary laughter from her, laughter that, after a moment, he joined. Then his face sobered. A voice in the back of his mind whispered, *Don't carry it any further. Don't let her know what an inadequate coward you really are. She's more than you can handle. Don't let yourself in for something that can only end in disaster.*

"I have to go, Meg." He looked at his watch. "I'm supposed to meet some people for drinks. See you Tuesday night."

He moved quickly away and left her standing there, wondering what to do with a ruined Saturday afternoon.

## Chapter 6

Meg was not in class on the following Tuesday and Jeff was surprised to find that he could not get his mind off the empty chair at his side. He could not imagine any logical reason for her absence. He he been so abrupt to her in the museum that she did not want to face him again? That was far-fetched: in spite of her occasional waif-like quality, Jeff had sensed from the beginning that she was a survivor. There was a tenacity about her that he felt would ultimately prevail. She was like a frail willow that would repeatedly bend but never break, even when giant redwoods were toppling around it.

He tried in vain to listen to Dr. Laglen's lecture, but it seemed only a drone. Laglen had raised his eyebrows when he called Meg's name at the beginning of the class and received no answer. Dr. Laglen did not like absences. Jeff supposed it was frustrating to the professor's Prussian temperament to have no real means of penalizing students for cutting class, since no one was taking the course for credit. His only means of retribution was sarcasm or a heavy silence.

"This Saturday," Laglen announced as the buzzer sounded for the end of class, "we take our first field trip. This time we go to Staten Island. I give you the details for meeting, and so forth, during our Thursday night class."

Jeff gathered his notes and decided to have a hamburger at McBurney's. Walking in, he remembered the night he had come here with Meg. Why was it so difficult to get her out of his mind? He had made his decision and every brain cell in his head told him it was the right one. So what was the big deal?

He ordered a hamburger, rare, with pickles and onions, and had an Irish coffee while he was waiting. The Irish coffee was almost finished when Louie the bartender came to his booth. "Hey, Jeff, I wancha to see sumpn' I took the last time ya was heah. It's good stuff, man." He took from the pocket of his white jacket an envelope of snapshots. Jeff knew Louie was an amateur photographer and not a bad one; they had compared notes often before. It was one of the reasons he liked the joint.

He examined the photos as Louie handed them to him, one by one. They were of various patrons of the bar: the two dissolute brothers; the tiny, servile man who always came in and nursed one beer; the old lady who appeared at three a.m. after she had sold the last of her gardenias to couples in the Village clubs. His hands suddenly trembled as Louie handed him the next photo —he had snapped Meg just as she was finishing a sip of Irish coffee. The white, foamy cream was still on her upper lip and she was trying to lick it away. Her eyes were laughing as she looked at Jeff mischievously. The lamp behind her backlighted her hair into a halo. He had never seen a more beautiful photograph.

"Nice, huh?" Louie was as pleased as if he had just been awarded the Pulitzer Prize.

Jeff didn't answer. He looked at the photograph for a long time without speaking, then handed it back to Louie. "Yeah. It'll do, Louie," he said, mocking his own understatement. "No, hell, I'm kidding you, Lou. It's a great shot."

"See, I thought a flash would wash it out too much. I just set the camera on the edge of the bar and did a time exposure. It turned out beautiful, didn't it?"

"Yeah. Beautiful. I'd like to have a copy."

Louie grinned. "Sure! I'll give it to you next time you come in."

He wolfed down the hamburger and caught a cab home. Without bothering to take off his coat, he went to the telephone and dailed Meg's number. In the cab, he had finally admitted to himself he was no match for the force that pulled him to her. The phone rang in her apartment. He must have let it ring a dozen times before he finally gave up and replaced it in its cradle.

Meg was in her usual chair when he arrived in class on Thursday night. He had tried to call her almost hourly on both Wednesday and today, with the same result he had had on Tuesday night. No answer. His heart leapt when he saw her. They were both early and he slipped eagerly into the seat beside her. There were only four or five other people in the room. The new Minolta was around her neck.

"Hey, I missed you Tuesday night. What happened?"

She looked at him briefly, cast her eyes to the opposite side of the room and spoke stiffly. "A death in the family."

"God, I'm sorry. Somebody very close?"

"My aunt." Her tone did not encourage further questions.

Jeff perservered. He had to let her know that his attitude had changed, that he was no longer fighting against the attraction she held for him. He wanted to tell her, no matter what words he used, that he was sorry for having been such a fool. "That's too bad, Meg. But I'm glad it wasn't anybody in your immediate family."

She looked at him as if he had struck her. "She and another aunt brought me up, Jeff. They were the only family I ever knew." Her voice was iced with contempt.

"If you'll excuse me, I think I'll move closer to the front. Dr. Laglen is sometiimes hard to hear."

Helplessly, he watched her gather her belongings and move to a seat in the first row on the far side of the room. He slapped his forehead with the heel of his hand. What an idiot he was! She had told him when they had first met that she had been reared by two aunts, offering it as an explanation for her inhibitions. It must have been very painful for her to articulate. And he had forgotten it completely and had made a jackass of himself. After such a show of insensitivity and carelessness on his part, he wouldn't blame her if she never spoke to him again.

But he couldn't let her believe that he was a total clod. Dr. Laglen entered and class began. He would try to make amends afterward. It was too late to do anything about it until class was over at ten o'clock.


When the bell rang, Dr. Laglen consulted his notes hurriedly. "Ladies and gentlemen, before you go, if I may allow my voice to be heard over this frantic rustling of papers—" He waited for and received the titter of obligatory laughter. "We meet for the field trip at the dock of the Staten Island Ferry at ten on Saturday morning. Bring, of course, your cameras—also filters, and if you have them, wide-angle lenses. We will study the use of this equipment. You would perhaps be wise to bring a sandwich for sustenance. Class dismissed."

Jeff waited outside the door. Meg came out without stopping and started briskly down the street toward her Lower East Side apartment. "Meg! Wait for me for a minute, will you, please?"

She turned and shot him a terse look of contempt, then continued on her way with hardly a break in her stride. Her walk was rapid and determined. She wasn't going to make it easy for him, that was for sure. He started running after her, jostling students on the sidewalk who were having a convivial final cigarette before making their separate ways to the bus or subway.

"Meg, please wait! I have to tell you something!"

Her steps slowed and finally stopped. She kept her back to him. He put his hands on the shoulders of her pea-jacket and turned her to face him. The smoky mist of their breath commingled in the cold air.

"What exactly do you want from me, Jeff?" Her eyes were both pleading and angry.

"Meg, I've been a damn fool in about a hundred ways that I can think of, for starters. I want to apologize and—"

"You haven't been a damn fool, Jeff. I have. But it doesn't matter. When they called me about Aunt Emma, and I had four days in Georgia with nothing to do but think, I got a whole different perspective on a lot of things. Including you. And all of a sudden, it doesn't amount to a hill of beans whether I can live up to your standards sexually or not. I mean, at the time I was really hurt. You see, Jeff, I'm not used to playing games. Even though we had known each other for such a short time, I thought there was something between us that was strong, and good. I guess I thought you had the same feeling. That's how foolish and naive I am, Jeff. I thought that if I felt that way about you, then it followed without a doubt that you felt the same way about me. So think again. You're not the fool, don't you understand? I am."

The tears that had been brimming in her eyes overflowed onto her cheeks. Her breath started coming in short, erratic gulps. She turned away suddenly and started running down the street.

She ran unheeding, at full speed. At Washington Square, she crossed the street without paying attention to the cars and cab that sounded their horns shrilly. She heard the frantic beeps from a distance but did not connect it with her headlong flight. The lights of the vehicles were yellow blurs through her tears. She had just reached the opposite sidewalk when a rough hand grabbed the back of her jacket and Jeff caught her arm in a vise-like grip.

"For God's sake, Meg, are you trying to get us both killed?" He looked at her unseeing eyes and slapped her—hard. "Come to your senses!"

She raised a trembling hand and blinked her eyes in surprise. "Why—why did you do that?"

"Because you're half out of your mind. Now let's sit down—I have a lot to tell you." He thrust her arm through his and pulled her back across the street to the square. They entered the park under the Washington Square Arch. The park was almost empty—only a few stragglers on their way home and a small hard-core contingent of winos and marijuana pushers were left. Jeff found a vacant bench and led her to it.

"You had your say. Now listen, while I have mine. First, I'm sorry I was such a clod about your aunt. The minute I said it, I remembered you had told me your two aunts brought you up. The news about your aunt's death came to me out of left field and for a minute I just didn't make the connection—that's my only excuse. I want you to tell me more about her later, because she must have been a remarkable lady to have been responsible for the woman you are."

He drew a deep breath and went on. "And I want to apologize for being a total creep the last time we were together. You're absolutely right. I left because I thought I couldn't stand the complications of a relationship with you. It was sheer cowardice on my part. But I *am* a devout coward and I have ample credentials to prove it. However," he continued hurriedly—he did not want to explain that last statement now—"When you weren't in class on Tuesday night, I imagined all sorts of hideous things that might have happened to you, from being raped and murdered to being asphyxiated by a gas leak. I must have tried to call you fifty times between Tuesday night and tonight when you finally showed up for class."

She did not look at him, nor did she move. She watched the dried brown leaves as they skittered along the walk in the late evening wind. Her eyes would follow one until it became indistinguishable among a drift of others, then would pick out another and fix her gaze on it with intense concentration. He had no idea what effect his recitation was having on her; her face was completely noncommittal. Was she listening, or was she in a numb and grieving world of her own? He plunged on.

"Meg, I've been going with a woman who is probably the most skillful sexual partner I'll ever have—" Now at last, she looked up at him, silently and contemptuously, but he refused to be silenced. "I've got to go on and tell you this. I called her the day after I had—been with you. Yes, I found the release I didn't find with you. But I also found that it didn't mean—"

Suddenly she was flailing away at his chest and shoulders with both her fists. When she spoke, her voice was strident, almost a shout. "Shut up! I don't want to hear any more from you, you conceited bastard! What are you trying to do—turn me into a basket case? How much more can I take from you? Go away and leave me alone!"

She crumpled in slow motion onto the bench, her head pillowed in her arms on its narrow wooden slats. He heard terrible, racking sobs. A late dog-walker looked idly at the couple and shrugged, chalking it up as a lovers' quarrel, then moved on down the path.

Jeff reached out to touch her cheek, to comfort her, but he reconsidered and slowly moved his hand back into his lap. She wept, half-sitting, half-lying, for perhaps five minutes. Then the sobs slowly died. She sat up, moving stiffly. When she saw Jeff still sitting there, her eyes flickered with surprise but she said nothing.

"Are you ready to go home?" There was a gentleness in his tone she had not heard before. She nodded and got to her feet.

He hailed a cab and gave the driver her address. In front of her building, when she realized he was getting out of the taxi, her mouth opened and she started to speak. He quickly put his finger lightly over her lips and shook his head. "I'm not going to touch you, Meg. I just want to be sure you get a good night's sleep."

He took the keys from her hand and unlocked the door. Once inside, he helped her off with her coat and shoes. Then he went into the bathroom and ran a tub of hot water. He came back to find her sitting on the sofa, glassy-eyed. He took her hand gently and led her to the steaming tub.

"Get in," he ordered.

She bit her lips, looked at him and nodded. He retreated to the living room, closing the bathroom door softly behind him. From an end table, he picked up a framed oval photograph of a wedding couple. Judging by the woman's clothing, he would guess it had been made during the late fifties. She was a raving beauty; the man was in a soldier's uniform. He replaced the photo carefully as Meg came into the room, her hair pinned into a topknot with wisps curling damply about her face. *My God*, he thought, *she is beautiful*. At that moment, she looked like a Botticelli angel.

She smiled at him tentatively. "I feel better. Thank you for suggesting that."

"There's one more thing I want you to do for me,"

he said. He rummaged around in his briefcase and brought out a small vial of capsules. "Take one of these."

"What are they?"

"A mild tranquilizer. You'll sleep better."

"I never take pills."

"Tonight . . . just one. Trust me."

A wan smile flirted with the corners of her mouth. "Okay, doctor. Just this once." She held the pill in her hand while he brought water from the kitchen, then gulped it down.

"You have any rubbing alcohol?"

"I don't know—there may be some in the medicine chest."

Finding it, he led her into the bedroom and turned on the lamp. Funny, he thought, this had all the earmarks of a standard seduction scene. But he felt something far more tender than sexual arousal. He wanted only to put her to bed and leave her serene and at peace with herself.

"Lie on your stomach, Meg."

She lay down unquestioningly. He moved the long shirt off her shoulders and began to rub her back with slow, firm strokes. She spoke to him only once, in a drowsy, childish voice.

"You sent me the camera, didn't you, Jeff?"

"Yes."

"I thank you. I'll try to use it well."

After a few minutes, her breathing slowed and he saw that her eyes were tightly closed. He put the cap on the bottle of alcohol, turned out the lamp and stood up.

Going to the doorway, he looked back at her. If he never did anything else for her, he had given her a night of badly needed rest. At least she would awake knowing he was her friend.

## Chapter 7

Jeff called Meg the next evening and was relieved to find her much improved after a solid ten hours' sleep. She had called her office to let them know she would be late and Mr. Benson had insisted she take the entire day off. Things were exceptionally slow, he said, and her caseload could easily be handled by her colleagues.

"So I've had a whole day to unwind, even though my conscience did bother me a little for not going in to work. The only thing was, they didn't expect me back till Monday anyway."

"Then I think you did the wise thing, Meg. All work and no play, you know. Say, Meg, about this field trip tomorrow—shall we go down together? Why don't I pick you up about a quarter to ten?"

"All right. But look, I think you'd better make it nine-thirty. We might run into traffic."

"Doubtful on a Saturday morning, but okay. Nine-thirty it is."

"Oh, Jeff, I'll bring lunch, huh?"

"Super. See you tomorrow."

He hung up, feeling vaguely dissatisfied with the conversation. He had wanted to ask her to dinner, but something told him not to rush it with Meg. She needed time to assimilate him into her life—to accept him as a friend. Then they could go on from there.

Before he could move away from the phone, it rang. Andrea, his stepmother, was on the line.

"Jeff, dear, had you thought about Thanksgiving?"

"Thanksgiving? No, not really. It's weeks away, isn't it?"

"Not as many weeks as you'd think. It comes early this year—the twenty-third. Timmy's been asking and asking when we're going to see you again, and I thought maybe we could bribe you out here for the holiday."

Timmy, Jeff's half-brother, growing up without a father, was another reason for Jeff's attacks of guilt. The boy needed somebody as a surrogate father and Andrea's never-ending parade of men friends was hardly qualified to fill the bill. Not the ones he had met, anyway. If Timmy had been asking for him, he would have to go.

"No bribe necessary, Andrea. You know that. I'll be there. I look forward to it. And tell Timmy he'd better start practicing his backgammon."

She laughed lightly. "Yes, I will."

"May I bring a friend?"

There was silence on the other end of the line. Then she asked coolly, "Oh, who? Jessica?"

"No. Uh, I imagine she'll be busy with her own family. But I'd like to bring someone else, if that's all right."

"Oh?" Andrea's upward inflection was too well-bred to betray naked curiosity, but he sensed it just behind the questioning syllable.

"Yes. A friend I met in the photography class I'm taking. She's new in New York and I'm sure she'd enjoy a real family Thanksgiving."

Another pause. "Oh. Then of course. I'll call in a week or so to set the particulars."

"Right. G'bye, Andrea. My love to Timmy."

This turn of events was unexpected, Jeff thought as he hung up. Five Thanksgivings had passed since the death of his father, and this was the first holiday invitation he had received from Andrea. He saw Timmy at intervals more infrequent than they should have been, and took the bright 13-year-old to the theater, the planetarium or to a ball game. But he usually met Timmy in town—since his father's death, he had been back only once or twice to Rosehill and then only briefly and on business.

Rosehill was the Long Island estate where Jeff had grown up, and where Andrea and Timmy now lived. Although Jeff, his late brother Robert, and Andrea had inherited the estate jointly when Jeff's father died, it was a matter of mutual agreement between Jeff and Robert that Andrea and Timmy should live at Rosehill until she remarried, if she did. Ordinarily they never heard from her till time to pay the annual property taxes. Neither brother had ever mentioned to the other that it was perhaps a bit unfair to be asked to pay taxes on property they never saw. The only part of their father's estate they ever went near was the small beach house on the North Shore, where one or the other had sometimes spent summer weekends, until Robert went to Vietnam.

Expenses for Rosehill would have been considerably less if Andrea had been willing to give up the McAllister stable of thoroughbred horses. Jeff had tentatively broached the subject only once, shortly after his father's death, when he had met Andrea in town to sign some legal papers.

"You know, Andrea, those horses cost a lot of money. Wouldn't it be easier if you sold them?"

Her eyes widened. "Why, Jeff, I'm really surprised that that would even enter your head. You know how much your dad loved those animals."

"But their feed, and the groom, and boarding them in Florida during the winter—"

She interrupted stubbornly. "Timmy enjoys them, too, you know. I'm teaching him to be a fine rider. It would be a major upheaval to—well, really, I don't think you ought to ask it of me."

So the bills for hay and oats continued to be forwarded to Jeff and Robert, and they did not mention the matter to her again.

Shaking off the depression that always accompanied thoughts of his brother or his father, Jeff settled back to read a photography magazine and to wait for midnight when he could decently retire for the night. He looked forward to the field trip with Meg; he also wondered whether she would accept the Thanksgiving invitation. If he did actually extend it, that is. He was not sure Meg and Andrea were each other's type.

Saturday dawned clear and nippy. Meg hastily put on a pair of jeans and a heavy red cardigan, tying a bandanna over her hair, gypsy-style. She had just swallowed the last bite of toast and jelly when the doorbell rang. She peeked into the hall, saw Jeff waiting on the front steps and motioned him she'd be right out. Checking the stove to be sure the gas was turned off, she grabbed her pea-jacket from the closet, gathered up the camera and its accessory bag, and walked out into the bright morning sun.

She was in an elated mood. Her grief for her aunt lay like a dark specter in the background that she was determined to keep dormant for today. She was looking forward to exploring Staten Island. Though she had ridden over and back on its famous ferry, she had never disembarked for more than the few minutes it took to buy a newspaper or a candy bar and reboard for the return trip to Manhattan.

Jeff, too, seemed excited by the prospect of the day's outing. He regaled her on the way to the Battery by doing a devastating parody of a confused tourist guide.

Pointing out the Woolworth building, he identified it as the Empire State Building; he blithely renamed the World Trade Center the Chicago Merchandise Mart and insisted that the Brooklyn Bridge was actually the Golden Gate which had been shipped intact by truck from San Francisco.

"The Brooklyn Bridge was bought in the late 60s by a wealthy Texas oil man who had it reassembled on his back lawn. His kid, you see, wanted it for Christmas. Then when the Golden Gate Bridge was moved to New York, San Francisco bought the one that used to be over Chesapeake Bay."

Keeping a poker face as the cabdriver gave him a startled look and Meg collapsed in a paroxysm of laughter, he continued, "What's so far-fetched about that? London Bridge is somewhere in Arizona, isn't it? People get tired of looking at the same old bridge day in and day out. It leads to monotony, which in turn can result in atrophy of the funny bone, which is responsible for all sorts of dread communicable diseases."

They met their straggling colleagues shivering at the loading dock. Dr. Laglen was attempting to keep them in an orderly group with notable lack of success. The first field trip had all the air of a holiday. The students' prior conversation during class had been limited mainly to "hello" and "goodbye," with an occasional, whispered comment on a pronouncement of Dr. Laglen's. Now the housewives had been released from a day of grocery-shopping or cookie-baking, the plump or plain students were not yet confronted with the misery of a Saturday night alone, and the widowers and retirees did not have to find an excuse for lingering at the corner newsstand to find someone to chat with.

Meg and Jeff joined the group, still laughing at the cabdriver's parting shot: "Buddy, I hope your girl friend finds somebody else to show her around this city.

If she don't, she's gonna be one mixed-up dame."

As the ferryboat chugged out of its berth and turned its prow toward Staten Island, Meg took Jeff's hand and pulled him to the stern. "Wait," he objected. "Let's go up front and let the spray blow in our faces and pretend we're Vikings."

"On the way back! I want to look at the Manhattan skyline on the way over."

It was surely one of the most breathtaking views in the world. Even the tall, up-ended boxes of the World Trade Center looked delicate from the boat. The entire concrete island could easily have been a mirage, for the sun was still half-shrouded by mist that clung over the water, although it had been brilliantly clear onshore. To their left, the Statue of Liberty appeared.

"I'll never get over the thrill of this city," she said. "People always talk about what's wrong with it, but it has to be the most alive city in the world."

"I won't give you an argument. I've loved it since I was a toddler, when my father used to bring me in on Saturdays to go to the Museum of Natural History and see the dinosaur bones. He always said—" Jeff stopped abruptly and his face darkened.

"Yes? He always said what?" Meg, who had been devouring the skyline with her eyes, had not noticed his change of expression and now pressed her face to his playfully. When she saw the look on his face, she moved back a step. "Jeff! What's the matter? Did I—"

He took her hand and moved it against his cheek. "No. I'll tell you about it sometime. Not today. Let's go and get coffee before we dock."

Dr. Laglen herded the class along the ramp that led from the ferry station to the public roadway, where they boarded a bus for Great Kills Park.

"What a gruesome name," Meg observed. "Did it used to be a place for hunters to stalk their prey?"

"No no. 'Kill' is a Dutch word meaning any sort of channel or inlet. As in 'Catskill.' "

"Oh ho! I'd never have made the connection."

"Possibly 99 percent of the people in New York never do. They think the name of those mountains has something to do with the talents of a feline."

"Oh, you're clever with words, you are."

"Naturally. The Irish have a gift of the gab, don't you know?"

"McAllister? I thought that name was Scottish."

"Could be either, actually. In my case, it's Irish."

There was so much she did not yet know about him. She didn't know where he had been to school, what he had been like as a boy, whether he had any rabid likes and dislikes, what his particular interests were—outside of stockbrokerage and photography. Somehow none of it seemed important. Jeff was Jeff. Since Thursday night, when he had taken her home and soothed her to sleep, she had felt a grateful, platonic fondness for him almost to the exclusion of any other feeling. Now, as they sat side by side on the jolting bus, he put an arm around her shoulders, and in an instant the feeling became quite different—an urgent wish that he could hold her tightly, that they were alone somewhere far from the magpie chatter of the others. The pressure of his hand on her shoulder tightened. Had he, through some mysterious alchemy, sensed her feelings?

She had never felt such a wild need to be touched, to be held, to be engulfed. The sensation was both delicious and frightening. She moved away from him with an almost imperceptible furtive motion. He looked at her with one eyebrow cocked and one corner of his mouth lifted. "Going somewhere? You'll never get away from me. Don't you know that, even now?"

Deep in her loins, she could feel an insistent throb. She smiled at him tenuously, then immediately looked away, out the window to the hilly street. "Oh, look! That little boy is riding his bicycle with no hands. He's really good, too."

At that moment, a dairy truck barreled out of a side street and screeched its brakes, narrowly missing the boy on the bike. Meg cut off her own involuntary scream by clapping a hand over her mouth. She held herself rigid until the moment of panic had passed.

"Meg! Honey, what's the matter? It's all right—the truck missed the little guy. There's no harm done."

When she uncovered her face, Jeff saw that she was deathly white.

"Oh, Jeff. My God, that reminded me so much of one of the worst moments of my life."

"You want to tell me about it?" He spoke quietly.

"I—yes. I guess so. I had just gotten a bicycle for Christmas—I think I was nine or ten years old. I went out to ride it—my aunts told me to be sure to get off and walk it across the highway. It was a fairly heavily traveled road just two blocks from our house. But I got on the bike, and I guess I felt drunk with power, or pride of ownership, or something. Anyway, when I got to the highway, I started riding across. I thought I had looked in both directions—I thought I was being very careful—but somehow a car zoomed out of nowhere and slammed into me.

"I remember seeing the car fender tear off the front wheel of the bike and I remember hitting my head on the pavement. I was conscious for a minute, and I remember being more concerned with the bike than with how badly I was hurt. But here's the strange thing: when I came to, three days later, I was in the hospital and I didn't remember anything at all about those three days!"

Jeff was puzzled. "But that's not so unusual, is it? It simply meant you were unconscious for three days. What was it—a concussion?"

71

"Yes, it was, but you don't understand. During those three days, I had been *awake*. I had been talking, eating, going through all the normal motions. My aunts had been in to see me during that time, I had asked them questions about my friends, about my pet rabbit and things like that. Then after three days, when I really got back to normal, I started asking them the same questions all over again! Neither they nor the doctors could understand it. It was the weirdest thing that's ever happened to me."

"That is quite a phenomenon." He squeezed her hand. He could see that she was still a bit shaken and he wanted to change the subject. "Well, don't worry—I won't let you forget *me*."

The bus disgorged the group at the park's entrance. Dr. Laglen gave them brief instructions about the kinds of photographs he wanted them to try for. He explained the uses of the different colors of filters—"Red gives very dramatic color contrasts, for instance"—and they fanned out into the park, exclaiming over the panorama of trees, sky and water.

"What body of water is that?" Meg pointed to the choppy inlet.

"It's the Lower Bay that separates Staten Island and Brooklyn, I think. Hell, I don't know. I've only been to Staten Island once or twice myself."

"Did you notice on the bus coming out here, it's almost like you'd suddenly been transported to the Midwest? The architecture of the houses, for example. They're very Midwest in feeling."

"I've never been to the Midwest," Jeff confessed.

"Never? My aunts used to drive across the country every summer for years. Just to get back to the grassroots, they said."

"How quaint," Jeff responded. Then, seeing the fleeting expression of hurt in her eyes, he instantly regretted the flip remark. "I'm sorry, Meg. My family used to indulge in that kind of barbed repartee all the time. They taught me bad habits, I'm afraid."

"I wish you'd tell me about your family sometime. You start talking about them and then, all of a sudden, you stop."

"I will. Someday when I'm in a masochistic mood." He focused his camera on a squirrel perched on the lower branch of a tree. "If I ever decide I really dig guilt, I'll tell you all about them."

## Chapter 8

By early afternoon, they had wandered to an isolated meadow protected from the wind by surrounding hillocks and warmed to some extent by the pale, autumnal sun. Meg was delightedly trying out the new camera on everything in sight.

Jeff smiled at her obvious pleasure. "I would have got you a Hasselblad, but you seemed to be in love with Minoltas."

"Oh, I think you did the right thing. I'm used to this kind. What time is it, by the way?"

"Ten after one."

"Ready for lunch?"

"Silliest question of the week. I'm ravenous."

She poured steaming coffee into plastic cups and began unpacking the luncheon. Fried chicken, potato salad, pimiento-cheese sandwiches, tiny sweet gherkins. Jeff stared with goggle-eyed wonder.

"You must sure as hell have a good deli in your neighborhood. That looks super-delicious."

"Deli? No, of course not. I made this—I told you I was going to bring lunch."

"Thought you meant you were just going to buy it and haul it." He bit into the chicken. "As they say on the telly, I have just two words for this chicken: 'Umm-umm.' "

"You like?"

"Not really." She looked up startled until she saw the grin. "It's just the best damn chicken I ever tasted."

"I'll tell you a secret," she said, pleased. "You have to soak the chicken in milk before the flour, use a heavy iron skillet and drain it on a brown paper bag."

"How did you learn to cook?"

"My aunts both taught school in a town twenty miles away from the little town where we lived. I got home earlier than they did, so I started having supper ready for them at night."

"Supper?"

"Well, yes. We had breakfast, dinner and supper instead of breakfast, lunch and dinner. You see, most people in the little town came home at noontime and that's when they had the big meal of the day. Supper was usually a lighter cold meal. Not in our case, though —we had the main meal of the day at night. But we still called it supper."

"Yours really sounds like an idyllic childhood."

"It was, a lot of the time. Typical small-town upbringing. I remember going barefoot all summer, walking along dusty lanes and smelling the tiny white hedge blossoms. In the summer, after supper, when I was a little kid, all the neighborhood children would gather in old Mr. Lambert's yard. He lived up on a hill and had a huge front yard. We'd catch fireflies— lightning bugs, we called them—and put them in fruit jars."

"What did you do with them?"

"The lightning bugs? Oh, I don't know. I guess when it was time for us to go inside, we turned them all loose again."

Jeff laughed. What would have been an exercise in futility for an adult furnished a child with hours of perfect happiness.

"How old were you when your mother died?"

Meg's expression changed, closed off. "I was—uh, five. My father was in the Vietnam War. He went in the early 60s, supposedly as an advisor. Six months later, my mother got a telegram that he was missing. It was in the winter, just after I was five. My mother started out walking, to tell her sisters—the aunts I lived with—and a car hit her."

"Where were you when it happened?"

"I was with her. They told me later—when I got old enough to understand—that she must have been walking on the edge of the pavement and I on the shoulder of the road. All I remember was the headlight —one of the headlights was out, they found out later. I remember the one headlight, and then I saw her lying there and I started calling her and she wouldn't answer me."

Meg had laid down her half-eaten sandwich and was staring straight ahead. Jeff was sorry they'd gotten started on the subject. He hadn't meant to make her live it all over again.

"I'm sorry, Meg. God, this is no day to bring back memories like that. I shouldn't have brought it up."

She smiled at him, picked up her sandwich and took another bite. "It's all right, Jeff. It was a long, long time ago, and time has a way of taking care of even the most painful episodes."

"Does it? Yes, I suppose so."

"You sound doubtful."

Jeff didn't answer. True, the doors in his past that he tried so hard to keep closed were much more recent than this one in hers, but he saw no signs of his pain easing. Maybe it would help if he could talk about it as openly as she did. But he could not—not yet anyway.

Determined, he grinned broadly and leaned over to kiss her. "My compliments to the chef. And I mean that with all my heart."

She understood exactly what he was trying to do— bring the conversation back to a mundane level. She crumpled the plastic wrap from the sandwich and stood up.

"Race you to that weeping willow." She sprinted away, looking back at him and laughing, her dark hair blowing over her mouth and out into the wind.

"Hey, just a minute! You didn't wait for the starter's pistol, you cheat!"

He caught her just as she reached the tree. He put his arms around her and hoisted her into the fork of a low branch. She began climbing higher. The still-green leaves of the willow obscured most of her body; he could see only the pale oval of her face and her enormous eyes, caught by the late afternoon sunlight. "Hold it! Don't move." Quickly he focused his camera on her face, framed by the chartreuse willow fronds. "That should be terrific, if I'm lucky."

He heard her disembodied voice from the leaves. "Help me down, Jeff. We'd better go."

"What?" he asked, with pretended surprise. "You don't want to spend the night among the ghosts and goblins in Great Kills Park?"

"Oh, shut up and help me down."

He put his arms around her waist to lift her off the limb. She jumped lightly to the ground, laughing, the jar cushioned by his supporting hands. Their arms went around each other and tightened.

"I love you, Meg."

His words caught her mid-laugh. The laughter died abruptly. "Jeff." Her lips sought his briefly, then she pushed herself away to look at him. "Jeff. Don't say that. I think it might work better if we were just good friends."

"Meg, why?"

How could she tell him that that was the only kind of relationship she felt comfortable with? That she was afraid to test her own inadequacies further? That she knew instinctively that it would be a minor miracle if she ever met a man patient enough to guide her to fulfillment? She could not tell him. Not that she did not want to—it was simply that the psychological complexities were too nebulous and subtle to articulate.

She remembered the frustration and incompleteness of their attempted liaison. She would not put him through that again. She would only try to keep him as a friend and let him find sex elsewhere. It was the greatest favor she could do him.

She shook her head. "It's better—for both of us. Let's join the others."

When they got back to their colleagues, they found them chilled and ready to go home. They boarded the return bus to the ferry and within minutes, Meg leaned her head against the seat and with an elaborate sigh, pretended to fall fast asleep. It was easier than trying to talk.

Through the remainder of the weekend, Jeff thought long and hard about their Saturday outing. Maybe he had been right the first time. Meg was obviously a neurotic who needed professional help in getting her head together. He would accede to her wishes; he would not see her again except as a friend.

Late Sunday afternoon, he called Jessica. Her maid answered and told him Miss Sterling had gone away for the weekend, but would be back later that evening. He hung up without leaving a message. Restlessly, he dropped into a movie late Sunday night—a highly touted comedy which was reputed to be hilarious. He could find nothing in it that amused him and left halfway through, to wander into a dreary coffeeshop for an overdone steak sandwich.

Meg spent Sunday getting organized for the following workday. After the confrontation with Mr. Gillespie when he had seemed to soften, she had hoped against hope for a miraculous transformation in his character. But no miracle had occurred, and Sarah Gillespie had at last decided she must leave her husband. Meg had found a potential employer for the woman. He was a garment manufacturer who usually spent the latter part of the day in the market; she had to call early before he left his office. She would try to make an appointment for Mrs. Gillespie to see him personally and Meg would accompany her there for moral support.

She felt discouraged. Mrs. Gillespie was a shy little woman who showed no aptitude for selling herself. Though she was bright and quick, Meg was doubtful that a first meeting would reveal those qualities. Well, she thought, sighing as she closed the heavy looseleaf notebook, she would do what she could.

Meg looked at the clock. Four-thirty. On impulse she decided to go to five-o'clock Mass. She had not been to church since she had been in New York. One of her objectives in coming to the city was to try to rid herself of the strictures of Catholicism. She knew that was also one of the reasons she had become a social worker. She resented the hold the Church had on her and felt if she substituted social activism for religion, she would be, to some extent, forgiven for her heresy. But now some primeval urge propelled her to the church down the block.

She sat in the dimness of one of the pews in the rear of the narrow church, its altar illuminated by the amber votive candles. She was early; mass had not yet started and only three or four people were in the church. Her thoughts were a jumble, but after she had sat for some minutes, a numb kind of peace seemed to wash over her like a tide. She felt that if she simply kept doing her best, things would surely work out.

After the brief service was over, she went home and had a light supper of tea, soup and toast. Climbing into bed, she shivered at the cold clamminess of the sheets. The bed felt like an empty wasteland.

Jeff saw Jessica on Monday night, but Jessica was in a hands-off mood. They went to dinner at the new restaurant Jessica had mentioned before, and through most of the meal, Jessica chattered about a man she had met through Sally, an old college friend with whom she had spent the weekend in Connecticut.

"You'd like him, I know, Jeff. He's an actor, darling, and talk about matinee idols! You know, I've always told you you look a little like Robert Redford? Well, this stud is the spitting image of Robert deNiro."

Jeff found himself wishing that Jessica talked more like a lady and less like a truckdriver. He supposed he was being old-fashioned.

She had not paused for breath. "You know—dark and brooding, and you feel there's something a little bit savage just underneath the surface?"

"Have you posted the banns?"

"What? What do you mean?"

"Have you set the wedding date?"

"Oh, 'banns.' You and your archaic expressions. Of course we haven't set the wedding date. He's nobody to *marry*, for heaven's sake. He has no money whatsoever. He's simply an attractive man with more sex appeal than practically anybody I know—present company excepted, of course, darling. Anyway, he's in a show—something Off-Off-Broadway. I don't know, I have to find out what it is so I can go see him in action. Monday night is his only night off. Wait a minute, this *is* Monday, isn't it? He said he'd call me on his night off, that dog, and we'd go out somewhere. Oh, well, actors are notoriously undependable, aren't they? You remember that singer Phoebe actually got engaged to? One day she woke up and found out he had left for California."

Jeff smiled ruefully and let her rave on. He knew she was making him pay for not having called after their last evening together. It made him feel better, knowing she was getting it out of her system.

"Do you want dessert?"

"I beg your pardon?"

"Do you want dessert? I think I'll have a cannole."

"You insensitive bastard. I sit here and try to make you jealous and you're concerned with nothing but your appetite. No, I don't want dessert. I'd like a brandy though."

By the time they were on their way home in a cab, Jessica's mood had changed and she became amorous. "You know, don't you, Jeff, that I was simply blathering on to make you feel bad. You know you're my one true love."

"Yes, Jess, I know." He put an arm lightly around her shoulders and started to kiss her, but he found to his surprise he didn't feel even remotely like making love to her tonight. "Why don't you put your head on my shoulder and have a little nap?"

"I'm not sleepy. In fact," she said huskily, "I'm very wide awake."

He cleared his throat and faked a cough. "I think I'm getting a bug or something. I'd better not come up—wouldn't want you to catch it." He hated himself for offering such a transparent excuse.

She jerked away from him. "You pig." She spat out the words contemptuously. "What the hell kind of game are you playing?" The cab stopped in front of her building and she got out quickly and unceremoniously.

Before she closed the door, she leaned in and spoke with slow intensity. "I'm not a puppet on a string, Jeff. Don't call me again. I think I'll go up and phone my actor friend. He might like a midnight drink. As for you, you can go to hell!"

She slammed the door fiercely. It was unlike Jessica, he thought in a detached way, to lose her cool so openly. But he could not really blame her. He had been a bastard.

He gave the driver his own address. His father had always assumed he and Jessica would someday marry, uniting the family fortunes. Now the break was open and probably irrevocable. Sorry, Dad, he thought grimly.

Then he smiled, in the dark back seat of the cab. Why feel grim about it? He had never truly cared for Jessica. If he had, he would not have been so cavalier in his treatment of her, which only added to his already overburdened sense of guilt. He could not let his father dictate his life from the grave. Jeff suddenly felt a sense of overpowering relief.

As for Meg, she thought she wanted only a platonic relationship. But he recognized, beneath the layers of her uncertainty and fear, a potential for deeply passionate response. Was he strong enough to slowly guide her to sexual freedom? It would not be easy, and he knew that failure would be damaging to both of them. His own self-esteem was precarious. But maybe. Just maybe. A wild surge of determination swept away his doubts. He would succeed—he would not stop trying until he did succeed—no matter how long it took. She meant that much to him.

He reminded himself that the situation was fragile. He would play her "platonic" game for a time, so as not to make her feel pressured. They would both know when she was ready for the next step.

He got out of the cab whistling, gave the driver a too-generous tip and bounded up the stairs two at a time.

# Chapter 9

On Monday morning, Meg placed a call to Mr. Danner of Danner and Stokes, Super Sportswear. Joseph Danner told her he would be happy to see Mrs. Gillespie if she could get to his office before eleven. When Meg relayed the message, Sarah Gillespie said she would be at Meg's office within half an hour. By the time she arrived, however, almost an hour had elapsed and Meg could only hope that Joseph Danner's trip to the market had been delayed and that they could still catch him in his office.

Arriving at the Seventh Avenue address, Meg stabbed the elevator button, and on the 30th floor pulled Mrs. Gillespie down the hallway behind her. Mrs. Gillespie was trembling with nervousness; Meg realized she was close to outright panic.

"It'll be all right, you'll see. You're a very intelligent woman, Sarah, you've nothing in the world to fear."

The receptionist, the woman whom Mrs. Gillespie would possibly be replacing, sat behind the desk filing her nails. She was leaving to have a baby, so why overwork these last two weeks? She looked up in annoyance as the two women entered.

"Mr. Danner, please."

"Which one?"

"Mr. Joseph Danner."

"He isn't in. Won't be back till late this afternoon."

"Oh." Meg looked at her watch. Quarter past eleven. Just then a man with a small, neatly trimmed beard, seemingly in his mid-twenties, emerged from the inner office.

"It's all right, Lucy," he said to the receptionist mildly. "I'll handle it." He turned to Meg and Mrs. Gillespie. "Miss Gardner?" Meg nodded. "My father told me he was expecting you and asked me to take care of you. I'm Michael Danner. Come in, please."

He led them into a small, unpretentious office with a rack of spring shirts, skirts and pants in one corner. "As you can see, winter is already over in the garment business. After being surrounded by spring things all day, sometimes I go outside in the evening and am amazed that birds are not chirping or trees budding."

He indicated chairs for them and continued to make small talk to give them a chance to settle themselves. He was quick and selfassured and seemed to be enjoying a chance to take charge.

"Now, Mrs.—" he referred to a paper in front of him—"Mrs. Gillespie, why don't you tell me a little about yourself?" He smiled benignly and settled back in the swivel chair.

Mrs. Gillespie told him haltingly that she was separating from her husband and needed a job to support her two children.

"Your husband is not able to contribute to their support?"

"Yes, some. But not enough to get along on, unless I work, too."

"I see." His attention strayed to Meg. "Uh, Miss Gardner. You're a relative, are you?"

"No, I'm the social services aide assigned to Mrs. Gillespie's case. And we're friends as well." She smiled and squeezed Sarah's hand to transmit to her a flow of confidence.

"I see. Have you any experience in the garment business, Mrs. Gillespie?"

Sarah lowered her head and brushed away an imaginary piece of lint from her dress. "I sold dresses parttime at Macy's before I was married."

"Good."

"And I do like people. I think I'd really enjoy the job once I learned the—the ropes."

"Well, perhaps that's more important than anything else. I sometimes get the feeling our present receptionist would often prefer to be elsewhere." He smiled faintly to show the remark was without malice. "Well, suppose I take you out and let Mrs. Shapiro explain some of your duties—provided we can come to terms, of course—and we'll talk more about it when you understand what's involved, hum?"

He led her to the outer office. When he turned back and saw that Meg was following, he motioned her to resume her seat. "Just be comfortable, Miss Gardner. Stay where you are. I'll be right back."

Meg would have preferred to be with Sarah, but she sat down again and waited. Michael reentered the office, closing the door behind him.

With preamble, he asked Meg, "Do you think she can handle the job?"

"Well, to be quite honest, she has no accounting or bookkeeping skills. But if it's just a matter of greeting people, answering phones and doing light typing, yes."

He came to Meg's chair and faced her. "If she does get the job, would you consider going to dinner with me tonight?"

Meg was stunned. When she found her voice, she asked coldly, "Are you making one condition contingent upon the other?"

He pulled back at once, recognizing the crudity of the question, and laughed easily. "No, no, don't get me wrong. I phrased that very badly. But would you consider going out with me tonight?"

Meg looked up at him. He seemed perfectly presentable—a middling-tall, black-haired, bespectacled man, dressed in the overly dapper Seventh Avenue mode. Although he had hastened to assure her that Mrs. Gillespie's job was not dependent on her answer, she was not altogether convinced.

"Yes, Mr. Danner. I'd enjoy seeing you tonight." Her tone was almost defiant.

He made a self-deprecating gesture. "Michael—or Mike—please. Good." He handed her a notepad. "Just write your address and phone, will you?" He stepped back into the reception room and summoned Sarah inside. "Do you feel you can handle it, Mrs. Gillespie?"

"I think—I think so. I'll certainly try my best."

"Good. That's the spirit we need around here."

They settled on a salary that seemed barely adequate to Meg, but Mrs. Gillespie found it acceptable, and Meg felt she could not object and perhaps bollix the deal by doing so. As Michael Danner ushered them out, he spoke to Meg in a low voice. "I'll pick you up about seven, all right?"

Meg nodded and on the return trip to the office, tried vainly to pay attention to the chatter of her elated and for once voluble companion.


Michael Danner called for her promptly at seven.

"Would you like a drink, Michael? Somebody left some Scotch here a week or two ago."

"Fine. With a splash of water, please."

"I didn't know what to wear because I didn't know where we'd be going."

"I'm sorry. I should have consulted with you about that. But you look fine. Do you like Italian food? There's a very good cafe on University Place. I used to go there when I was a student at NYU."

The place turned out to be Pete's Tavern, a vintage eating spot in a building where O. Henry had once lived and written. The ambience was family Italian, with a lively bar in front, and in back a happy crowd of diners. Meg soon learned why: the food was delicious.

"What a find!" she said, spinning a web of linguini around her spoon.

"Haven't you been here?"

"No. In the first place, I like to cook. And in the second place, I don't like to go to restaurants alone."

He leaned across the table and took her hand. "A woman as beautiful as you should never find herself in that position."

She laughed at him to hide her slight unease. He was coming on a bit strong, and had apparently worked to perfect his approach. His overtures were so different from Jeff's openness.

"Thank you. But the men I know are mainly my colleagues at the office. They're as overworked and underpaid as I am."

"Would you like a job in the garment business?" His tone was offhand as he concentrated on buttering a roll.

"I don't know anything about the garment business."

"You could model. We need showroom models quite often, and so do most of the other firms in the building."

"Oh, no. I don't think that's quite my cup of tea. You misunderstand, I'm not unhappy in my job. It's just taken for granted that everyone complains."

"Okay, but if things should ever change, keep it in mind. I'm serious. You'd make a very good model."

After the meal, he suggested a movie in the neighborhood and they slipped inside the dark cinema just minutes before the feature started. She had to give him credit—he had planned beforehand to see that the evening moved smoothly. He must have checked out the movie clock in the newspaper and the location of a movie that would be both enjoyable and convenient. She admired such efficiency in a man. Maybe she was behind the times when it came to women's liberation—she had no doubt she was—but it was relaxing to be with somebody who had taken the trouble to plan ahead.

The only thing was—maybe he was a little too efficient. He seemed to have it down to a science. She wondered what he would have done if she had demurred and suggested a different movie. She had an idea he wouldn't have been pleased.

After the film, they strolled along Fourth Avenue looking into the windows of the second-hand bookstores that lined the street. She saw a book of Cartier-Bresson photographs and swore she'd commit larceny to have it.

"Is that a hobby of yours?"

She told him about the class at the New School. "If I ever decided to get out of social work, I think I might like to try my hand at becoming a professional photographer."

"You know, I think you should seriously consider changing your profession."

"Oh? Why?"

"Because you've expressed discontent with your job twice tonight."

They had reached her apartment. Mulling over what he had said, she absent-mindedly opened the door and found him entering behind her. She had intended they should say goodnight in the hallway.

"I'm tired, Michael. Will you forgive me if I say goodnight now?"

"I'll just come in for a short time," he said firmly, and pushed his way past her into the room.

She made the drinks in silence. She really wanted to

be alone, and she had not liked his overbearing intrusion. She groped about for a safe conversational topic, and referred to his suggestion that she might change careers.

"I don't know," she said slowly, a line of worry creasing her brow. "I suppose it's possible you might be right."

"Think about it. It might be fun to consider modeling. And you get a healthy discount on clothes, you know. That ain't hay." He reached for her hand and pulled her onto the sofa. She was so startled by the sudden move that her drink spilled on her skirt.

"Michael! Look what you've done!" She was not feigning her distress. The drops had already darkened the beige crepe, one of the few presentable things she owned.

"Forget it," he said crisply. "Send the cleaning bill to me." He grabbed her shoulder and pulled her close to him. Without warning, he kissed her. The kiss was brisk, efficient and thorough. She felt distaste rise in her throat, and with an effort, pushed him away. He had no right to kiss her, she thought, she belonged to—She stopped in confusion. Her mind had been about to complete the sentence: "—to Jeff." But she didn't. She had told Jeff to think of her only as a friend. In fact, she had insisted on it.

Then why was her mind playing such tricks? Her thoughts were interrupted by Michael's second attack. He pulled her to her feet, his hands holding both her wrists in a vise-like grip. As she tried to pull away, he warned her between clenched teeth: "Don't reject me. I don't like women who reject me. Now come on and be a good girl. I'm a nice guy. You don't have to be afraid of me."

Again his arms were around her, pulling her to him, hard into his body. One hand was on the back of her head, pressing her face inexorably closer to his own. An image of Sarah Gillespie flashed into her mind. If she antagonized Mike Danner, Sarah might lose the job before she even got started. She realized she was in a difficult situation which would require the utmost diplomacy. She submitted to his kiss momentarily, while she tried to think of some way out of her dilemma. When she felt his grip relax, she pulled back and looked at him. "How about one for the road?"

"Wait a minute. What do you mean—one for the road?"

"Well—just that."

"I'm not hitting the road, baby. I'm staying here tonight."

"You are not invited to stay here. Not for the night, not even for another moment."

"You're damn right I've been invited. I've been invited by that body—all evening." His eyes, behind their hornrimmed glasses, were suddenly hard. "You're damn right I've been invited," he repeated, more forcefully.

He took the two empty glasses she had been holding, set them down on the coffee table and pulled her roughly into the bedroom. "Take off your clothes and lie down," he said. His manner was almost businesslike. He shed his clothes immediately and turned down the bed. When he saw that she was standing in the center of the room dumbfounded, he said impatiently, "Come on to bed, for Chrissake. You'll freeze your ass."

"You get out of here." He ignored her frantic command, took her hand and pulled her down onto the bed. She felt instant panic as his hands moved over her breasts. She flailed her hands against him like a frantic bird beating its wings against the sides of its cage. But he caught both her hands in one of his, and with the other hand unbuttoned her blouse and loosened her skirt. His actions were as automatic and efficient as an office machine.

What would happen, she wondered, if she started screaming? Before she could consider further, his hand moved between her legs, opening them, and then he was above her, trying to plunge himself inside her. As she felt a scream rising in her throat, his mouth came down upon hers with bruising force. She felt his beard scraping her chin and thought of the obscene beard in her dream. Frantic, she tried to move from under him but his weight held her prisoner. She made an incoherent plea for deliverance to unseen, unknown gods.

At last he moved his mouth away from hers, breathing heavily. She started to scream, but instead the sound inexplicably emerged as an insane snicker. Then she burst into a full laugh. Peals of laughter racked her body, and once she started, the situation seemed genuinely comic in its grotesqueness. Hysterically, the ferocious laughter continued. His movement slowly ceased and he lifted his body from hers. She sat up, groping wildly for the covers, her face still contorted with sobbing laughter.

Stunned, Mike Danner reached for and found the switch to the bedside lamp. Blinking against the sudden light, he looked at her as one would look at a dangerous lunatic who had managed to escape its strait jacket. After a moment of speechless amazement, he grabbed her shoulders and shook her violently.

"You cunt." The words hissed from between teeth held tightly together. "Is this the way you get your kicks?"

The laughter died in her throat as abruptly as it had begun. She looked at him blankly, as if awaking from a nightmare.

He buttoned his shirt and whipped his tie savagely

around his neck. She sat on the bed, her icy feet dangling on the hardwood floor. He must have finished dressing in less than two minutes. He left the room, not looking back at her. She followed him to the bedroom door without speaking, only staring numbly as he scooped his topcoat from the back of the chair. He opened the door into the hallway, then turned back to her and shot her a look full of contempt.

"I feel sorry for you. You sure got problems—big problems."

If she had had strength left, she would have laughed again at the unintentional irony of the remark. But she did not. The door closed behind him, and Meg was left standing, staring at the dark brown door with blank unseeing eyes.

# Chapter 10

On the following evening after class, Jeff asked her out for a drink. She was dazed from the nightmarish incident with Mike Danner and from lack of sleep, but she felt she could not face going back to her empty apartment just then. The ghost of Mike Danner would be in every room.

After he had left, Meg, moving like an automaton, had torn the sheets off the bed, put on fresh ones and had a hot shower. But the scent of Mike Danner's cologne still hung in the small and stuffy room. She finally wrapped herself in a quilt, took one of the pillows, and spent the rest of the night on the living room sofa.

Now, as she and Jeff sat again in the familiar warmth of McBurney's, she relaxed a little for the first time that day. She wanted to tell him about Mike Danner, but decided she could not. He already pitied her for her inadequacies . . . the Danner episode would only worry and anger him and add to that pity.

Jeff was feeling ebullient, being with Meg again. He did not notice her air of troubled remoteness. "What have you been up to, Meg? God, it seems ages since I've seen you."

She averted her eyes. "Oh, nothing. Work, eat, sleep, you know. How about you?"

"Same here. Oh, listen, Meg, one reason I wanted to talk to you—my stepmother has invited me out to her place on Long Island for Thanksgiving, and says I can bring a friend. Would you like to join us?"

"Thanksgiving?" she asked blankly. "When is Thanksgiving?"

"In about two weeks."

"Really? I didn't realize that. I hadn't even thought about it, I guess."

"Well, what do you think? Before you make up your mind I'd better tell you a little about Andrea. She's very chic, very bright, very 'with it.' I'm not sure you'd be on the same wave-length at all, but I'll more or less have to be there and you'd be doing me a favor if you'd go, too."

*Very chic, very bright*, thought Meg. *And he's not sure we'd be on the same wave-length.* She summoned up the nerve to make a limp joke of it. "Thanks for the compliment," she said drily.

"Oh, come on, Meg. You know what I mean. There's so much more to you than that. Andrea is okay, but maybe a little shallow—that's what I meant."

When she saw his distressed expression, she was remorseful. "I know. I was only kidding, Jeff."

"And Timmy—her son, my half-brother—Timmy, you'll love. He's the greatest kid."

Meg looked at Jeff's lips as he spoke, and remembered the feeling of Mike Danner's brutal, demanding mouth on hers. "Uh—how old is Timmy?"

"Thirteen. It's really for his sake I'm going. He never had a father, really."

"How long has your father been—when did he—?"

"Five years ago. But he was more or less estranged from Andrea for a couple of years before that."

"I wish you'd tell me about it sometime, Jeff. Maybe we should try to talk to each other more. About things that aren't so easy to talk about." Perhaps if he opened up about his father's death, she would find it less difficult to tell him about Mike Danner.

"I don't want to talk about it," he said. Then, his tone softening slightly, "I'll tell you about it sometime, Meg. But not now."

She sighed. Tonight they seemed almost strangers. Was he merely honoring her request for a platonic relationship? Or was each of them living in a secret, half-hidden world, without the courage to reveal it to the other?

"Let's go, okay?" she asked abruptly, and without a word, he paid their check and led her into the street.

"Would you like to walk?" he asked.

"Yes, I think I would."

"Good. So would I."

They walked silently for several blocks, Meg confronting the enigma of their relationship. Jeff, too, was in deep thought. The silence deepened. When they reached her apartment, she turned to say goodnight. Without warning, Jeff found himself embracing her, and was surprised when she pushed him away violently, her eyes as wide and terrified as an animal at bay.

"Don't, Jeff! Please! Don't do that!"

He looked at her in amazement. In spite of her problems, she had never before been violent in her rejection of him. "What's the matter, Meg? That was just a friendly goodnight hug."

Tears sprang to her eyes. She looked troubled, defeated. "I'm sorry, Jeff. I guess I'm just on edge tonight. I'm sorry."

He looked deeply into her eyes. At the beginning of the evening, he had felt invincible . . . positive his feeling for her was strong enough to surmount any obstacle. And now they seemed back to square one—even beyond it. The knot of hopelessness in his stomach grew heavier. At last, with a small, crooked smile, he struck a playful blow off her chin, turned and left the building.


It was Friday afternoon, and almost time for Meg to leave her office. She sat at the desk, clearing up paperwork and looking forward to the weekend. Anne Woody, a classmate in the photography sessions who had proven to be likable and congenial, had suggested a photographic expedition on Saturday to the Cloisters, the medieval museum in upper Manhattan. Meg had never been there, but Anne's description made it sound like a soothing retreat from the mad scurry of midtown.

The office was empty except for herself and Edgar, a conscientious young beanpole of a man who was trying desperately to phone a family who had been burned out of their home to tell them he had news of an affordable new apartment. Meg organized her papers in order of importance to be tackled on Monday morning, took her coat and knitted cap from the coat clost and was just closing the door when she heard the phone ring. Edgar answered and called after her.

"Meg! Phone."

"Oh, dear. Just as I was about to make my escape."

On the other end of the line, she heard a frantic Mrs. Gillespie. "Miss Gardner, I've been fired! Mr. Danner called me in just before five and said I hadn't worked out to his satisfaction."

A knot of fury formed in Meg's throat, but she tried to keep her voice even. "Which Mr. Danner was this, Sarah?"

"Mr. Michael—the young man. He seemed so angry—I must have been doing a really awful job."

"No, Sarah, that may not be it, at all. It may be my fault."

"Your fault? But Miss Gardner, you got me the job! It couldn't be your fault. It's just that I don't know where to turn—"

"Listen, Sarah, just keep calm and let me think. You see it may have been my fault, because I went out to a movie with Mr. Michael, and I think maybe he wasn't pleased with my—my behavior. So he may have been getting back at me through you, do you see?"

"No, I don't think so. I think I just wasn't bright enough to learn the job the way he—"

"Sarah, stop that! If anything you were too good for the job. Now, listen, if you'll just stay calm over the weekend, I'll see what I can do on Monday morning. Obviously, I can't do anything at five o'clock on Friday afternoon. You'll work your two weeks' notice, is that right?"

"No! He's giving me two weeks' severance, but he said he didn't want me back in the office. That's why I thought I must be really bad—"

"And I'm explaining to you that it was not your fault —I'm sure of it. All right. You have two weeks' pay, so there's no reason to panic yet. I'll try very hard to help you get another job before the two weeks is out. So trust me. Go home and have a good weekend, and I'll talk to you on Monday. Okay?"

"Yes. All right. I feel better having talked to you. Thank you, Miss Gardner."

"Goodnight, Sarah."

Standing in the aisle of the crowded bus, crushed between jostling passengers, Meg felt again an impotent rage. How could Mike Danner use an innocent person to vent his wrath against her? And where was she going to find another job for Sarah Gillespie? Then a thought occurred to her: maybe Jeff had a place in his office, or knew of someone in his firm who needed a receptionist or clerk. It was worth a try. She would call Jeff when she got home. Then, trying to be honest with herself, she wondered if she were looking for an excuse to call him. After he had turned and left her apartment hallway on Tuesday night, she recalled the expression in his eyes—a look of puzzlement and pain.

She had been very foolish to let a split second of panic, of unwelcome memories, lead her to push him away so forcefully. She should have explained about Mike Danner. At least Jeff would not have left misunderstanding the situation. She had decided she would make an effort to explain on Thursday night, but Jeff had not appeared in class.

Reaching home, she threw her coat aside, picked up the phone and dialed before she lost her nerve. The phone had rung several times and Meg was just about to hang up when it was picked up and she heard a woman's voice on the other end.

"Hello?" Meg said, puzzled. "I must have the wrong number—I was trying to reach Jeff McAllister."

"No, this is his number. But Jeff's out right now. Could I have him call you?"

The voice was cool, slightly nasal, and inflected with what Meg had come to recognize as an Eastern finishing-school accent. She guessed at once that it must be Jessica. Her heart seemed to shrink and wither.

"No. No. I'll call again later."

"May I tell him who phoned?" The voice was politely persistent.

"Meg. Meg Gardner. But it can wait till later. Thank you." She hung up, feeling lightheaded. She wondered if he and Jessica were going away together for the weekend.

Well, apparently he had not been as hurt and upset as she had thought. In any case, he had made a rapid recovery. But wasn't she being unreasonable to expect him to spend months or even years trying to nurse an emotional cripple back to health? Particularly since she had dreamed up her little scheme of friendship and friendship only? No, Jeff was absolutely right to find comfort and affection elsewhere. He probably had been no more than fond of her to begin with, Meg thought. As he would have been fond of an appealing stray dog whom he might stop to pet briefly on the street.

## Chapter 11

Over the weekend, Meg convinced herself that she had been overly sensitive about the phone call to Jeff. In the first place, she had no way of knowing that it really was Jessica. It could conceivably, she supposed, have been a maid. In the second place, she should be glad he was occupied with someone else, since she seemed to respond to his physical advances only with blind, unreasoning panic. She felt terribly confused and ambivalent.

But the need to help Sarah Gillespie was still a very real one. She owed it to the fearful little sparrow of a woman to find another job for her, since she herself was responsible for the loss of the first one. On Monday evening, she phoned Jeff's home again. He answered at once.

"Meg! What a nice surprise! Good to hear from you."

"I missed you in class on Thursday."

"Yes. Well, something came up. Nothing serious."

"Oh. Well, I tried to phone you Friday night, but you weren't in." Why had she found it necessary to make that gauche remark?

"Oh." There was a slight pause. "Right." There was no further explanation.

"Well. I just had an idea. How do you feel about having supper with me after class tomorrow night? I know you once mentioned you'd never had real Southern barbecue and would like to try it. I'm making some tonight and I'd love to get your reaction."

"Sounds great to me. I'll see you in class tomorrow, then." And he hung up.

Had he been in a hurry to get off the phone? Or was she becoming totally paranoid? She shrugged in annoyance with herself and put on her coat to go to the grocery. She picked up the items she would need for the barbecue—a pink loin of pork, brown sugar, red pepper, potatoes, pickles, onions, cabbage.

The evening of cooking was therapeutic. She roasted the pork slowly and gently, basting it frequently with the fiery sauce. While it was baking, she made potato salad, confetti-bright with the golden flecks of hardboiled eggs and the bright red and green of pimientos and pickles. She would do the coleslaw the next day.

She was very nervous about cooking for Jeff. She was sure he dined often in New York's most illustrious temples of *haute cuisine*. She hoped he would find her efforts adequate.

On Tuesday night after an unusually dull class, Jeff and Meg walked out together to find a light dusting of snow on the streets. The flakes were drifting down lazily and lightly. It was, as Jeff remarked, a "friendly snow." They stopped off at a delicatessen where Jeff, at Meg's suggestion, picked up a carton of Mexican beer. Carta Blanca and barbecue were a perfect combination.

Sitting down at the table, Meg cautioned him. "I made two kinds of sauce, hot and hotter. You'd better try the less hot first. Other people I've made it for have accused me of trying to demolish the lining of their mouth."

"Oh, I'm fearless," Jeff laughed. "When I got on to Szechwan food a couple of years ago, I became a real addict about spicy foods. I'll take the hot-hot."

"All right," she said doubtfully, "but don't say I didn't warn you."

He slathered the thinly sliced pork generously with the devil-red sauce and took a large bite. Coughing and sputtering, he reached for his beer to cool the raging fire that filled his mouth and throat. "My God, Meg, what are you trying to do to me? I've never tasted anything so hot in my life."

"Have some potato salad," she said sweetly. "That should help." She could not hide her amusement.

"Oh, I'll get used to it," he blustered manfully. "Just came as something of a surprise."

He did get used to it, very quickly, but he treated it through the remainder of the meal with much greater respect. His compliments to the chef were extravagant and sincere. Meg beamed with pleasure.

Over coffee, Meg broached the subject of Mrs. Gillespie. "Jeff, I got one of my clients a job a couple of weeks ago. Friday she called and said she'd been fired." She went on quickly. "It wasn't anything she did. It's my fault really."

"Yours?"

"Yes. Well, I—" She found herself, without plan or forethought, pouring out the story of the incident with Mike Danner. She had thought the trauma of the evening was behind her, but as she talked, she found herself pacing the room with nervous, jerky movements.

Jeff's eyes narrowed as he listened. "That bastard. I should look him up and punch him out."

"No, Jeff, please! I just want to forget it as soon as possible. Truly I do. You see, I didn't even mean to tell you. I knew you'd be angry. I knew it would only make you pity me. More than you already do."

He stared at her in disbelief. "Pity you? My God, Meg, I love you. Don't you know that by now?"

She stood still and looked at him. "Jeff. Don't. You couldn't."

He came to her then, and held her, very lightly. Again

she reminded him of a small wild bird poised for flight. He must remember to be gentle with her—he would have to tiptoe.

"But I do, Meg. You've got to believe me." She looked at him uncertainly. "I'll convince you. Just give me time." He released her and went back to the sofa, in deep thought. "So that's why you were so frightened and repelled the other night—"

She nodded. Her voice was almost inaudible. "That was the night after—after it happened."

"You just need some time," he said after a moment.

"Yes. I guess so."

"Well, I've got plenty of that, Meg. And it's all yours for the asking." She gave him a shy, wondering glance, then lowered her head. Jeff sensed he had pushed her far enough for one evening. "Now back to your Mrs. Gillespie. What's she like?"

Meg was relieved that the conversation had turned less personal. Her emotions were still in a tumult. "She's very conscientious and she really needs the job. She isn't very aggressive, but she's brighter than she knows. I just wondered if anyone in your office would be needing a receptionist or file clerk."

"I don't know of anyone offhand, but why don't you send her down tomorrow? I'll take her up to the personnel department and see what they can do."

"Oh, Jeff, thank you. That's good of you, really. I'll call her early in the morning."

Gradually they both relaxed and talked of trivial things. Meg felt almost at peace. She was very glad she had told him about the Danner incident after all—in so doing, she seemed to have exorcised it. Jeff reached over casually and gently took her hand. It was almost as though they were an old married couple, Meg thought. Except in the bedroom.

"Have you given any more thought to

Thanksgiving?"

"What?"

"Thanksgiving. Going to the Island with me for the day."

Meg was silent for a long moment. She had thought when he extended the invitation that she would not go. It was not her milieu. But Jeff had changed all that when he told her, almost casually, that he loved her. She had not yet had time to even digest it. But she felt that now, she would be unafraid anywhere.

"Oh," she said at last. "Yes. I think I'd like to go."

He shifted his position and cleared his throat. "Ah, by the way, Meg, I'd better fill you in a little bit with some background material before you meet Andrea."

His tone had changed so abruptly to one of reluctant confidentiality that Meg's listening antennae were immediately and acutely tuned in. The forthcoming conversation might provide her with some clue about what deeply troubling matter lay buried in Jeff's psyche.

"When my father died, it wasn't from a heart attack, or cancer, or illness of any kind. Andrea had been living alone—I mean just with Timmy and the servants—in the house for months. My father had been staying at his club in town. For some weeks, there had been rumors in the neighborhood of prowlers. A few days before this particular Friday night, Dad called Andrea and said he'd like to come out and spend the night in the guest room, because the following morning he was taking Timmy on a weekend fishing trip and wanted to get an early start. Andrea agreed. But apparently she forgot the plan, and when Dad—he still had a set of keys—was letting himself in the front door, Andrea grabbed a rifle from Dad's collection and shot through the door. He was killed instantly."

Meg was stunned. She had thought the story, when it

came, would be full of strained pauses and halting phrases, perhaps even tears. Instead, although the facts were more shocking than she could have imagined, Jeff's narration of them was delivered in a dispassionate monotone. Then she realized that that was the only way he could have got through it—to separate his emotions from the horrifying events.

"How awful that must have been for everyone," she whispered. "Were you there at the time?"

His answer was a sudden explosion. "Hell no, I was nowhere to be found! If I'd been there, it would never have happened." The traumatic passion that had been absent to this point surfaced with frightening intensity. "I was the one who was supposed to take Timmy fishing. Dad always hated fishing and knew very little about it. When Timmy was very little, Dad taught him to ride, I taught him to fish. Fishing trips were always *my* department.

"But a friend of mine in school was a big mountain-climbing enthusiast; I was just getting into it. He had the use of his family's cabin in Vermont near a place famous for its climbing, just for that one weekend. He talked me into going up with him. When I told Dad about it, he insisted he would take Timmy fishing himself, so the kid wouldn't be disappointed. I let him do it. That's how steadfast and strong I am. A regular Rock of Gibraltar."

Meg sat silently. She sensed that Jeff did not require nor even want any sort of response from her. He continued pacing for another few minutes, then suddenly turned away from her and leaned against the wall. Dry, heavy sobs began to shake his shoulders. She moved behind him and put her arms around his waist.

He continued in a muffled, strangled voice, "If I had been any kind of man—if I had been anything except a sniveling, selfish adolescent, my father would be alive today. That's the one fact I can never change or forget."

"Jeff," she said at last, "you're being much too hard on yourself. There's no way in the world you could have known—"

"I killed him, Meg. I killed him as surely as if I'd pulled the trigger myself."

"No, you didn't, Jeff. No, you didn't. It was a horrible thing to have happen, but it wasn't your fault. You must believe that." She led him back to the sofa, and they sat for a long time without speaking. Meg reviewed the facts of the hideous accident in her mind and at last spoke again, deliberately keeping her voice detached.

"If anything, the fault was your stepmother's, Jeff. I mean, wasn't she a bit hasty—to say the least?"

Jeff sat up and turned his head away from her with a sharp jerk. "Oh, she went to trial. There was talk—plenty of it. Everybody knew they hadn't gotten along for some time. But she was aquitted. The whole process just made the thing even more ghastly."

"I can imagine." She spoke softly.

He went on as if, now that he had started, he wanted the entire episode out in the open. Meg knew that it was an important catharsis for him. She said nothing more until he had subsided into a long silence. The final part of the narrative seemed to be the most difficult.

"The thing was that Dad had told a business associate —I didn't know this until it came out during the trial— that he was going to change his will and leave Andrea with just enough to live on. The major part of the estate would go to me and my brother and into a trust fund for Timmy. The executor would not have been Andrea, but Robert and me." He frowned and let his head drop into his hands, as if pondering the enigma all over again. She waited, but he sat as motionless and silent as a stone.

Finally, she spoke.

"Did Andrea know that?"

"What?"

"Did Andrea know he planned to change his will?"

"I don't know. She said she didn't. But I don't know." There was another long silence.

"Jeff," her voice was tentative. "In the light of all this, isn't Thanksgiving going to be rather difficult?"

"Well, maybe. It'll be the first time I've been around Andrea for more than a few minutes since Dad— I've just met her a few times to go over business matters. I had no right to ask you to share it. That was another selfish move on my part."

"No, it wasn't!" Meg's voice was sharper than she intended it to be. But she felt that he needed a jolt. "You're being unselfish, because you're doing it primarily for Timmy—you told me that when you first mentioned it. Now stop the self-pity—it's destructive and misplaced."

He looked at her in surprise. Her vehemence had accomplished its purpose; he was irritated and indignant. She knew both emotions would be therapeutic for him right now.

"Well," he said. "I'm sorry I've taken up so much of your time with my self-pity."

"Stop it! You know I didn't mean it that way. But you're killing yourself with guilt and I won't let you do it. You mean too much to me!" Her arms were around his neck, and now she was crying, too. Slowly, his arms enclosed her. They stood together like that for a very long time—not moving, merely feeling the beat of each other's heart. The embrace was so tender, so mutually comforting, that Meg felt none of the fear that had assailed her the week before. Her spirits lifted—maybe the worst of the trauma was over.

His face was buried in her soft, dark, flowing hair.

"I'd never told anybody about it before. I couldn't. But it must leave you with a pretty poor opinion of—"

"I'm not going to listen, Jeff," she warned. "I'll listen to anything except your telling me how worthless you are."

He pulled away from her slightly, looked at her and managed a rueful smile. "You're right." He released his grip and moved away to the coat closet. "I'd better go. It must be late."

Meg glanced at the clock. Two-thirty. "Jeff, would you like to stay here tonight? Just to have someone near?"

He understood her perfectly. There was no sexuality in the question—it was merely an offer of warmth and comfort, as it would have been tendered by an old, familiar friend. "Yes," he said finally, "I would."

Meg undressed in the bathroom and when she returned, Jeff was already in bed, lying on his back, one arm thrown over his face. She climbed in beside him and he reached for her hand. He clutched her fingers tightly, almost painfully, for a moment. "My brother, too," he whispered.

She sat upright, startled by a subject apparently unrelated to the evening's conversation. "What, Jeff?"

He moved his hand away from his eyes and looked at her in confusion. "What did you say?"

"No, I asked what you said. You just said something that sounded like 'my brother, too.'"

He raised himself on an elbow. For a moment there was a blank stare on his features. "That's another story. But not tonight, not tonight, darling Meg." He lay down again, still holding her hand. "Oh, God," he breathed, "let me sleep." Within minutes his grip loosened and she heard the heavy, regular respiration that denotes deep sleep. She gave a long sigh of relief.

She lay awake for another hour, remembering how

sophisticated and sure of himself Jeff had seemed the first time they had met. She had envied and been in awe of his easy self-confidence, his humorous, carefree manner. And to think of the burden underlying that quick and facile charm! She hoped the spectre of his terrible guilt had been laid to rest. She was not sure the cure would be permanent, but she knew the evening's conversation had been of help to both of them. There was only one thing that still puzzled her. What had his cryptic remark meant at the end of the evening: "My brother too"?

Well, they both had a lot of problems still to be worked out, but at the moment she felt invincible. They would fight their way clear together. She was sure of that. Or was she? Tonight the matter of sex had been of no importance to either of them. But when that facet of their relationship arose again, what would she do? Maybe the unfortunate experience with Mike Danner had traumatized her even further.

But Jeff knew her problem, and he had not deserted her. He lay beside her now. The flinty pioneer perseverance that was a part of her heritage asserted itself and refused to be daunted. *By God*, she thought, *I love him, and somehow, we'll make it*.

As sleep drifted into her mind like smoke, she wondered if the courage to acknowledge her love stemmed from the revelation that Jeff needed her as much as she needed him.

## Chapter 12

Thanksgiving Day dawned clear and cold. Meg had been hoping for a big snow, picturing in her mind an old-fashioned trip to "grandmother's house," or its modern equivalent. She saw Jeff and herself arriving by sleigh, warmed by lap robes, and on arrival joining a group of immaculately turned-out children for an idyllic snowball battle. She saw Andrea dressed in modest black, her hair in a neat bun at the nape of her neck, proffering helping after helping of crisp-skinned turkey and homemade sage dressing. As she showered, she imagined the entire family grouped around the living-room piano, singing romantic ballads and relating warm and funny childhood incidents.

Of course she knew this was solely an imaginary version of what the day would be. They were not, after all, back in the nineteenth century, and Andrea, whom Jeff had described as very chic, was hardly likely to have a bun at the nape of her neck. But Meg had, the night before, been so carried away with the vision of a real, old-fashioned holiday that she had baked both a pumpkin and a pecan pie. In Martinsville, Georgia, one did not go empty-handed to a neighbor's Thanksgiving dinner.

Jeff picked her up at noon. She was watching for him, and when the Mercedes pulled into a space just across the street, she raised the window and yelled to him. "Come on in, Jeff. I want you to help me carry something."

He came inside and she proudly displayed the two pies. He smiled rather faintly and she asked, "What? Is something wrong?"

"No, love, nothing. I just hope Andrea has the good taste to appreciate them."

"It's an old Southern custom," she said gaily. "People always take something when they're invited for dinner—especially on holidays."

"I'm sure everybody will be delighted. Particularly Timmy."

The Long Island Expressway was, for once, almost deserted. Apparently everyone else had already arrived at wherever it was they were going.

"How is Mrs. Gillespie working out?" Jeff had found a job for her in an associate's office.

"Fine. I hear nothing but good about her. She seems to be a very hard worker."

"I knew she'd be good. She's a bright lady, if someone could only talk her into believing it."

"Thornburg is good at that. He's very patient with his people."

"I'll never forgive—" Meg brought the sentence to an abrupt halt.

"What? Never forgive who?"

"Nothing."

Jeff did not pursue it further. His mind was on other things. He hoped the day would go smoothly. He had never, since his father's death, spent any social time with Andrea. He hoped desperately that they could find something to talk about and that the day would not be filled with awkward pauses and half-finished, pointless stories.

Meg seemed to be in high spirits. As they drove, she hummed her way through the entire score of "Camelot." But beneath the elation, he sensed a kind of feverish nervousness. At one point, she said out of the blue, "Was it Jessica who answered the phone that night I called?"

"Who? Jessica? I don't see Jessica anymore. When?" He glanced at her sidewise, frowning in bewilderment.

"One Friday night—the Friday night before last, to be exact. I called you because that was the day Sarah Gillespie got fired and I was anxious to help her find another job. A woman answered the phone. She was very curious as to who was calling. And now I'm very curious as to who was answering."

He laughed suddenly. "No, no. You know who that was? It was Andrea."

"Andrea?"

"Yes. Funny coincidence that it should happen that way. She had been in town shopping, and happened to pass by my apartment. On the spur of the moment she rang the bell and came up. Wanted to fill me in on when she expected us for dinner today, what time we'd eat, and so forth. When she started to leave, she discovered something was wrong with her car. I went down to take a look at it and she stayed in the apartment. But it's funny—she never gave me a message that anyone had called. She probably got too busy nipping into the martinis."

"Did you get her car fixed?"

"There didn't seem to be anything wrong with it. I got it going with no trouble at all."

Meg felt a surge of relief. She had not realized till then that the episode had been gnawing away at her. But the lifting of her spirits told her it had.

"This should be a lovely afternoon, Jeff."

"Let's hope so," he said. But Meg could not help noticing a certain tightness around his mouth.

They were greeted at the door by a petite maid, her apron starched to frilly perfection. As they entered the room, Jeff's mouth opened slightly as he gazed about in astonishment.

"What is it? What's the matter?"

"The furniture is different. There's hardly a piece that was here when my father—"

The furniture was mostly chrome, glass and bleached wood. The room was furnished in monochromatic oyster, beige and white. The floor was lacquered a glossy white with deepy fluffy white area rugs. The room's stark modern appearance was distinctly at odds with the traditional Tudor exterior of the house.

"Even the leaded windows are gone. Dad had them shipped over from England," he said, unbelieving. One entire wall was a picture window; the others were modern casements.

After showing them in and taking their coats, the maid had disappeared. Jeff's face was pale, his hands clenched into fists at his side. Meg was dismayed that their visit should have started so inauspiciously.

"What kind of furniture did it used to be?"

"More or less an eclectic mix. But there were some beautiful antique pieces my father had searched out one by one. I could kill that bitch." His tone was suddenly flat, cruel.

"Jeff! Don't let it get to you. People have different tastes."

"But what did she do with it all? How could she have disposed of it without even letting me know? Without even giving me a chance to *buy* it from her, for God's sake?"

Their conversation was interrupted by Andrea appearing on the stairs. She was a stunningly beautiful woman, clad in a floating gray chiffon afternoon dress, her hair impeccably dressed. Though her hair was worn in a knot, it was a far cry from the Whistler's Mother bun that Meg had pictured. Instead, a glossy blonde French twist was pulled high onto the back of Andrea's head, which showed off her long, pearl-draped neck to perfection. Meg glanced down at her own pleated wool skirt and felt like a ragamuffin.

Andrea went directly to Jeff, took his hands and kissed him on the mouth. "So glad you could make it, dear," she said warmly and turned to Meg. "And this is your friend? Welcome."

Jeff did the honors with formal restraint. "Meg Gardner, Andrea McAllister. Oh, Andrea, Meg brought some desserts. Shall I take them back to the kitchen?"

Gingerly, Andrea lifted the aluminum foil from the pies Meg was holding. "What in heaven's name?" She seemed nonplussed.

"It's pecan pie, Mrs. McAllister. A Southern specialty."

"Oh?" The syllable ended with a slight, questioning intake of breath. "Well. I've always preferred a very light dessert after a holiday dinner, but perhaps Timmy will enjoy it." She rang a small glass bell on the desk and the maid reappeared. "Janie, put these away, please."

"Yes, Ma'am."

"Oh, and Janie, send Sanders in, will you? I think we'd all like a drink."

Meg glanced at Jeff. He was sitting tensely on the edge of the sofa. He returned her look briefly, then turned to Andrea bluntly.

"When did you do the redecorating?"

"Oh, that's right! You haven't seen it. A couple of years ago, I guess. The furniture in this room was getting terribly shabby and I just felt a need to go in another direction. Do you like it?" She smiled.

He ignored the question and asked one of his own.

115

"What happened to the other furniture?"

"Why—let's see—oh, I let a friend of mine have most of it. He's gone mad over antiques. Or so-called antiques. Very few pieces were really worth anything, you know."

"Did it ever occur to you that I might have liked some of it?" Jeff's voice was cold.

"Why, Jeff, dear, no, it didn't. I had no idea you were interested in such things at all. Had I known, I would certainly have given you first choice. But you've always seemed so disinterested in Rosehill." She offered a small regretful smile. "Please forgive me," she said, with extravagant humility. "I suppose I was horribly thoughtless. Would you like me to get in touch with my friend and reclaim it for my angry stepson?" She walked to him langorously and ruffled his hair.

"After two years, that would be a little awkward, don't you think?" Jeff asked. He changed the subject abruptly. "Where's Timmy?"

"He went off early this morning to play tennis with a friend. He's just discovered tennis, and he's gone mad over it. But he should be back soon."

As if on cue, the front door swung open and a panting, red-faced boy entered. Meg was struck by how much he resembled Jeff. Their features were almost identical—it was only the coloring that differed. Whereas Jeff's hair was auburn—almost red—Timmy was an unabashed towhead. His complexion, too, was fairer. There was a delicacy about him that was absent from Jeff. He was of a slighter build, with an air of great vulnerability.

"Timmy, here's Jeff. And meet his friend, Miss—I'm sorry, dear, I'm so bad with names. Miss—Baker, is it?"

"Gardner," Meg said simply. "Meg Gardner."

"Oh, dear, yes, of course. Baker, Gardner—how silly

of me. I did remember it was one of those peasant occupations, though, didn't I?" She smiled.

Meg gave her a level stare. "Yes," she said, "you pegged the socio-economic class right on the nose."

Andrea returned her look with a lifted eyebrow. Meg was surprised by her own response. She had no desire to make the afternoon a battle of wits; she had always loathed cattiness in any form. So she turned instead to Timmy.

"How was your tennis game?"

"I lost one set, won one. But that's not too bad. See, Bunky—my friend I was playing with—has been playing since he was about six. I just took it up a year ago."

"Under those circumstances, you must be terrific! You'll probably be entering tournaments in another year."

"Do you play?" he asked, warmed by Meg's interest.

"No, no!" she answered in mock horror. "I tried to learn in school till everyone gave up on me. But ping-pong's a different story. I could probably beat the socks off you at ping-pong."

"Oh, yeah? There's a table downstairs. How about a game?"

"When will I ever learn to keep my mouth shut?" she groaned. "I didn't know I was going to get an instant challenge."

"Nah, I'm only kidding. I'm pretty much all in from the tennis."

"And you have to shower and change for dinner," Andrea interrupted. She had not seemed to particularly enjoy the interchange between Timmy and Meg, Jeff thought. Jeff was delighted that they had hit it off so well. He decided not to pursue the furniture contretemps further. It was done and could not be undone. But he also decided that this would be his last visit to the house. He would hereafter arrange to see Timmy in town alone.

The butler appeared in the doorway. "What would you two like?" Andrea asked. "I'll have a vodka martini, Sanders."

"I'll have a Bloody Mary. Meg?"

"A glass of white wine, please."

"Oh?" Andrea's tone was disappointed. "Sure you wouldn't like something a little more—robust?"

"No. White wine will do nicely, thanks. I have to work tomorrow," she explained.

"What do you do?"

"I'm a social worker."

"Ooh, how depressing! What ever made you choose to go into that?"

Meg thought the question rude, but answered as best she could. "I suppose I was rather idealistic. I thought maybe I could be of help to people. I realize now it's a very complex situation—the whole system. It's awfully difficult to bring any lasting change into these people's lives. Although there are two or three whom I do have some hope for—"

Andrea raised a crimson-nailed hand. "Oh, spare us the details. This is a holiday. I don't think we should spend it talking about those poor, unhappy people."

Anger rose in Meg's throat and the words spilled out without conscious thought. "I would never have brought it up at all. But you asked me a question. I was trying to give you the courtesy of an answer."

"You're quite right, dear. It's all my fault." Andrea's tone was patronizing.

The drinks were served and a strained silence ensued. The butler put a tall pitcher of martinis on the table at Andrea's side, from which she frequently replenished her glass.

"We'll have dinner about four. If that meets with your approval?" She looked from one to the other, an eyebrow slightly raised.

"Of course," said Jeff shortly.

Timmy came downstairs, looking dapper and self-conscious in a navy-blue blazer and gray flannel slacks. He was going to be a very handsome young man, Meg decided. Jeff smiled at him conspiratorially. "Has your girl friend seen you in those elegant threads?"

"Nah. I got no girl friend."

"Don't lie to your big brother, Timmy. I'll bet they're fighting over you night and day."

"Nah." But he reddened with pleasure at the implied compliment.

The maid had just announced that dinner was served when the telephone rang. "I'll get it, Janie," Andrea said hurriedly. She picked up the phone impatiently.

"Yes? . . . Well, where in hell are you? We're just about to sit down to dinner . . . I told you about four . . . I see . . . no, forget it." Her voice suddenly lifted harshly. "I said forget it, don't you understand English?"

Jeff led Meg into the dining room and motioned for Timmy to follow them. He did not want to listen to any more. Andrea had obviously invited one of her lovers to dinner, and the gentleman obviously wasn't going to show. Jeff only hoped she was discreet, with Timmy around. At that moment, Andrea entered the dining room and swept the fifth place setting from the table. She set it angrily on the credenza and rearranged the four remaining settings.

"I'm sorry for that little display. I had asked Laz Brennan, an old friend of mine, over to join us, since he has no family of his own. He ran into—complications and won't be able to make it. So there'll be just the four of us. Well, that's cozier anyway, isn't it?" She smiled and motioned them to sit.

The dinner was an elegant repast, which included

roast goose (Meg missed the traditional turkey), chestnut souffle, asparagus au gratin and hothouse tomatoes which Andrea assured them had been especially flown in from Mexico to her favorite gourmet grocer. For dessert, there was lemon mousse. Meg's pies were nowhere to be seen.

Conversation at the dinner table was less strained than Meg had expected. Andrea, loquacious after the pre-dinner martinis and the champagne she poured throughout the meal, regaled them with stories about her busy, hectic life at Rosehill.

"Of course, you're here at exactly the wrong time of year. The roses won't be in bloom till spring and the horses are all in Florida for the winter. Jeff, you must really bring Miss Baker—"

"Gardner," Meg corrected. "Meg. Just call me Meg, please."

"Yes, dear, I'm sorry. Anyway, you must bring, er, Meg out when spring comes. Do you ride, dear?"

"Not very well, no."

"What a shame. You're missing the most glorious experience. I love to ride with the wind in my hair . . . just gallop away at a tremendous speed and forget the whole damn world. Striker—my favorite horse—is a demon. He won't let anyone ride him but me. Did you ever see him, Jeff? No, you wouldn't have. I bought him after your father—that is, when he was just a tiny colt. He's almost five now and gets more beautiful every day. But I like to have the horses winter in Florida. Even Striker, who doesn't race. I think he appreciates the warmth. And I really don't care much for winter riding. I like to work up a good sweat in the summer."

The phrase was incongruous, coming from such an impeccably lacquered creature. Meg looked at her and realized that Andrea couldn't be much over thirty. She was probably less than ten years Meg's senior, yet her worldliness made Meg feel like a child.

They left as soon as it was decently possible. Andrea walked them to the car, pointing out the rose garden, the pruned and dormant bushes now covered with burlap wraps. Meg could imagine how magnificent the garden would be in bloom; it must have stretched for almost half an acre. Even now, in the winter, it reminded her of home. Aunt Emma and Aunt Bess had been rose fanciers, too. The bushes lined both sides of their house; she could remember waking to the scent of roses all during the spring and summer.

Jeff and Timmy were walking behind the two women. Meg could hear Jeff asking Timmy if he'd like to spend the following weekend in the city. At Timmy's enthusiastic affirmative, Jeff asked Andrea's permission. She gave it willingly, almost eagerly. Jeff sensed that Timmy must sometimes get in Andrea's way.

Andrea went to Jeff as he started to open the car door. "Kiss your old stepmother g'bye?" She smiled at him with a lifted eyebrow, challenging him to resist her.

"Of course." He kissed her briefly and had started to move away when her arms twined themselves around his neck and she pulled him back to her. She held his lips against hers for a long moment, then released him, laughing. "You don't mind my borrowing him for a second, do you?" she asked Meg. Then she threw up her hands in mock horror.

"Oh, your pies, dear! I forgot them completely—I'm so sorry. Look, why don't you take them back with you?"

"Oh, no, I couldn't—I brought them for—"

"Now come on, I won't hear of it. They're far too fattening for me. They'll just go to waste." She turned and yelled for Janie, who shortly appeared in the front door. "Bring those two pies Miss Baker brought out, Janie. She wants to take them back with her."

Meg looked at Jeff; he shook his head and shrugged. He was very angry but tried not to show it. Why get Meg more upset than she already was?

At last they were on their way. For the first few miles, neither of them spoke. At last Jeff broke the silence.

"I'm so sorry, Meg. I had no idea I'd be putting you through an ordeal like that. I hated to leave Timmy so soon, but I just couldn't take any more of it."

"You'll be seeing him next weekend. That'll more than make up for it."

"I hope so. It's too bad Dad ever got mixed up with—"

"Don't say it, Jeff. You'll only feel sorry later on. After all, she is Timmy's mother. She seems to have done a pretty good job with him. He's wonderful."

"Yes." He took her hand and squeezed it, then his tone changed. "Meg, I can't go on with this platonic business. I need you, and want you—tonight."

At once she felt both excitement and fear. She could not pretend to feel platonic toward Jeff any longer either. At the same time, she was panicked by the thought of again proving to be unresponsive and inadequate. But she knew him better now, she was more at home with him. She had been very successful at erasing the Mike Danner incident from her mind.

She knew now beyond all doubt that she loved him. Surely that would make a difference. Hope kindled in her like a warm fire. Yes, this time it would be all right. He would guide her—there was nothing to be afraid of.

"Yes, Jeff," she said. "I want you, too." Her eyes were full of faith and love.

## Chapter 13

Meg's unpretentious apartment had never looked more beautiful to her than it did when they reentered it on that cold Thanksgiving night. Jeff slipped off his shoes and padded about comfortably in his stocking feet; Meg at once pulled on a pair of faded jeans.

"You liked Timmy a lot, didn't you?" he asked.

"He's terrific—reminded me of the kids I grew up with. I felt very much at home around him."

"You've got to help me entertain him next weekend."

"Love to. What do you think he'd like to do?"

"Why don't we do all the things out-of-towners do in New York? The Christmas tree in Rockefeller Center, the top of the Empire State Building. If the weather's good, the boat trip around the island?"

"Hasn't Timmy done those things?"

"I doubt it. If he has, he probably did them with Dad when he was tiny. Andrea doesn't bring him in very often. When she's in the city, she's always busy shopping or lunching with friends."

"What a treat! I love to show people around town. I don't know it that well myself, so it gives me a good excuse to explore."

Jeff looked at her, and her eyes and cheeks were glowing with anticipation. His arms were suddenly about her tightly. Then the glow faded and her eyes became troubled. She looked up at him, pleading silently for understanding.

"What is it, darling?"

"It's just—I'm not—I'm no good in bed, Jeff. You know that."

Gently, he moved her onto the sofa and sat beside her. "Listen, Meg. When we went to bed together that first time, I admit I left here pretty frustrated. In fact, I called up Jessica the very next day. I'm not particularly proud of that, but I did it."

"I don't blame you." Her voice was barely audible.

"But listen to me, Meg. I tried to tell you this once before, and you got angry, but I want you to understand. After it was over with Jessica, there was no real feeling of satisfaction, because there was no love in the act. It was only mechanical. It's different with you. It's going to be different from now on. Because I know now that I love you."

"Don't say that yet, Jeff. Please don't say that yet. I can't let myself hear that yet. I don't want to be responsible for that yet."

He smiled at her with tenderness and humor. "Not even if there's a great big happy voice yelling it inside my body? My God, Meg, I want to shout it from the top of the world. I want to get a megaphone and drive through every block of Manhattan, screaming, 'I love Meg Gardner, do you hear me, folks? I love that girl!' "

Meg managed a half-laugh. "Oh, Jeff. I want you to be able to love me with no reservations . . . none at all. But as long as—" Then she realized that dissecting their problems was possibly the worst thing she could do. She took his hand and wordlessly led him into the bedroom.

For awhile, they lay fully clothed on the narrow bed. He began to kiss her, at first lightly and aimlessly, then more urgently. Within Meg, conflicting feelings were engaged in a searing battle. Her body strained toward his. She wanted to abandon herself to him with every ounce of muscle, blood and bone in her body. But the fist-hard knot of anxiety in her stomach threatened to explode into panic. She remembered the hysteria during the episode with Mike Danner. It had been on this very bed that she had dissolved into maniacal, helpless laughter.

She knew that she was safe from that with Jeff. Tears, maybe, certainly not laughter. Well, wasn't one as bad as the other? Then, as Jeff reached inside her sweater and moved his hand over her breasts, all thought was washed from her mind. She whispered, "Take me, Jeff. Do what you want with me."

She sat up and he pulled the sweater lightly over her head. Then he unfastened the pale, lacy bra. He moved his mouth to her nipples and caressed them with his tongue. Quickly, he brought his lips against hers, and her tongue sought his. He was very patient, very deliberate. It was several minutes before he reached, with agonizing slowness, for the zipper of her jeans. She helped him tug them off, her panties discarded with them.

In the dim light filtering from the living room, he could see her nude body. Perfectly formed, sensuous, waiting. He took off his clothes and lay back down beside her. She was quite still, but her body seemed relaxed. There was not the tenseness there had been before. He began to caress her thighs, softly, slowly, lightly. His hand moved inside her leg. She moved her legs slightly apart. She was not looking at him; her eyes were closed. She hardly seemed to be breathing. As though in slow motion, he moved above her. He began to open the lips with his hand and felt the smooth soft liquid inside her. His hardness became a persistent throb. But he could not hurry; he must be sure she had all the time she needed. God, he loved her. Her hair, as black as night in the dimly lighted room, was spread around her like a fan. Her eyes were still closed. She had not moved except for the slight relaxing of her legs. He must not rush. . . .

Meg waited. She could not feel the bed beneath her body. She was in a limbo inhabited by neither time nor space, but only feeling. The one real thing in this dreamlike world was the feeling of Jeff's hands and lips. Below her softly curved belly, inside her body's depths, was a void aching to be filled. What he was doing was wonderful, but she wanted more. Her body cried for more. She felt him begin to enter her. The void was filling, was about to be filled at last. From nowhere, out of the night, crashing into the glorious limbo, she heard Frank Pittman's taunting question: "Do you know what I could do to you with this?"

In terror, she pushed down the panic that rose in her throat like bile. If ghosts of the past would give her no rest, she must at least protect Jeff from them. He was now fully inside her. But now Frank's chant continued in her head, spinning in her brain senselessly over and over, like a record repeating itself on a long-forgotten turntable.

"Go ahead, Jeff," she said in a whisper. "Any time you want to."

"I want to wait for you," Jeff said, his voice muffled in her naked shoulder.

"No!" The word was a harsh moan, torn from her throat. "No! Just do what *you* want to."

He reached a hand between their bodies and caressed the bud above the open lips. Meg felt an indescribably vivid stimulation from his touch, and then another taunt began: "I saw you pee! I saw your thing!" The sensation he had aroused withered and died. She only wanted him to be done with it. She tried mechanically to match his rhythm as it increased in rapidity and intensity. But her timing was not right; it was not something one could achieve consciously and clinically. She sensed that fact, even as she worked to predict his tempo and his need. He began to moan softly and murmur incomprehensible words to her. She attempted to imitate his sounds until quite suddenly, he fell against her, spent.

They lay together silently, his arm around her shoulders. She thought she had brought off the subterfuge successfully until he spoke.

"You didn't make it, did you?"

"Yes, I did."

"Don't lie to me. I know you didn't. I'm sorry."

She jerked away from him. "Please don't say that. It's not your fault. You're the most patient and understanding lover any woman could want. It's me, Jeff. I'm sorry."

"Well, it can't be a very happy experience for you. I should have taken more time."

"No, no, it's not that. It's something else—" But she stopped. What good would it do to talk about it? "Anyway, Jeff, I'm not complaining, am I? Truly, it's enough for me to make you happy."

"No, it isn't enough. But don't worry, darling, we'll work it out—I know we will."

"I told you, I'm not complaining!" Her words were bitten off, sharper than she meant them to be. She softened her voice to a whisper. "Really, Jeff. If I can make you content, that's all I ask for."

"We'll work it out," he said again. "I love you, Meg. Nothing can change that." He patted her shoulder as one would comfort a child, and that, she thought, hurt more than anything.

She felt tears brimming over her lids and was glad Jeff had not turned on the light. How long would he go on loving her with her ridiculous neurosis dashing all hope for real fulfillment?

The following week, Jeff was lunching alone at the Staunton House when Peter Jamison breezed in. Though Peter was Jeff's closest friend in the firm, his office had been moved downstairs and they had not seen much of each other lately. But today, Peter looked particularly healthy and fit.

"Where'd you get the tan?" Jeff inquired enviously. "You look like a candidate for a beach movie."

"Man, I feel like one. Just got back from my week's winter vacation, and it was a blast."

"How so?"

Peter consulted the menu, summoned the waiter and gave his order before continuing. "We went to Caracas. It was gorgeous! Perfect weather, great food, casinos, the race track, discotheques, beautiful beaches—what more could you want?"

Jeff groaned. "And me stuck up here in this slush and ice, followed by ice and slush. Well, my vacation is coming up Christmas week. Would you suggest I call for reservations right now?"

"I would, sport, and I'm not kidding. It's a great place to visit and I think I might even like to live there. Those Latinos know where it's at."

"You mean Lisa didn't go with you?"

"Sure she went. That's what I'm talking about. Listen, I've seen so little of you lately, you may not have known about my family problems. For the last—oh, six months or a year, Lisa and I have been having a bad time of it. Since the baby was born, she wasn't giving me the time of day. I mean, all of a sudden, she was a Mother, with a capital M, and 'wife' didn't seem to interest her any more at all."

"You mean in your physical relationship?"

"That's exactly what I mean. Judging from her attitude you'd have thought I was the hunchback of Notre Dame. But once she got out of the house and into that Caribbean sun, wow! She sure made a 180-degree turnaround."

"I take it the baby didn't go along."

"No, my mother kept her. It was like a second honeymoon, only more so. And the thing is, now that we're back home, the glow is still there. It's wonderful."

The talk turned to other things then, and Peter ate hurriedly and left, saying he had an early-afternoon business appointment.

Jeff sat at the table with a second coffee, pondering Peter's conversation. He had been seeing Meg almost every night, but they had not again ventured into the domain of the bedroom. They had done what used to be known as "heavy petting," but when Jeff found himself getting too much aroused, he put on the brakes. He did not want to burden Meg with the feeling that he was seeing her for sex, or even that sex was particularly important to him. He did not want to foster an encounter which would leave her feeling frustrated and unhappy.

Meg, in turn, did not want to invite Jeff into circumstances which might leave him feeling that he was less than a superb lover. Though she knew the difficulty was of her own making, Jeff seemed to add it to his already heavy load of guilt. It seemed to be a no-win situation for both of them.

He wondered if a change of scenery would work with Meg as well as it had obviously worked for Lisa. Of course, the origin of the trouble was different—Lisa had just become temporarily preoccupied with her role of mothering. But maybe the result would be the same.

He and Meg had not really talked about Christmas. Andrea had invited him to spend it with her and Timmy, but that was out of the question. He had no desire to repeat the Thanksgiving fiasco. He did not know whether Meg planned to go to Georgia for Christmas or not. Perhaps he had been afraid to ask her, for fear her answer would be yes.

Impulsively, he went to a pay phone in the back of the long, narrow restaurant and dialed Meg's number at work. But the voice which answered relayed the information that Miss Gardner was "in the field." He supposed that meant she was calling on clients. He hung up dispiritedly. For a moment, it had all seemed so simple.

That night, in class, she was a little late arriving and pushed breathlessly to her seat.

"Did you call me today?" she whispered.

"Yes."

"Anything special on your mind?"

"I'll tell you after class."

She nodded with a smile and turned her attention to the lecture.

Back in McBurney's, again over Irish coffee, Jeff was trying to figure out how to ease into his Caracas sales talk when Louie came over with another stack of his photographs. After they had given him an appropriate measure of admiration, he sauntered away again, his ego inflated by their extravagant compliments.

"We haven't talked about Christmas, Meg. You know, I get Christmas week off, and I'd like to do something special. How much time do you have?"

"Two weeks."

"Are you going home?"

"To gorgeous Georgia?"

"Yes, to gorgeous Georgia."

"I haven't let Aunt Bess know yet. But I'd like to—I mean, it's the first Christmas she'll be without Aunt Emma and I think I should be there."

"I understand that. But—wait a minute! What if I

could exchange Christmas week with one of the guys for the week *after* Christmas? That should be no problem at all. Christmas week is the week everybody wants, especially men with families. If I could get New Year's week, instead, you could spend Christmas in Georgia and then join me somewhere for the week following!"

She looked wistful. "Well. Maybe."

"A friend of mine at lunch has just come back from Caracas. He raved about it. Does that appeal to you?"

"Venezuela? I don't know. I'd never thought about it." Her lips parted with mounting pleasure as she considered it. *God*, he thought, *she is so beautiful*.

"They flew to Miami and took a boat from there. He said it was the most glorious vacation they'd ever had. And I was thinking this afternoon . . . why don't we take the trip as man and wife? Say, a small civil ceremony just before we leave?"

She looked at him, touched, and then her eyes clouded. She bit her lips and looked at the worn tabletop, where couples' initials inside hearts had been carved for so many years there was no room for others. She wanted nothing more in the world than to be Jeff McAllister's wife. It would have been the embodiment of her wildest and most romantic girlhood fantasies. But she could not do that to him.

"I—I don't think so, Jeff." When she saw his face, she raced on. "It's not that I don't love you, darling, it's *because* I love you. Don't you see? It could never work until I could be a real wife to you, in every sense of the word."

"Meg, I've tried to make it clear to you that it's you I love. Not going to bed with you, but the essence of you. Your mind, your sense of humor, your warmth and kindness. . . ."

"I know, I know." She shook her head wearily. "I know, Jeff. There's not one man in a million who would put up with me the way you have."

He felt they were on a treadmill and there was no way of getting off. They had had this conversation over and over again, and it always ended with both of them starting explanations and assurances, and windng up with half-finished sentences and self-recriminations.

"All right." He ran a hand through his wind-touseled hair. "All right. Will you come with me, then, without benefit of clergy?"

"I'll have to lie to Aunt Bess." Her forehead puckered into a frown.

"Lie? Why?"

"Jeff, she'd never consent to my running off with a man to South America. She doesn't know you; she doesn't know how I feel about you. Of course I'd have to lie to her."

"Are you willing to do that?"

She sat weighing her words for a moment, then gazed at him steadily as she answered. "Yes," she said, "I am."

## Chapter 14

Meg spent a quiet, mostly uneventful Christmas with her Aunt Bess. The older woman was frailer than she had been when Meg was home for Aunt Emma's funeral less than three months before. Aunt Emma had always been the mover and shaker in the family and Aunt Bess seemed to have lost her zest for living since her sister's demise. One of the most delightful things about Bess had always been her dry, elfin sense of humor. Now, if she made a joke at all, she seemed to have to force herself to do it. Meg grieved for her inwardly.

She had brought her aunt a shawl she had seen one day at Lord and Taylor's, a gossamer drift of cashmere and lambswool, its delicate, ombre colors melting one into the other. She had also tried to find things uniquely available to New York shoppers: a fat, raisin-and-fruit filled *panettone* from an Italian bakery on Bleecker Street, a tiny twelfth-century Buddha she spied one day at an art gallery in Soho, a box of carved Belgian chocolates, a set of coasters with reproductions of Aunt Bess's dog, Jinx. The coasters had been made from a photograph Aunt Bess had sent Meg.

Bess exclaimed in delight over each gift as it was unwrapped; for a time she seemed her old self as she sat luxuriating in the shawl and nipping at the chocolates. She and Meg went to midnight mass at the tiny Catholic church (which, in that Protestant stronghold, boasted less than a hundred members), and dutifully attended mass again on Christmas Day. After mass, they drove to the cemetery and placed a pot of scarlet poinsettias on Aunt Emma's grave.

The remainder of the week they spent quietly, but Bess seemed more cheerful as the days passed. Meg told her aunt she was going to Caracas for a week, and though she did not directly lie to her, she did nothing to disabuse Aunt Bess of the impression that she was going with a girl friend. Bess seemed genuine in her hope that Meg would have a splendid vacation. "You need one, you know, my dear. You're too thin. I think you've been working too hard. Now when you get to Caracas, don't worry one minute about your crotchety old aunt in Georgia. In fact, wipe out any thoughts that might stray into that brain of yours, and just run your motor on instinct."

They were at the dinner table when Bess made that remark, and Meg was so startled that she very nearly dropped a forkful of mashed potatoes into her lap. Her aunt could not have given her better counsel if she had been a psychiatrist to whom Meg had confessed her problem and related her life history. *Run your motor on instinct*. If she could only manage to follow that advice! Did Aunt Bess, in her unassuming, quiet way, know more than Meg had guessed she did? Was she running her own motor on instinct, sensing the source of Meg's restlessness? Meg would never know, for in the Gardner household, such things were never discussed.

On Saturday, the older woman drove her to the Atlanta airport to catch a plane leaving for Miami a little before noon. She and Jeff had booked their flights (and got passports and vaccinations) before she left New York, and she had asked Jeff not to call her while she was in Georgia. She did not want to plant any suspicions in Bess's mind that would have worried her needlessly. She was meeting Jeff in Miami International Airport: they would go directly to the cruise ship, and sail that evening at six.

As they entered the Atlanta airport, Meg said, "Don't try to find a parking place. Just let me off at the front entrance, and I'll get a skycap to help me with my bags. Then you can head right back to Martinsville."

"Hush. I'm coming with you just as far as they'll let me. You can't stop your Aunt Bess, once she's made up her mind."

Meg smiled. That statement displayed more spirit than Bess had shown the entire time Meg had been there. Maybe her visit had been good for both of them. She hoped so.

They walked down a long corridor, Meg fighting back tears, Bess making a gallant effort to be cheerful.

"Drop me a card if you have time, snookums. But on the other hand, don't worry about it if you don't. Get some sun and eat well. And turn the switch off in your brain. You think too much."

Meg laughed and started through the metal-detector. Just before she entered the closed ramp that led to the plane, she turned. Aunt Bess was a very small figure half-hidden by a scurry of passengers hurrying to board. But she was waving energetically, her flailing hand holding a crumpled, lace-edged handkerchief.


The plane lifted sharply and the no-smoking sign went out. Meg's heart soared even higher. To think—in less than two hours, she would be with Jeff! She stared out the window and the thought of Aunt Bess brought her down to earth again. She was sorry Bess's life was not happier. Then she told herself she was being a sentimental fool. She could hardly expect Bess to be deliriously happy three months after the death of her sister—the woman she had lived with all her life. But Aunt Bess was pretty resilient. It was easy to see that she had felt much better by the end of Meg's visit. She would send her aunt a really nice gift from Venezuela. *Meanwhile*, Meg told herself, *stop this maudlin wallowing*.

The clouds outside the window of the plane were like pink-tinged cotton candy spun for a giant. She thought if she jumped onto one, it would hold her weight and bounce her gently back in the air like a trampoline. She smiled to herself at the childish conceit. Lunch was served but she hardly touched it. Excitement was growing in her with every mile the plane covered. The tray was removed and the stewardess inquired if anything was wrong with the food.

"Oh, no. I just wasn't very hungry." She smiled at the attractive black girl. "What time will we reach Miami?"

"One-forty-five. Looks like we'll be on time, too."

"Thank you."

Meg closed her eyes and tried to sketch in her mind's eye every detail of Jeff's features. First, the shock of thick, disheveled, auburn hair. Then the strong, heavy brows; the hazel eyes, crinkled at their corners. The straight, long nose, the light brown freckles sprinkled over it; the mobile lips, the stubborn chin. Did such a paragon really exist in this imperfect world? Was she on her way to meet a phantom—a man who was literally too good to be true?

Her whimsical daydreams were interrupted by the captain's voice, telling them they had started the descent into the Miami Airport. Meg looked at her watch. In fifteen minutes, give or take a few, she would be with Jeff McAllister. She felt like the heroine in a romantic film scenario. The camera would zoom in on the lovers, running wildly to meet and embrace each other. There would be a long, long kiss and the director would yell "Cut." Then he would congratulate the actors on their realistic and convincing portrayals.

Jeff should already be waiting—his plane had been scheduled to arrive at one o'clock. Oh, God, what if something had happened—what if there had been an accident! They would not have heard of it on the plane—it was not the sort of thing an airline pilot would be eager to announce. My God, what if something like that had really happened? It was not impossible, it happened every day.

The plane set down with an almost imperceptible jog, and they were taxiing along the runway. Now the pilot was maneuvering into his space near the terminal. She looked frantically out the small window. She saw a group of people waiting to greet passengers as they clung to the wire fence that separated them from the plane area, but she could not discern Jeff in the group. Unless—as the plane moved nearer, the figures dissociated themselves from each other and became individuals —unless—it *was*! It was Jeff. He had somehow managed to change into warm-weather clothes. He was wearing tan slacks and an open-necked white shirt. His skin seemed to have already absorbed the Florida sun—he looked almost tan.

The wait for the plane's doors to be opened seemed an eternity. She did not know what the delay was. The other passengers, too, were shuffling their feet restlessly, packed into the aisles with their baggage, boxes and now burdensome winter wraps. Then she saw light ahead of her at the front of the plane and realized the passengers were being discharged at last. She moved ahead as rapidly as she could without physically maiming the people in front of her. Down the ramp, through the gate, and she was in his arms. "Jeff. Oh, Jeff, it's been so long."

But her words were cut off by his kiss. He held her close to him, so that she could not separate the racing of her own heart from the beating of his. He released her and took her hand. "Come on, we've got to get you out of those heavy clothes. You'll be a puddle of warm and very sticky perspiration in about two seconds flat."

"What's the temperature here?" She had not even noticed the heat.

"Eighty-two. Let's find you a ladies' room. They have those private baths—you can even shower if you want to."

"I'll just splash some cold water on my face. You look wonderful, Jeff. Did you have a good Christmas?" They walked hand-in-hand toward the baggage claim area.

"I was going to spend it alone. Just have a nice, lazy day doing nothing, then a good dinner out somewhere."

"Oh, Jeff, I would have hated to think of you alone. I thought you were going to your friend Peter's."

"He and Lisa decided on the spur of the moment to go skiing in Vermont. He called me with profuse apologies, asked me to go along with them. But I decided I'd rather spend the day poring over travel pamphlets and thinking of you."

"So—that's what you did?"

Jeff took Meg's bags off the conveyor belt before he answered. "Andrea called at six o'clock Christmas morning. Does that register with you—six o'clock? She said the cook was ill, and wanted to know if I'd take her and Timmy out to dinner."

"And—did you?"

He grimaced. "Well, I didn't have much choice, did I? Unless I wanted Timmy to think of me as the original Scrooge. Yes, I took them out. Actually, it wasn't so bad. Andrea was on her best behavior. She can be fairly amusing when she wants to be. And she looked terrific, as she always does."

In spite of the heat, Meg felt a sudden chill. Andrea

was, after all, an exceptionally beautiful woman. "Oh, look, there's the ladies' room over there. I'll be out in five minutes."

She dug through her suitcase and settled on a yellow-and-white striped cotton pantsuit. The top was a sliver of a camisole, with thin straps that tied over her shoulders. She took off her panty hose and exchanged her heels for flat yellow sandals. She put on her sunglasses and went back to Jeff.

"Think we might have time for some lunch?" he asked.

"Didn't you eat on the plane?"

He shook his head. "Had a late breakfast and wasn't hungry. Yours was a luncheon flight, too, wasn't it? Well, you can have iced tea and watch me eat."

She laughed. "Aren't you going to feed me? I didn't eat anything either." They looked at each other and grinned, each knowing why the other had suffered a sudden loss of appetite.

They took a taxi, which maneuvered the East-West Expressway, and delivered them to the pier their ship would be sailing from in Biscayne Bay. It was in its berth, dazzling white and glamorous—*The Sea Queen*. They could not board till four but were told they could leave their luggage and it would be loaded aboard. Then they set out in search of a good seafood retaurant.

It seemed an enchanted afternoon. They found the perfect spot for lunch—a restaurant whose interior had been outfitted with fishnet and hurricane lamps to look like a South Sea Island shack. There was a long veranda that wrapped around three sides of the weathered clapboard building, and there Meg and Jeff sat, sipping a daiquiri and watching the sailboats, schooners and cruise ships in the bay. Plates of crusty, golden-fried shrimp were set in front of them, followed by a luscious avocado salad.

Jeff looked at Meg as she bit into a shrimp. "Happy?"

"Oh, Jeff, of course."

"Me too. Oh—I brought some books about Caracas. We can read them on the way down."

"Okay. If you can get me out of the pool. I'm really looking forward to swimming a lot." She suddenly focused her camera toward the bay.

"What do you see?"

"A crane—or maybe a heron—perched on one of those pylons. He's standing on one leg, see him?" She clicked the shutter once, wound rapidly, then clicked again.

"Are you a good swimmer?"

"Pretty good. When I was growing up, the swimming pool was our only source of amusement in the summer."

"What'd you do in the winter?"

She thought for a moment. "What *did* we do? Oh, made fudge, roller skated, played monopoly. Martinsville was maybe fifty years behind the rest of the world. I suppose my childhood was almost Victorian."

He reflected on her statement. Perhaps it was that quality of an earlier-day innocence he loved in her. At the same time, he realized that such a background was a large part of her sexual problem.

Jeff looked at his watch in sudden surprise. "Do you have any idea what time it is?"

"No. Three, maybe?"

"Four-twenty, my girl. Let's get on board our ship and get settled in."

While Jeff paid the check, Meg tried a panoramic shot of the bay. The light was slanting over her left shoulder, and the shadows of the ships on the water created a mottled, dramatic effect. They walked together down the rickety steps and into the sand of the dockside. A white-uniformed man with a brisk military air checked their tickets and summoned a steward to show them to their staterooms. Jeff had insisted on observing the proprieties and had reserved two rooms with connecting doors. Though she supposed it was a silly pretense—she was certain no one on board would care—she was still glad he had arranged it that way. Her Martinsville upbringing again, she thought wryly, as the steward put her bags on the rack at the foot of the bed.

"Thank you very much." She gave him a dollar and wondered if it were enough. But he smiled broadly and wished her a pleasant voyage.

There was a knock on the connecting door and she opened it to let Jeff in from his room. "Come and visit me," he said. She followed him in to his room—a little smaller and less grand than hers, but comfortable and attractive. They went together to the porthole and peered out. The deck was bustling with activity. An orchestra was playing sentimental love songs; there were bursts of laughter, the pop of champagne corks, exuberant shouts. The sun had plummeted low on the other side of the ship.

Meg was struck by a sudden idea. "Let's go up on deck and see the sunset."

"Wait a minute," Jeff said peremptorily, and began to rummage through his suitcase. He held up a bottle of Bollinger champagne, with two small silver goblets.

"Jeff," she said haltingly, "let's save that for midnight."

"Midnight? Why? This isn't New Year's Eve. Besides," he winked at her slyly, "I have another bottle of champagne for New Year's Eve."

"I know, but humor me, okay? I'd like to have it at midnight."

He laughed indulgently. "Okay, consider yourself humored. Let's go."

They went up to the main deck and leaned over the rail, watching the red ball of fire drop over Miami. The clouds that hung lowest on the horizon were an incendiary red; the higher ones shaded to rose and mauve and ivory.

As she stood regarding the spectacular sunset, she reflected again on Aunt Bess's advice: *Wipe out any thoughts that might stray into that brain of yours, and run your motor on instinct.*

She was determined to remember that.

## Chapter 15

The ship sailed a few minutes after six. Meg and Jeff were still standing at the railing, eyes only for each other. But after the sharp blasts of the ship's whistle, with a sense of excitement and adventure, they watched the luxury hotels on the Miami shoreline become miniatures, like pieces on a Monopoly board.

At dinner, they were seated at a table for eight, with three other couples. Two of the couples were evidently taking the cruise in order to play bridge, the third were middle-aged Hispanics who were going to visit their daughter in Caracas. Though both spoke fluent English, they were native Venezuelans and they regaled Meg and Jeff with sights they must not miss while in the country.

"Be sure to take a *teleférico* up Mt. Avila. You can see both the Andes and the Caribbean—the view is *fabuloso*! Oh, and save some time for shopping along the *Calle Sabana Grande*. The gold jewelry is exquisite. Did you know there is a replica of Cristoforo Colombo's ship in Caracas? It is at a place called *Parque del Este*—Eastern Park. Let me give you my daughter's number. We would love to have you come out and have dinner with us one evening."

The petite lady—Señora Raimundo—was a bundle of ebullient energy. She evidently felt very maternal toward the two young Americans. Meg liked her very much, but hoped she wouldn't feel smothered with affection before the cruise was over.

After dinner, they wandered into the lounge, where an attractive pop singer was holding forth with a medley of torch songs. "Let's go when there's a break," Jeff whispered. "I'm not in the mood for sad songs."

Neither was Meg. They returned to the deck, where an orange moon was just rising. It hung low on the horizon, its reflection rippling in a long line over the water. Jeff considered going below for his camera, but thought better of it. This evening was to be theirs alone. He put his arm around Meg's shoulder. Her skin was cool and fragrant. Wine had been served with each dinner course and Meg saw and felt everything with a heightened awareness.

"That feels good, Jeff. Your arm around me." The breeze was brisk and her dress was thin. Jeff took off his dinner jacket and slipped it over her shoulders. "That feels even better," she said.

He took her chin and lifted it to his face. "I'll always remember this night, Meg. As long as I live, I'll remember this moment."

She said nothing. She merely nodded, too full of love to speak.

"Let's go below, shall we?" His question was casual, unpressured.

She nodded again and he followed her belowstairs to their rooms. In his own room, he changed into a light robe, wrapped a towel around the bottle of champagne and took it with the two silver cups into Meg's room. She was sitting at the dresser, dressed only in one of the ship's oversized bath towels. He was mildly surprised by her deshabille, but delighted. She had turned on the radio and strains of unobtrusive music provided a background for the discreet pop of the champagne cork.

"Oh," she said with a disappointed frown. "I thought champagne corks were supposed to go off with a bang."

"No, my dear,' he announced grandly in a pseudo-French accent. "A sommelier at *21* assured me they should be removed gently. Like children, they should not be heard."

Sipping the dry, tingling wine, they leafed through the literature about Caracas and began to plan their time there, after they landed at Caracas' port, La Guaira. They agreed they could probably get some wonderful photographic shots from the *teleférico*, or cable car, that climbed the side of Mt. Avila. Then perhaps a trip to the beach.

"And I'd like to go to Margarita Island while we're there," said Meg.

"Of course." He poured another inch of champagne into her glass. "Let's see if the moon is still up."

They strolled arm in arm to the porthole. The moon had disappeared behind a bank of dark clouds. The deck was semi-illuminated by the ship's lights, streaming onto it from the lounge and dining room directly above their cabins. But beyond the gleam of the ship's railing, all was inky black. They could hear the waves rushing against the sides of the ship with monotonous, powerful regularity. Now that they were further out at sea, the ship was rocking like a giant hammock. The darkness and the rocking somehow hinted of danger, and the effect on both of them was like a powerful aphrodisiac.

He touched her glass lightly after he had poured out the final drops of the champagne. The clear, metallic ring of the silver was like a summoning bell.

"To my darling Meg," he said. "I love you. I will love you forever."

They finished their drinks and spontaneously touched glasses again. Then he took the silver goblet from her hand and placed it on the dresser. "Come," he said simply. He led her slowly to the bed.

He was even gentler and more deliberate than he had been the last time they had been together. Tonight he was determined that everything should be pefect. He sensed a difference in Meg as well. The passionate abandon he had sometimes barely glimpsed in her, deeply covered by repression, tonight seemed closer to the surface. She responded to his kiss willingly, eagerly. She let his tongue enter her mouth and lap at her own tongue. Then her tongue searched his mouth as though she would siphon the very juices from his body.

They had left on only the nightlight near the door. After the dinner wine and the champagne, the pale blue glimmer made the walls of the stateroom seem remote— indeed, nonexistent. His hand slid slowly down the length of her body. He felt the concave curve of her waist, the slightly convex mound of her belly, the soft triangle of pubic hair. He pushed his hand into the inner thigh and felt her legs open for him. Her right arm slid under his left, and she caressed his chest. Then, shyly, tentatively, her hand followed his body to the erect and stiffened rod which now lay upward against his abdomen. She massaged it; there was a gentle question in her touch.

He kissed her breasts, sucking them deeply and tenderly. His right hand cupped them to his lips, first one and then the other. His left hand found the opening lips of her body, damply receptive. She inhaled sharply as he let his finger play lightly over the bud above the lips. . . .

Meg stopped stroking as the sensation inside her began to become more and more intense. She was on an island where nothing existed except sensation. Only Jeff was there with her. An island where there was no horizon, no sky, no sea. She touched him again. Only Jeff was real. She struggled to move one hand under his shoulder and around his neck. From very far away, she heard a child's jeering voice, "I saw your thing." But she could not remember its source and the voice faded.

A momentary image of Mike Danner entered the back of her mind, but instantly vanished as she felt Jeff move above her and lie on her lightly.

"Inside me. Get inside me," she whispered. Oh, the smoothness of him, the gliding smoothness of them both as they met and melded into each other, like white-hot metal that fuses and becomes one entity. For a world of time, she felt the delicious thrusting inside her yearning body. No, not a world of time. For now time did not exist for her. There was neither world nor time. There was only the strength and hardness of her lover inside her, as close as one human being can ever be to another. But it was not close enough—she wanted to consume his entire being, and she wanted him to consume hers. It was not close enough, and she, with a spontaneous, rhythmic lifting and falling of her pelvis, tried to put her body inside his, tried to exchange bodies with him.

"I saw your—" The voice, so faint, intruded again. She could hardly decipher the words; she remembered only the cruel, triumphant singsong. "No!" she whispered. "No!"

"What, darling?" Jeff's voice immediately banished the other hated ghost of a voice.

"Nothing, Jeff. Hold me." She did not know whether she had spoken the words or only thought them. It didn't matter. As he moved inside her, Jeff's hand was again caressing the tiny opening bud above the deep inside of her. His breath was like a warm and intimate breeze across her face, and smelled of peppermint. The world had receded again, and there was only instinct and feeling. Her movements became faster. She wanted—what did she want? The sensations she was feeling were a thousand times more intense than anything she had ever felt before, or even imagined. But there was more, she was sure. She wanted . . . she wanted. . . .

And then, starting inside her belly, and moving deliciously downward, there was a feeling of wanting nothing. For nothing could be more blissful, more all-consuming than this feeling now overtaking her. There seemed to be waves of purple satin all around her. They seemed to be coming one after another and endlessly, faster and faster, out of a grotto of deepest iridescent blue. She did not hear the moans in her throat, nor did she hear Jeff's fragmented words of love, as his ecstasy rose to meet hers. The waves of glittering purple satin crashed against her body and into her body and outward from her body until there was, finally, a wave so high she could not even fathom where its crest might be. It lifted her to the top swiftly, heart-stoppingly, held her cradled for a long and blissful moment. She felt she was literally outside and above the world, looking down on a miniscule and insignificant Earth. An eon of time passed before she started the breathless, gentle downward slide.

Her eyes closed, the waves of purple satin receded, and she imagined herself descending slowly, as if from an invisible glider, into an idyllic grassy valley. Then she felt the deep, thick, billowing grass cushion her body. She had never imagined there could be a feeling of such total, rapturous well-being.

They both reentered the world slowly, so slowly.

Meg was in a stupor of contentment, but inside her heart there was singing. The taunting, long-ago phantom voice had been banished at last. She knew she would never hear it again. She wondered if she could have managed tonight's achievement if Aunt Bess had not made that almost accidental remark about instinct. . . .

. . . . Jeff had never been so happy. He had never even come close. From the beginning, he had sensed in Meg an incredibly passionate nature, and he had been right. To know that he had been the instrument of release for her increased his joy a thousand-fold. Now nothing lay in their way. The future was a straight, broad avenue with no more detours. Only bursting happiness for both of them.

He adjusted his head on the pillow and spoke softly. "Do you suppose your Aunt Bess would be horrified if we got married in Caracas?"

Meg looked at him and laughed, a full laugh that bubbled irrepressibly from her throat. "I think she'd probably survive."

"Meg, are you serious? Because I am."

She became thoughtful. "I guess it's something to be considered. You've no family at all you'd want to have to the wedding?"

He shook his head, musing. "An uncle in California I haven't seen in years, a couple of distant cousins in Canada. Timmy, of course. But don't you imagine a thirteen-year-old would rather die than be roped into going to a wedding?"

"Probably. Well, let's talk about it tomorrow. We'll have nothing to do but talk about our wedding—and love each other."

# Chapter 16

A brilliant, endless morning of shuffleboard and sunbathing was followed by a smorgasbord lunch that was just as endless. They exclaimed with incredulous delight over the elaborate display of lobster, shrimp, crabmeat, thinly sliced roast beef, salads and heaping mountains of fresh fruit. Shaded from the sun by a green fiberglass awning, they devoured the luscious meal ravenously.

"Wait a minute, Jeff—where'd you find that crab salad?"

"Right next door to the salmon mousse. I was trying to keep it a secret from the starving masses."

"Of which I am one?" she asked in mock indignation.

"Well, if you're going to make a nasty issue of it, here's half my portion." Carefully, Jeff piled a large helping of flaky white crabmeat, flavored with dill and capers, onto Meg's plate.

With both their mouths full, they looked at each other and grinned. Then the ebullient grins became mutual glances of desire.

Jeff laughed. "This reminds me of the eating scene in *Tom Jones*. Did you ever see that movie?"

"No. But speaking of movies, there's one being shown this afternoon I'd like to see."

"Seems a shame to desert this sunshine."

"Maybe. But you're looking a little like a lobster as it is."

"Flatterer. What's the movie?"

"Can't remember the title, but it's about a young War veteran and the problems he has when he comes home."

Jeff said nothing for a moment, and Meg looked at him with a question in her eyes.

Finally he spoke hesitantly. "Doesn't seem like the ideal subject for a cruise movie. We're supposed to be squandering our time in riotous living."

"I know," Meg smiled. "But the reviews all said it was one of the outstanding movies of the year. And I do think we've probably had enough sun for one day."

So after a shower and change of clothes, they entered the darkened ballroom which was serving as the afternoon's screening room. Meg became almost instantly engrossed in the film. It was a story of a Vietnam veteran who returns home to find that life's everyday problems have become strangely unimportant, and of his psychological difficulties in adjusting to an ordinary, almost forgotten lifestyle.

Perhaps an hour into the movie, she became aware that Jeff was squirming in his seat. She leaned over to him and whispered, "You don't care for this, do you?"

"It's all right. I'm all right," he said, not moving his eyes from the screen.

She turned her attention back to the movie. It showed the young soldier standing on a bridge at midnight, staring into the black water. There was a closeup of the flotsam and jetsam of the river—an old tree, beer cans, a log. Gradually the scene transformed. The audience, seeing through the soldier's eyes, watched the log turn into a mermaid of bright and beckoning beauty. Meg held her breath to see if the soldier would be seduced into make the fateful leap.

Suddenly, Jeff sprang from his seat. When she looked up at him, she saw that his forehead was gleaming with perspiration. He muttered to her, the words barely audible, "I'll be in the cabin," and bolted from the room. His departure was so precipitous that the couple sitting next to him exchanged a look.

Meg sat for another minute or so, wondering if she had read more into his leaving than she should have. Could it be that he had simply not cared for the film? No, she decided. Something was wrong. Quietly she left, whispering apologies to the people whose view of the screen she was momentarily blocking.

She knocked at the door to Jeff's room. He answered with a muffled, "Come in." She entered to find him stretched face down and full-length upon the bed. She sat down on the bed beside him.

"Jeff. What's wrong?"

He turned his head only far enough toward her to make his words audible. "Go away, Meg. I'll be all right in a little while. That movie just wasn't the sort of thing I was in the mood for today."

She said nothing for a long moment, wondering why this sudden, impenetrable wall had been flung between them. Why had she ever suggested the movie? Such a complex and unhappy story was obviously a very bad choice for a day like today. Why would the cruise people ever have booked such a movie, she thought, turning her anger toward them. Probably because it was a major contender for an Academy Award. Well, the mistake had been made. She would have to see what she could do to rectify it.

"Jeff. Please talk to me. Whatever it is that's bothering you, let me hear about it and share it with you."

"If you'll leave me alone, I'll be all right. There's no reason to burden you with something you can't do anything about."

"But how do you know, unless you tell me?"

"Goddam it, Meg. Get out of here! This is something

I have to face by myself." His head was once more buried in the pillow.

She got to her feet and looked down at him. She did not want to desert him. But if he truly wanted to be alone, she would be doing him a favor by leaving him for a while. Resolutely, she walked into her own room, closing the adjoining door noiselessly behind her.

She picked up a paperback book she had bought at the ship's newsstand and tried vainly to interest herself in it. At last, she threw it across the room and tried to write a few postcards. She wrote two, reread them, found them stilted and uninteresting, and threw them into the wastebasket. How could life, which only yesterday had seemed cloudless, suddenly taste of ash?

At that moment, she heard a deep, prolonged moan from Jeff's room. She jumped to her feet and raced through the connecting hallway. He was sitting bolt upright in bed, with a look of terror in his eyes. She sped to him and enveloped him in her arms. He did not react, either to welcome her embrace or to push her away. His body was rigid.

"Jeff! Please tell me what's wrong. Please don't shut me out any longer—I can't bear it." Tears streamed down her face. "I love you, Jeff. You've got to let me share this with you, whatever it is!"

He began to rock back and forth in her arms very slightly. He closed his eyes and let his head rest on her breast. "I had a nightmare. I'll be okay." Beneath the new sunburn, his face was pale, and when she let her hand brush his forehead, she found it very warm.

"Are you ill, Jeff?"

He managed a faint smile. "No. Sick at heart, that's all."

"Then will you tell me what's wrong?"

"Are you prepared to have your vacation ruined?" The bitterness in the question seemed to be self-directed.

"I'm prepared for anything. I only want you to feel there's someone around who wants to help."

He sighed, then got up without a word and went into the tiny bathroom. From the open door she could see him splashing water on his face. When he finally turned off the tap and came back to her, she thought with relief that some of his natural color had reappeared. He sighed again and sank down into a bedside chair.

He sat silent for a few minutes, hands clenched in front of him. Then he rose and restlessly paced up and down. "Would you like to take a turn around the deck?"

His voice was almost distant, as one might address a chance acquaintance. She swallowed with difficulty and tried to make her smile bright. "Yes. I'd like that."

Once on deck, they walked for a time without speaking. He did not touch her, not even when a high-spirited child jostled against her, knocking her momentarily off-balance. The sounds of the afternoon —the cry of the gulls, the splashes from the pool, the wooden thumps of a shuffleboard game—seemed to emanate from a world they were no longer a part of. She did not question him further. She would have to wait until he was ready.

They reached a corner of the deck from which the sun had already disappeared. Nearly all the deck chairs in the area were deserted; there was an elderly man dozing, his newspaper over his face.

"Sit down, Meg."

She sat at once. He took the deck chair next to hers and passed a hand over his eyes wearily. She waited, hardly daring to breathe.

"I don't know how I struck you when we first met. But I know that most people think I'm one of the luckiest people alive. I guess they have reason to think so. My surface qualifications would seem to bear that out—I don't have two heads, I'm reasonably intelligent, I have enough money to be comfortable for the rest of my life, even if I should choose not to work at all.

"But fate—or karma, or whatever—has seen fit to deal the bitter with the sweet." He shook his head impatiently. "Ah, let me get off this philosophical meandering and give it to you straight. I told you about my father."

"Yes, and I realize how much guilt you've carried with you over that, Jeff."

He motioned her words away. "That may be true, but my brother's death was—well, I was much more directly responsible."

"How could that—"

"My father's death was painful, but I was beginning to get straightened out about it. I went into therapy for a while, and the therapist made me finally realize that those things do happen—that there are things we can't foresee or control. But with Rob, I should have seen from the first—"

"Jeff, why not wait until—"

"No, I want you to hear. I should have told you long ago. You could have decided then whether you wanted to attach yourself to one of the biggest cowards and most selfish bastards that ever walked God's green earth."

She shook her head in protest, then subsided into an uneasy silence. She had never seen Jeff in this bitter, self-hating mood before. When he had told her the circumstances of his father's death, there was pain, true, but also a certain resignation. His present mood betrayed a virulent streak of deeply embedded guilt.

He squinted his eyes, trying to decide whether the triangular speck of white on the horizon were a boat or a figment of his imagination. "Rob was so changed that it was like dealing with a stranger. He was like that from the moment he came home. So much like that movie. That's why I couldn't take it any more."

His voice assumed a half-mesmerized, remote quality. Meg could see that he had again retreated into the world of the past—the world of three years ago. . . .

Jeff knew from the moment he met Robert at the airport that his brother had changed significantly. Before his stint in Vietnam, Robert had been the ebullient one, the rakish one, the one whose thirst for life and laughter seemed to remain unslaked. Jeff had been rejected by the army for that most hackneyed of medical reasons—flat feet.

Jeff went alone to meet his brother. Watching him come down the ramp of the military plane, he felt another pang of guilt that Robert had been the one to go. As his brother neared, Jeff was shocked to see the familiar, jocular features screwed into a grim, unsmiling visage. The first few days in his brother's melancholy company confirmed that first unhappy impression.

Robert moved into Jeff's apartment in the city and his depression increased after he found that his former girlfriend had married someone else less than a month before his return. Jeff lived at the time in a fifteenth-floor flat on Riverside Drive, a rambling suite of high-ceilinged rooms with a sweeping view of the Hudson River. Robert would sit by the hour with a pair of binoculars, scanning the Jersey shore. Looking for what? Jeff never found out. When he asked, Robert would simply turn him off with a flippant or cryptic reply.

One day Jeff came back to the apartment after a long and very tough day at the office. Robert was sitting in his accustomed chair with the binoculars. Jeff felt his patience wearing thin.

"You haven't been out all day?"

"Now why would I go out?" his brother asked, with a crooked smile. "Am I not master of all I survey, right here in the depths on the fifteenth floor?"

Robert's speech was slightly slurred, and Jeff noticed then the half-empty glass of amber liquid at his side. Jeff sat down on the sofa and fixed his brother with a level stare. "You know, Bobo," he said, using the pet name Robert had somehow picked up as a child, "you're not doing a hell of a lot to help yourself. I know Vietnam was no picnic, and I sympathize, God knows I do. But for Pete's sake, try to find something, somewhere in this big, wide world, to take an interest in."

"That's the trouble, baby brother. This big, wide world. It's amazing how much bigger and wider it gets every day. And deep. 'No, 'tis not so deep as a well, nor so wide as a church door, but 'tis enough, 'twill serve.' "

"What are you talking about?"

"The wound, the wound."

Jeff could make no sense of the conversation. He stood up impatiently. "Let's go have something to eat, Bobo. You'll feel better when you get some food in your stomach.'

"I'd feel better if I had another drink."

"You've had enough. Come on, let's get something to eat."

Robert winked at him drunkenly. "Baby brother, food is the least of my worries. I shall now refresh my libation." He went to the serving bar and poured a generous measure of Scotch into his glass, then lifted it in a mock toast to Jeff. "The elixir of life," he said and took a deep draught.

"All right! I've had enough. I'm going out for dinner. If you want to stay here and drink until you kill yourself, kill yourself!" Jeff picked up his jacket from the chair and walked out.

When he returned from a neighborhood restaurant an hour later, he found the room empty and a chill, April wind blowing the sheer white curtains back from the open window. On the table at one end of the sofa, weighted down by the empty glass, he found a scrawled note: "I thought I might stay here and drink, but then I decided to kill myself."

He did not even have to look fifteen floors below. He went to the phone and called the police.

## Chapter 17

The story of his brother's death had spewed out of him in bitterness and self-loathing, but once it was told, Jeff seemed to feel a great burden had been lifted. Though it had been a wrenching experience, Meg was glad she had been there to listen and to try to comfort.

He was pale and ate little at dinner, but seemed in control. As she watched him with love and concern, she thought he was like a patient who has been seriously ill, but one for whom the crisis is past. He was still a little fragile, as convalescents are fragile, but mending. Señora Raimundo was again her loquacious, animated self, and Meg was grateful for her chatter, because the quartet of bridge players had apparently had a falling-out over their afternoon game and were barely speaking.

The señora leaned over to Meg with the air of someone who was about to deliver a top-secret gossip item. "We were listening to our short-wave transmitter just before we came in to dinner. There is a big storm east of us."

"Really?" Meg was surprised. The day had been brilliantly clear. "I hope we aren't in its path."

"No, no, no. It is veering to the north, they say."

Señor Raimundo spoke sharply to his wife. "Maria, I told you not to alarm people with tales of that storm. It has nothing to do with us." Turning to Meg and Jeff, he said expansively, "Why you not join us for some after-dinner cognac in our stateroom?"

Meg looked at Jeff. A relaxing half-hour with the Raimundos might do him good, she thought. But he smiled at the older couple, replied that the sea air and the sun had done him in, and requested a raincheck. He and Meg left the table shortly thereafter and returned to Meg's room.

Several hours later, Jeff was awakened by the slamming of something metallic against the porthole. He got quickly out of bed, and when he stood up, realized the ship was rocking rather violently in what seemed to be choppy seas. Steadying himself by hanging on to the furniture, he went to the porthole to find the source of the slamming. He opened the curtains and looked out, but beyond the lights of the main deck, he could see nothing but a black void. He opened the porthole slightly and found the rumbling of the surf loud and angry. The slamming sound continued, but he could not find the source. He saw a booted and slickered crewman hurrying along the deck, and wondered why he was dressed for rain, since there was none. The captain was evidently expecting some heavy weather.

Should he wake Meg? He looked at her and his face softened into a protective grin. She was sleeping with a vastly contented smile on her face, one arm clutching her pillow like a teddy bear. He could not know that in her dreams, she fancied the pillow was Jeff. Wake her and tell her what? he thought. Let her sleep. He closed the window and the watertight porthole shut out almost completely the sound of the sea. Jeff turned out the lamp and got back into bed. His eyes took a moment to adjust to the dimness of the blue night light.

He lay awake for a few minutes, listening to an occasional yell from a crewman. Once he was back in bed, the rocking of the ship was hardly perceptible. Indeed, it was like a soothing hammock-sway, lulling him into drowsiness.

He was in the last moment before sleep when he almost pitched from his berth. The ship was being battered by a giant sea. He heard muffled cries and scuttling noises along the passageway outside the stateroom. He lay there, undecided about whether to get up and investigate, or remain where he was until someone gave explicit orders as to what the passengers were to do. Then he told himself he was being an alarmist. Obviously, it was nothing serious, or the captain on the bridge would have announced it over the ship's loudspeaker, which reached every public room, every stateroom, every work area of the vessel.

Meg began to toss restlessly. He had been holding her when the ship lurched, so he had cushioned the jolt for her and she had not awakened. But now she turned and muttered something that sounded like a question.

"It's all right, Meg. Go back to sleep."

She murmured drowsily and turned over. He wrapped his arms around her and, in a moment, her regular breathing told him she had followed his advice. The waves continued to batter the sides of the ship. He heard a commotion on deck and wanted to go to the porthole. But he did not want to risk waking Meg.

There was a hum as the loudspeaker came on, a few bursts of static, and then the captain's voice, calm and matter-of-fact. "Attention, all passengers. This is Captain Jorgensen. We are entering some rather heavy seas. If the motion of the ship has wakened you, please stay in your cabins. There is at present no cause for alarm. Repeat: please stay in your cabins. There is, at present, no cause for alarm. We will keep you advised."

Jeff breathed a small sigh of relief. At least someone was staying on top of things, although the phrase, "at present," had a slightly ominous ring. He, too, turned over and was about to doze off when the ship was tipped at a forty-five-degree angle, hanging there helplessly. Then it slowly sank into a trough of water and stabilized itself. Meg moved into his arms. Her voice was suddenly alert.

"What's going on, Jeff?"

"I don't know. We seem to be in a storm." And indeed, he could hear now the crashing surf and the howl of the wind even through the closed porthole.

"Maybe we should get up and dress, Jeff."

"The Captain announced a minute ago that we should all stay in our rooms. So we might as well relax as much as we can."

"Jeff. Hold me. Hold me tight."

Again they heard the static of the loudspeaker, and again the Captain's voice: "Please do not—repeat—do not leave your cabins unless you are so instructed. Our crew is very capable, and the situation is being efficiently handled. Please remain calmly in your cabins."

They could hear, on the deck outside, the sound of running footsteps and an occasional yell, which could be discerned only briefly before it was carried off by the wind. Underneath the melange of sounds there was the low, steady hum of the ship's giant engines.

Jeff and Meg held each other close. Her love for him had never seemed so overwhelming. She held him to her with savage possessiveness. Life was now complete for both of them. It occurred to her how much her life had changed within the last twenty-four hours. She now felt whole as a human being, and she was determined, with a steely resolve, never to lose the preciousness of what life had so recently yielded. She was now certain that she could make Jeff happy for the rest of his life.

After perhaps half an hour, the wind seemed to lose much of its force, and the violent rocking diminished. "Let's try to go back to sleep, darling," Jeff whispered against her shoulder. "Everything seems to be under control. I guess the worst is over."

"What time is it?"

Jeff craned his neck to see the tiny travel clock at their bedside. "Four-thirty. Let's try to sleep so we can enjoy ourselves tomorrow." They snuggled into the sheets and both slept almost immediately.

Meg awoke first, and it was not sound which brought her back to consciousness, but silence. She blinked several times, wondering why the room seemed different. Then she realized that the blue night light and gone off. And something else was different, too. There was no muffled hum of the engines. The entire ship was held in a vast stillness. She did not know why, but the silence was more unsettling than the sounds of the storm had been. It was something a ship's passengers took for granted and rarely consciously considered, but whatever else was going on, the life of the ship was dependent on the muted hum of the engines, emanating from deep within the craft's bowels. And now that hum was stilled.

She wondered if she should wake Jeff. Perhaps they had cut the engines to do some repair work—perhaps the storm had damaged the engines in some way. She had never traveled by ship before and had no knowledge of the vessels' workings. As she considered whether to rouse Jeff, he moved against her and opened one eye.

"What's going on?"

"Oh, nothing. Go back to sleep. It's just that the ship's engines have stopped, and I guess that's what woke me."

Jeff, more experienced at ocean travel, was alert and wary in an instant. He knew, as Meg did not, that there is nothing more pathetically helpless than a great steam-driven ship dead in the water. At cruising speed, a liner will still go more than a mile before it can be brought to a stop, even under full reverse power. Jeff also knew that the steam from a ship's engines not only moves the ship; it heats the galley's ranges, and creates the electricity for lights, refrigeration, air conditioning and public address systems. Without the steam that powers the entire ship, Jeff realized that they were sitting in the middle of an elephantine, 25,000-ton corpse.

Quickly, but without hope, Jeff tried to switch on the bedside lamp. Nothing happened. Meg, sensing his alarm, tried to keep her voice steady as she framed the question. "Are we in trouble?"

"I—the storm must have caused a malfunction in the engine. Let's hope they get it going again soon."

"Is it dangerous? I mean, for the engines not to be running?"

"Not per se. But without the engines' power, the captain has very little control of the ship." Though his voice was soft and even, Meg realized with a shock the import of his words.

"Maybe we'd better get dressed."

"You don't have a flashlight, do you?" His tone was not hopeful.

"No. No, I don't—yes, wait a minute, I do." She felt in the pitch-black room for her handbag, and drew out a tiny, pencil flashlight on her keyring. It had been one of Aunt Bess's gifts to her when she left for New York. They dressed hurriedly by the faint and narrow beam of the flashlight. As they started to leave the room, Jeff reached for his wallet and said without explanation: "Bring your handbag. And any valuables in your suitcase."

For the first time, Meg was frightened. She looked at him but his face did not encourage questions. Then his expression softened. "I don't think it's necessary. Just an extra precaution."

He waited at the door while she got a small jewel box from the pouch compartment of her luggage. When they opened the door into the corridor, they could see the glow of matches and cigarette lighters down the length of the hallway. Passengers were standing in small clusters, waiting to be told what to do. They were murmuring in hushed voices—the same voices one hears at a funeral or an accident. At that moment, the emergency lights came on, and the ship's social director, a young blonde woman dressed in a windbreaker, slacks and sneakers, came down the hallway, instructing the passengers to follow her.

Her voice exuded false cheerfulness. "Don't be upset. We've temporarily lost power, but things should be all right very shortly. We're all going to the Main Ballroom, and have a wee-hours party. So just be calm, and you'll have quite an adventure story to tell your friends when you get home."

When they reached the companionway beyond the corridor, the wind seemed to have risen again. Or perhaps they were simply closer to the deck and so were able to hear it more clearly. The ship's listening began again, at first gently, but before they reached the end of the alleyway, Jeff was forced to take Meg's arm as she lurched sharply against the wall. Other passengers, too, found it difficult to keep their footing. Jeff heard an aborted scream from a woman behind him. He turned and saw that she was being supported by her husband; she was apprently on the verge of fainting. He looked at Meg. Her face was pale, but she seemed composed. He had never loved her more than at that moment. Yes, he thought, there was a core of fine-tempered steel within her, which stood her in good stead in times of crisis.

Walking was becoming almost impossible. The social director instructed them to join hands and form a human chain. Finally, in this manner, they reached the doors to the ballroom and entered. The group was now almost completely silent. Even the social director had lost her vivaciousness and was grimly efficient as she led her charges inside the cavernous room. The emergency lights cast an ominous glow over the shrouded grand piano. The opulence of the room itself, with its gold sconces and wine-red curtains, was wildly incongruous.

"It might be a little rough for dancing," she announced, with a stretched expression on her lips which in other circumstances might have passed for a smile, "but does anyone here play the piano?"

No one spoke. Jeff looked at Meg, then rose. "Not well, but I'll give it a go." Meg's mouth opened in surprise. He had never mentioned that talent. He made his way unsteadily to the instrument and removed the sheet that covered it. He launched into a medley of Broadway show tunes, all liltingly upbeat. The spirits of the group brightened as the music shut out the sound of the gusting wind.

Through the broad floor-to-ceiling windows of the ballroom, Meg could see nothing but the gray mist. Even the sea was no longer visible. She wondered where the other passengers were. Perhaps many had elected to stay in their cabins. She wondered, too, why no further instructions had been offered over the speaker system. She could not know that at that moment, technicians and engineers were working frantically to try to find out why the auxiliary sound system had not been activated when the regular one went out. Occasionally crew members, in various stages of uniformed dress, would scurry through the ballroom on their way hither and yon, all, she noticed, with carefully expressionless faces.

Jeff continued his impromptu recital. Kathy, the social director, stopped a young steward and asked if any brandy were available. He promised to investigate and hurried into the bar next door. Meg thought he looked as if he could use a pick-me-up himself. Jeff asked for requests, and someone who had been able to hang on to his sense of humor suggested "Slow Boat to China," and was greeted with good-natured jeers. Jeff launched instead into a swinging, syncopated version of "Everything's Come Up Roses."

Suddenly, there was a grinding jolt. The ship hung motionless for a long second and then lurched backward. Meg tried to clutch the table to keep herself from falling, but the table moved suddenly and slid across the floor. The scene was tumbling, changing before her eyes like pieces shifting in a nightmarish kaleidoscope. She tried to sight Jeff, and caught the briefest glimpse of him before she was knocked over and found herself on the cold, bare ballroom floor.

She thought she heard a scream, but it faded quickly into a dark void of nothingness.

## Chapter 18

At the instant of impact, Jeff was trying to catch Meg's eye. But a crew member had stopped at a table directly between them and was attempting to calm a distraught passenger. So when the ship went aground, snapping the piano leg and sending the heavy instrument crashing down on Jeff's leg, he could not see what happened to Meg. He felt a sharp pain in his right thigh, then numbness.

The emergency lights had now gone out, and only the first gleam of a raw, windswept dawn illuminated the room. The entire ballroom was tilting crazily at a thirty-degree angle; all of the furniture not bolted to the floor was sliding toward the long row of French windows. The piano alone was too massive to slide more than an inch or two; the full weight of it remained on Jeff's leg.

The scene was one of total confusion. Jeff, still fully conscious, could hear screams and shouts. With a sense of impotent, hopeless fury, he struck the piano keys wildly and the discordant bang seemed a fitting punctuation to the cacophany of sound. He began calling Meg's name, but so great was the turmoil that he could hardly hear his own voice.

With a great tearing, sucking sound, the windows collapsed outward onto the deck. The noise was oddly musical, like an enormous set of glass windchimes. The boat righted itself slightly and the passengers took advantage of the moment to cling to anything available —the ballroom curtains, a built-in serving bar at one end of the room. Then the boat listed sharply to one side again and Jeff, on the topmost side of the room, saw one panel of the curtains tear away from their rod and the man and woman who had been clutching them slide smoothly across the deck and into the sea. That horrifying tableau would be frozen in Jeff's mind for many months to come.

The ship righted itself again and Jeff saw the first sign of hope. Crew members had managed to lower two lifeboats into the sea and several fluorescent-orange life vests were beng thrown overboard. Perhaps only fifteen or twenty people of the original fifty or so were now in the ballroom—or what had been the ballroom. They were huddled into one corner, those close enough clinging to the still-intact serving bar, the others clinging to them. Jeff could not see whether Meg was a member of the pathetic clump. He tried to call out for her again, but a brilliant arrow of pain shot through his leg and he succumbed to unconsciousness.

When thought returned to him, he realized he had been wakened by water and stillness. The water covered the lower half of his body and was inching upward toward his face. The ballroom floor was on an even keel; he could see that from the water level. For a fraction of a moment, he felt grateful that the ship's listing had ceased; then he realized the import of that fact. The ship had stopped rocking because the water was *inside it*, serving as ballast. It was slowly sinking. The realization came to him in a confused and fragmented way, punctuated by stabs of pain in his leg. He tried to find the corner where the tiny group of passengers had been huddled, but apparently the piano had shifted its position slightly and its bulk was now between him and that portion of the room. He could no longer see the expanse of water through the windows, but only endless gray-green sky.

Gradually he became aware of noise which evolved

into distinct and separate voices.

"Hey, wait a minute! There's somebody else in here."

"Where?"

"Under the piano."

"Is he alive?"

He was semiconscious as two pairs of white-clad arms pulled him with difficulty from under the heavy instrument. He realized dimly that he was being rescued. He squinted to make out the features of his two saviors: one was bearded and dark-skinned, the other sandy-haired and spectacled.

"Meg! Did you find Meg?" He thought his voice was completely audible and the words perfectly articulated, but the men looked at each other with an expression of puzzlement.

"What'd you say, Buddy?"

"Meg! Did you find Meg?"

The second man shrugged slightly and muttered to the first as if in answer. "Beats me."

"Take it easy, Buddy. Everything's gonna be all right."

Why couldn't he get through to them? Through stiff, cracking lips, he tried to form the question once more, but the ship shuddered briefly and the movement sent another stab of pain coursing through his thigh. Then he passed again into a world without color, light or noise.


He woke fitfully as he was transferred from the mortally wounded vessel into a lifeboat. Consciousness returned again momentarily as he was lifted into a police boat. Then (it seemed days later; he was sure that it was not) he found himself on an operating table, staring into an unbearably bright white light. He seemed separated from the world by layers of gauze, but he could hear a low buzz of conversation and he managed to pick out a few distinct words.

"He under yet?"

". . . few minutes."

"Let's go . . . others . . . waiting."

When he returned, finally, to an almost normal waking state, he was lying in a hospital bed and a red-haired nurse was making notations on a chart at the foot of his bed. When she saw him looking at her, she smiled and moved to his side.

"How do you feel?"

He considered the question at length. He noticed for the first time that his right leg was in traction, lifted off the bed by a harness-like contraption and suspended ludicrously in the air.

"I don't know. I'll live, I guess, won't I?" Full, horror-stricken consciousness suddenly flooded his mind. "Where's Meg? Did they find her?"

"Who?"

"Meg! My—my girl. Did you find her?" He instinctively tried to get out of bed, but the sharp, jerking motion signaled such an onrush of pain that he collapsed onto the pillow, lightheaded and weak from the effort.

The nurse was holding his shoulders, her hands a gentle pressure. "You really can't do that, you know." Her tone was lightly chiding, as one would reprimand an unruly but lovable child.

He tried to frame the question more sensibly. "How can I find out what happened to one of the other passengers?" Perspiration broke out on his forehead; his hands were knotted into fists. "What day is it? How long have I—?"

She smiled again. He decided he hated that capable, condescending smile, but he forced himself to lie quietly while she framed an answer.

"It's Tuesday, the thirty-first of December. Your ship went down very early yesterday morning. You've been—"

"Never mind. How can I find out about another passenger?"

"Well." She mused over her answer for an unreasonable length of time. "Many of the other passengers are in this hospital. Some weren't hurt seriously enough to be hospitalized. And some are in St. Joseph's Hospital a few blocks from here."

For the first time, Jeff realized he had no idea where he was. "Where am I? I mean what city?"

"Willemstad." Seeing the blank look on his face, she elaborated. "Curaçao."

"How can I find out where Meg is?"

Again she hesitated. "One of the Red Cross ladies will be in soon. I'll have her come by and see you."

"But maybe Meg's right here in this hospital. Couldn't you check that?"

"Of course I can check our list here. But I don't think—" Her voice trailed away indecisively.

"Well, would you do that, please?" His mouth was very dry. "Gardner. Meg—Margaret Gardner."

"Yes. All right. I'll be right back."

When she returned, he could see the results were negative. She shook her head. "No, I'm afraid not."

"Well, could you call the other hospital? Or is there a phone here—I'll call them—" He looked around but saw the room contained no telephone.

"I have to make rounds now. But when I have a minute, I will call them. If Mrs. Van den Aker hasn't got here by then." She turned quickly and left the room as if relieved of an onerous assignment.

Jeff was stewing with anger, frustration and fear. She certainly had not supplied him with any great amount of information. He didn't even know whether all the passengers had survived. With that thought, his anger turned to cold terror. Oh, God. No. No. That couldn't be. More likely, Meg hadn't been hurt at all. But if that were the case, she would surely have been to see him—would be here now. He rang the bell and a different nurse appeared.

"Yes, Mr. McAllister?"

"Has anyone been here to see me?"

"You mean today?"

"I mean since I've been here." God, one nurse more stupid than the next.

"Not that I know of. Not while I've been here."

"Would there be any record of visitors?"

"No."

They were interrupted by the appearance of an angular woman with a horsy face and kind, perceptive eyes. She wore a gray Red Cross Volunteer's uniform. She stepped into the room briskly and came to shake Jeff's hand at once.

"You're Mr. McAllister, right? I'm Karen Van den Aker. Can I do anything for you?"

"Yes. God, yes. I'm trying to find out what happened to another passenger. Another passenger from *The Sea Queen*. Meg Gardner. Could you get any kind of list for me, do you suppose?"

Mrs. Van den Aker dug into a commodious tote bag. "Yes. I have a list of passengers. Who was taken to what hospital and so forth." She began to run her forefinger down the roster of names. "What was the name again?"

"Gardner. Margaret Gardner. Meg Gardner."

Her eyes followed the finger slowly down the list. She stopped at the very bottom of the page. Her eyes left the paper reluctantly, her finger still marking a name.

"Has your family been notified? Will they be coming

down to join you—"

"I don't know, goddam it! What's happened to Meg?"

"You see, it's better if—"

His voice was almost a shout. "I have no family to speak of. What's happened to Meg?" He tried to tear the paper from her hand, but with a slight reflex move, she turned her body so that it was out of his reach.

"Please. Just be calm, Mr. McAllister. I'll tell you." She pulled the bedside chair an inch or two toward him and sat down. "Miss Gardner is—unaccounted for."

"Un . . . accounted . . . for." He spoke the words as if they were in an unknown language, as if he could make sense of them only if he digested them syllable by syllable.

"Yes." As Jeff started to speak, Mrs. Van den Aker continued hastily. "Now remember, Mr. McAllister, the—er, accident happened only yesterday morning. We know only that—er, Miss Gardner is not at St. Joseph's nor at this hospital, and that she was not treated at Emergency Central where they took the passengers not requiring hospitalization. But we know of at least four passengers who were picked up by small private craft which happened to be in the area. It's entirely possible that something of that sort may have—"

He shook his head firmly. "No. I would have heard from her by now."

"Remember, the whole area has been in a state of great confusion since the accident. So not necessarily, perhaps."

"How many people are—" he paused, reluctant to use the phrase—" 'unaccounted for'?"

"At the beginning, twenty or so. But twelve, I believe, have turned up alive, and four others have been—found."

"Found?"

"Their—er, bodies recovered."

Jeff turned his face to the wall. He could feel the tears, hot and salty, drop onto the pillow.

"I'm sorry, Mr. McAllister. But the important thing is not to give up hope. As I said, some of the passengers were rescued by small boats in the area and it's quite possible that—"

Jeff, his head still turned to the wall, nodded curtly. He wanted the woman to leave. He wanted to be alone with his bewilderment and grief. At the same time, he realized his feelings were unreasonable, that he was being rude and ungrateful for the information she had given him. *Better to know than to lie here and wonder*, he mused bitterly.

"Can I get anything for you, Mr. McAllister? Some iced tea or ginger ale?" Her voice was soft, as though she were reluctant to intrude on his privacy. She seemed genuinely concerned.

He turned his head to look at her. He felt contrite. After all, she had done what she could. He looked at her helplessly. "Is there anything else we can do? Any other sources we could check?"

After a moment's thought she shook her head. "No, I really can't think of anything. Just don't believe the worst right now. She could turn up at any moment. You must keep believing that."

Jeff looked at her, then lowered his eyes to the metal traction-frame. "If I could only get out of here." He looked at the apparatus speculatively, as if trying to figure out how to escape from it.

Mrs. Van den Aker must have thought he was delirious enough to try some sort of escape, for a few seconds later she excused herself from the room. Shortly thereafter, the red-haired nurse returned and gave him an injection, and within a few minutes he fell into a heavy, stuporous sleep.

# Chapter 19

When the ship, with its power gone and floundering like a helpless leviathan in the water, hit the submerged reef, Meg was knocked to the floor of the ballroom. She tried to scramble back to her feet to reach Jeff at the piano, but the craft's heavy listing made it impossible to do anything but slide toward the lower end of the smooth, cold expanse of wooden floor. Finally, she was unable to move at all and found herself clinging to the ankles of a huge, powerfully built man who was holding onto the corner serving bar.

She tried to get to her feet, but her legs seemed made of rubber and would not hold her up. She looked toward the piano and saw that its legs had given way. She screamed once, a sharp, primal scream of agony. At that moment, the man to whom she was clinging saw that one of the lifeboats was being lowered. He scooped Meg up in his arms as though she were a sack of potatoes and by turns crawling and sliding managed to get onto the deck. People were racing in panic toward the lifeboat.

Meg tried to tell him she must find Jeff but he brushed her protests aside peremptorily. He obviously considered her hysterical. Seemingly in a state of shock, he moved like an automaton. He swung over the side of the ship, Meg still in his arms, and grabbed the sides of the rope ladder. For such a large man, he was surprisingly agile. The lifeboat was already full of people, who began shouting at them frantically. Meg could not hear what they were saying; their voices were lost in the wind.

Then she heard the man utter a bitter, accusatory epithet and saw the lifeboat pulling away from the ship.

". . . bastards!" The large man was screaming at the people in the boat. The rope ladder now led nowhere, its bottom floating aimlessly in the empty water. The man stopped. They were about midway down the side of the ship. Then, slowly and painfully, he began to climb back up.

"Can you make the climb on your own?" he gasped. He was panting with exertion. "I don't think I can make it carrying you."

"Yes, I can." Meg clambered above the man's shoulders and reached for the sides of the ladder. Now she could go back and find Jeff. But at that moment the ship gave a violent shudder and the rope ladder was knocked furiously into its side. Meg's head hit the metal ship and flaming pinwheels spun through her brain. She was sent flying through the air like a rag doll and into the angry sea.

When she surfaced, brought back to consciousness by the shock of the water, she saw that the man, too, had lost his hold and fallen. He was in the water not far from her, flailing away in panic, mouth agape. Meg realized with dismay that he could not swim. She swam frantically to him and put one arm around his waist, the other under the collar of his bathrobe. They stayed like that for what seemed an eternity, she treading water, the man trying to expel the salty sea from his gaping mouth.

"Close your mouth! Breathe through your nose!" she screamed.

Then there was a thud on the water and she saw the bright orange life vests. She tried to swim to them, holding onto her human burden, but the man's weight was too great. She could not tow him with her; the vests were drifting away. She had no choice—she was forced to release him.

"If you can relax, you'll float. If you can't, kick your legs. I'll be back with the vests," she spluttered.

She swam to them, grabbed them and started back. But when she looked at the spot where he had been struggling, there was no sign of him. She paddled furiously to what she thought was the exact location, but the sea was empty. She dove beneath the surface and tried to search for him, but there was only bottomless darkness.

She got into one of the vests, deflated the second one and fastened it around herself as well. She might need a spare. Or there might be someone else in the water. Buoyed by the life vest, she lay still, drained and exhausted. Her head hurt terribly.

When she looked at the ship again, she saw that it was much lower in the water than it had been. Hadn't she read somewhere that when a ship sinks, it creates a force of suction that takes anything in the area down with it? She began to paddle away from the doomed vessel. She could see two lifeboats not far away and three or four other small craft on the distant horizon. She headed desperately for the nearer lifeboat, but the distance between herself and it never seemed to narrow.

After a time, the sun came out and beat through the haze down onto her head and shoulders. The top of her head felt as though it would explode. She would have to rest for a minute. . . .


The chugging in the water grew louder and louder. Was it real or was she hallucinating? She opened one eye wearily. Pulling alongside her was a sleek cabin cruiser. Two men on its deck were looking down at her curiously. They conferred with each other briefly and one shook his head emphatically. Meg looked up at them blearily. She still could not decide whether the cruiser was real or a mirage.

She tried to call up to them but no words came out. She wanted to tell them what had happened. With a shock, she realized then that she was not sure herself what had happened. She remembered that she and a very large man were in the water and that she had tried to save him and failed. But why was she in the middle of the ocean?

When she heard the men raise their voices in argument, she decided they did in fact exist. They were both deeply tanned and dressed in faded jeans, without shirts or shoes. Finally, the taller one made a gesture of angry dismissal to the other and jumped into the water. With strong, sure strokes, he swam to her and began pulling her toward the cruiser.

"Don't worry, you'll be all right." By the time he had reached the motorboat, the second man had disappeared into the cabin.

"Yanni! Come here and give me a hand, goddam it!" The second man reappeared from inside the cabin. He looked dark and surly and provided the needed assistance with tightlipped disapproval. But at last Meg was lifted over the side of the boat and deposited on its deck. She lay there semiconscious, knowing only that her survival was no longer solely in her hands and thankful for deliverance. She closed her eyes and tried to will the pain out of her head.

"Goddam it, she's hurt. I told you not to get messed up with this." The angry voice spat out the words contemptuously.

"What are we going to do—let her die out there? I man not be a saint, but I don't want *that* on my conscience."

"All right, we've got her on board. Now you take

care of her." Meg opened her eyes groggily, in time to see the smaller man disappear again into the boat's interior. The man who had rescued her bent over her and examined her head wound.

"Nasty bump you got there, lovey," he said cheerfully. "But we'll get you fixed up in no time." He went away and returned a moment later with a tin basin and a first-aid kit. He began to wash her temple. His hands were very gentle.

"By the way, I'm David." His accent was peculiar, Meg thought. Almost British, but not quite. "Wondering where I hail from, are you?" Meg smiled faintly as if to confirm his guess. "Down under. Australia."

"Oh." He was brandishing a pair of scissors. "What are you doing?"

"Sorry. Have to cut a bit of your hair." Then he put an odorous ointment of some kind on the wound. Another throb of pain stabbed into her head.

"Do you have any aspirin?" she asked weakly.

He dug again into the first-aid kit. "Here we go. Wait—let me get some water." He brought a glass of water and Meg realized for the first time how thirsty she was.

"More?" he asked.

"Please." It was hard to hold her head up. There was something she was trying to remember and couldn't.

"Here we are." He was back with another glass of water. "I'd drink that sort of slowly, if I were you. Otherwise, it might make you sick. Or so they say."

"Thank you. And thanks for saving me."

"Anytime. What's your name, by the way?"

"My name?" Meg frowned and slowly sat up. Another bolt of pain rammed into her head. Still frowning, and now bewildered as well, she looked at David and then averted her eyes. "My name is—Peggy." That didn't sound right. But if Peggy was not her name, what was? The strange thing was she couldn't remember!

David laughed. "Well, blimey, I thought for a minute you weren't going to tell us! Peggy, eh? That's a nice name. And what's your last name?"

She opened her mouth, then closed it. She did not know. She looked at the sunburned face before her and shook her head. "I don't know." The words were spoken in an embarrassed whisper.

The man called Yanni came back on deck. He had put on a dark shirt and canvas shoes. David called to him. "I say, come over, Yanni. We've got a bit of a mystery on our hands. She doesn't remember her name!"

Yanni snorted impatiently. "What kind of bloody game is this?"

Meg looked at him helplessly. "I just—can't remember."

David looked at her brightly. "It's the knock you got on the head. You're just momentarily confused. A good night's sleep and you'll be all right." He turned to Yanni. "Is dinner about ready? Maybe some food is in order for our mermaid."

"In a minute." Yanni disappeared once more. Meg became conscious that it was almost dusk. She was somehow sure that she had been on the ocean almost the full day, though she could not have explained how she knew that. Some inner timepiece ticking the hours away, perhaps.

Yanni brought out steaming plates of seafood stew that was quite delicious, but after a few bites she could eat no more. She was still disoriented. "Where are we?" she asked.

David started to frame an answer. "We're headed for—"

"Shut up, Davey!" Yanni's voice was sharp with

authority.

"But she's got to know—"

"I said shut up."

The two men seemed very strange to Meg. Why did they not want her to know where they were or where they were going? The water looked somehow tropical. South America. She could not imagine why she suddenly thought of South America—the name came to her from nowhere.

"Are we near South America?"

Yanni looked at David briefly and shook his head. David said softly, "No."

She gave up trying to figure it all out. It hurt her head to think. But a few minutes later, she knew she had to try. Maybe if she knew where she was, it would bring back—other things. "Is this the Caribbean?" she asked David.

Yanni jumped in before David could answer. "No," he said firmly, "it's the Gulf of Mexico."

David looked at the bedraggled figure sympathetically. "Peggy, you don't remember anything before we picked you up? Nothing?"

Meg closed her eyes, struggling to meet the challenge. When it proved helpless, she shook her head wearily.

"Do you remember how you got in the water in the first place?"

"I remember being in the water with a fat man. Two life jackets came from somewhere." She could remember only seeing them fall from the sky. "I tried to save him, but he—I couldn't."

"And what about before that?"

"I don't know. I don't remember anything."

"Nothing?" Yanni repeated David's question, his voice incredulous and, it seemed to Meg, relieved.

David spoke with sudden inspiration. "Yanni, you know American accents better than I do. Can you tell where she might be from?"

"Don't know. I've only been in the country three years myself, remember."

Night fell quickly, shutting them into a tiny universe bounded by the circle of light on the deck and the narrow but powerful beam of the steering lights across the dark stretch of water. When Yanni announced he would steer the boat and keep watch while Meg slept and David caught a catnap on the foredeck, she was numbly grateful. She crawled into the bunk, thinking how good it would be to fall asleep and not have to remember anything. But after they had doused the lights and settled down, sleep eluded her. She had taken more aspirin before going to bed. The ache in her head had subsided to a dull throb, but sleep was far away. How strange wakefulness is when there are no memories! She could think back only on this one half-delirious day.

After a time she heard the two men talking in low, angry voices. At first she could not distinguish what they were saying, but after a little, their voices rose slightly and scattered words became audible.

". . . what the hell to do with her."

"She's obviously American. Put her ashore when we land—"

"No! Somewhere else. Lucky . . . doesn't remember. Where . . . lifejacket? Had the name of—"

"Overboard."

"Good."

". . . let the police handle it."

"Christ no! Are you crazy? They got the mother ship! If they find out we were in those waters . . ."

"Then what?"

"Leave her in Santo Domingo."

". . . give her enough money to get to the States, for God's sake, Yanni . . ."

"Okay . . . do it your way."

Meg was frightened and confused. What was it Yanni and David were trying to hide? The most likely possibility occurred to her—they were smuggling drugs. That would explain why they did not want the police involved. She was a distinct liability to their plans, and though they had given no sign of harming her, she had seen the resentment in Yanni's eyes ever since she had been brought on board. In any case, she thought, there was nothing she could do. She'd better just lie low and give them as little trouble as possible.

When David came into the cabin to wake her, full morning sun streamed through the door. Although she did not think she had slept at all, she must have dozed off at some point during the night, for she felt terribly groggy.

"Peggy, wake up. We're going ashore, and we're going to put you on a plane back to the States."

"Where—where are we?"

"We're putting into Santo Domingo. Here are some clean jeans and a tee-shirt. I think you can wear them all right—Yanni isn't that much bigger than you are."

"Where are my own clothes?"

"Lovey, they were in shreds—I threw them out." Seeing her expression of distress, he added, "You couldn't have got on a plane in them."

"There might have been some identification—"

"Well. Too late now, love." He cleared his throat. "Get dressed and we'll try to find some shoes for you in town."

"But where am I going?"

"Back to your own country, which is obviously America. When you get back there, I'm sure your memory will be jogged and you'll be all right again."

The previous day—bizarre and unreal—came flooding back to Meg's mind. The second impact which registered was the absence of any memory before that.

She felt as though she were back in a desolate, empty sea—but this was a sea of the mind and many times more terrifying than the body of water in which she had drifted yesterday.

She never found out whether they were smugglers or simply did not care to get involved with the police for other reasons. Later, she had a hazy, confused memory of buying tennis shoes from a French-speaking saleswoman, of being driven with David and Yanni in a battered taxi to a small airport, of being handed a plane ticket to Miami and five hundred dollars in cash, of getting off the plane an hour later in the blinding glare of the Miami airport.

As she walked down the ramp of the plane, she looked at the terminal building with a faint echo of recognition. Had she been here before? She bought a comb and some lipstick at a drug counter. Then, as though guided by an unseen hand, she went directly to a ladies' room which contained a number of private baths. Her head had ceased throbbing, but she felt as though it were wrapped in cotton. The women in the restroom seemed unreal, like lifesized mannequins that miraculously moved and spoke.

She took a tepid bath—hot water was too uncomfortable on her sunburned skin—and wondered what she should do next. She felt uncertain about everything. She had no past and no way of knowing what form the future would take. She did not even know her name. What was the name she had made up for David? Oh, yes, Peggy. She was Peggy somebody, or would henceforth *be* Peggy somebody. Peggy who? Her eye fell on the tube of lipstick she had purchased. "Elizabeth Arden." That name was as good as any. She would be Peggy Arden.

## Chapter 20

Jeff managed within twenty-four hours to get a telephone installed in his room and stayed on it for the next twenty-four, calling the steamship line, the local police and the Curaçan equivalent of the Coast Guard. None of them was able to give him much concrete information, although at first the cruise line was very solicitous indeed. A representative called on him to assure him they were doing their utmost to account for all passengers. Thereafter, however, they could only repeat, in answer to his numerous calls, that according to their records, Miss Margaret Gardner was not yet accounted for. They also reminded him with increasing briskness that they had his hospital number and would certainly report to him any further information the moment it was received.

On the day after the accident, Andrea had seen an account of it in the newspaper, which included Jeff's name among those injured. Through the cruise line, she managed to locate him in the Willemstad hospital, and after being told that he was not accessible by phone, left an urgent message to have him contact her. After the phone was installed in his room, and he had exhausted all avenues in trying to find Meg, he telephoned Andrea reluctantly. He did not really want to talk with her, but he could not remain incommunicado forever. And there was Timmy to consider.

"Jeff, darling! I couldn't have been more shocked. I didn't even know you were going by ship. You only casually mentioned something about Venezuela to

Timmy." Her voice was vaguely reproachful. "Are you badly hurt? Your voice sounds strong."

"A broken leg."

"Oh, poor dear. Well, as soon as I hang up, I'm going to make a reservation for me and Timmy to come down and take care of you."

"Oh, no, Andrea, please don't. I'll be all right—it'll just take a little time to heal, that's all. And Timmy will have to be back in school soon, won't he?"

"He has a few days yet. In any case, you can't be down there all alone. Were you traveling by yourself?"

"No. No, I wasn't. Meg was along."

"Who?"

"The girl I brought out Thanksgiving."

"Oh. Yes." Andrea's voice was cool and casual. "Is she all right?"

"She's—up to this point—unaccounted for."

"Oh, my dear. I'm sorry. Well, anyway, you can expect me tomorrow."

"Andrea, please. I'm very serious when I say—"

"Shush. I won't have you down there without anyone to turn to. Bye." And she hung up quickly, leaving Jeff in a state of confusion.

He wanted to be free, when he got out of the hospital, to pursue the search for Meg on his own. By that time, of course, weeks would have elapsed and chances would grow slimmer with every passing second. He realized that it was possibly an exercise in futility, but it was something he had to do before he left the area.

On the other hand, a strange hospital in an unfamiliar city, surrounded by personnel who spoke Dutch more readily than English, was undeniably a lonely experience. It would especially be good to see Timmy. And considering the fact that he could not forcibly restrain Andrea in her determination to make the trip, he had no choice but to welcome her.

He had just finished dinner on the following late afternoon when the red-haired nurse, whom he now knew as Hilde, ushered in a radiant Andrea and an excited Timmy. Andrea carried a large bouquet of flowers and a gift-wrapped package which contained an elegant silk foulard dressing gown. She sank into the easy chair and imperiously motioned Timmy to take the smaller chair on the other side of the bed.

"You look marvelous! I expected to see some pale shrunken invalid. You look like you're ready for a bash!"

He smiled wryly at her penchant for exaggeration. "Not quite. How you doing, Timmy?"

"Okay. 'Cept we were worried about you."

"Well, now you see there's nothing to worry about. Just have to let the old bones knit."

Andrea lighted a cigarette and looked at the traction frame. "Where is the break, Jeff?"

"Just below the thigh."

"How long before you can get out of here?"

"They think about four more weeks. Then I'll probably be ambulatory, with crutches."

"Oh, how ridiculous. You shouldn't have to stay here that long. Don't they have ambulance planes or something? Tomorrow I'll see what I can arrange."

Andrea took complete charge of the situation over Jeff's weak protests. He did not have the physical or emotional strength to dissuade her, for she seemed fiercely determined that he should be taken back to Rosehill, with herself and the servants to care for him, as soon as possible.

In the end, a small private plane was chartered and outfitted with all the necessary medical equipment and an attendant nurse. During the ten days between Andrea's arrival and their departure from Curaçao, Jeff made more despairing phone calls about Meg and ran into the same blank wall he had encountered from the first day he awoke in the hospital.

Until the very moment he was rolled out of the room on the stretcher and into the waiting ambulance that would take them to the chartered plane, he thought that miraculously, the phone would ring and he would hear Meg's voice on the other end.

The girl who now called herself Peggy Arden soon found that five hundred dollars would not last long in Miami. It was the height of the season and even the small, inexpensive hotels were filled to capacity. She took a room in a boarding house, counted her money every night and tried to decide if she had made any unnecessary expenditures during the day. She also tried doggedly to ward off despair. She had bought a summer cotton dress, which she laundered each night in the bathroom basin, a pair of low-heeled sandals and some underwear. She ate breakfast at the boarding house, had a hamburger for dinner and usually went without lunch. But in spite of her rigid economy, the money dwindled at an alarming rate.

She started combing the want ads, trying to find a job classification that sounded familiar to her. What had her vocation been? She did not know. However, one day she saw an ad for a "social services aide," and something about the phrase rang a bell. She went to the address indicated and told the receptionist she would like to apply for the job.

"Fill out this form, please."

She took the application to a corner of the room and began to write. But after she had filled out her name and the address of the boarding house, she saw at once it would be impossible to answer the further questions: "Experience (give last job first); Educational Background; Personal References." She crumpled the paper in her hand and mumbled something to the receptionist about not feeling well. "I'll come back another time," she said.

The woman stared after her disdainfully. These hippies who showed up in Miami to enjoy the winter sun didn't really want a job. They only made a halfhearted stab in that direction to keep themselves eligible for unemployment insurance. She shook her head indignantly and went back to her typing.

One night in bed, trying vainly to sleep, Meg was startled by a sudden flash of memory. It was vague and half-formed in her mind, but she was sure it was connected in some way to a bicycle accident. Hadn't she lost her memory before? The only thing vivid about the recollection was a pale green hospital room and a sweet, cloying aroma that came in at night through the screened windows. Honeysuckle? She thought so, but was not sure why she thought so. Nor could she really remember what honeysuckle smelled like. It was simply a name she connected to the remembered scent. What had they called it when she had lost her memory that time? Amnesia. She supposed she must be suffering from the same thing.

But after that childhood accident, she remembered the word always being spoken in a hushed voice, as if it were a source of shame. She gathered it was something not to be talked about in that place, wherever it had been. It had been spoken in the same tone used when illegitimacy or venereal disease were being discussed.

Had she ever told anyone about that peculiar event? Another flash entered her brain for only a fraction of a second. She was on a bus, riding through a small, hilly town somewhere, and she was telling someone about the accident, someone receptive and sympathetic. Someone who, she sensed, had been very important to her. But who? Before she could remember more, the blank gray curtain came down again and the memory was gone.

She looked one night in the mirror and realized with dismay that she was thinner than ever. Her hair, which had suffered from the effects of the sun, wind and water, hung limply about her face. She thought it made her look sad, almost hangdog. She ran her hand through it with disgust. With sudden determination, and elated that she was able to come to a firm decision about anything, she ran downstairs and knocked on the landlady's door. Mrs. Feliciano, a sharp-eyed but not unsympathetic Cuban woman, opened it at once.

"Mrs. Feliciano, have you a pair of scissors I could borrow?"

"Sí. But you return them *esta noche*, huh?"

"Yes. I'll bring them back in half an hour."

She cut the sun-reddened hair until it formed a short frame that reached just beneath her ears. She stepped back and surveyed herself in the mirror. She looked quite different. It had somehow been an act of penance; for what she didn't know. It also seemed fitting; a new hair-style to go with her new life. And it would be easier to care for—these days she had no extra energy to expend.

The following morning she checked the classified ads carefully again. After her experience at the social services office, it was obvious she would have to seek a job that required no previous experience and no references. A small ad in the top lefthand corner of the page caught her eyes.

"Cocktail waitress. Good pay, free dinner included. No experience required."

The ad gave no phone number, but only an address, with instructions to apply after noon.

She took a bus, and at a few minutes before twelve, found herself in one of the more luxurious hotels on

Miami Beach. The cocktail lounge, to which the hotel desk clerk directed her, looked out onto the ocean. Its deep green carpeting served as background for white rattan chairs and yellow tablecloths. On the walls was a line of portraits of nudes. But they were not blatant and it would have been difficult for anyone to find them offensive.

A bartender was at his post, desultorily filling small bowls with cherries, olives and lemon twists.

"Help you?" he inquired carelessly.

She dug the clipping from her straw bag. "Yes. I'd like to apply for this job."

"Minute." He continued the slicing for a moment, then disappeared into an adjacent room marked "Private." Within a few seconds, a corpulent man puffing a cigar came out and ushered her into his office.

He asked her only the most basic of questions, then peered at her sharply through the billowing circles of smoke. "I know we said no experience necessary, but just for the record, do you have any?"

She shook her head. "Not really. But I know I could do a satisfactory job. I don't mind hard work and—" Suddenly the room felt very hot. She put a hand to her forehead and leaned an elbow on the desk.

"Hey, kid, are you okay?"

She tried to make her smile look convincing. "Yes. Oh, yes, I'm fine. But could I have a glass of water, please?"

"Sure." He opened the door and called out to the bartender, "You, Jerry! Glass of ice water in here. Pronto!"

He watched her closely as she drank. "Care for somethin' a little stronger?"

"Oh, no." The thought of alcohol was repugnant. "Thank you."

"Are you sure you're strong enough for this work?

There's quite a bit of tray-carrying and running around, you know. It's not just lookin' good, although you're a very good-lookin' girl.''

"Oh, yes, I'll be fine."

"Very good-lookin', as a matter of fact. We might be able to arrange it so that you wouldn't have to carry trays. That's always possible. Cashier, say, or—"

"I don't mind, really." *Cashiers don't make tips*, she thought in desperation. "If you'll just give me a chance—"

He nodded impatiently. He'd try her out. If she couldn't do the job, he'd have to find somebody who could. But she was gorgeous-lookin', no question about that. Even though she looked like she could use a good meal.

Mr. Callios settled on a salary, told her she would have her dinner each afternoon at four before her shift started at five, would work six days a week, Mondays off, uniforms furnished, be back at three-thirty to get squared away. She got up and started out. She turned at the door to thank him, but he was already dialing the phone and acknowledged her gesture with the merest nod of dismissal.

# Chapter 21

Jeff was forced to admit that his bedroom at Rosehill was considerably more comfortable than his room at the Willemstad hospital. Andrea was never in evidence until late afternoon, Timmy was away at school, and during the earlier part of the day, Jeff had plenty of time to think. He had finally obtained the name of Meg's Aunt Bess from the cruise line. Along with her address and telephone number, it was tucked into a book that lay in the drawer of his bedside table.

Several times a day, he got the name and number out, looked at it, and on a few occasions actually started to dial the phone. But how would he explain his interest? He knew that Meg's aunt had been under the impression her niece was traveling with a girl friend. He also knew she must be intensely bereaved by Meg's disappearance. He could not bring himself to phrase it any other way than "disappearance." The alternative was not acceptable.

As soon as he could get about, he would go back to Curaçao, if only for a few days. When he was thinking most lucidly about it, he admitted to himself that it would probably do no good whatsoever. But it was something he had to do for his own peace of mind. He waited restlessly for the day when he could walk.

He and Andrea usually had a drink together before dinner. Often, if she were not going out for the evening, she would have her dinner, too, sent up on a tray and dine with him. Almost without realizing it, Jeff had come to look forward to those evenings. Andrea's vivacious, sometimes overbearing presence was a welcome change from the companionship of his camera and books. From how many angles could one photograph the four walls of a room?

One night about two weeks after their arrival from Curaçao, he felt he needed to talk to someone seriously. A few of his friends and colleagues from the office had visited him, but Peter Jamison, the only one in whom he would have wanted to confide, had been sent to the firm's London branch for a few months. So when Andrea came in that evening, Jeff had already decided he would force her to listen to him so that he could get some sort of outside perspective on the situation.

She swept in with a new coiffure. "Isn't it nice, Jeff? Do you approve? Don't you think it has a certain *je'ne sais quois*?" She came close to the bed; he could smell her distinctive musky perfume.

"Yes, very nice, Andrea. Did you go to the hair stylist you were telling me about? The one who's all the rage, as you said?"

"Yes, my dear. Titian. Can you believe he swears that's his real name? Isn't that too much?"

"Sit down, Andrea. I want to talk to you about something."

There was a compelling seriousness in his voice. Her smile faded almost at once and her expression changed to one of eager concern. She sat down and picked up the waiting cocktail on the silver tray. "Of course, Jeff. What is it?"

"I'm thinking of calling Meg's aunt."

She paused, then spoke with careful deliberation. "Oh, dear, I think that would be a mistake. Just look at it this way: if Meg were back with her aunt, she would certainly have contacted you. And if she isn't back, what possible good could it do?"

Jeff took a thoughtful sip of his own drink. Her

arguments were irrefutable. It would only mean prolonged unhappiness for both of them, and additional worry to her aunt. Sheltered as her life had apparently been, when she found her niece had been jaunting around the world with a man, it would merely intensify her grief.

"Jeff, I don't want to sound unfeeling about this," Andrea was continuing, "but sometimes we have to accept the inevitable. I know it isn't easy to do, but you must realize it's been over a month since this thing happened. If you were going to hear anything at all, don't you really think you would already have done so?"

Jeff could not deny the sense of her remarks. But there was a stubborn nagging inside him that would not yet let him rest. "Then I suppose you think I would be extremely foolish to go back to Curaçao?"

"For what, my dear? Really, for what? You don't think she would have magically reappeared and taken up residence there, do you? Without even trying to contact anyone? It just doesn't make any sense."

Jeff was silent. Andrea, of course, was right. Not being personally involved, she could see things with a clarity he had not yet been able to muster.

"Really, you've got to take your mind off these things. They only make you and everyone around you unhappy." Her face brightened and her blonde hair shone as she tossed her head. "Now, how about a game of honeymoon bridge before Janie brings up dinner?"

A few nights later, however, when Andrea was out and Jeff was once more fingering the paper on which he had written Aunt Bess's number, he began to quite methodically press the digits on the push-button phone. He wanted to complete the action before inhibition or rational thought could interfere. At some length, a hesitant, rather faltering Southern voice came on the line.

"Miss Bess Tilton? This is Jeff McAllister. You don't know me, but I was a friend of your niece, Meg Gardner. I—I met her on the cruise to Venezuela. I was just wondering if you had heard anything more at all about her—her disappearance."

The woman coughed gently, but no words came.

"I know this may seem odd, but I liked Meg very much and I was anxious to know—"

"I'm sorry, Mr.—was it McAllister, did you say? I don't understand. Of course I don't have any news. No. We held a—a memorial service yesterday for Meg. I surely don't mean to be rude, but I think you can understand—I'm still a little shaken from that. And I'm not well myself. I just—there's not a thing more I can tell you."

"I see. Well, thank you, and I'm very sorry. Just—just please know that she was a very lovely person whom I—whom I liked very much."

"Yes. She was. Well. Thank you."

"Mrs. Tilton, if you should hear—" he began, but he heard the soft click before he could finish the sentence.


From that point on, the idea of Meg's death became more real to him. The fact that a memorial service had been held gave substance to the thought that up to now he had so adamantly refused to accept. Hope fled, and with it the energy to conjure up emotion of any kind.

A physical therapist now came in daily and Jeff worked conscientiously in exercising and relearning to walk, but his actions were those of an automaton. The therapist, Harvey Spector, was a martinet in his early fifties or so. He was a man of few words, those few usually in the form of a terse command. Jeff's hours with Spector were grimly concentrated sessions, devoid of small talk and unleavened by humor. It was an ordeal for both of them.

For his part, Harvey Spector would have liked to chuck the whle thing, except that Mrs. McAllister had somehow found out he had learned his trade in a prison infirmary. She had him where she wanted him, the bitch.

Andrea seemed to be going out less and less in the evenings, but Jeff became more and more withdrawn. Timmy was in a boarding school in Connecticut and Andrea's overly vivacious chatter began to grate on Jeff's nerves. He welcomed the time when he would be able to move back into his own apartment. He should be getting back to work as well, but he did not look forward to the brokerage firm. The truama and grief of the accident had made the buying and selling of stocks seem trivial.

But in making such a decision, he felt an overpowering need to talk to someone, and Andrea was the only one around.

"I feel trapped there, to tell you the truth, Andrea. I never particularly liked the business, but my father built that firm almost from the ground-up. I feel if I left it, I'd sort of be selling out—betraying him."

Andrea surprised him completely by her reaction. He had thought she would consider the idea of his switching occupations ridiculous. But she sat for a few moments in deep and serious thought, musing over his statement.

Finally she spoke. "What would you want to do instead?"

"I don't know. Stock-brokering is all I'm really prepared for. Unless . . ."

"What?"

"Unless I could somehow go into photography professionally. I know it sounds wild, but that's the subject that's always fascinated me."

"It doesn't sound wild at all. Not if that's what you want to do. You're still young."

He smiled. At that moment, Andrea sounded very maternal. She was probably not more than four years older than he.

A few nights later, she stuck her head in the door of Jeff's room and asked if he would mind having a third for dinner. Jeff acquiesced politely and decided Andrea was about to do him the honor of introducing him to one of her men friends. But the man who followed her into the room could not be in that category. Although impeccably tailored, he was rotund, balding and at least three inches shorter than she.

"This is Ricardo Cavullo. You've probably heard the name."

"Yes, it sounds very familiar," Jeff murmured, hoping he would be forgiven for the small social white lie.

"Mr. Cavullo is the country's—probably the world's—most famous fashion photographer. He knows you're interested in the subject, and since he's an old friend of mine, he very kindly consented to have dinner with us tonight."

"Very kind indeed," echoed Jeff. He was not interested in fashion photography and couldn't imagine that he ever would be, but it was thoughtful of Andrea to arrange the meeting.

Ricardo Cavullo proved to be enjoyable company. Jeff had imagined that a man who spent his time photographing beautiful models in expensive clothes would be rather shallow. But Ricardo spoke with humility of his chilhood in Nicosia, a poverty-stricken village in Sicily, his emigration to America at the age of fifteen and his apprenticeship in the alien and highly competitive world of New York fashion. He was without pretension of any kind, nor did he try to hide his peasant background. He looked at the experimental photography Jeff had been doing from his bed with quiet interest. By the end of the evening of listening to Cavullo's conversation on an astonishing variety of subjects, Jeff felt more alive than he had in weeks.

When Ricardo Cavullo got up to say goodnight, he went to Jeff's bed and shook his hand warmly. "In addition to my own work behind the camera, I am trying to start a photographic shop. I would like to do some things that have not been done before. I could use an imaginative associate. When you are able, why don't you come in and talk to me about it? My card."

Andrea went downstairs to show him out. Jeff turned out the lamp and settled back on the pillow. He felt the chemistry between himself and Cavullo was promising. He thought he could be happy running such a shop. At least it was a step in the right direction. But time enough to make final decisions later. When he was well, he could stop in and talk further with Mr. Cavullo.

He saw the narrow shaft of light fall across the carpet. He sat up in bed, startled. Andrea, hearing his movement, murmured softly, "Don't be alarmed, Jeff. It's only me."

"What is it, Andrea?"

"I just came in to say goodnight."

"Oh." Jeff turned on the bedside lamp. "It was very nice of you to bring Cavullo along. I liked him very much."

"Good. I thought you would. He might be of help to you." Andrea picked up the remains of her brandy. "Shall we have a nightcap to celebrate?"

"I guess." Jeff wanted to be alone with his thoughts but he could not seem ungrateful. He watched while Andrea poured a generous snifter of the dark amber liquid and handed it to him.

She sat down on the side of the bed. Again he caught

the scent of her expensive, potent perfume. "You know, Jeff, I know you were never very fond of me. But I like to think I've grown up a little myself in the last few years. That's why I wanted to do something meaningful for you—something that might make some difference in your life."

"I appreciate it, Andrea. As I said, it was damn good of you to arrange the meeting."

"Since you've been here, I've come to realize how much we've missed by not getting to know each other better."

"Yes. I suppose that's true."

Her movement was sudden, feline and totally unexpected. Her arms were around him, her mouth pressed against his. Her lips parted hungrily. Jeff took her shoulders firmly and held her away from him.

"God, Andrea, what are you doing? This is crazy."

"I don't see why. Of course, I know you're still a convalescent. But what's wrong with a little affection between us?"

"Look, you've been very good to me, Andrea, and I appreciate it. But—"

"But I'm still the wicked stepmother, as far as you're concerned?" She laughed huskily. "I just wonder if I can ever change your mind about that."

"Don't be silly. I didn't mean that. You've been awfully good to me since I—"

"Then I suppose you're still grieving over your lost love, the poor little country girl." She paused. "I'm sorry. That wasn't necessary." She picked up her glass again. "It's just that the men I used to go out with don't seem to interest me very much anymore. You're so much more attractive than any one of them. But I'll play your game, Jeffie. And we'll see who wins."

She looked at him over the rim of the snifter, then threw back her head and drained the glass. She left the room, closing the door quietly behind her. The clinging scent of her perfume floated back to him.

Jeff lay still, reviewing the import of the last few moments. He decided he must redouble his efforts with the physical therapist—he wanted to get well enough to leave Rosehill very soon.

# Chapter 22

Meg found her work at the Mermaid not too demanding, sometimes even pleasant. Mr. Callios was not around very often—apparently running the bar and restaurant was only one of several of his occupations. Jerry, the bartender who had been on duty when she applied for the job, was officious and not well liked by any of the other waitresses over whom he held sway in Callios's absence. But Pierce, the barman who came on duty after nine in the evening when the bar began to fill up, had become her friend.

Pierce Graham was a medium-tall young man in his early twenties, who willingly served as surrogate psychiatrist to many of the bar patrons who frequented the Mermaid. He was sandy-haired and suntanned. He had worked as a lifeguard until his curriculum at the University of Miami (where he was indeed majoring in psychology) made it necessary for him to take a night job. He hailed from New Hampshire and had the New Englander's traditional laconic taciturnity. But Meg soon discovered that this covered a delightfully off-beat sense of humor, as well as a great deal of patience with the foibles of the human race.

She had moved from the boarding house into one of the small rooms at the hotel reserved for its employees. Many of them, who had worked at the hotel for years, had families and homes of their own in the area. This accounted for the vacancy into which Meg moved. The room was on the second floor, with the dining-room kitchen below and central utility room above. At almost any hour she was likely to be awakened either by the slam of pots and pans below or by vehement disagreements over supplies from above. However, she was delighted to have her own private space, tiny as it was. After she had gone on a shopping spree with her first paycheck and bought plants, curtains and prints, she thought the room looked welcoming and cheery.

One night just after the bar closed, Pierce asked her if she would like to take a swim. The idea of a late-night dip was irresistible to her. The evening had been a long one, not helped by a rather belligerent customer who had argued with her over his check. "Just let me get my suit," she told Pierce. "I'll be right down."

She found Pierce waiting at the bar. When he saw her through the glass jalousies, he came out and took her hand companionably. They walked to the shoreline. The amber lamps from the hotel veranda lighted the water dimly.

"Last one in," he yelled, as they approached the water. Laughing, she followed him into the placid surf. The water was unimaginably refreshing. She let it wash over her, reveling in its effect of instant rejuvenation. The fatigue seemed to drain from her body; the waves were playful and buoyant. She closed her eyes and floated blissfully.

Unexpectedly, a wave much more powerful than the preceding ones slapped her body and sent her spinning under the surface. With the impact of the wave, she experienced another of those strange phenomena that she had come to think of as "memory flashes." She saw a grand piano against a backdrop of ornately molded walls, crystal and gold chandeliers and deep red curtains. She heard a shrieking cacophony of noise and saw the piano crumple as if in slow motion. She did not know why, but the sensation was one of wrenching, terrifying loss.

What had begun as a delightful ocean dip turned at once to panic. She tried to stand up in the water and discovered she could not reach the bottom. She could vaguely make out Pierce's figure swimming rapidly toward her. She heard a frightened scream still hanging in the air and realized with astonishment it had been her own.

"Peggy! What happened?"

"I've got to get out of the water. Help me, please."

He put his arm around her waist and led her to shore. Once there, she collapsed on the sand and lay with her eyes closed, her breathing labored. Pierce sat beside her quietly, not speaking, letting her collect herself.

After several minutes, he moved to her and gently pushed a lock of sodden hair away from her eyes. "What is it, Peggy?" He waited, but no answer was forthcoming. "What happened?"

She shook her head dumbly and started to rise. But the shock of this most recent trauma, plus the pressure of living the past few weeks as an imposter of sorts, suddenly inundated her like the wave. She lay back down on the sand and, with one finger, started tracing nervous circles into its damp graininess. Still she did not speak.

A faint streak of mauve on the horizon heralded approaching dawn. She felt a sense of sudden urgency—she had to talk to somebody, and it would be easier while they still sat in the shadows of the night, alone on the deserted beach. "I want to tell you something, Pierce. But promise you won't think I'm crazy."

He laughed. "I've heard a lot of crazy stories since I began bartending."

"But not like this one." She paused. "For starters, I don't think my name is really Peggy Arden."

"Come again?"

"Yes. I warned you it was strange. This is the middle

of February, isn't it? My life as Peggy Arden began around, I think, the first of January. There must be some significance in that. New Year, new life." Her mind idly toyed with the concept for a moment. Then she continued, eager to get across the gist of the story as quickly and unemotionally as possible. "I was found in the middle of the sea. I don't even know where. They said the Gulf of Mexico, but I was taken to the airport at Santo Domingo, which doesn't seem logical. They gave me a plane ticket and five hundred dollars."

She could see Pierce's hunched shoulders silhouetted against the lightening sky. But it was too dark to read the expression on his face.

"Found? Who found you? And who took you ashore?"

Meg sat up. She sighed at trying to make someone believe the series of phantasmagorical events. "Two men on a cabin cruiser. They put me ashore and gave me the money. They threw away the clothes and the life vest I was wearing. My life began, really, at the Santo Domingo airport. I mean, the only life I can remember."

Pierce looked at her, her face barely lighted by the fingers of dawn. He still could not quite believe this was not some uncharacteristic practical joke. But a close look at her bewildered expression put that suspicion to rest. He felt a sudden surge of immense sympathy for the beautiful, lost woman before him. "Why didn't they take you to someone who could help? A doctor or—the police?"

"I don't know. The only reason I can think of is that they were doing something illegal by being there in the first place. I mean, I heard them talking and they seemed to think going to the police was out of the question."

"Dope, probably."

"That's what I thought, maybe."

"If they let you off at Santo Domingo, you were right in the middle of "Smugglers' Lane." They may have been coming from Colombia, or meeting a mother ship coming from there more likely. And they never told you where they were headed?"

She shook her head. She felt better for having confessed the truth to someone. She sensed Pierce's level-headed compassion.

Once he had accepted the incredible premise of her tale, his mind turned at once to practical solutions. "You know what you've got to do now—go to the police."

At the idea, she felt a strange combination of shame and stubborn pride. "I know I probably should, Pierce, but I keep thinking if I just concentrate on it, I'll start remembering more and more. Already, two or three times, I've remembered little fragments of things."

"What were they?"

She shrugged helplessly. "Just vague impressions."

"Islands of memory, they call them. Peggy, I've been studying amnesia in Abnormal Psychology. You're obviously suffering from retrograde amnesia, which means it affects the memory processes of the time *before* the trauma. Not much is known about the process, but one thing that is known is that the longer the condition lasts, the poorer the chances of recovery."

Amnesia. Retrograde amnesia. *Abnormal* psychology. All these clinical terms frightened and confused her.

Pierce was continuing in his slow, calm way. "Why not go to the police and see if they can find out who you really are?"

"The thing is," her words were slow, "I keep thinking I'll wake up some morning and remember everything, all at once. Who I am, where I belong, where I came from. This will all be over, like a bad dream."

"But it's more difficult the longer you wait. I don't understand why you're willing to leave everything to chance. Or if not the police, why not see a doctor?"

He was making her feel like a mental case. She wished she hadn't talked to him about it. She was getting along fine, even in this strange new world. She wished she had kept it completely to herself until she felt more able to cope with its ramifications.

As they stood facing each other on the empty beach, he saw the dark shadows of fatigue under her eyes, which heightened the exquisite structure of her cheekbones. She was very different from the coeds at the university or the nubile young tourists who converged on the bar in high-spirited two or threes. There was something almost other-worldly about her—a feeling heightened, he supposed, by the incredible tale she had spilled out.

"You need some sleep, Peggy. Let's go in."

She nodded and, without a word, held out her hand for him to take. He found her extremely attractive, and yet the momentary physical tingle he sensed at her touch was almost instantly replaced by a protective, almost parental, emotion. She was like a rare, exotic creature, threatened by the randomness of fate. He hoped she would be strong enough to survive its assaults.


The next Friday night, the bar was exceptionally crowded. A convention of businessmen was quartered in the hotel, most of them apparently intent on drinking up a goodly percentage of the bar's liquor supply. She noticed the lone dark man sitting in the corner because his casual, almost arrogant, repose was so at odds with the frenetic shouts and laughter from the conventioneers. She thought he had been in before as an occasional, but not steady, customer. He was exceptionally handsome, his face not swarthy but darkling and saturnine. His blackish hair was combed straight back and, when she caught his hawkish profile, it was like the face on an antique Roman coin.

He exuded effortless authority. Meg was not serving his table—the short, vivacious waitress called Binky was working his station—but she noticed that when he wanted service, he raised one finger almost imperceptibly from the tabletop and somehow Binky instantaneously appeared.

After the bar had closed that night, she and Binky were the last to leave the waitresses' locker room. With idle interest, Meg happened to remark on the silent, solitary customary who had been in Binky's corner.

"Don't you know who he is? He's Mr. Callios's boss or has some hold on him or something. Anyway, every time he comes in, Mr. Callios goes into his bowing-and-scraping act."

"You mean he owns the hotel?"

Binky looked blank for a moment, then laughed. "No—at least not that I know of. The bar here is a concession or something. But he apparently owns the concession."

"But Callios wasn't around tonight."

"No, he's away on another of his sidelines, whatever they are. Jerry says he's due in tomorrow."

Meg got up late the next day—later than she had intended. When she looked at the clock, she found it was almost two in the afternoon. She'd hoped she would have time for an errand or two before going to work. But she had to do her laundry and she had found that on Saturday afernoons the laundry room was usually all hers. She finished her coffee and toast and started piling her clothes into the laundry bag.

The telephone rang. Meg had not yet had an outside phone installed, so it was someone inside the hotel. She picked it up and heard the gruff, rasping voice of Mr. Callios.

"Peggy? Callios. I want you to come down and have lunch with me and a friend of mine."

It sounded more like an order than an invitation, she thought. "Thank you, Mr. Callios. That's very nice of you, but I was about to—"

"Don't argue with me, Peggy. This is important. I'll see you in my office in half an hour." The conversation was cut off with a decisive click.

Peggy showered and dressed in a state of annoyance and puzzlement. Though she did not particularly like Callios, he had never before interfered with her private life or time. She found while she was dressing that she was very nervous. She could not keep her fingers from shaking as she tried to catch her hair with a yellow ribbon. She finally gave up, reflecting that her hair was still so short the ribbon was unnecessary anyway. She did not wait for the elevator, but took the backstairs which opened into the hallway directly off Mr. Callios's office.

Two men stood in the corridor. The afternoon sun blinded Meg for a moment so that she saw only the two silhouettes, but she at once recognized the profile of the dark, quiet man who had the evening before occupied the corner table.

"Peggy!" Mr. Callios greeted her with uncharacteristic cordiality. "Want you to meet a friend of mine, Johnny Pack. Johnny, Peggy Arden, the star of this establishment. Everybody loves Peggy."

Johnny Pack took Meg's hand in his, lightly. His black eyes examined her with unhurried thoroughness, moving over each feature of her face. His brows were sharply defined and shaped like inverted *V*'s. There was something tightly controlled and calculating about Johnny Pack. When he brushed her hand fleetingly with his lips, she caught a glint of brilliance from the ring on his little finger.

"Mambo's, right, Johnny?" asked Mr. Callios. "My car's in the driveway."

She was ushered into the low-slung black car between the two men. Johnny Pack had not yet spoken. Callios's conversation was made up of fragmentary nonsentences to which Pack responded with grunts or nods. He spoke only once during the drive. When Callios made a right turn, Pack pointed out briefly that Collins Avenue would have been a simpler route. Callios sighed through his teeth apologetically.

Once inside the sleek, dimly lighted restaurant, however, Johnny Pack's mood changed. He greeted the maitre d' familiarly and introduced Peggy as "Miss Arden" with a gallant flourish. The maitre d' seated them at the table to which Johnny Pack had pointed, then scurried away. Pack asked Meg without preamble if broiled lobster would be agreeable. Meg could only nod. She was waiting for the bizarre situation to begin to make some sense.

"Miss Arden," said Johnny Pack after a nervous waiter had taken their order, "let me come right to the point. Rico," he indicated Callios with a curt, sidewise nod, "takes the long way around. I don't. I watched you last night in the bar and I liked what I saw. You've got what is generally called class. I have to do a lot of socializing in my business. It's easier if I have a woman on my arm. I need a companion—a companion with class. I'd like you to be it."

Meg was stunned. She had not imagined that a conversation like this could take place outside the movies of the 1930's . . . movies she sometimes watched on the late-late show. After a moment she was rescued from speechlessness by her own anger at the man's presumptuousness.

"Mr. Pack, I am not for hire. I have an honest job and I like it that way—"

He laughed—a surprisingly warm laugh. He reached for her arm. His touch was light but there was a hint of steel underneath. "Maybe I explained myself badly. I'm not trying to make you a kept woman—not in the usual sense. Except that I would of course pay you a generous salary. This would be strictly a business arrangement. Ah, here's our lobster. Good. Have you been to Mambo's before, Miss Arden?" Meg shook her head, her mind reeling. She was not sure whether she should be enraged or flattered by this incredible man.

Johnny Pack and Mr. Callios dug at once into the huge, succulent lobsters. Mr. Callios ate the same way he talked, brusquely and without regard for protocol. The lobster on his plate was soon reduced to crimson rubble. He wiped a trickle of lemon butter impatiently off his chin.

By contrast, Johnny Pack's table manners were fastidious. He dissected the lobster with the economy and skill of a surgeon. When he saw that Meg was picking ineffectively at her shellfish, he effortlessly and quickly extracted the rosy chunks of meat for her. As they finished lunch, he leaned to her once more. "I know this is unexpected. You'll want some time to think it over. I'm flying back to New York this afternoon, but I'll be back in Miami on Saturday—a week from today. I'll get your answer then."

Callios and Johnny Pack drove her back to the Mermaid after which, she gathered, Callios would drive Pack to the airport for his afternoon flight. In front of the restaurant, Johnny Pack insisted, over Callios's protests about lack of time, on seeing Meg to the door.

"You've no idea how beautiful you are, do you?" he

asked bluntly as they stood in the sun-flooded entrance. "That innocence makes you all the more special." Meg started to speak, but he motioned her to silence with the barest gesture of an immaculately manicured hand.

"Before you make a decision, remember this. I won't make any demands on you that you're unwilling to fulfill. If you should ever want to call off the arrangement, I'll give you no trouble. That's a promise. And Johnny Pack never goes back on his word."

He disappeared into the interior of the highly polished black automobile, and it glided away noiselessly down the concrete drive.

Meg went through her duties that evening like a robot. As she served the roistering conventioneers and assorted tourists, her brain whirled with the events of the afternoon. She was forced to admit that Johnny Pack held an undeniable fascination for her. But when she tried to analyze it, she came to realize it was the same fascination one would feel while watching a panther—lithe, dark and taut—lying in wait for its unsuspecting prey.

He seemed to move in another world—a world so alien she could not even imagine what it must be like. But a signal spelling danger kept coming through to her. She knew instinctively, though he had been courteous, even gallant, that he was not a man to be trifled with.

By nine, she had made up her mind. She must find out who she really was at the earliest possible moment, and there was only one course which offered any real hope.

When she saw Pierce take his station at the end of the bar, she ignored a customer trying to catch her eye and walked hurriedly to the green-coated bartender. He watched her approach with a smile of surprise and pleasure.

"Peggy, hi! I think the man in the plaid jacket—"

"Pierce, I've made up my mind. You were right. I'm going to the police with my story."

"Do you want me to go with you?"

Meg nodded gratefully.

"When?"

"Could we go tomorrow?"

# Chapter 23

Andrea was negotiating for the purchase of a thoroughbred horse at a neighboring estate, and had become very fond of its owners, the Gundersens. One night as she and Jeff were having their usual predinner cocktails, Andrea snapped her fingers in sudden inspiration.

"I've a terrific idea, Jeff! Now that you're able to move around a little on your crutches, why don't we celebrate by having a dinner party?"

Jeff smiled. So far, he was able to walk very slowly along the upstairs corridor, but that had been the limit of his ambulatory activity. "I don't know whether I'm up to an orgiastic blast, Andrea."

"Oh, silly, I don't mean a cast of thousands. But I really like the Gundersens very much. They're related to the Vanderbilts, you know. I think you'd enjoy them, too."

"And you think if you had them to dinner, you might reach more favorable terms on the purchase of that horse."

Andrea allowed a mischievous smile to cross her face fleetingly. "Well, I wouldn't have put it so crudely, but—no, they're lovely people, really. Besides, you must be bored to death just sitting around with me. Wouldn't it be fun to introduce a little new blood into the household? How about Friday night?"

"So be it." Since Jeff was nominally only a guest at Rosehill, he was in no position to argue.

"Good! I'll go call them right now."

She returned in great good spirits. "They'll be here! Let's see, a crabmeat souffle is always good for starters. Then maybe that *bouef daube* Janie does so well—you always enjoy that, too, don't you? Oh, this is going to be fun. We've been living much too dull a life lately. I know you're not ready for a discothèque yet, but I think a little socializing might do you good."

For the next couple of days, Andrea was busy with her party plans. She was having an extra maid sent out, fresh flowers were ordered, and Sanders and Janie were kept busy polishing and scrubbing. Jeff could not help but find her childish anticipation attractive, almost touching.

On Thursday night, she was regaling Jeff with all that had been accomplished and what a truly lovely party it was going to be when Sanders knocked discreetly on the door and summoned her to the telephone. When she returned she was in a cold fury.

"Do you know what's happened? This is unbelievable. That call was from Timmy's headmaster. Timmy was found smoking marijuana, and he's being sent home for a week!"

"Well, Andrea, that isn't exactly good news, but on the other hand it's not the end of the world."

She said more calmly, "No, I suppose not. But this week of all weeks! Now he'll be underfoot tomorrow night—"

"Wait a minute, Andrea. Back up a little, there. What's wrong with having him at your party? He's not a one-year-old who'll have to be fed strained carrots at the table."

She was immediately and ostentatiously contrite. "Oh, dear, Jeff, you're right. That sounded terrible, didn't it? I didn't mean it that way. It's just that you prepare yourself for one kind of evening, and then. . . ." She let the sentence trail, and soon after, excused herself.

After she had left the room, Jeff felt that perhaps Timmy's problem was more serious than it had seemed. Otherwise, why would they send him home for an entire week? Jeff had been so preoccupied with his own grief that he had probably been more neglectful of Timmy than he would have otherwise. When Timmy came for weekends, Jeff was always glad to see him and they had enjoyable games of scrabble or gin rummy. But he had not really taken the interest in the boy he should have. *Oh, God,* he thought, *another burden of guilt*? He lay restlessly in bed for several hours before sleep finally came.

When Timmy arrived on Friday afternoon, Sanders met him at the station and brought him home; Andrea had gone to the florist's to check on the flowers before they were delivered. Timmy came in to Jeff's room feverishly elated.

"How are you, Timmy?"

"Glad to be away from Simon Legree for a while."

"Simon Legree?"

"The stinking headmaster."

"What's the matter with him?"

"He's an A-Number-One creep."

Jeff looked at the boy intently. Timmy's flip, sneering manner was completely unlike the boy who, a few months ago, had been habitually shy and soft-spoken.

"Hey, Jeff, I'm going over to Hughie Keene's for a while. I'll see you later."

"Oh? I thought we might have time for a game of gin or something."

"Yeah. Well, maybe later."

"You know Andrea's having guests for dinner tonight."

"Yeah. She left me a note."

"She wanted me to remind you it's at seven sharp."

"Yeah. Well, see you later."

At six o'clock, Jeff managed to slowly maneuver the winding staircase and help Andrea greet the Gundersens. George Gundersen was a tall, bucktoothed man; his wife Maria a diminutive brunette. They both had the earthy, unpretentious manner of the very rich whose money is very old.

Seven o'clock came and went, but there was no sign of Timmy. Andrea glanced covertly at her watch and sighed. "Why don't we all go ahead with the first course? My son's usually punctual manners seem to have deserted him tonight."

The dinner conversation was animated, but Jeff detected a forced gaiety in Andrea's voice. She also replenished her wine from the decanter more often than usual.

They had almost finished the excellent *daube* when Sanders entered from the kitchen and murmured something inaudible into Andrea's ear. She excused herself and went to the phone in the library.

When she returned, her face was taut and strained. She waited until the Gundersens were momentarily engaged in conversation with each other, then muttered to Jeff, "That was Hughie Keene's father. It seems that Hughie and Timmy have taken one of the Keene cars and disappeared."

"Good God," said Jeff softly. "Have they called the police?"

"I'm sure by now they have. They wanted to check here first."

"How old is the Keene boy?"

"Fifteen, I think. He's too young for a driver's license, I know that."

"Don't worry, Andrea. They're sure to be picked

up."

Dinner over, Andrea ushered her guests into the library for brandy and coffee. Her chatter was even more vivacious than usual, but there was an edge to her laughter and Jeff knew she was extremely upset. He did what he could to keep the conversation flowing; if the Gundersens were aware that anything was wrong they gave no indication of it. Mr. Gundersen launched into a very long anecdote about a race track in England and Jeff was grateful that all he need do was smile and nod at appropriate moments. Andrea occupied herself by refilling her glass and those of her guests at frequent intervals.

Timmy was brought in by the police about midnight. Hughie Keene had piled the car into a tree on a cross-country parkway. Neither boy was seriously injured, but both were shaken up.

The Gundersens, at last sensing the tension, soon said their goodnights and left. Andrea, who had been warm and gracious until the door closed behind them, turned to Timmy in a cold fury.

"What the hell do you mean by doing this? Have you lost your mind? You're asked to leave school for a week and then you almost kill yourself in a goddam car wreck! What are you trying to do? You spoiled the entire evening. The Gundersens will think we're absolutely disreputable. The one night I try to have a nice dinner party you make a shambles of it. I'll never forgive you!" She whirled out of the room and ran upstairs.

Jeff patted the boy's shoulder. "She'll be all right tomorrow. She was just worried about you. Help me upstairs, will you, Tim?"

Together the made their way to Jeff's room. He got into bed at once; the pain in his leg had become acute. Timmy's forehead was bruised slightly; otherwise he showed no phsyical effects of the accident. He sat down next to Jeff's bed, chastened and subdued. Finally, Jeff looked at him and spoke soberly.

"Timmy, I'm sorry I haven't given you more of what you needed. I've been preoccupied with my own problems and—"

"Nah. Wasn't your fault, Jeff."

"Why'd you do it then, Tim?"

"Well, for one thing, I got the idea Mother would be just as happy if I didn't show up for her fancy dinner party."

Jeff moved uneasily. He could not in all honesty contradict the statement. He looked at Timmy closely; the boy's eyes seemed unnaturally bright. "Timmy, you haven't been fooling with anything more serious than marijuana, have you?"

Timmy looked at him briefly, then averted his eyes. He finally answered in a small voice, "Just some uppers sometimes."

Jeff shut his eyes in anguish. On every weekend home, Timmy had been making a wordless appeal for help and Jeff had been deaf to it. He had contributed to the boy's being fatherless in the first place, and he had been blind to his silent supplication. In his grief for Meg, he had closed his eyes to a desperate need right under his nose.

After a few more minutes, Timmy started talking. His words were at first faltering, but Jeff was gradually able to etch in the portrait of a badly confused adolescent trying to cope with the changes of puberty, an alien new school away from home, and peer pressure from comparatively daring classmates—all this while surrounded by unseeing, self-centered adults. Jeff would have to find some way to make amends to the boy. What Timmy needed above all, of course, was a father.

Jeff got up early the next morning and dragged himself downstairs. Perhaps he and Timmy could find something to do together. He was surprised to hear voices from the kitchen. He entered to find Andrea and Timmy having French toast and sausages together. He knew that Andrea, after the previous evening, must be suffering from a severe hangover. He had to admire her for so quickly turning over a new leaf.

"Come join us for breakfast," she smiled brightly. Her face was rather drawn; otherwise she looked composed and put-together.

"What's on the agenda for today, Timmy?"

"Mother's gonna take me shopping for a moped."

Jeff felt a twinge of disapproval. So Andrea was trying to buy back Timmy's love—to bribe him into "behaving himself." He wanted to shake her, to shout at her: "Andrea, that isn't the way to do it! Timmy needs your time and your love, not expensive motorized bicycles." But perhaps Andrea was responding in the only way she knew how, so he said nothing.

During the week, Jeff and Timmy sat on the terrace a couple of afternoons when the late-February weather turned unusually warm. Jeff was doing some experimental photography of flagstones, flower pots and individual leaf-shapes, and giving Timmy some informal tutoring in the subject. Timmy was an apt and eager student, and as they worked together, the boy opened up to him like his old self. Jeff's conscience was partially mollified.

On Monday afternoon, Washington's Birthday, before Timmy was to return to school the next morning, Jeff felt the boy was at a definite crossroads in his life. They were sitting in sweaters, having hot chocolate on the flagstone terrace. There was a nip in the air, but the sun was strong.

"Hey, Timmy, no more uppers, eh?"

"Nah. I guess that's a pretty stupid way to go."

"You're damn right it is."

"It's just that—well, they make you forget all your problems."

"Come on, Timmy, you've got no real problems. I know adolescence is a tough time, but—"

"I wouldn't mind it so much if you were around. I mean all the time."

Jeff glanced at Timmy surreptitiously. The boy was sitting hunched over, rubbing his hands nervously, his eyes wistful.

"Timmy, you know I can't be around all the time. But I promise you this. I'll be around a lot more often than I have in the past. Will that do for starters?"

"Yeah, Jeff. Sure." Shortly afterwards, Timmy excused himself and went upstairs.

Jeff remained on the terrace. A light wind had sprung up and the sun had disappeared. It seemed much colder. He reached for his crutches, hefted his weight onto them and followed Timmy inside.

# Chapter 24

The nearest police precinct was in a white stucco building on a quiet residential street. Meg and Pierce walked up the stairs and into the building shortly before noon on a blindingly brilliant day. Though it was only late February, the air was summer-sultry. The heat seemed motionless and stagnant, its presence almost palpable. Meg could feel the thin material of her sundress clinging to her back, as much from nervousness as from the heat itself, she thought.

She and Pierce had sat up together most of the night, talking about what action the police would probably follow and how she would convince them her story was true. As they talked, Meg wondered how she would feel at the moment of discovering her true identity. Then she gave up trying—there were too many variables, too much uncharted territory.

At the reception desk sat a rather small and scholarly-looking policeman. It was a slow midday Sunday and he was whiling away the time with a large volume which looked like a textbook. Certainly not the stereotypical cop, thought Pierce. As they approached, the officer closed the book, keeping his finger in place, and Pierce got a glimpse of the title: "Building Your Own Boat."

"Excuse me," he addressed the man. "I wonder if we could talk to you."

"What's your problem?" The policeman was neither hostile nor encouraging. His tone was incurious and matter-of-fact.

"My friend here wants to talk to you." He indicated Meg with a tentative gesture.

A flicker of weariness crossed the cop's features. "Shoot. That's what I'm here for. First things first—what's your name?"

Meg and Pierce looked at each other. Meg opened her mouth, closed it, opened it again and took the plunge. "I've been going by the name of Peggy Arden—"

"I need your real name. We'll get around to aliases later."

"No, you don't understand. I don't know what my real name is."

The man removed his horn-rimmed glasses and rubbed his left temple. "Wait a minute. You don't know what your real name is."

"No. That's why I'm here. I—I seem to have lost my memory."

The cop impaled her with a pair of cool gray eyes. "Just a minute," he said, and dialed his desk phone. "Sarge, could you come front a minute, please?"

In a few minutes, the sergeant appeared, a portly man who wore his salt-and-pepper hair in a crew cut. He entered briskly and strode to them at once.

"Yes sir. Can I help you?" he asked Pierce. Pierce gestured toward his companion. Better if Peggy told her story directly.

She spoke quietly, haltingly. "I'm Peggy Arden. Or rather that's the name I've been going by. I don't know what my real name is. About two months ago, I was picked up in the Gulf of Mexico. I don't know how I got there."

"Um hm. Just swimming around the Gulf, were you?"

Meg's ire was roused by the flip rejoinder. "I was in a life vest. I guess I was semi-conscious."

The sergeant, apparently contrite, scanned Meg's face

with a practiced eye. "Come on into my office, Miss. I need to ask you some questions. I'm Sergeant Monroe, by the way."

They went into a small, unpretentious room with chipping paint and a smell of disinfectant. On a table that had seen better days was a coffee urn, steaming and sputtering. "How 'bout some coffee?" He poured himself a cup, lacing it liberally with sugar.

"No, thank you," Meg said. The idea of hot coffee on a day like today repelled her. The sergeant's office was not air-conditioned. "Could I—would it be possible for me to have a glass of water?"

Sergeant Monroe wheeled toward her. "You from the South, aren't you?"

"Well, that's just it—I don't know. I guess I must be. A few people have told me I sound Southern, but I have no memory of being from any place."

Sergeant Monroe disappeared briefly into the hall and came back with a paper cup of water. It was ice-cold and delicious. Then he settled back in his swivel chair, his coffee before him, and carefully placed his fingertips together, church-steeple style. "Now, little lady, would you mind startin' once more from the beginning?"

Meg told the story, trying to keep her head clear and her voice dispassionate. After she had finished, the sergeant asked her to tell it all over again, which she did. If he was looking for discrepancies, he found none. The memory of those events were too indelible for her to falter over details.

"Now I want you to think long and hard before you try to answer this one," Monroe said. "Have you got any glimmering, never you mind how small, of anything at all that happened to you before you found yourself in that water?"

Meg sat silently. When Pierce had asked more or less the same question that night on the beach, she told him she remembered nothing. But now she made a desperate effort to dredge up anything she possibly could, no matter how trivial.

"I—it won't make any sense."

"Never you mind," Monroe said excitedly. "Just give me any pictures that enter your mind."

"But they're such fragments, really." Her voice was almost a whisper. "But I remember—I think I remember—being in some kind of bicycle accident a long time ago and when I woke up, I had a—what I guess you'd call a memory blackout."

" 'Member anything about the weather? Whether it was hot or cold?"

"Ye-ess," said Meg slowly. "It must have been hot, because I remember the hospital windows were open at night. I remember the smell of some kind of flower. I thought it was honeysuckle, but now I can't remember what honeysuckle smells like."

Sergeant Monroe nodded. "That sounds like the South. Anything else?" He made a note on his yellow pad.

"This is even odder."

"Never you mind. Go on."

"I remember a big room and a piano falling. And then a big man carrying me across someplace like a porch."

"Hmm. Not much to go on, but you never know." He scribbled again on the pad, asked her a few more questions which led to nothing but dead ends. Then he found out she was self-supporting. "Well, we don't have cases like yours very often, Miss—Arden, as you can imagine. But if you have a job, I see no reason to keep you here. Tomorrow I'll get in touch with social services and also our photographer will be here."

"Photographer?"

"Sure. As I understand it, most of these cases are

solved when the victim's picture runs in the papers. Somebody comes along and sees the picture and knows who it is. Then usually the patient's memory begins to return."

"Oh," said Meg. But she had had long hair when she was picked up. She remembered how much trouble it had been to comb out the tangles. She must remember to tell the photographer that.

The sergeant uttered a sudden expletive, then apologized. He stabbed a forefinger into the desk calendar. "Tomorrow's Washington's Birthday. Won't be nobody around but a skeleton staff. I mean, the officers'll be here, of course. But the photographer won't unless there's an emergency, and the social services'll be closed. Our hands are tied till Tuesday. Come in Tuesday abut nine."

"But—" Meg stopped in confusion. Johnny Pack would be in town on Saturday. He would be expecting her decision. Time was of the essence—every day counted, every hour. But she could not explain that to Monroe; it was too bizarre. Besides, she had not even told Pierce. Her personal dilemma with Johnny Pack had nothing to do with either of them.

Sergeant Monroe had risen; he obviously considered the interview at an end. He looked at her questioningly. "Was there somethin' else?"

"No," said Meg. "No, that's all. I'll come in Tuesday."


Timmy went back to school on Tuesday, seemingly determined to stay out of trouble, but still with a melancholy wistfulness in his eyes as he told Jeff goodbye.

Jeff and Andrea entered the house together, shivering from having stood outside in only light jackets. Jeff was now ambulatory, but barely—the pain in his leg remained constant and he moved very, very slowly.

"Let's have our drinks in the library tonight, shall we, Jeff? It's cozier and I'll ask Sanders to build a fire there. Brrr." Her lips ruffled to make the familiar sound signifying chilliness.

"Yes," said Jeff. "Or B-R-R, as they say."

"What?" Andrea's voice was puzzled.

"Nothing. 'Bee-are-are.' Just a corny joke I picked up somewhere." He remembered, with a stab of pain more hurtful than any physical ache, the night he had said that to Meg, the night they first met. He remembered she had been slow to get it, but how hard she had tried to convince him she thought it really amusing. Then he forcibly and impatiently brought himself back to the present. As Andrea had reminded him, loss is a part of living.

He had begun to feel closer to Andrea than he would have thought possible a few months ago. She could still be vain and sometiimes drank too much. But during the last week she had really tried to do something about the latter vice. She now had no more than two cocktails before dinner and sometimes made those wine rather than martinis. She had also been surprisingly open to the idea of his changing his vocation to photography, while many people would only have scoffed. She had gone to the trouble of bringing Ricardo Cavullo to dinner. Jeff was reminded now, putting his crutches aside and sinking gratefully into the deep leather lounger, that he must get in touch with Cavullo next week. He thought soon he could manage the trip into town, even with the pain such exertion would undoubtedly bring.

Andrea was looking at him as though waiting for an answer. "Did you say something, Andrea?"

"My word! I've heard of daydreaming, but . . ."

Jeff smiled a little sheepishly. "Just trying to sort some things out. What'd you say?"

"I said I'd like to give Sanders and Janie the evening off tonight and display some of my own culinary skills. After all, they had extra work while Timmy was here—they deserve a mini-vacation, don't you think?"

"Whatever you say. But you realize I won't be much good as assistant chef."

"You won't have to be. I'm a whiz. I took a course at *Cordon Bleu*, one summer when I was young and ambitious in Paris."

He looked at her. Her use of "young" in the past tense was ludicrous. Today, in well-cut French jeans and a cranberry-red turtleneck, she looked about nineteen.

That evening, after Janie and Sanders had decided to drive to the village to see a movie, Jeff came downstairs, looked into the library, found it empty, and followed the clatter of dishes into the kitchen. He watched in amazement as Andrea deftly managed, in the course of half an hour, to turn out a simple but sumptuous meal: artichokes vinaigrette, cheese fondue and cherries jubilee.

"Your days in Paris were not wasted, Andrea," he noted approvingly as he ate. She answered with a wry grimace. "What were you doing in Paris anyway?"

"Just seeking fame and fortune."

"And did you find them?"

She shrugged ruefully. "I found that French noblemen are often not only penniless but penurious. He did stake me to the course at the *Cordon Bleu*, though, so it wasn't a total loss."

"So you came back to America a sadder but wiser girl."

"No, neither. I would be better off if I had come back one or the other, wouldn't I?"

Jeff glanced at her surreptitiously. It was the only time he had ever heard her speak in a tone of such naked regret. The context implied that the days of marriage to his father were part of that regret, though he was sure she wasn't aware of the implication.

They had their coffee in the library where Sanders had gotten a crackling fire going before he left. Jeff adjusted the lounger and leaned back. He felt almost at peace for the first time in months. A twinge in his leg reminded him he was not yet ready to run a four-minute mile.

"I can't understand why this damn thing doesn't start feeling better," he grumped. "It's been almost two months."

"I think the break was just one of those complicated ones. I'm sure within a few more weeks you'll be as good as new."

"Lately, I feel worse after the therapist's visit than before."

"Well," she cooed soothingly, "maybe that's only natural. He's supposed to be the very best, my doctor said."

"Best at cracking the whip, I'll say that."

Andrea laughed. "Are you comfortable now?"

"Yeah. Resting pretty easy." He closed his eyes.

"Jeff."

Her voice was quiet, but something in it made Jeff open his eyes instantly. "Yes?"

"I wish you'd stay here. Timmy would be so much better off. I know I've made a lot of mistakes, but what he really needs is a father."

"I really can't fill that role, Andrea. You know that."

"You could come very close. He worships you. It would mean so much to him, just during this next year or two."

She was standing behind his chair, her arms on his shoulders. Again he caught the smell of her musky perfume. "That perfume must drive your men friends wild," he said.

"I don't have any men friends any more, Jeff." She rubbed a cool hand across his forehead

"No?" He felt wonderfully relaxed from the food and the heat from the open fire. He opened his eyes lazily to find her watching him intently. "Where'd they all go?"

"I kissed them goodbye and told them to find themselves another girl. You've changed me a lot, Jeff. I think I've grown up a lot since you've been here. Not enough, maybe, but I'm making progress."

"Maybe we're growing up together," he said slowly. "I need to do some more growing, too. Stop orbiting in dreamland and reenter the real world."

He felt her arm around his shoulder. She moved to the side of the chair. He could feel the heat of her body. He saw the deep vertical shadow between her breasts. The smell of the perfume was hypnotic. He felt her fumbling with the buckle of his belt. He raised his hand to stay her movement, but could not find the power to do so.

"You won't have to do anything, darling," she whispered urgently. "I'll do it all. Just lie back." He felt the lounge chair slowly descend to its horizontal position. He felt Andrea's hair fall over one side of his face.

"My God, Andrea. Don't—please—I—" His voice stopped as her mouth covered his ravenously.

## Chapter 25

Meg went alone to the police station on Tuesday morning. Pierce had offered to get up early and go with her, but she felt she had imposed on him enough. And although her feeling for Pierce was strictly platonic, lately she had begun to sense a possessiveness in him which indicated he'd like their friendship to develop along closer lines. She felt perhaps she had unintentionally misled him by confiding in him and by allowing him to accompany her to the police on their first visit.

Sergeant Monroe greeted her heartily in his bluff, Southern fashion. It was not often that he became involved in a case of such exotic dimensions, nor that he was called on to help a "client" as beautiful as this. He introduced her to the photographer, whom he called only Buttons, a rail-skinny man with a shock of the most flaming red hair Meg had ever seen.

Buttons went about his work expertly but silently. It was early in the morning after a holiday weekend, and he had consumed more alcohol on the previous evening than he would have cared to admit. As he put a new roll of film in his camera, a faint whisper of memory stirred in Meg's mind. Something about cameras seemed significant. She watched Buttons closely; his actions were somehow familiar to her.

She picked up the cardboard case from which he had taken the cartridge of film. "ASA 400?" she asked, and was immediately surprised at her question. How had she known that ASA 400 was unusually fast film?

"Yeah," he said carelessly. "I use nothing but. A lot of times I need to catch fast action."

"Oh, really? I would have thought police work involved mainly just doing those—what do you call them—mug shots?"

"I freelance for a newspaper and do a lot of sports features."

"I see."

She felt elated by her knowledge of the ASA number. Somewhere in her background, she had learned something about photography. She was suddenly excited by the prospect of getting hold of a camera again. She wondered whether she was a good photographer. How strange to have to make that discovery all over again! But at the moment, there was a more pressing curiosity to be satisfied.

"Once these photos are developed, what happens to them? I mean, how will they be distributed?"

"Be sent to the wire services." The answer was laconic.

"Will a lot of newspapers use them, do you think?"

"Depends on whether it's a heavy news day. Sometimes they do and sometimes they don't. They'll also be sent to police headquarters in major cities."

Meg felt disappointed. If she were going to discover her true identity, certainly her best chance was having someone who knew her see her photograph. Now it seemed a matter of random accident, depending on the mood of an unknown city editor in some remote newspaper office. But in any case, there was nothing she could do about it.

Buttons snapped a half-dozen photographs, asking her to move slightly from one angle to another. The job done, he replaced the camera in its case and began packing up his equipment.

"When will I be able to see them?" she asked eagerly.

"Possibly tomorrow. I'll finish this roll of film this afternoon, prob'ly."

She thought the procedure rather lackadaisical, but refrained from comment. "Well, thank you. I'd like to thank Sergeant Monroe, too, before I leave."

"Stick your head in his office. He's in there."

Monroe motioned her to a chair. Buttons had already made a hasty exit. Suddenly Meg remembered. "Oh," she said, "I meant to tell Mr. Buttons something."

"What's that?" Sergeant Monroe asked alertly.

"Just that I—when I was—found, I had long hair. I looked different then."

"Hmm." Sergeant Monroe took a long sip of his ever-present coffee. "Well, not much he can do about that."

"I thought maybe a retoucher."

"Unfortunately, Miss Arden, we don't have one on the payroll. That's a highly skilled and highly paid job." He smiled at her comfortingly, his weathered, ruddy face arranging itself into an expression of solicitude. "Never you mind. I wouldn't worry too much about it. I don't think a new hair style would make you unrecognizable."

"I suppose not." She rose. "Well, thank you for everything, Sergeant Monroe. May I come in and see them tomorrow?"

"Is that when Buttons said they'd be ready? Sure you may."

Meg left the precinct station feeling frustrated and helpless. Of course neither Monroe nor Buttons knew she was in a race against time. She had hoped the photographs could be distributed that very afternoon and used in the Wednesday papers. Then she would have three days to wait for concrete results before Johnny Pack returned to Miami on Saturday. Of course, he had made no threats nor issued any ultimatums. It was ostensibly a free choice on her part to accept or reject the strange arrangement he offered. But instinctively she felt that rejection of Johnny Pack was a decision which should be made with extreme caution.

When Meg saw the photographs, which were finally ready late Wednesday afternoon, she felt like weeping. The extremely fast film Buttons had used might be ideal for sporting events, but in photographing her it had produced a grainy quality which left much to be desired.

And finer points of photography aside, Meg was startled by the features of the woman who stared out at her from the black-and-white glossy. Short, curly hair, sun-darkened skin, high, stretched cheekbones, haunted eyes. She looked like a stranger, even to herself.

Monroe promised they would be mailed off the following morning when his clerical help came in and could conceivably appear in some newspapers as early as Friday evening. Meg left the stationhouse feeling as though she were on the brink of yet another unknown and quite possibly dangerous adventure.


The photograph of Meg was ignored by many newspapers because of its poor quality. It was used in only a handful of Georgia newspapers, none of them in the Martinsville area. But remarkably, it did run in the newspaper with the largest circulation in America, the *New York Daily News*. This happened for two reasons: the *News* was consistently and avidly on the lookout for human-interest stories, particularly when the subject was a beautiful woman (and Meg's beauty was evident, even through the graininess). Secondly, that particular Friday evening, when the Saturday morning edition was being asembled, was a dead news day. The president had made no profound pronouncement; the international situation was momentarily quiet; there had been no sensational fire, no flaming plane crash, no lurid murder.

So Meg's photograph duly appeared in the *New York Daily News* on Saturday morning, February 27, accompanied by a two-paragraph story. It was not predominently featured—it was on an interior page otherwise filled with a furniture-store ad—but it was there.

On that morning, Andrea got up early to visit her new pet, the horse she had purchased from the Gundersens. She was nervous about keeping him in the Rosehill stables during the winter. The building was not well insulated since the Rosehill horses always spent the colder months in Florida. But she checked the chestnut colt carefully and he seemed to be in fine fettle, nipping her fingers playfully. In a few minutes, the hot walker whom she had hired the previous week would be in to exercise him. Relieved, she started back to the house and decided to stop off at the mailbox. She might as well save Sanders the trouble of walking down the long hill for the morning mail.

The house was very quiet. It was barely eight o'clock; Janie was either still sleeping or had already gone on her morning jaunt to the greengrocer's. One reason Andrea had been able to keep the servant couple was that she never insisted on early risings. She herself usually slept late, and on those infrequent occasions when she did get up early, she enjoyed having the house to herself for an hour or so.

She went into the kitchen and made coffee. She lit a cigarette and sat down at the breakfast table with the bundle of mail. She sorted through the bills and junk mail and shoved them aside impatiently. She picked up the newspapers and turned to a *Daily News* columnist whom she admired. She was glancing desultorily through the rest of the paper when a blurred photograph suddenly and inexplicably caught her eye. There was something about the girl's face. She read the caption: "Florida Mystery Girl," then went on to the story that followed.

> "This woman calls herself Peggy Arden, because she does not know her real name. Thought to be in her early twenties, she was rescued from the Gulf of Mexico about two months ago by two men—thought to be drug runners—who put her on a commercial flight to Miami. She has since worked in that city as a cocktail waitress. Apparently a victim of severe amnesia, Miss Arden says she remembers nothing of her life prior to the day she was plucked from the sea. Anyone with any knowledge of her true identity is urged to contact the Miami Police Department at once."

Andrea narrowed her eyes thoughtfully. Two months ago. That would have been around the first of the year. That was exactly when Jeff—no. It was too fantastic. Besides, she remembered distinctly that the girl who had accompanied Jeff to Rosehill at Thanksgiving had had very long hair and a strikingly pale complexion. The girl whose face stared up at her from the paper had close-cropped hair and tawny skin.

She read the brief article a second time. The Gulf of Mexico. Then that settled it—it was inconceivable that a cruise ship on its way from Miami to Venezuela would have been in the Gulf of Mexico. Still—could it be that the "mystery girl" was confused about the area where she had been rescued? What if by some outlandish coincidence—"

Andrea did not care to pursue that train of thought. In fact, she adamantly refused to do so. The relationship between Jeff and herself was far too promising. She would not allow a nonentity from the past to spoil it for her. And, she rationalized, to keep the knowledge from him was hardly a criminal action. The girl, whoever she was, had apparently established herself in Miami; the newspaper story stated she had a job. She appeared to be healthy except, of course, for her strange mental state.

Even if she were the girl for whom Jeff had grieved—was still grieving—she was not right for him. She had neither polish nor sophistication. Suppose the accident had not happened and Jeff had married her. In years to come, Andrea was certain he would have grown weary of her naivete and embarrassed by her social blunders. Now that he was beginning to get back to normal, she, Andrea, would actually be doing him a favor by not allowing him to be drawn again into past entanglements.

She took another sip of coffee and grimaced to discover it had grown stone-cold in the cup. She must have been sitting in a deep reverie for a long time. She shook her head as if to clear it of indecision. Then she resolutely rolled the newspaper into a cylinder and went quietly through the kitchen and down the back stairs.

The old-fashioned furnace stood in the far corner of the dim, concrete-floored room. With difficulty she swung open its heavy iron door. The dull red embers leapt hungrily into yellow flame as they devoured the unexpected fuel. With the satisfaction of one who has accomplished her mission with inarguable finality, Andrea began to rub the newspaper ink from her fingers as she retraced her steps up the stairs.

## Chapter 26

On the morning of February 27, Johnny Pack strode restlessly up and down the VIP lounge of one of the major airlines at Kennedy Airport in New York City. His plane, scheduled to depart for Miami at ten that morning, was being held up by mechanical trouble. It was already close to eleven and no one had even been allowed to board. Johnny Pack was impatient with delays. He ran his life on schedule and expected others to do the same. But there was nothing he could do but wait. He remembered with a rueful half-smile a part of the creed he lived by: "If you can't do anything about a situation, don't let it worry you."

Trying to heed his own philosophy, he sat down in an upholstered chair, sighed and opened his briefcase. He took out a thick sheaf of documents the *consigliori* had handed to him last night and began to thumb through them. But he found it difficult to concentrate with the public address system blaring in his ears every few seconds. He replaced the papers, closed the briefcase and restlessly left the lounge. In the main waiting room, a headline in the *Daily News* caught his eye and he folded a copy under his arm, tossing a half-dollar into the change dish on the newsie's counter.

His flight finally left shortly after eleven. Johnny Pack sank back into the wide, first-class seat and tried to relax. The odd thing—one which friends had often noted about him—was that even when he was at ease he did not look relaxed. He possessed an innate, steely tenseness which never left his body.

Once airborne, he glanced again at the *News* headline: "Mob War Believed Imminent." He smiled contemptuously and turned to the story to see what kind of hash the police and media combined had made of it. Scanning it rapidly, he congratulated himself for having surmised correctly. Not more than ten percent of their statements bore any relation to fact. Good. So much the less to worry about.

He began to flick swiftly through the inside pages, finding little of interest. Though Johnny Pack was a highly intelligent man with an intuitive shrewdness, he did not trouble to keep abreast of current affairs. Not, at least, those which did not concern him, his associates and his livelihood directly. He flipped a page and was about to flip the next when his hand stopped in midair. There was something strikingly familiar about the woman in the small, grainy photograph. A second look and a quick scan of the caption convinced him he was indeed seeing the face of the girl he knew as Peggy Arden.

As he read the story, his hands began to tremble slightly. He was a man of wide-ranging experience, but this was so fantastic it was unreal. Even the girl herself had no idea of her origin or background? Incredible. He put the paper down and began to review the situation. He wasn't sure it was wise to become involved with a completely unknown quantity. Depending on who her family turned out to be, it might lead to sticky complications. Like most people, he knew next to nothing about the causes or cures of amnesia. Before he saw Peggy again, he needed to find out more. He found Peggy Arden unusually appealing but he had not attained his present status without hardheaded pragmatism.

When the plane landed, he did not go to the hotel which housed the Mermaid bar, but checked in at another a few miles down the beach. He was, however, as well known at one as at the other and was accorded the same instant privileges, no matter how esoteric his wants. Usually, Johnny Pack's wants were not especially esoteric except in the field of food. He had a highly educated palate. Fine food was one of his passions and indifferent viands offended him. On this disappointingly gray Saturday afternoon, though, his mind was not on food.

Still in his impeccably tailored suit, but now tieless, he picked up the phone and was put through at once to the manager.

"Sheldon, I need a little research done. This afternoon, if possible."

"Of course, Mr. Pack. How can we help you?"

"Do you have someone in the stenographic pool who knows her way around a library?"

"I'm sure there's someone qualified in that respect, yes sir."

"Ask her to come to my room in half an hour."

"You do realize this is Saturday, Mr. Pack?" the man inquired nervously.

"She'll be paid three times what she ordinarily gets."

"Right."

In exactly 27 minutes, a buxom blonde who introduced herself as Suzy appeared. She looked as though she had never seen the inside of a library, but after he had questioned her briefly, he found she had been a major in library science at one of the country's outstanding universities. She had had to leave school in midterm of her senior year when her father died, leaving the family almost no money.

Johnny Pack had no interest in whether her story was true or a cock-and-bull figment of her imagination. When he told her what he wanted to know, she suggested medical journals as a good source and her subsequent suggestions also made sense. He thought she could do the job.

"I'll have to hurry, though," she said. "I'll have only a couple of hours before the library closes."

"Then go." He extracted a slim alligator wallet from the breast pocket of his suit and took out a twenty. "Take a cab," he said briefly.

She came back at five-thirty, entering his room flushed with victory. From the huge beach bag she carried, she extracted three black-bound books and four medical journals.

"I had to steal these," she said. "They were all in the reference section—not supposed to be taken out. They should be returned."

He smiled slightly over her qualms about making off with a few library books and reassured her. "I'll be through with them by Monday morning. I'll leave them at the desk and trust you to return them, okay? Will this cover it, including the extra trip on Monday?" He proffered her a hundred-dollar bill.

Her eyes widened with delight. "They'll be put back exactly where I found them. That's a promise." She opened the door into the hall. "If you should ever need anything else, just whistle," she lilted. He had already turned away, but raised one hand over his shoulder which she recognized as a gesture of dismissal. Disappointed, she closed the door.

He dove avidly into the books. When he looked up from his reading, he was amazed to find it was after ten in the evening. He didn't feel like going out for dinner. He called room service, and gave minutely detailed instructions for the preparation of his chateaubriand. Then he had a long hot shower, slipped into a brown moiré robe and resumed his reading as he waited for dinner.

Meg did not know what to expect nor when to expect it. She only knew that her nerves were strung taut, her stomach was churning, her head felt giddy and light. At any moment, one or both of two things might happen. The police could contact her, saying that she had been identified by someone seeing the newspaper photograph. Or Johnny Pack could walk in the door. She felt, not without reason, that her entire future depended on which of those events occurred first.

As it transpired, nothing at all happened over that anxiety-ridden weekend. She served her customers, forcing herself to be pleasant, even making a few attempts to be jocular. For the most part she succeeded, although at one point things became a little unpleasant.

A customer insisted that his stinger was a single instead of the double he had ordered. Meg relayed the message to Pierce and delivered a second drink to the man. Again he complained of its weakness. Meg took the glass from the table and set it irately at Pierce's end of the bar.

"Why don't you learn to make a decent drink, Pierce? New England stinginess?"

Pierce set down the cocktail shaker in his hand and stared at her. It was the first time he had ever heard her make an unkind or sarcastic remark. He opened his mouth to retort in kind but thought better of it. She had been under terrific tension for the last few days; she deserved to let off a little steam.

"Yep, that's me," he said cheerily. "The original Scrooge."

Before the end of the evening, Meg found an opportunity to apologize to him and Pierce was amazed to see tears in her eyes. "I'm sorry, Pierce. I should have picked on anyone rather than you."

He gave her hand a hurried squeeze. "I understand, Peggy. It's okay." God, he hoped something would come of that police photograph. She was living in a limbo, and the strain was beginning to show.

Johnny Pack read far into the night. Not that there was much material on amnesia—knowledge about it was surprisingly limited. But he was looking for a particular bit of information, and finally, in one of the medical journals, he found it.

The journal stated that amnesia that lasts for a period of more than a few days is unlikely ever to be fully cured. "It would appear that the longer the amnesic state continues, the less likelihood there is of return to full mnemonic health." Certain case histories were cited; in no case where the amnesia had been present for a period of months was memory ever fully restored. He felt a sense of relief that family entanglements seemed unlikely as a result of a liaison with Peggy. But it was tempered at once with sympathy for her, for Johnny Pack was not an unfeeling man.

He also realized that he had probably been brutally curt in his unusual proposal to the girl. If she were already in a state of confusion about her identity, his approach must have seem grotesquely abrupt. He would have to be much gentler henceforth.

As he continued to read, he found himself fascinated by the world of the amnesiac. Surely amnesia was one of the most bizarre and least understood of maladies. He learned that there are two general kinds: that caused by a cerebral disease such as a brain tumor, and "traumatic" amnesia caused by an accident—a blow to the head, for example.

He assumed Peggy was suffering from the latter. He wondered how she had come to be found in the Gulf of Mexico. Perhaps a sailing accident? A victim of some sort of kidnap plot that went awry? The possibilities were numerous. He supposed it was possible that no one would ever know, not even Peggy herself.

It was after three in the morning when he closed the books and stacked them neatly on the dresser to remind himself to have the bellboy take them to the desk the following day. After he got into bed, he tried to imagine what it would be like to have no previous memory. With all past recollection gone, would one wind up in the same general circumstances as if one had never suffered the loss? Or would one's lifestyle bear little resemblance to his or her earlier mode of living? Would one choose the same kinds of friends? Would one's socio-economic level be similar or vastly different? They were intriguing ideas to ponder.

He would not see Peggy tomorrow. He was sure she would be grateful for the respite—he must have startled her badly. And he wanted to find out whether anyone would respond to her newspaper picture. She might even be married, with a family. But if no one had contacted her within 48 hours, say, it was unlikely that anyone would. Nothing is forgotten more quickly than yesterday's newspaper.

When Andrea reentered the kitchen, Jeff was just sitting down at the breakfast table with a bowl of cereal, his crutches propped against the wall. He looked at her in surprise as she entered through the backstairs door.

"Where'd you come from?" he asked.

"Oh! I—didn't you hear the water pipes clanking and gurgling all night long?"

"No. Didn't hear a thing."

"Well, the plumbing was acting up. Before I called anyone to see about it, I wanted to see if I could get some idea of the trouble."

"Andrea the engineer," he said jokingly.

"That's me," she agreed as she poured out the cold coffee and refilled her cup.

"Have you seen the *News*?"

She smiled brightly. "No, I didn't watch this morning."

"I mean the *Daily News*, smart guy."

"*The Times* is right there."

"No, I wanted to see the *News'* center photo spread of the football game last night."

Andrea elaborately searched through the stack of papers. "I guess it didn't come today. Isn't that odd?"

"Very. Sanders bring in the mail?"

She paused. "No—come to think about it, I collected it this morning."

"You?"

"I was up early. Wanted to check on the new horse. He's a darling, by the way. His conformation is superb."

"Good. What time are we leaving?"

"Leaving?" Her tone was puzzled.

"Don't tell me you've forgotten, Andrea. We're driving up to see Timmy this afternoon."

"Oh, how stupid of me. Of course we are—it had slipped my mind for the moment."

"He wants us to be there for the parents' tea at four. Why don't we leave a little early and have lunch somewhere on the way?"

"Oh, that's a wonderful idea!" she agreed.

"After all, it's my first real trip out of the house since the accident. We should make an occasion of it."

"By all means! That is, if you feel up to it."

"Sure. And I can pick up a copy of the *News* on the way, before they've sold out."

"Why—yes."

Her tone changed so abruptly that he looked at her quickly. "What's the matter?"

"Matter?" she echoed,

"You just sounded—odd."

"No," she laughed lightly. "Well, I'd better start getting dressed. Should we leave about noon then?"

"Seems about right."

"Then I'll meet you in the library a little before. I'd better remind Sanders we'll need him to drive, too."

She ran upstairs to her room and closed the door. She was breathing hard and sat down on the side of the bed for a moment to recover. Then, moving noiselessly she went to the phone and dialed.

"Harvey Spector, please." She waited, drumming her crimson fingernails on the glass-topped bedside table. Her expression suddenly became alert and she lowered her voice to a whisper. "Harvey. I want you to come out here right away.... To see our patient, that's why.... He wants to go on a driving trip this afternoon and I'm sure the exertion will be too great. I want you to tell him so."

During the ensuing pause, her greenish eyes narrowed dangerously. "And I say he's *not* able to go.... Of course I want him to recover, but according to my timetable.... Before you start arguing with me, Harvey, you'd better remember who signs your paychecks and whether you ever want a recommendation for another job.... That's better. Be here by ten-thirty at the latest."

# Chapter 27

Timmy McAllister sat on the long, low stone fence that overlooked the visitors' parking lot. Since he had been at the Huxley School in September, his mother had paid him three visits. The first time, she was on her way to New England to see the fall foliage and had stayed less than an hour. The second time, she was en route to a tri-state bridge tournament in northern Connecticut and the third time she had appeared unexpectedly with a Mr. Somebody who embarrassed Timmy by telling the other boys exactly how much he had paid for his Silver Shadow Rolls-Royce.

But he was really looking forward to her visit this afternoon because Jeff would be coming with her. Today would be a real family get-together. He couldn't wait for them to get here—recently he had been lonelier than ever. Since his and Hughie's escapade in the Keene family car, Hughie had not come back to Huxley, but had been sent South to a military academy famous for straightening out difficult rich boys. Timmy hoped they wouldn't change Hughie completely. Hughie was kind of wild, but he was a lot of fun.

Timmy adjusted his position on the rough stones. He looked at the scaled-down Cartier watch his mother had given him for Christmas. After three-thirty. He wanted to give Jeff and his mother a chance to freshen up in his room before they went downstairs for the parents' tea. It was the third such tea of the year and it would be the only time he had had a parent there. This time he would have two, more or less. Of course Jeff was really his brother—half-brother—but he treated Timmy like a son and Timmy felt almost like his son. He no longer remembered his father very distinctly at all. He had been almost relieved when his father left the house to go live at his club. He remembered when that happened, because the fighting stopped.

He started thinking of Hughie again. Hughie wasn't afraid of anything. And Timmy felt that he, Timmy, was afraid of everything. He would be 14 in June and he was still afraid of everything. He had been flattered when Hughie started singling him out. He would have followed Hughie on any adventure, no matter how daring. Maybe Hughie liked him for that reason—because he knew Timmy would do anything Hugh wanted him to.

He wished Jeff and his mother would marry. If that happened, he would have a father all the time. At all the parents' teas, he could introduce Jeff and Andrea together and everyone would probably think Jeff was really his father. He would be a little younger than most of the other boys' dads, but that wouldn't matter.

He got up and snapped a small twig off one of the low-hanging branches. He began to pull off the leaves, one by one. He looked down at the parking lot. Most of the parents had already arrived, but he could see two or three cars disgorging mothers and fathers, sometimes with younger siblings. He looked at his watch again. Ten minutes after four. If they didn't get here soon, they would be too late to go through the reception line. The Huxley School considered protocol very important.

Maybe they had had car trouble on the way. But he didn't think that likely, the way Sanders babied the black Cadillac. Sanders had said to Timmy more than once as he drove him to or from school: "Your father, rest his soul, told me the day he hired me, 'Sanders, buy a good car and take care of it. Then you won't have to trade it in every year, like these show-off Charlies.' " At that point in the story Sanders would invariably chuckle. "I always got such a kick out of your father, God rest his soul, using that expression. He was always so dignified. I couldn't hardly keep from laughing out loud when he'd come out with that expression, 'show-off Charlies.' " And Sanders would chortle again. Timmy liked Sanders. He and his young wife Janie were both shy, but they always asked Timmy how he was doing, and seemed to really care.

Timmy came out of his reminiscences with a start. He saw a long black car pulling slowly into one of the parking spaces with one figure in the front seat and two, a man and a woman, in the rear. That would be Sanders, Jeff and his mother. He loped down the stone steps that curved to the parking lot. Midway, he stopped. The man and woman getting out of the car were ancient. They must be someone's grandparents. Certainly they bore no resemblance to Jeff and Andrea.

He looked toward the parking-lot entrance drive. He could see no other cars entering, nor even a single automobile on the long stretch of country highway that led to the school. Maybe something had happened after all. Maybe he should go back to the dorm, in case they were trying to phone him.

His room, when he entered, was so neat that it looked like a stranger's room. Then he remembered he had spent an hour that morning dusting the furniture, washing the window sills and getting his dirty gym clothes out of sight. Yesterday he had even caught a ride into the village and bought a nice print and two burnt-orange cushions to brighten up the place.

He left the door to his room ajar so he could hear the hall phone. But the bell in the clock tower chimed five and still the phone remained stubbornly silent. It was then he went into the bathroom, where, two weeks before, he and Hugh had stashed a few spare quaaludes, taped to the underside of the removable top of the toilet.

Half an hour later, Andrea got through to him.

"Timmy? I'm sorry, darling, I've been trying to reach you since three o'clock. Where were you?"

His mother was a wonderful liar, he thought. What had she been doing for the last hour, when he had been in his room? "I went out to wait for you," he said carefully. "Where were you?"

"We—the therapist came by and thought Jeff shouldn't make the trip. Jeff insisted he could and we actually started out twice, but the pain was just too great. I couldn't let him do it. I didn't call till three, because I thought perhaps we'd be able to manage after all."

"I've been in my room for quite awhile."

"Oh? Well—I didn't call after four because I thought you'd be at the tea. I'm sorry, darling. You must not have stayed long. Wasn't it a nice party?"

"Fuck the party," Timmy said, slowly and distinctly. "And fuck you, too." Then he hung up.


On Monday morning, Johnny Pack woke up feeling great. He lay in the apricot silk sheets planning his strategy for the day. First, he had found out from Callios that Monday was Peggy's day off. So much the better that he had not contacted her over the weekend. When he did see her, he would have an entire day to woo her at leisure. A corner of his mouth curled in wry self-deprecation at the use of the word "woo." For no one—not his business associates nor childhood friend nor his still-living parents—knew Johnny Pack's most closely guarded secret: he was frightened to death of women.

Johnny Pack had grown up in a houseful of sisters—five of them. They were all older than he, and all high-spirited and strong-willed. Johnny was born four years after the last of the female children, the identical twins Jeannette and Joanna, arrived on the scene. Put into a position of inferiority not only by age but by early physical frailty as well, Johnny learned quickly to cover his fear by silently holding his ground and staring them down. That quality served him well in later business dealings. But what he never learned was how to feel at ease with women.

The fear of his sisters extended to other female acquaintances during high school. The feeling was so strong that it negated any possible physical attraction to women. During college he gained a reputation for magnanimity. He was always willing to take a classmate's obese or unattractive sister or cousin to an important dance or football game. He never got a date on his own. An apocryphal story was generally accepted among his peers that Johnny had been desperately in love with a childhood sweetheart who died of tuberculosis at fifteen.

By providing lonely ugly ducklings with his handsome and gentlemanly company, and by never denying the dead-childhood-sweetheart myth, he accomplished two things at once. He laid to rest any conjecture that he might be homosexual and he gradually accumulated a sizable stack of social IOU's from his college chums.

After his college graduation (magna cum laude), he tacitly let those men know that they could repay his social favors with business ones. As a result, he rose quickly within the loosely allied illegal and quasi-legal organizations which formed a vast network throughout the country. Now he was in a top-echelon position which required a woman as a social appendage.

Numerous business associates were eager to provide him with the most desirable women of their acquaintance, and Johnny often found it convenient to escort them. But the typical woman in his circle of friends was brittle, lacquered and aggressive. In her company, he covered his fear with an arrogant silence. Perversely, this only made him more attractive to the women, but Johnny writhed inside with a feeling of inadequacy. He never dated a woman more than once or twice, because after that she either insinuated or openly suggested that they should go to bed together.

He finally decided after a particularly awkward incident following a large and drunken Christmas party that the situation was untenable. He would have to find a woman innocent and unspoiled enough to make no demands on him. She would, of course, also have to be beautiful. It was not an easy bill to fill. He could perhaps have found a girl of sixteen or seventeen, but he had no desire to be considered a cradle-robber. No, she must be of a suitable age—over twenty, at least.

He had almost given up his search when he dropped into Callios's bar, the Mermaid, in late January and saw Peggy for the first time. He had certainly never expected his search to end in a Miami cocktail bar! But thereafter, when in Miami on business, he made it a point to visit the Mermaid, take a corner table and unobtrusively watch her.

She was arrestingly beautiful, even with the severely shorn locks which did not seem to fit the rest of her face. She was surprisingly innocent—once or twice he had overheard a customer make an off-color remark and her reaction astounded him. Instead of laughing with too-hearty enthusiasm or returning the remark in kind, Peggy would stare with widened eyes, give the customer a shy, disappointed half-smile and turn away. She was not being prudish, he saw; she was simply reacting honestly. Johnny Pack was captivated. He would have nothing to fear from such an unassuming, straightforward girl-woman as that.

Johnny Pack noticed the sun rising higher through the frosted-glass jalousies and kicked off the silken sheet. He dialed Callios, asked for Peggy's number and swore under his breath when he was told she had no outside phone. Then he had a better idea, and quickly picked up the phone again to make another call.

On Sunday night, when Meg's shift in the bar was finally over, Pierce suggested they drive to a place on the bay, have a seafood omelet and watch the sun rise. But Meg at that moment wanted only to be alone. She felt wrung out physically and emotionally.

"Sorry, Pierce. I'm not up to it tonight. I'm going to bed, if I can make it to my room without falling on my face from exhaustion."

He smiled. "Okay. A raincheck then. Sleep well."

Meg called after him, "Maybe we can catch a movie tomorrow, Pierce."

"Can't. Mid-semester exams this week."

Meg went directly to her room, undressed and fell into bed. But it was one of those nights when she was so tired that sleep was impossible. Her body was infinitely weary, but her mind kept speeding in faster and faster circles. Until she found herself alone in the darkened room, she had not realized how much she had been counting on the newspaper photograph to solve the mystery of her identity. Sergeant Monroe had told her she should hear within a day or two if she were going to hear from anyone at all. The photograph had been released on Thursday and it was now early Monday morning. Hope grew dimmer with every passing hour.

The tears, when they came, surprised her. She had

thought she was beyond tears. But they slid down the sides of her face in steady salty streams and dampened the already clammy pillow. She made no effort to wipe them away; she lay passively and let the outpouring continue until they abated at last and sleep came.

Just as dawn was beginning to lighten the room, she sat bolt upright in bed and slowly realized she had been jolted awake by a dream. What was it? It had been unpleasantly vivid. Painstakingly, she was able to assemble the fragments:

She was walking down a city street, thronged with strangers. The buildings on either side were incredibly tall and formed an ominous canopy over the sidewalk that almost completely shut out the light. The look of the city was somehow familiar—was it a Manhattan canyon? The air was thick and gray; she found it difficult to breathe. There was something she had to find out from the strangers on the street, but as she approached them, one by one, a swirling mist shut out their faces. She could see their clothes—one man, in particular, was dressed in a brown suede jacket with tweed trousers and an Irish country hat. She could even see his wavy auburn hair at his ears. But the mist spread over his face and became only a blank halo of light. Just as the mist began to dissipate, he turned a corner and was gone.

She felt a sense of irretrievable loss and turned to the next stranger. But then they all began walking away from her quickly, in unison, as if they had been given simultaneous orders. And she was alone on the street that had been, the instant before, packed with humanity. That was when she awoke, startled out of the dream and into a sense of desolation.

She turned on the light and went into the kitchenette for a glass of water. The mundane reality of the lit room reassured her, and slowly her uneasiness subsided. After a time she went back to bed, and this time, her sleep was dreamless.

The knocking became louder and louder. She had become accustomed to assorted clatters and shrieks from the utility room, but this was a different sound. She opened her eyes and realized it was outside her door. Moving heavily, she put on her robe and opened the door.

The small, wiry messenger stood almost at attention. He held an armful of white roses and an ivory-colored envelope, which he offered her ceremoniously.

"I'm to wait for an answer, but he said you'd need some time. I'll be back in half an hour. Okay?"

Meg nodded dumbly. The messenger bowed and closed the door. She had never seen so many roses, long-stemmed, still dewy. Astounded, she began to count: four dozen. Since she had nothing to put them in, she laid them in the bathtub temporarily and filled it with an inch of tepid water. Then, with puzzled curiosity, she opened the creamy envelope.

> "Dear Miss Arden,
> I have reviewed with some dismay our conversation of the Saturday before this past. I believe you may have gone away with the erroneous idea that I was proposing a dishonorable arrangement to you. Please know that that was the furthest thing from my mind. Would you do me the honor of having dinner with me tonight so that I may clarify the matter? If so, I will call for you at six.
>
> Sincerely,
> Johnny Pack"

There was probably not a woman in the world, Meg thought, tapping the envelope nervously against her fingers, who would not be flattered to get such a note. Its tone was one of old-world courtliness. It was charming in its modesty. And its arrival could not have been more timely. Meg felt so abandoned when she awoke from her dream that the prospect of a day alone was grimly unsettling.

The letter made her feel quite different about Johnny Pack. He was no longer threatening; indeed, the whole thrust of the letter had been to remove any hint of threat. He might be unorthodox in his approach but he was no longer frightening.

She sat down at her dresser, which doubled as a desk, and wrote a careful reply, faintly embarrassed that the plain white typing paper she used was so utilitarian.

> "Dear Mr. Pack,
> Your note was very kind. I will look forward to seeing you at six o'clock.
> 
> Sincerely,
> Peggy Arden"

She hoped it did not sound abrupt, but there was really nothing more to say until he had given her a more complete explanation of his extraordinary proposal.

## Chapter 28

After the parents' tea fiasco and Timmy's final telephone rejoinder, Andrea and Jeff held a "family" conference. Jeff agreed that the boy must have resumed his drug-taking or he would not have made that astounding remark to his mother.

"I think you should bring him home, Andrea. Let him go to school here. He obviously hates it at Huxley."

"Yes, but Timmy should be learning how to handle independence. And Huxley is such a fine school—Huxley boys always have an edge in getting into whatever college they choose, and later, whatever job they choose."

"The local schools are not exactly one-roomers. And how much good will Yale or Harvard do him if he's strung out on quaaludes or angel dust? For God's sake, Andrea, get your priorities straight."

"But will he be any better off at home? He has no father to provide a strong hand and I don't seem to be able to do anything with him. Sometimes I think he hates me."

"Don't be melodramatic. He doesn't hate you at all—he's just going through a very trying time. Adolescence is difficult for the best of us. God knows it was for me."

"If you could only stay on through this school term, Jeff. He adores you. If you were here, it might make all the difference. If you were here, I'd be willing to bring him home."

"You know I'm starting with Cavullo in a week or so, this leg permitting. But I'll try to come out every weekend, or almost every weekend."

"It isn't the same. He needs somebody around who can help him over the day-to-day rough spots. You're comfortable here, aren't you, Jeff? Why don't you try commuting into the city for a few weeks?"

"I won't be working from just nine to five. Once I get involved with Ricardo, my hours are going to be long and hard. And I want them that way."

"Look, if it'll help, I'll lend you Sanders. He'll drive you back and forth. I'll make do with the MG and drive myself around."

"Such a sacrifice," he noted, with wry admiration. He meant it, too. Andrea had often said that happiness was having a chauffeur at hand. She loathed driving and Jeff knew it. "No, Andrea, I wouldn't think of taking Sanders away from you. I can cope with the Long Island Railroad."

"Then you'll stay?" She came to him and kissed him lightly on the cheek. "At least till the school term ends in June?"

It was not until that moment that Jeff realized he had talked himself into a corner. But the next few months might be crucial for Timmy. When the school term ended, he could leave with a clear conscience. "Yes," he said finally. "I'll stay till the school term ends."

From that point on, it seemed, Jeff's leg improved steadily. Harvey Spector was trying a new technique which seemed to produce much happier results than the strenuous exercises and massages he had used previously. By April, Jeff had put aside his crutches, was maneuvering the stairs quite well, and was even able to join Timmy on moderately paced hikes, so long as they didn't go more than a half-mile or so. Timmy, now enrolled in a local school, seemed much less restless, even content.

In mid-March, Jeff had started his creative partnership with Ricardo Cavullo. He became director of the new photographic shop, which incorporated a unique feature. Clients (Ricardo hated the word "customers") could bring in samples of their work and Jeff would evaluate it in terms of composition, exposure and development techniques. In the beginning, he made these critiques under Cavullo's tutelage. But the older man soon saw that Jeff possessed a superior eye and an instinctive knowledge of what qualities transform a good picture into a great one, and he soon left Jeff to his own devices.

Andrea, at last, was taking a deeper, more consistent interest in her son. Frequently, when Jeff came home in the evening, he would find Andrea and Timmy playing one of the electronic games Timmy was so fond of or watching television or, most gratifying of all, simply talking together.

One evening in early April, Jeff happened to let himself in so quietly that neither of them heard him approach. He opened the door into the library and was struck by the domestic tranquility of the scene. Andrea and Timmy were sitting cross-legged on the floor, working to solve a gigantic crossword puzzle. Andrea had one arm loosely draped over Timmy's shoulders. The lamplight turned the two blond heads into golden halos. As he stood watching in silent appreciation, Andrea, sensing his presence, looked up and smiled. He realized in that moment how far she had come from the restless, driven woman she had once been.

He sat down with them until the puzzle was finished.

"Three heads are better than two," said Andrea, yawning. "My God, it's after ten o'clock."

"Oh, no!" Timmy scrambled to his feet. "I wanted to watch that documentary about that new electric car."

"Then hurry upstairs and turn it on," Andrea laughed. "It's only a few minutes after—you won't miss much."

"He's going to be an engineer," Jeff predicted after Timmy had left.

"Looks like," Andrea agreed amiably. "Want a nightcap? Sorry you didn't make it home for dinner."

"Cavullo had a rush job and wanted me to develop some of the work."

Andrea whistled lightly. "You must really have made a big impression. He's famous for keeping control of every step from A to Z. That's how he got his nickname, 'The Czar.' "

"Yep, I was a little surprised myself."

He was helping her tidy the room. They both reached for the same ashtray at the same split second and it spun to the floor, spilling cigarette butts and spent matches over the Danish rug. On hands and knees, they began picking up the debris. Andrea suddenly seemed to lose her balance and fell on her side, laughing at her own clumsiness. Her blonde hair fanned against the rug's autumnal copper and gold. Jeff took her hands to help her up and somehow she was in his arms. Again the scent of musk. He felt a deep, throbbing ache that began in his loins and spread throughout his body.

He sank his face into the fall of golden hair. "Oh, Andrea," he murmured. "God, Andrea—" With difficulty he broke the embrace, but she insinuated herself quickly into his arms again.

"Timmy won't be down again, I'm sure," she whispered. "But I'll lock this door anyway—just in case."


A few nights later, Jeff was surprised to find Andrea waiting up for him when he arrived home from work past eleven.

"Have something to drink with me," she said as he

entered the library. "A nightcap."

"All right. I could use one. I'm beat." He settled onto the sofa and she brought him a generous dollop of brandy. The fiery liquid helped wash the fatigue from his body.

"I'm worried about Timmy again," she said. "I found some pills in a drawer in his room. I know what's worrying him."

Jeff was immediately concerned. "What, for God's sake?"

"He knows you're going to leave when the school term is over and it's bugging him already."

"Andrea, I've told you and I've told Tim I'll be out here most weekends."

"He needs the security of knowing you'll be around all the time."

"But—"

"Would you consider marrying me, Jeff?" She glanced at him and smiled. "Don't look at me like that. I know you're still in mourning for your lost love. It would be just a semi-business arrangement, for Timmy's sake. Although you don't find me too unattractive, do you?" She nestled against him and touched his temple, very lightly.

He cleared his throat. "I find you all too attractive, Andrea. You know that."

"Well, then?"

"Let me think it over." Then he snorted ruefully. "My God, that sounds patronizing. I'm sorry."

"Think it over," she whispered. "But let's not do any more thinking right now." She wrapped her arms around his neck and pulled him to her imperiously.


Jeff and Andrea were married on Friday, April 13. Andrea insisted 13 was her lucky number and thus the date boded well.

It was a small, private wedding, attended only by Peter Jamison and his wife (now back from London), Ricardo Cavullo and a favorite aunt of Andrea's who had driven up from Pennsylvania.

Although it was still early in the season, they decided to take a short wedding trip to Bermuda. Andrea had wanted to go by sea if they could book a cruise, but when she mentioned that idea to Jeff, his face darkened. "No. No more cruises for me, Andrea. At least not for a while."

"Oh, of course, darling," she said quickly. "That was insensitive of me. Of course. We'll fly."

In Bermuda, it rained every day. Later, Jeff would wonder if things would have turned out differently had it not been for that ceaseless rain. Andrea seemed delighted with the inclement weather, content to stay in their suite of rooms, eat, drink and make love. But Jeff soon found himself staring restlessly out the window at the sodden pink sand and wishing he were back in the photography shop with his clients and friends. He could not understand his own restlessness. Andrea was a skillful and always willing sexual partner. Her body was slim and beautifully proportoned, her skin fair and smooth. Why, then, once the physical release was attained, was there such an inexplicable sadness in him?

When they woke up at noon to the fifth day of rain, Jeff hurled himself out of bed. "Look, Andrea, it's silly to be defeated by the weather. We may not be able to sun ourselves on the beach, but we could get out and explore the island."

Andrea yawned and stretched herself. "Oh, Jeff, I've seen the island. Quaint, but nothing I'd slosh around in the rain for." She turned over and burrowed her head in the pillow.

He managed to talk her into going downstairs for

brunch, rather than ordering it from room service. The maitre d' who seated them inquired politely whether they were enjoying their stay.

"Yes, of course," Jeff replied with equal courtesy. "But I wouldn't mind seeing a ray of sunshine now and then." The man shook his head in sympathy. "Yes. Really bloody awful. Too bad. Spring showers, as the saying goes."

"I didn't even bring a raincoat," said Jeff ruefully.

"Oh, not to worry. I have a mackinaw in my locker. Use it any time."

"Thanks. I may take you up on it later this afternoon."

"I'm sure we can outfit the lady in one as well."

Andrea smiled stiffly. When they returned to their room, she was furious. She had concealed the extent of her irateness as long as they were in public. But once behind closed doors, her anger spilled out in a stream of invective.

"What kind of honeymoon is this? I think it's humiliating for you to announce publicly that you're so bored you're dying to get out of here. To get away from me."

He was taken totally by surprise. "Andrea! I'm not dying to get away from you. You said this morning you had no interest in going outside—that you'd seen it all before."

"That doesn't mean I want to sit cooped up in this room alone! I should think you'd have more tact. Everyone in this place knows we're on our honeymoon."

"Andrea, don't be like that, please. All right, if it upsets you that much, I won't go, that's all. I haven't made any appointments—I don't have to meet any deadlines."

"There's no need to resort to sarcasm, either," she

said shortly. "Go if you want to. I don't want you to feel I'm keeping you prisoner here."

The remark was close enough to the truth to sting. "All right, I will go. I think we'll both be better off if I get a little fresh air. Sure you don't want to go along?"

She shook her head firmly. "No. But you go on and enjoy yourself. I don't want to interfere with your pleasure."

He threw up his hands in a gesture of helplessness. "Damned if I do and damned if I don't!" He walked out quickly.

Andrea was white with anger. She had started her campaign to marry Jeff because it would mean greater financial security. As the senior McAllister's widow, Rosehill was on loan to her only until she remarried. As Jeff's wife, she would be in solid possession of the entire McAllister fortune. And after a time, the project had become more than a search for financial well-being. The longer Jeff stayed with her at Rosehill, the more attractive he had become. She had endured marriages to two older men whom she did not love, because their wealth could make her forget the miserably shallow, scrimping childhood she had had.

When circumstances dropped Jeff in her lap, so to speak, she felt as if fortune had smiled on her at last. He was vital, talented, attractive and *young*. During her earlier marriages, Andrea had arranged discreet and hasty trysts with virile young men here and there, and it had not always been easy to be discreet. She felt she deserved at last to *own* someone who could satisfy her sexual needs—someone whom she would not have to send away at dawn.

Now! Married five days and the honeymoon was over. She had followed Jeff's restless pacing, had seen the wistfulness in his eyes as he watched the surf pound in from the gray Atlantic. And she had known where his thoughts were. It was maddening and humiliating. She looked outside the window. The rain was coming down in buckets. Good. Let him get soaked. The idea of going out for a walk in weather like this was insane. The glint of the tequila bottle caught her eye. They had bought it their first evening here, when she had said a margarita sounded like a good idea. A drink now might not be a bad idea. The room was not cold, but dampness hung unpleasantly in the air.

Jeff walked along the shore. He felt defeated. He had thought that he and Andrea could have a contented marriage, if not a wildly happy one. Their common interest, of course, was Timmy. They would work together to see him grow into a confident and successful young man. Perhaps subconsciously, Jeff felt that by marrying Andrea, he would be atoning for the guilt he felt in his father's death. He would be taking his father's place in a very real sense, and he felt the elder McAllister would have been grateful.

Marriage to Andrea would open a new life and help him forget the old one. For Meg still haunted his dreams, and many of his waking moments. Her place in his mind was marginal—he could not bear to admit her to the center of his thoughts. Once Meg's Aunt Bess had told him of the memorial service, Meg's death had become ineluctably real.

Now, standing on the raw and windswept beach, he faced his memories of Meg head-on. He remembered a certain fluttering motion she made with her fingers when she was trying to remember something and couldn't. He remembered her startled eyes when he first introduced himself. He remembered her quiet reserve and sudden, unexpectedly gutsy laugh. More than anything, he remembered the evening they had made such exquisite, liberating love on the first night of the ill-fated cruise, and how triumphant, loving and womanly she had been afterwards.

He realized he had been standing still for quite a long time. He brushed the rain out of his eyes and the unsettling memories out of his mind. He'd better head back to the hotel.

He straightened his shoulders. What was he doing, alone on a rain-soaked beach, mooning like a ten-year-old? And wallowing in self-pity, because he and Andrea had had a minor disagreement? He started jogging along the dunes. He would go back to the inn, buy Andrea flowers in the lobby, have a hot shower and pass the rest of the afternoon in peace. Probably by now she had cooled down as well. Perhaps if the rain stopped by nightfall, they could venture out somewhere for dinner.

He bought an armful of daisies for her. They were not Andrea's type of flower, but today they somehow seemed right. They looked fresh and unpretentious. He took the elevator, then walked down the hallway to their room and let himself in with his key.

Andrea was standing nude in the center of the room. The radio was blaring and she was dancing alone, lazily and sinuously. She held a drink in her hand.

"Come in, come in. The daring explorer has finally returned from his global travels. Neither rain nor snow nor sleet nor dark of night shall stay this stud from his appointed—"

"What the hell are you doing, Andrea? Have you been sitting here drinking all afternoon?"

"Sitting here? No. What a silly idea. I'm not sitting here—can't you see that? I'm da-a-an-cing!" She tried to execute a pirouette, lost her balance, and steadied herself against the foot of the bed.

"Come on, Andrea, let's have a cold shower." He grabbed her arm and headed for the bathroom.

"Both of us?" she asked kittenishly.

"Yes, both of us. All right." After being in the rain, the last thing he wanted was a cold shower, but he also did not want to argue with her.

After she got out of the shower, she fell immediately asleep and he was grateful. Let her sleep it off. Maybe when she woke up, she'd have come to her senses and they could salvage at least a part of the evening.

He turned on the television set and absently watched the tiny figures move meaninglessly across the screen. What a hell of a mess.

## Chapter 29

Since she had been working at the Mermaid, Meg had accumulated a decent, if not extensive, wardrobe. But as she flicked through the dresses in her closet, nothing seemed quite right for the evening with Johnny Pack. She had no idea where they would go, but assumed they would be having dinner somewhere.

She had been extremely frugal since working at the bar. Her take-home pay was more than sufficient for her needs and she had several hundred dollars in a bank account. She had not tried to acquire credit cards because she knew proof of identification would be impossible. But her checkbook should be sufficient for her shopping. She tucked it into her straw handbag and left her room.

Collins Avenue consisted of block after block of the smartest boutiques in Miami, an extension of Bal Harbour and Palm Beach. Or were they an extension of it? In any case, the shops were exclusive and expensive. Meg headed for one whose clothes she had always admired—Trout's. Its interior was cool and understated; the dark wall paneling, brass sconces and beige carpet served as an unobtrusive background for the clothes. The atmosphere was vaguely European.

"May I help you, Madam?" The voice was smoothly modulated, British.

Meg turned. "Oh—yes. I'd like to see something for evening. Not—er, formal, but just to wear to dinner."

The blue-haired saleswoman took in every detail of Meg's appearance without seeming to notice it. She said coolly, "Sit over here, please. I'll be back in just a moment."

She reappeared with four dresses. Meg asked hesitantly, "What size are these?"

"You're an eight, are you not, Madam?" Meg nodded. "These are your size."

Meg examined the dresses. One was turquoise, a color she had never liked. A second was a filmy summer black, but Meg was not in the mood for black. The third was white linen and, though it was undeniably lovely, Meg thought it too impractical. The fourth was a smoky plum color, almost indeterminate in its subtlety. She fell in love with it at once. "I'd like to try this one, please."

"Of course. This way, please." The woman led her into a small fitting room and discreetly disappeared. The room was walled on all four sides with mirrors. Meg looked at her mirrored image. The dress was perfect. Its bodice was closely fitted, the skirt a whispering fall. The neckline slashed straight across her throat in front, but in back swooped into a low cascade almost to her waist.

The saleswoman magically reappeared.

"This is perfect, I think," Meg said.

"Very nice indeed. It's a de la Renta."

"Oh—how much is it?"

The saleswoman examined the coded tag. "Four-fifty," she said offhandedly.

"Four hundred fifty dollars?" Meg was incredulous.

"Yes, Madam," the woman responded coolly.

The saleswoman was not unkind, and the openness of Meg's shocked reaction was refreshing. "Of course, you'd look charming no matter what you wore. There's another dress which arrived just yesterday. Let me show you that one." She returned with a pale beige jersey. While it was not as spectacular as the plum-colored creation, Meg felt it would do quite nicely. Its lines were simple and graceful, and the color was becoming to her tawny skin.

Its price tag of ninety dollars was still extravagant but affordable, and Meg walked out with the box tucked under her arm. As she left the shop and continued down the broad palm-lined avenue, she decided she would never be able to spend nearly five hundred dollars for a dress. It seemed wrong, no matter how much money one had. Besides, she had better plans for her money. She stopped at the window of a camera shop. Her eyes gleamed as she looked at the wares. She had been reading about a new Nikon, just on the market, which was surprisingly inexpensive. She was tempted to go in the shop and ask to examine one, but restrained herself. She had done enough shopping for one afternoon and she must get dressed.

Once back in her room, she decided to have a leisurely bath. Then she remembered the dozens of white roses in her tub. She ran upstairs to the utility room and wheedled four tall vases out of the housekeeper. After she had arranged the flowers, she could not help but laugh. The reckless lushness of the floral display was so at odds with the cramped little room that the roses looked as though they had wandered in by accident.

She dressed carefully, again noting the fit of the dress with approval. At five minutes after six, someone tapped softly at the door, and she opened it to Johnny Pack.

He smelled of an expensive after-shave—that was her first reaction. Then she noticed his masterfully tailored summerweight gabardine suit. "We're almost twins," she cried, with nervous cheerfulness. She indicated the nearly identical colors they were wearing.

"Yes, I see we are," he smiled. "Something in common already."

He led her to a silver-gray sedan and helped her into

it. "I'd like to take you to a place a few miles out of town," he said.

"What sort of place?" she asked ingenuously, not realizing her question could be construed as rude.

Johnny Pack laughed. He was trying to imagine any of the other women he knew blurting out such a direct and spontaneous question. "A restaurant. I think you'll enjoy it."

"Oh."

They spoke little during the half-hour drive to the restaurant. Meg had no idea where his interests lay and Johnny Pack, although he had felt completely comfortable with her from the moment of her naive inquiry, was reluctant to launch into a conversation of trivial small talk. He sensed this relationship was going to be too important for that.

The restaurant to which he took her overlooked Biscayne Bay, between Miami and Coral Gables. It was built on a jetty in the water and was glassed-in on three sides. It was like dining in a transparent ship at sea. As they were seated at a window table, Meg felt a nudge of recollection. What was there about the look of the dark night sea? Then, almost at once, the memory receded— impossible to hold onto, like a drop of mercury in one's hand.

The place was enchanting. On each pink damask tablecloth was a miniature candelabrum holding five pink tapers and a small vase containing one perfect gardenia. The flatware was not silver but golden, and the china was white and gold. Each place was set with an imposing array of tableware, including three wine goblets of assorted shapes and sizes. The dining chairs were upholstered in a dusky rose velvet. The effect was dazzlingly romantic.

Johnny Pack inquired smoothly, "May I order for you?" Food was the one social area where he was completely in command, even in the company of the most overpowering woman. "Perhaps an aperitif?"

"Yes, I—what do you recommend?"

"Why not one of their exotic tropical specialties? Something served in a pineapple or coconut?"

"I—it sounds terribly sticky." Meg wanted to be agreeable, but she didn't feel she could cope with a huge sugary drink before dinner.

Johnny Pack shot her an approving look. "Very wise. I've never cared for sweet drinks, but many women do. Why don't we settle for champagne?"

"Fine." For once, Meg really looked forward to a drink. She had no idea how she was going to make dinner-table conversation with this man for an entire evening. She had never been exposed to anyone remotely like him. Their previous meeting had been unusual, to put it mildly. Who knew what the second would bring?

The champagne was brought promptly in a frosty silver bucket and two tulip-shaped goblets were set before them. As the waiter poured the champagne, her eye caught the label on the bottle: Bollinger. Again, a faint bell sounded in her head. It was the same sensation which had assailed her as they entered and she looked out into the moonless sea. Something stirred in the back of her mind—almost, but not quite, a memory. It was both intriguing and frustrating. She was almost sure that Bollinger champagne had been a part of a very important moment in her past. If only she could cling to the intuition, materialize it into a specific background, with flesh-and-blood people. No, not people. *Person*. One person. But who?

The echo of memory was lost. Conceding defeat, she reached for the wine goblet, but before she could bring it to her lips, Johnny Pack reached across the table and touched his glass to hers. The faint crystal *ping* hung in the air like a promise.

"You've been somewhere very far away, I think, Peggy," he said quietly. "In your mind, I mean." His voice held conviction without accusation.

Meg was startled by his perception. "Oh, just daydreaming, I suppose."

"Of some—lover? Of happier days?"

"Oh, no. Nothing like that. Honestly." She was accutely uncomfortable. She did not want to go into the tortuous complexities of her baffling loss of memory tonight. She changed the subject with sudden false brightness. "Oh—I forgot to thank you for those beautiful roses! But you needn't have sent so many. Of course," she amended lamely, "you needn't have sent any at all."

His laugh was full-bodied, a rarity for Johnny Pack. "It gave me a great deal of pleasure. There are so few women who deserve the purity of white roses." He stirred in his seat and there was an awkward pause.

Through sheer nervousness, Meg began chattering inconsequentially. "I went shopping this afternoon and saw the loveliest dress. I can't even tell you what color it was—it was like purple smoke, in a way."

"Where did you see it?" he inquired casually.

"A place on Collins Avenue. Trout's—one of those very exclusive places. I've never shopped there before, and I probably never will again."

"Why not?"

Meg laughed. "The dress was four-hundred-fifty dollars. Need I say more?"

Johnny Pack smiled. She was an adorable woman—girl-woman. Her surprisingly robust laugh indicated a spontaneous sense of humor beneath the shy veneer. It was a disarming combination.

"Ah," he said lightly, "our *coquille St. Jacques*."

The scallops, brimming in a sherry-touched cream

sauce, were delicious. The next course was *pompano en papillote*—a white-fleshed fish baked in parchment, which gave it a flavor unlike any Meg had tasted.

"I hadn't realized how hungry I was," she said. "Or maybe it's just that this food is so good."

"We must send our compliments to the chef."

"Yes. And to the gentleman who ordered it." She indicated Johnny Pack. She suddenly felt quite giddy.

He nodded. "Thank you." His tone shifted abruptly. "Peggy."

Something in his voice made her lay down her fork immediately. "Yes?" she asked hesitantly. She knew the conversation had become dead serious.

"I'm afraid the other day, when I broached the unusual arrangements I had in mind for you, I may have alarmed you by my suddenness. I mean, by coming on too strong, as they say."

"It's just that—well, I was taken by surprise. It isn't the usual kind of thing—"

"I know that. I think I overwhelmed you. Tonight I'd like to explain in a little more detail just what I intended. Without going into all the personal reasons, let me just say that I need, at certain social functions, to be accompanied by an attractive and charming woman." He saw the question in her eyes and forestalled it. "I don't want to be married—again for reasons I won't go into. But as I told you, I will never make any demands on you that you're unwilling to fulfilll. And if you ever wish to end the arrangement, you may. Johnny Pack is a man of his word. Not even my worst enemy would deny that."

"But, Mr. Pack—" It was the first time she had called him anything and he raised a hand in quick protest.

"Johnny, please, Peggy. We should at least be on a first-name basis."

"Johnny." But the name sounded alien on her tongue. She hesitated, then continued without using any name. "I'm just totally perplexed. I mean, you don't know me—"

"I know you very well. There's nothing like watching someone handle a trying job to find out what that person's made of." He was very, very sure of himself as a character evaluator. His judgment had never proven wrong.

"What exactly would I be expected to do?" Her voice was still puzzled. The pieces somehow didn't fit together.

"But I've told you. It's extremely simple. You would simply accompany me to social engagements . . . parties, dinners and so forth. You would be hostess on those occasions when I was expected to entertain my—my colleagues. And that is the sum total. No physical involvement at all would be entailed."

Meg sat in stunned silence. He seemed quite sincere—she could not imagine that this was some elaborate and convoluted kind of seduction. She was sure that Johnny Pack would have found that kind of ploy unnecessary in any case. At length she found her voice again. "Where—where would I live?"

"In New York. Occasional trips to Miami, Las Vegas, a few other cities might be involved. But principally, New York."

New York. Suddenly the dream of the previous night flashed into her brain with burning clarity. She remembered the feeling of the tall buildings around her, arching miles over her head. For no rational reason, she had been sure she was in Manhattan. Had she lived in New York? If so, perhaps if she returned there, she could find some trace of who Peggy Arden was.

Johnny Pack sat back and watched the wheels turn in her mind. He had a pretty good idea of what she was thinking. He had, of course, no earthly idea of whether she had been a New Yorker. But if she considered it a possibility, as she apparently did, she might be more willing to accept his unorthodox offer. It would give her an avenue to further the search for herself.

She remained in deep thought and he did not intrude. During the course of the evening, their perceptions of each other had altered sharply. Johnny Pack was now unwilling to set a definite deadline for her decision because he knew instinctively that she could, in time, mean much more to him than any other woman ever had. Meg, who after their initial meeting had considered him a cold and frightening man, now sensed an odd vulnerability in him which abolished any trace of fear on her part.

"I'll be in Miami a few more days. Why don't you think about it?"

"All right." Meg found herself agreeing before she realized the implications of that agreement. If she were going to sever this strange relationship, this moment would be the perfect time to do it. He had already stated, and stated unequivocally, that he would make no demands of her that she was reluctant to comply with. Why hadn't she simply declined to see him again? But the reason she now said yes when she felt that perhaps she should have been saying no explained why Johnny Pack had reached his present eminence in his organization. He was a master persuader without either himself or the other party being consciously aware of it.

On the drive home, Johnny was content to let her have her thoughts to herself. He had been looking only for a female companion. After this evening, he realized he had found much more. If he were capable of normal man-woman love, Peggy Arden would fill that place in his heart. Perhaps someday, it might work out that way.

He parked the car expertly and walked Meg through

the hotel lobby and up to her room. As she let herself in with her key, he said, "I'll call you tomorrow."

"Yes," said Meg. Then, "Oh, you can't. I've only a house phone in my room."

"All right. What time do you get up?"

"Usually about eleven."

"Right. Goodnight."

"Goodnight—Johnny. It was a—an awfully nice evening."

"Right. Goodnight."

The next day at precisely noon, Meg opened the door to a knock and found a deliveryman from Trout's. Inside the box he handed her was the plum-colored dress There was no card.

# Chapter 30

When Johnny Pack boarded the big 747 that left Miami on a Friday evening in mid-April, Meg was with him. She looked out the window and watched the white skyscraper hotels, the turquoise ocean and the scalloped shoreline disappear. The plane banked and circled and the mirage-like city was no more.

She felt a turbulent pull of emotions. She was leaving the only life she remembered and plunging into an unknown world with a man she had seen, really, on only three occasions. If a sane observer had known only the external facts, he would have thought her a lunatic. But if one had been privy to the gentleness and consideration with which Johnny treated her when they were together, the onlooker would have been forced to revise his opinion.

First, there had been the staggering gift of the plum-colored dress. Every day thereafter, at exactly noon, a single white rose was brought to her door by a uniformed messenger. Otherwise, there was no communication from Johnny Pack. Meg continued her work at the Mermaid, but her wonder grew at his mysterious absence. One week lengthened into another, then another. The single white roses continued to arrive, but Johnny Pack himself did not.

More than a month had passed since their dinner at the seaside restaurant when Meg went into work one Thursday afternoon and found Johnny Pack at his habitual corner table. She stared at him as if seeing an apparition.

"Hello, Peggy."

"Oh! I didn't expect to see you. I mean—"

He came to her and took her hand lightly in his. "I had to go back to New York unexpectedly. There was a business crisis of sorts. But it's getting straightened out. Besides," his dark eyes pierced her own, "I thought you might need some time to yourself. However, since I'm back . . . don't you think it's time I saw you in that dress you say is made of purple smoke?"

"Do you think it's quite suitable for serving cocktails in the Mermaid?" she asked with a flash of humor. Suddenly, her heart had lightened. She herself was surprised by the sweep of elation that filled her.

His hawklike features turned serious. "Would you see me tonight, Peggy? I'm sure Callios can find a substitute."

She hesitated briefly. "Well, I'll ask him if it's—"

"There's no need. It's already arranged."

"What if I had said no?" she countered, her indignation only partly feigned.

"Then the substitute would have had to find her evening's employment elsewhere," he smiled.

They dined on a starlit roof terrace atop one of the larger hotels in Miami proper. From their vantage point, the hotels on Miami Beach were like a vast tiara, set with imperial jewels of light.

"You know, Johnny," she found she now felt comfortable with the name, "you've never told me where you work."

"An oversight." He brought out a business card from the thin alligator billford. She examined it with interest. "Executive Vice President - Marathon Funding." The title and company name were followed by a Park Avenue address.

"What does this Marathon Funding do?" she asked.

"Oh, it's too complicated to go into. It's a holding

company for ventures that require commercial funding—that sort of thing."

She nodded vaguely, trying to appear knowledgeable. "I see."

"It's too beautiful a night to talk about me and my dullish business career. Would you like to dance?"

There was a small bandshell on the terrace and a six-piece dance orchestra filled the warm night with discreetly muted beguines and tangoes.

"I wouldn't, really, Johnny. Do you mind?"

"Not at all," he answered, and she felt his smile of relief was genuine. "I much prefer to look at you. The dress, by the way, is stunning. More accurately, you are stunning in it."

Now, in the plane, Meg remembered the remark and a faint smile lifted a corner of her mouth. She had known from that moment of gallantry she would be on the plane with Johnny today. Or perhaps she had known from the moment yesterday afternoon when she saw him as she walked into the Mermaid. There had been something in his posture. He was sitting patiently, but with that spring-like tautness just below the surface. He exuded both strength and vulnerability, a combination difficult to resist.

She realized her throat was dry with excitement. Johnny was going through papers in his briefcase—papers he'd told her he must review carefully before they landed in New York. Dinner was served, but neither of them touched it. Johnny hated airline food and Meg was too much on edge to eat. She thought the sensation she felt at the moment was probably much like an actor feels just before going onstage in a demanding role on opening night. Elation and panic. On the threshold of triumph or disaster.

After they landed, they were led into a private anteroom at Kennedy Airport at Johnny's request. Meg wondered at the royal treatment—she was sure total privacy was not proffered the average passenger.

"Why are we waiting here, Johnny?"

"Just stay put. I have to make some phone calls."

"We can bring you a phone, sir," said an alert nearby attendant.

"No, thanks. I'll use a public phone."

It was more than half an hour before he returned and they took a cab into the city.

"Er, Johnny—where will I be staying?"

"I'll show you." He seemed preoccupied and she did not persist further.

The taxi pulled up before a steel-and-glass skyscraper on upper Fifth Avenue. The doorman rushed out to see to the bags and Johnny led Meg through an elegant lobby and into a paneled elevator, which rose quickly and silently to the thirty-first floor. He led her into a very large room carpeted in white, with pale blue draperies at the oversized windows, their swags cascading in extravagant ripples to the floor. The furniture was ornate—a sofa upholstered in blue-and-lavender brocade, a magnificent Chinese chest beneath the windows, a fragile, gold-leafed desk. On the low, inlaid-wood coffee table was an outsized bowl of fresh fruit, and white roses were in tall vases everywhere. Outside, the illuminated city glowed with brilliant scattered dots of light from adjoining buildings.

Johnny looked at her questioningly. "Do you like it?" There was almost a shyness in his question.

For a moment Meg did not speak. How could she tell him that although it was probably the loveliest room she had ever seen, it was completely foreign to her natural taste? She could not. He was too obviously eager to have it please her.

"Yes. It's exquisite, of course." She hoped she was able to inject a suitable degree of enthusiasm in her voice.

"Good." That established, Johnny at once became businesslike. "Well, you can explore the rest of it on your own. There are two bedrooms—it might be necessary, occasionally, for me to stay over. There's a small kitchen—you'll find it supplied with orange juice and coffee. Anything else you'd like you can order up from downstairs. I've got to run."

"You're leaving—now?" She was dumbfounded.

"I have to, Peggy. I have to be at a very important meeting in—" he glanced at his watch—"exactly forty-five minutes. It's out on the Island."

Meg protested uncomprehendingly. "But it's ten o'clock at night, Johnny! I thought we could go out together and walk around a little bit—"

He picked up his briefcase with quick efficiency. "I'm sorry. I'll call you tomorrow. If you'd like to see a movie or anything, just have the doorman put you in a cab. Goodnight, Peggy."

Meg was left alone in the middle of the room. Already fatigued from the trip and now discovering she had been left alone in a strange city, she felt slightly disoriented. When they got off the plane she had been ravenous, but now she had no appetite.

She wandered through the bedrooms and found them furnished much like the cavernous living room. She glanced into the compact but well-equipped kitchen. What in God's name would she do with herself rattling around in these beautifully furnished but somehow lonely rooms?

Restlessly, she took a warm shower and got into a robe. The thin material did not take the chill out of he bones. April in New York is hardly midsummer, she thought wryly. She was not prepared for the cool briskness of the air she had felt briefly getting into and out of the cab. Tomorrow she would have to get some warmer clothes. New York-weight clothes.

She opened one of the sliding closet doors to begin hanging up her things. Inside were half a dozen women's garments. How careless, she thought, that a place of this caliber would not have had the room checked. Then she saw the note pinned to one of the sleeves.

> "Peggy:
> I had my secretary buy these. I think they'll fit. Hope they'll tide you over until you have time to do your own shopping.
>
> Johnny"

There were three dresses, a suit, a nightgown and a satin-quilted robe. There were suitable shoes for each of the dresses. She put on the satin robe and sat down thoughtfully on the edge of the bed.

Johnny Pack was undoubtedly the most puzzling man she had ever met. It was fantastically considerate of him to have these clothes for her. And yet he had left for a meeting late at night with little explanation. There was something about it all that didn't make sense. She got up and restlessly began to move up and down the room. Then a thought occurred to her. If she had indeed lived in New York, shouldn't she try to find out whether she could find any familiar landmarks? *Yes*, she thought, *and the sooner the better*.

Weak with excitement, she put on the suit and surveyed herself in the mirrored door. It fit perfectly—she could not have made a better choice herself. The pearl-gray fabric was meltingly soft. Looking at the label inside the jacket she found that it was cashmere. No wonder. She checked her handbag to see how much money Johnny had thrust into it while they were on the plane. Three hundred dollars. That should take care of walking-around money for the evening, she thought with a helpless head-shake at his generosity.

She took the elevator downstairs and the doorman found a cab immediately.

"Where to?" the cabby asked briskly.

"I—just want to see some of the city. Could you just drive around for a little while?"

He put the car in gear, then stepped on the brake and turned to look at her. "Just drive around the city, huh?"

"Yes. I've—never been to New York before. I just want to see different sections of it."

"Different sections," he repeated. "Sure. Be glad to, lady." He started the car down the avenue. "Want me to point out things along the way? Or would you rather just ask me things as we go?"

Meg was inordinately grateful that she had fallen into the hands of a congenial tour guide. "Oh, yes, please. Point out things. You see, I don't *think* I know the city, but—" What had possessed her to make that foolish remark?

The cabby turned in his seat and peered at her sharply. She didn't look drunk, but—.

"What's that building?" asked Meg quickly, pointing to her right.

"Empire State. See, we're headed straight downtown."

They drove in silence for a few moments.

"How's your luck been today?" he finally asked.

"What do you mean?" Meg was puzzled.

"It's Friday the thirteenth. My luck's been rotten. I'm beginning to believe in that kind of stuff. Had a flat before I even started out, a guy stiffed me for his fare—" The driver went on reciting the litany of woes which had befallen him on this hapless day.

Meg saw the lighted arch directly ahead of her with a

tingling jolt of recognition. "What's that?" There was a tremor of excitement in her voice.

"Oh, Washington Square Arch. The beginning of Greenwich Village." He turned again to look at her. "You've heard of Greenwich Village, ain't you?"

"Yes. Greenwich Village." Meg's head was spinning. She felt an overwhelming sense of *déjà vu*. She knew without doubt she had been here before. "Could you drive around this area for awhile? Just drive around slowly?"

"Sure thing." The cabby cruised the streets slowly, noting points of interest as they passed. This was a great way to make a buck, he thought with satisfaction. A beautiful, polite little lady who had no interest in watching the meter. No better combination than that.

"What's what?" his passenger questioned sharply. She was a little strange, though, he had to admit. So excitable all of a sudden. He wondered idly if she were on drugs. You never knew with some of these rich-looking broads.

"What's that? Which place you talking about?"

"Those buildings we just passed. Back on the right." She sounded out of breath.

"New School, I think they call it. It's not a regular high school or nothing. Some kind of special deal for adults."

"New School," she repeated slowly. "New School," she said again.

"Yep. Now here on your left is—"

"Stop, please! I'll walk from here." She got out of the cab and slammed the door with violent nervousness. Once outside, she remembered the fare and spun back to him. "How much is that?"

"Five seventy-five, lady." He was nonplussed to lose his goldmine so suddenly.

She thrust a ten at his outstretched hand. "That's all

right—keep the change," she yelled after him and started down the street, running awkwardly in her high-heeled shoes.

She stopped in front of the main entrance to the green-and-buff building. She walked slowly up the concrete walk. Had she traversed these steps before? A wisp of a memory floated back. She seemed to hear the echo of a Germanic accent making a rude remark. It had something to do with a camera, she thought. A broken camera? She should have brought the new Nikon Johnny had got for her. No. This was not the time to concentrate on anything except remembering—trying to recall what this particular place had meant to her.

A rush of cold April wind skittered through the still bare trees. "B-R-R," she muttered to herself, then stopped short. Why had she said it like that, spelling out the letters? It was eerie. It was also maddening, for try as she might, the ghosts of the past remained just that—elusive fragments of feeling.

She looked at her watch. It was after midnight. Except for an occasional dog-walker, the street was entirely empty. She'd better be getting home. Home! A palace of empty rooms. She had never felt so alone, so bereft of meaningful communion with another human being. Chilled and dispirited, she walked to the avenue ahead, where she could see a steady stream of traffic, and hailed a passing cab.

## Chapter 31

After the Bermuda wedding trip, Jeff became increasingly absorbed in his work at the Cavullo shop. He and two other photographers began discussing a collaboration on a book of geometric photographs of New York street scenes. The book would be a pictorial essay of the poetry of such unpoetic objects as playground fences, garbage cans and cobblestone streets. The idea was to photograph them in such extreme close-ups that the pictures would be only a series of geometric forms. Cavullo himself was interested in the project and, though such photography was not his forte, he scrutinized, with a flawless eye, each candidate for inclusion.

Jeff's leg was now almost completely back to normal. It was only after a hard-fought tennis game with Timmy (who now sometimes bested him) that he realized that he tired much more quickly than before the accident.

Andrea's horses were now back from Florida and took up most of her day. Her favorite, the gray gelding Striker, had a cough for a week and she was up early each morning, cross-examining the veterinarian and berating the groom for having carelessly exposed the animal to a draft.

Since the exhibition in the Bermuda hotel room, Jeff had never seen her drunk. But her drinking pattern had subtly altered. She sipped drinks very slowly throughout the day. At least that was her way of life on weekends, and weekdays were obviously no different. When he was home in time for dinner, Andrea would make a valiant effort to enter the conversation at table but, once the demitasses were cleared, she would yawningly excuse herself and disappear to her room. Since their schedules were now so divergent, separate rooms were an arrangement mutually agreed upon.

On the nights when Jeff was not home for the evening meal, Timmy was left to his own devices. Jeff worried about this, but the boy seemed to be surviving quite well. He had somewhere picked up an old Corvette engine and had managed to intall it on the back utility porch. On most evenings, he could be found with it, tinkering and polishing with single-minded dedication. It seemed that engineering was truly to be his vocation in life. His grades in school showed continued improvement, and Jeff had reason to hope the boy's flirtation with drugs had been a brief and now-forgotten affair.

One Sunday afternoon, Jeff and Timmy had just come back from a hike through Long Island's glorious springtime woods. They were crossing a field that adjoined the Rosehill property when they saw Andrea almost literally flying down the lane on Striker. Her blonde hair was streaming behind her and she had not bothered to put on riding clothes, but was in a shirt and jeans. She was goading the horse on with sharp flicks of her crop. They both watched the hard, punishing gallop with astonishment.

As she came nearer, she saw them standing by the gate that led to the stables and drew the horse up. The animal's neck and hindquarters were awash with sweat. She looked at them defiantly and grinned.

"I should have been a jockey! I'm sure we must have done five furlongs in about a minute. He's a damn good jumper, too."

Jeff was unsmiling. "I don't know what you were doing in how many furlongs, but you sure as hell were risking your neck—as well as the horse's. That lane is full of ruts and you can't always even see them."

"Oh, pooh, killjoy. Striker knows that lane like the back of his hand—if he had a hand. Clay!" she yelled for the groom. "Come take Striker. Give him a good walk to cool him down."

The groom led the horse away, his face carefully bland, and Jeff, Andrea and Timmy started back toward the house. Halfway there, Timmy had an idea. "Hey! Why don't we all go to the club for a swim?"

Jeff looked at Andrea. It would probably be good for them, he thought, to do something as a family group. It seemed a long time since they had.

"Sorry, baby," Andrea said to her son, carelessly ruffling his hair. "I'd like to take you up on that, but it's almost cocktail time. I'm going to wrap myself in a shower and then around a dry martini."

Jeff threw her a sidelong glance. She seemed to have already "wrapped herself around" several. He had hoped they could have a pleasant evening, but if she kept drinking she would be out of it by dinnertime.

"Jeff?" Timmy's voice was wistful. "How about you—are you game?"

Jeff sighed. The hike had left him pretty much all in. "Well, don't expect me to race you fifty laps, but sure, Timmy. I'm game."

The water proved refreshing and Jeff was glad he'd joined Timmy. As it happened, Timmy didn't really need his companionship, because he was introduced to somebody's visiting cousin Susan, a sassy thirteen-year-old charmer who captivated him right away.

On the way home, Timmy was full of excited conversation. "Maybe I could have a party, Jeff, and invite Susan and her cousin. Do you think?"

"We might be able to arrange that. How long is Susan going to be in town?"

"She's moving here! That's what's so great. Her

dad's been transferred here."

"Well, she certainly ought to be properly introduced to polite society," Jeff said gravely.

"That's what I thought. We'll ask Mother when we get home, okay?"

"Okay. And then it's back to the drawing board for you. Haven't you got some homework you ought to get done before tomorrow?"

"Yeah."

But when they reached the house, Andrea had already gone to her bedroom. Jeff knocked on her door and, getting no answer, stuck his head in. She was lying nude on the bed with an almost empty glass on the floor beside her.

"Andrea, we're home." Jeff tried to keep his voice pleasant. "It's almost dinner time. Why don't you wash your face and join us?"

She frowned and squinted at him. "I don't feel good. And I don't want any goddam dinner."

He left the room without another word, closing the door noiselessly behind him.


During the days that followed her arrival in New York, Meg found herself almost completely on her own. In the first two weeks of her stay, she had seen Johnny Pack only twice. On those occasions he had taken her out to dinner and apologized profusely for his neglect, promising that as soon as the present business crisis was over, he would be able to entertain her properly.

"But I don't understand, Johnny. I mean, it isn't even during business hours you go to all these meetings."

"No," he admitted, "but we're—we're taking over a couple of companies abroad. We have to transact business on their time schedule. That means our hours are crazy. Uh, how does the *veau blanquette* sound to you? Okay? Good, that's what we'll have." And the conversation drifted inevitably away from his business life.

Meg had been back to the New School and the Village area several times, but her memory never seemed to go beyond the blurred impression that she had been there before.

One early evening in late May when Johnny was again otherwise engaged, she gravitated once more to Greenwich Village. She had dismissed the taxi at the lower end of Fifth Avenue and was strolling about the streets aimlessly. It was one of those New York days when the air was warm and hazy. She could see the twin vertical blocks of the World Trade Center, their tops shrouded by the smoky mist. Breaking through it were pink streaks of sunset. Her camera was slung over her shoulder and she stopped on the street to try to capture the subtle melting colors of the skyline. She tried several exposures, hoping that one of them would produce the elusive perfect shot.

Snapping the camera back into its case, she realized she was very hungry, then remembered she had had no lunch. She looked for a place where she could have a quick snack. A few doors down, there was a bar and restaurant which looked fairly respectable. She walked inside and found herself in a long, narrow room with a handsome mahogany bar on the left. A pang of familiarity stirred within her, but she told herself it was simply because it looked like half the other small cafes in that neighborhood. She sat down in one of the high-backed booths.

The room was almost empty. Apparently the sandy-haired bartender was doubling as waiter, for he came to her booth with his order pad ready.

"What'll you have? Wait a minute! You're—God, I

haven't seen you for ages! How are you?"

How could she explain her dilemma to someone who to her was a total stranger? Maybe—just maybe—she wouldn't have to. "I'm fine. I've been out of town. How are *you*? I'm sorry, I've forgotten your name." She could not believe she was mouthing the evasions so smoothly.

"Great. I'm Louie, remember? I used to be a good friend of Jeff's—I mean we compared our photographs."

"Oh. Yes." Then carefully, casually, "How *is* Jeff?"

"I get it," he said with a half-embarrassed shrug, "you're not seeing each other any more. Sorry. I thought maybe you'd both moved away. I haven't seen him, I don't think, since the last time you were in here together."

"About when was that—I can't quite remember."

"Gee, I dunno. Last of the year, I'd say, or around there. I dunno."

She laughed lightly. "You know, you'll think this is silly, but I've forgotten his last name."

He looked at her, disbelief covered with a veneer of politeness. "McAllister."

"Oh, of course. Jeff McAllister." She repeated the name slowly. Did she imagine the lightning-like vision of hazel eyes and auburn hair that vanished almost as soon as it appeared?

"Wait a minute! I think I've still got some of the shots I took of the two of you. Let me check." He scurried away to his cache of photographs behind the bar.

Jeff McAllister. The half-remembered coloring that had appeared only to disappear, the nebulous intuitions of wonderful happiness that were almost memories but not quite—they had a name now. Jeff McAllister.

Louie brought over four snapshots. The first two

were of her alone, her long hair framed in the backlighting, her lips covered with a froth of whipped cream.

"You've cut your hair. I almost didn't recognize you."

Meg looked up at him. She had forgotten he was still there, holding the two other photographs. Slowly, she turned over the snapshot in her hand. The inked-in caption on the back was difficult to read, but slowly she made out the faded lettering: "Meg with Irish Coffee." *Meg*. Her real name was Meg.

She took the other two snapshots with a trembling hand. The face that stared back at her overwhelmed her with a series of kaleidoscopic impressions. There was a feeling of fighting against desperate odds, and then a sense of thrilling triumph. There was a strong remembered sensation of deep love, followed by a feeling of desolation and loss.

She looked at the face for many moments, searching for the key in her mind that would unlock the secret. This was the man—the something—she had been seeking. This was what had made her life as Peggy Arden seem so devastatingly incomplete. Something in the expression behind his eyes was haunted and hidden. It had something to do with his father and his brother. She had no idea how she knew that, but she was positive.

The second photograph was smiling, and gave her an unmistakable feeling of being wrapped in the security of his devotion. She tried to blink away the hot tears that sprang to her eyes.

"So you know—have you any idea where he is now?"

"Nope. As I said, he hasn't been in here since you have. I thought maybe you'd both jumped ship and decided to live in South America."

"Louie. Do you have time to sit down with me for a minute or two? I want to tell you something, and then ask you a lot of things."

Louie's eyes swept the room—still almost deserted. He slid into the opposite side of the booth and said with a baffled but willing expression, "Shoot."

When Meg left McBurney's a little more than an hour later, she went directly to the New School. The solution to the puzzle was not complete, but several important pieces had fallen into place. During the short walk she reviewed the newly discovered facts: her first name was Meg but she did not yet know her last name; she had been involved with a man named Jeff McAllister, and she knew she had been very deeply involved; they had attended a photography class at the New School which met on Tuesday and Thursday evenings. Jeff McAllister was a stockbroker, but Louie could not remember the name of his firm.

She and Jeff had left for a cruise to Venezuela, departing around the first of the year.

Her only source of further information was the New School. Surely they could give her more information. When she approached the registrar's office, she put a hand against her ribs to control the wildness of her heart. But the office had closed for the night and two students in the hall told her it would not be open until business hours on the following day.

The next morning she was waiting outside the door when Mrs. Buxton, the registrar, appeared for work. Meg told her without preamble or apology the facts of her situation and the woman, once her skepticism had been allayed, was helpful. She produced Jeff's records at once, including his home address and telephone number.

"You don't know your last name. Heavens, that *is* a challenge. But we'll manage." She began a painstaking search through the files. Students of photography were all filed in one section, and the search did not take as long as Meg was afraid it might. As she waited, she felt as if her entire rib cage was enclosed in iron tubing. She could breathe only with great difficulty.

Mrs. Buxton went through perhaps twenty folders, then paused and extracted one. "This has to be it, I think. Gardner, Meg." She handed her the folder. "There's no other Meg or Margaret here."

"Gardner," Meg repeated. "Meg Gardner. Yes! I'm sure you're right!"

Examining the folder, she could find no employer's name listed, but she did find her East Side apartment address. She wondered if the apartment had been left intact or dismantled by an angry landlord. But there was nothing of value in it anyway. Somehow she was sure of that.

She wrote her and Jeff's addresses and phones on a slip of paper. She noted with wonderment that her handwriting looked spidery and unsteady, as if it had been executed by a very old woman. Then she thanked the registrar, left the building and raced to the nearest telephone to call Jeff's number. Her fingers were trembling so badly it took her three attempts to make the connection. When at last she did, the phone rang endlessly, forlornly. Then she remembered it was ten in the morning. Of course! He would be at work; she would try again that evening.

Meg dialed his apartment day after day but there was no answer. At last she realized the number she possessed must be obsolete. She had seemingly reached a dead end.

Her memory of Jeff, her recall of his total character and personality, did not return with full impact until she was deeply asleep one night, when some buried subconscious instinct took over. He was standing before her and their love for each other was as palpable as the field in which they stood—a field of billowing grass and sheltering trees. The sunshine was incredibly brilliant, but not hot. They were laughing, tumbling, running, as innocent as children in a sinless paradise.

Bathed in the afterglow of the dream, she awoke to full consciousness, but magically the memory remained with her, intact. Jeff McAllister was now as real and close as her own body. The details of their past were hazy, but the memory of their love was absolute.

A terrifying thought jolted into her consciousness. If she had been found alone in the sea, had Jeff been found at all? It was inconceivable that he had not. No. She would not believe that until she had incontrovertible proof. Her next step was to find him, however long it took and in whatever way she could.

# Chapter 32

The private detective had no trouble at all. The information Meg gave him was a blueprint compared to the snippets of data he usually had to work with. On the late afternoon of the third day, he called her and asked her to meet him in a nearby bar. Over the years, he had learned to meet clients only in public.

Meg was there before him. He entered with a file of papers and spread them on the table. He told Meg she had grown up in a small town called Martinsville, Georgia. Her last living relative, an aunt, Bess H. Tilton, had died two months ago on March 23. What little estate there was she had willed to her church.

"I'm sorry to be the one to tell ya." His stubby fingers riffled the papers nervously. He didn't want to have to cope with a hysterical woman. But the thin, beautiful girl opposite him sat dry-eyed and unmoving. Only a slight tremor of her lips betrayed emotion. He continued, relieved.

"Now about this Jeff McAllister. It turns out he's in partnership with a Cavullo—Ricardo Cavullo. They have a photography store in the East 50's. Here's the address. He's usually there from around ten in the morning until eight or nine at night."

"Mr. Draco, I really appreciate this."

"Glad to be of help. Well, you can keep these copies, see if there's anything else of interest." He pushed the folder across to her and looked pointedly at his watch.

"Oh, yes," she said bemusedly, "I must settle your bill. How much do I owe you?"

"Twelve hundred."

"Twelve hundred. I don't know if I have that much—" Johnny had opened a bank account in her name. But since it was only for incidentals, he had considered a thousand-dollar deposit sufficient and she had thought it excessive. "But don't worry," she hurried on, "I can get it without any problem. But I may have to wait a day or two."

She did not have a number where Johnny could be reached; he insisted he would keep in touch with her. But he called almost every day; she was sure there would be no problem.

Draco ran a hand through his thinning hair and gave a tired sigh. "How much could you come up with now?"

Meg checked her bankbook. "Nine hundred? Would that be all right?"

"Okay. I'll give you a call in a couple days to collect the rest."

She wrote the check hurriedly, which he stuck into a bulging, untidy wallet. Then he plucked his damp cigar from the ashtray and left. She looked at her watch. Twenty past four. She started to take a cab to the East 50's address, then realized it was only a few blocks away and decided to walk. Perhaps on the way, she could get herself under control. She was shivering violently, though the weather had turned quite warm.

As she walked, she began to remember her Aunt Bess, the images returning in dissociated flashes. She would go to Martinsville soon to try to put together the shredded images of her childhood. But not yet. First, she had to see Jeff McAllister.

The store was not at all like the other mirror-and-chrome boutiques on the street. It was rather like stepping into an old-fashioned living room. On entering, the visitor was welcomed by hanging plants and deeply cushioned chintz sofas and chairs. Meg was too dazed to examine the furnishings closely, but she had a general impression of homey comfort. She took a few steps inside and was met by a smiling young man with thick spectacles and a prominent Adam's apple.

"May I help you?"

She heard herself blurt breathlessly, "Is Jeff here?"

"Mr. McAllister? He's doing some work upstairs. I can't disturb him in the darkroom, but he should be through in about half an hour, if you'd like to wait." He gestured toward the nearest sofa.

Meg nodded dumbly and the young man disappeared. She sank into a corner of the sofa. She thought the pounding of her heart must be audible throughout the store.

The wing back of the sofa hid most of her face from anyone approaching from the rear of the shop. She sensed rather than heard, the footsteps behind her. She should get up at once, she thought, but she could not move.

"Mr. Caldwell said you wanted to see me?" The voice was pleasant, distant.

Meg stood then and turned to face him. At first there was a polite, waiting look on his features. During that split second, when she saw his face, she was overwhelmed by the rush of the past. She remembered the time they had spent in her Lower East Side apartment. She vividly recalled the photography classes. The breath-catching memory of that one perfect night of lovemaking made her gasp. She reached out to steady herself against the arm of the sofa.

"Jeff?" Her voice was a ragged whisper.

Jeff's face slowly changed and she watched it as if in slow motion. The noncommittal mask one uses in confronting a stranger dropped away. Disbelief, suspicion, skepticism, faint recognition, and at last full acceptance of the impossible. She watched the whole range of emotions transform his face in what seemed an eternity, but must have been no more than a few seconds.

"Meg? Meg? God, am I seeing things? Meg?"

"Yes, Jeff. It's Meg."

And they were in each other's arms. They held each other so tightly she thought her heart would surely burst from her body. Neither of them spoke for a long, long moment.

"Meg. I thought you—what happened to you? Where have you been? I thought—"

"Oh, Jeff, it's such a long story. I think I'll have to tell you a little at a time. Otherwise you'll never believe it at all."

"Wait a minute. Let me tell them I'm leaving. I know a place where we can talk. God. Meg."

An hour later, sitting at a back table in a dimly lit hotel bar, Meg stopped talking for the first time and took a long sip of her white wine. Jeff had listened in almost stunned silence to her long narration.

Midway through the story, Meg became conscious of the fact that his eyes were faintly troubled. From time to time, he would glance away, then tap his fingers nervously on the table.

"Well, that's the way it happened. It's staggering, isn't it? Oh, Jeff, throughout the whole thing, when I couldn't really remember anything specific, I knew a part of me was lacking. I knew I had lost something priceless and I hadn't the faintest idea how to get it back." She laughed that glorious, full-throated laugh. "And then, through some kind of crazy miracle, I find myself back in New York and we're together! Can you believe it? I think it's going to take me about a month before it all sinks in. We're actually sitting here together!"

There was a pause before he spoke. "How about your Mr. Pack?"

"Oh. I suppose he'll be sorry. But it really was a business arrangement with him, truly, Jeff. I was—just a social amenity. In other circumstances, I never would have considered it. But I was so alone, with not even *memories* to cling to. I was in a hideous limbo—"

"I understand."

"Now tell me about you, Jeff. I'm so glad you've gone into photography professionally. You should be very happy. Are you?"

"Oh, the shop is working out very well. We're going to have to start thinking about expanding soon, as a matter of fact. Yes," he repeated, "the shop is working out very well."

"You must have moved to a new apartment. I couldn't reach you at the old one."

"No. I still have the apartment but I—I'm living on the Island. Oh, Meg, I don't know how to tell you. I wish I didn't have to. But I do. And I suppose the blunter the better. I'm married. Andrea and I were married in April."

Under the suntan, all color drained from Meg's face. She picked up her wine glass, put it down again, picked it up once more and took a slow sip. She glanced at him for the merest fraction of a second, then averted her eyes as if the sight of him was too painful to contemplate. He watched helplessly as she struggled with her emotions. She finally raised her eyes to his and looked at him searchingly, as if to be certain it was not an ill-conceived joke. His tormented eyes gave her the answer.

When she spoke, her lips hardly moved and her voice was nearly inaudible. "I see. It never occurred to me that. . . ." The sentence trailed and died.

"Meg. I thought you were—I thought you were not coming back—ever. Timmy was in trouble. He seemed to need a stronger hand than Andrea could supply. I don't know—it seemed life was just putting one foot in front of the other anyway. Without you, there wasn't any meaning to anything. The one area of my life that wasn't a total blank was Timmy. I thought if I could help him—"

"I see," Meg repeated. "I guess I shouldn't have looked you up. I've only caused trouble for everyone, myself included. If I hadn't found you again, I wouldn't have known what I was missing, would I?" She smiled a dark, bitter smile.

She rose from the table. Jeff pulled her back into her chair with fierce urgency. "Meg! Wait a minute. You don't know what you're talking about. I'll tell Andrea what's happened. She'll understand—I know she will. She's known all the time how I felt about you."

Meg shook her head. "But you cared enough about her to marry her. I don't want to be responsible for—"

"Meg, for God's sake! She and I are both miserable—you're not breaking up anything—it's already broken! It has been, almost from the day we married."

Meg rose again, this time determinedly. From her handbag, she took a small notepad. "This is my phone number, Jeff. If Andrea *is* willing—if things work out so that you're free, I'll see you again. But please don't call me until then."

"Don't you think you're being a little rigid, Meg? Consider the circumstances when I married her. I thought you were dead!"

"We can't build anything solid on someone else's unhappiness, Jeff. Maybe I am being harsh and straitlaced. But I can't help the way I feel. I'm sorry."

She turned quickly and tried to find the outer door through a blur of tears. Frantically, Jeff signaled the waiter for the check and flung a bill on the table. But by the time he reached the street, Meg had disappeared.

# Chapter 33

It was almost midnight by the time Jeff reached Rosehill, and Andrea was asleep. He went into her room and turned on the dim dresser lamp, then walked to the bed and shook her shoulders gently.

"Andrea. Wake up, please. I've got to talk to you."

"Wha—what?" She sat up in bed, groggy and disoriented. "What in hell you mean, coming in here middle of the night waking me up?"

"I've got to talk to you, Andrea. Please get up and come downstairs."

"Go to hell. You're crazy." She turned over and promptly fell asleep again.

He could not rouse her. At last, trying to be philosophical, he turned out the light and left the room. In her condition, the conversation would probably have been futile. Tomorrow he would try to get home early.

The next morning, he left a note on Andrea's dresser, saying he would be home early and needed to talk with her. When he got home shortly after six, Andrea was in the living room, not the less formal library. She was wearing a flowing black caftan and her hair was swept up sleekly. She looked very beautiful.

"I've asked Janie to bring our drinks in here tonight," she said graciously, as one might greet a congenial but not intimate friend. "I hope that's agreeable."

Jeff put his briefcase on the lacquered table and sat

down on the end of the sofa. Janie came in with the pitcher of drinks and silence ensued while she poured one for each of them and left.

"Andrea," said Jeff stiffly, "I don't quite know where to begin—"

"I believe," she said wryly, "the usual place is at the beginning."

"Yes. All right . . . yesterday afternoon, in the shop, I was told someone was waiting to see me. I went downstairs and—Andrea, it was Meg."

She took a swallow of her drink and a long drag from her cigarette. Then she looked at him and smiled. "Who?" The question was a polite social inquiry.

"Meg Gardner, Andrea. Don't play games—you know who I'm talking about."

She finished her drink and poured another, spilling part of it on the table. Jeff realized then she had started her drinking earlier in the day. "Well," she said flatly, "that *is* news. How did Miss Gardner escape drowning in the waters of the Caribbean?"

He looked at her. He had imagined many reactions from her, but not this display of controlled sarcasm. He ignored it and answered her question.

"It's a long story, but to make it short, she was picked up by two men in a boat, presumably smugglers. They got her back to Miami, but she was suffering from amnesia. She's just now beginning to pull out of it."

"How did she get back to New York?"

"She was brought here by a businessman. She works for him. As a sort of—social secretary."

Andrea laughed softly. "Do you expect me to believe that? And did she really con you into believing it? Oh, Jeffie, you're more naive than I thought you were."

"Of course I believe it—why would she lie about it?"

She countered his question with another. "Why would a businessman bring a social secretary all the way from Miami? She was probably shacking up with him, he dropped her, and she was forced to get in touch with you."

He went to her, pulled her up from the sofa and shook her furiously. "Don't you ever say anything like that about Meg again, do you hear me? You don't know her. I do."

She writhed out of his grasp, reached for her glass and refilled it in silence. Finally, she turned back to him. "All right, Jeff. Have it your way. Only don't get so excited. Can't we discuss this in a civilized fashion?"

He sat back down, his fists clenched into knots. "I hope so."

She spoke calmly and very quietly. "There's no big problem. You didn't get the little country girl out of your system, so you'd like to continue your fling with her for awhile. What's the big deal? Just try to be discreet about it, for Timmy's sake."

He breathed deeply for a moment. "I'm afraid you don't understand, Andrea. I wouldn't have arranged this conversation to tell you I wanted to have an affair. I don't want a 'fling' with Meg. I want to marry her. I'm asking you to give me a divorce."

With sudden ferocity, she flung her glass across the room and shattered it against the white wall. He watched the thin rivulets of liquid trickle slowly down the snowy plaster. Then she picked up the small silver bell and rang.

"Janie, there's been an accident. Would you bring another glass for me, please? And don't bother to clean up those pieces now—you can do it later." She turned to Jeff and said, in the same pleasant tone, "If you think I'm going to give you a divorce, you're dead wrong. I'll never give you a divorce."

The contrast between the quietness of her voice and the expression on her face was grotesque, for her eyes were feverish and her cheeks two dots of crimson. He saw that she was seething with hurt and rage.

Janie brought in a fresh glass amidst silence. After she had left, Andrea went on, "You're the first man I ever really cared for. Until I met you, I always had to be concerned about—practical considerations."

"Including my father?"

Her brief laugh was bitter. "Your father most of all."

"But why?"

"Do you know what it's like to lie in bed with someone whose every caress makes you physically ill? And to go through that night after night after night?"

Jeff's voice was strangled. "I wasn't aware my father was a monster."

"He wasn't a monster. He was worse—an impotent old man with bad breath and dentures."

"He produced Timmy."

"Yes, just before the prostate operation, he produced Timmy. The final irony." She poured another drink. "Well, it's all over now. Thank God for that at any rate."

"Andrea, we're—don't go on like this. Maybe we can talk tomorrow—"

She gave him a sly, sidelong glance. "I took care of that."

"What are you talking about?"

She looked at him as if to gauge his hurt against hers, then spoke defiantly. "I took care of it, that's all."

"How did you take care of it?" Jeff was careful to keep his voice bland.

"I set it up right. I don't care if you know. You never gave a damn about me anyway. I thought I could make you care, but—"

"What did you set up, Andrea?"

A perverse pride entered her voice. "All those phone calls to the police about a—prowler."

"Are you saying what I think you're saying? When

you shot through that door, you knew it wasn't a prowler?"

She gave an explosive snort. "Yes! I don't care if you know—there's nothing you can do about it now. That would be double jeopardy. Yes, I knew!"

"My God." Jeff's body sagged. "What are you made of, Andrea? What is a woman like you made of?"

"Do you really want to know? Then I'll tell you something else. I knew about your precious Meg. I knew she was alive months ago."

His voice was a numb whisper. "How?"

"I saw her picture in the paper. About her anmesia. I burnt it before you saw it."

"My God."

"So go to your darling Meg. But you'll go to her as my husband." She stood up abruptly, opened the bar cabinet, took out a bottle of gin and went to the door leading into the hallway. "I'm going to bed now. There's really nothing more to talk about, is there, dear?" When he did not answer, she repeated each syllable slowly. "Is there, dear?"

"No, Andrea," he said in weary surrender. "There's nothing more to talk about."


Toward dawn Jeff slept perhaps an hour. Until then, he lay in the dark and stared at the ceiling. A welter of tormenting emotions assailed him. He felt at moments he was on the verge of insanity. That he had comforted and aided Andrea in what he believed to be her hour of bereavement for his father was one of the most unbearable of his memories.

And a new wave of grief had been released by her disclosure about his father. What poor fools they had both been, to have been taken in by her relentless scheming.

He could not even think of Meg. He was too exhausted to try to fathom how that could ever be resolved. He needed to sleep; if only he could sleep, he would be able to think with a clearer head tomorrow. After hours of tossing, he mercifully dozed off.

When he awakened, the room was no longer black but touched with the first gray of dawn. The damp sheets were knotted beneath him in hopeless disarray. He got out of bed to make an effort to straighten them. Perhaps once he got them smoothed, he could fall asleep for another hour.

But it didn't work, and after a few minutes he knew that he could never rest in this house again. He got up and threw a change of clothes into a suitcase. He wrote a note to Timmy saying that he would soon be in touch with him and slipped it under the boy's door. Then he drove to his East Seventies apartment.

Jeff spoke to a lawyer, and found that Andrea was right about double jeopardy—she could not be tried for the same crime twice. He was also told that getting a divorce without her consent would be a long, painful and inevitably public process. He could not stigmatize Timmy with that.

During his every waking hour, he longed to pick up the phone and call Meg. But he had seen that tempered steel core of strength she possessed. Though he considered her decision dreadfully wrong-headed, he knew he could not change it. He tried to immerse himself in his work, but in the middle of analyzing the composition of a photograph, he would find Meg's face superimposed on the print.

At later times in his life, Jeff would wonder how he had physically survived that period of agony, and could only conclude that man's capacity for self-preservation is unlimited.

Meg did not leave the Fifth Avenue apartment for a week. She sat by the phone day after day and waited for the call that would allow her to begin living again. When Jeff did not phone within that period, she decided that he and Andrea must have agreed to try to make a go of their marriage after all.

She contacted Mr. Cohen, the landlord of her old apartment on the Lower East Side and found that miraculously, he had kept it intact. When she met him to give him a check and pick up the keys, she asked him curiously, "Didn't you think it odd that I just disappeared?"

"Not partic'ly. Happens alla time. I—there was just something about you—I was pretty sure you'd be back."

"It didn't occur to you to contact the police or anyone?"

"Never in a million years would I have thought of it. People in New York—they come and they go. I just thought you'd be back when you got ready to be back."

Meg was touched by the stoic equanimity with which Johnny Pack accepted the news of her leaving. He urged her to keep the suite as long as she needed it, even though she had told him of her hopes for a life with Jeff.

"The company pays for it anyway. Why let it sit empty? Stay."

"No."

He let it drop and changed the subject. "I knew about your amnesia, Peggy. I mean Meg."

"You knew? Why didn't you tell me?"

He shrugged. "What could I have done? I thought maybe you'd rather I didn't mention it."

Meg considered the statement, then nodded. "I suppose so. What could you have done?"

He showed no emotion at all until he got up from the table in the restaurant where they had been lunching. Then he touched her shoulder amost shyly. "If things had been a little bit different—nah. The only thing I regret is the timing. The corporation is straightened out now—we got control of those other companies. I'd be able to spend a lot more time with you now." He cleared his throat. "Well, in the well-known words of what's-his-name, here's lookin' at you, kid. All the luck in the world." Two days later, she got a notice from her bank that five thousand dollars had been deposited in her account.

There was one thing more she must do. She took a noon flight to Atlanta one July day and from there a bus to Martinsville. As the bus driver helped her off with her luggage in the center of the dusty little town, she heard someone behind her speak her name.

"Meg Gardner! My gosh, I thought I was seein' a ghost!"

Her heart leapt. As she turned, she wondered: would the face be familiar? Would she remember?

"Millard Sutton!" He had been a classmate of hers all through high school who lived a few miles outside the city limits.

"I thought sure you was dead, not bein' here for your Aunt Bess's funeral and all." He apparently did not know of her own memorial service.

"No, Millard. But I was real sick for awhile. Too sick to come to the funeral."

She stopped in at Bradley's drugstore and asked if she could leave her luggage there for an hour. There were more exclamations about her sudden reappearance and she explained again that she had been so ill she was unable to let anyone know she was even alive. If they thought her story odd, they were too polite to say so.

She walked to the Martinsville graveyard past hedges full of tiny, fragrant, white blossoms. The smell was a part of her childhood, and brought back with aching sharpness those days of scuffing barefoot along the dusty summer streets.

She went to the family plot, which now contained four rectangular mounds—an uncle she didn't remember, her mother, and now her two aunts. She knelt in front of the large tombstone engraved with the family name.

She did not weep, but remained there quietly for a time, remembering all they had given her and all they had tried to give her. Then she retraced her steps to the drugstore, reclaimed her bag, and Dr. Bradley helped her flag down the next bus back to Atlanta.

## Chapter 34

Sanders had set the clock for five. He wanted to have the car lubed, and he knew from experience it would mean a long wait unless he was there when the garage opened at six. Especially on the day after Labor Day, when everyone was back from vacation and getting into high gear for fall.

When the alarm went off, he began to move about the dark room as quietly as he could, groping for his trousers and socks beside the bed. No use waking Janie—she wouldn't have to be up till eight. And probably not then—recently Miss Andrea hadn't been downstairs till noon or after. Stayed up all night drinking and roaming around the house. Over this long holiday weekend, it had been especially bad. It was a shame, for her own sake and even more for the boy's. Since Mr. Jeff had left, the little fellow looked like he had lost his last friend. Half the time, Miss Andrea didn't seem to know he was even around.

He found one black sock and put it on. Where the devil was the other one? Suddenly, he heard the whinny of a horse. His and Janie's bedroom was just across the courtyard from the stables. Dimly curious, he went to the window and pushed aside the draperies. In the half-light of the breaking day, he could see a figure trying to saddle a horse. When she turned, he saw that it was Miss Andrea with that horse she was so crazy about—the gray gelding, Striker.

It looked like the horse was not in the mood to be

saddled; she was having trouble with the stirrups. Sanders watched her uncertain movements for a few moments and it became clear to him that she was very drunk. She must have been up all night. He'd better try to stop her; it wasn't even daylight.

Hastily, he slipped into his loafers without bothering to find the other sock, raced down the stairs and out the back door. But by the time he reached the courtyard, Miss Andrea and the horse were gone.

He jumped into the big black car, dug the keys from their accustomed hiding place under the mat and wheeled down the lane. It was still so dark that he needed the headlights. The lane curved over a low, rolling hill and sloped easily down into an indentation which could barely be called a valley. A narrow stream snaked its way through the dip and emptied into Mr. Hathaway's duck pond. Because of a long spell of dry weather, the stream was now only a trickle of brackish water. The land flattened here, and offered a good view of the countryside. He stopped the car, got out and looked in both directions. There was nothing to his left except an expanse of pastureland and a grove of scrub oaks, clustered by the dried-up stream. To the right, a patchwork of greening farms which ended at the duck pond. There was no sign of Miss Andrea.

He got back in the car and maneuvered a painstaking U-turn on the narrow road. He had come almost two miles; she couldn't be ahead of him. He was about to shift into forward and give up the search when something entered his field of vision to the right. He jerked his head around and saw Striker bolting wildly out of the grove of scrub oaks, neighing with pain. The horse was limping badly; his right front leg must be broken.

Sanders got out of the car and ran past Striker into the copse of trees, then through them until he came to a small clearing where some landowner or poacher had raggedly axed down most of the timber. He did not see Andrea until he was almost upon her. The tan of her suede jacket and the khaki color of her jodhpurs provided almost perfect camouflage against the cracked buff-clay of the dry stream bed. She lay in a heap, inert and motionless. He thought she must have tried to force Striker to jump the banks and had failed to make it.

He bent over her and tried to lift her as gently as he could, but when he did so, her head fell to one side at a grotesque angle from her body. It reminded him of that marionette he had fixed for Timmy years ago, when one of its strings had broken. Sanders could see that it was useless to try to find a pulse, but he did so anyway, without hope, for several minutes. Then he picked her up and laid her very carefully into the long back seat of the sedan.

After the small, private funeral, Jeff ordered his business manager to sell Rosehill at anything approaching a reasonable price. Janie, Sanders and the groom were given generous severance pay and excellent letters of recommendation. The horses would be disposed of at the next auction, excluding Striker. The gelding's cannon bone was shattered, and he had had to be humanely destroyed.

Jeff brought Timmy to live with him in the city. The boy was bewildered and grieved by the freakish accident which had claimed his mother's life, but he adjusted to the change remarkably well. Jeff introduced him to the Museum of Natural History, and thereafter Timmy visited it almost daily. Inside its vastness, he found healing diversion and a certain degree of tranquility.

The day after Jeff got Timmy settled in, from his office in the photography shop, he dialed the number

Meg had given him. His heart was pounding with the turbulence of his emotions as the phone began to ring. But an operator almost immediately broke in and stated that the number had been disconnected. Hope sank like a stone within him. He replaced the phone in its cradle and sat for a long time with his head in his hands, feeling impotent and hopeless.

Against phenomenal odds, they had been reunited, and now she was lost to him again. Had she left the city, disillusioned by his faithlessness? Had she stayed with Johnny Pack and perhaps gone back to Miami? In this teeming, restless city, where could he even begin to look?

Suddenly he straightened. There was only one possibility, and it was a chance in a million. Grappling with a recalcitrant sleeve of his coat, he ran out of the store and hailed a cab. The driver looked askance at the Lower East Side address. This dude didn't look like he belonged in that neighborhood.

The cab pulled up in front of the dingy brownstone. Jeff thrust a bill at the driver and ran up the steps. He looked at the names on the row of brass mailboxes. 1-A. Gardner. Her name was still there! Either she had come back to her old digs or the present tenants hadn't bothered to change the name. With a shaking hand, he stabbed the buzzer. For a moment, there was no response. Then he heard the sound of a door open, and he pressed his face against the streaked glass of the outer door.

Meg peered into the hallway curiously. She was not expecting anyone, and she never buzzed anyone in unless she knew who it was. She had been pickling peaches—the last of the summer crop. After mid-September, they would have disappeared from the Korean-run fruitstands that dotted the neighborhood. She could see only dimly the outline of a male figure on the doorstep. She moved into the hallway and tentatively cracked the door.

At the moment of mutual recognition, they did not speak. Jeff stepped inside, and they moved into each other's arms. Their coming together was as natural and inevitable as the tide. For a long time they said nothing at all, and when Jeff spoke at last, it was to make one short, declarative statement: "This time it's forever."


Out of respect for Timmy's feelings, they did not marry until the day after Christmas. The wait was long and at times almost unendurable, but they were both sustained by the memory of that first sentence Jeff had spoken in the grimy hallway on East Ninth Street.

Jeff wanted Meg to join him in the photography shop as an assistant but, surprisingly, she declined.

"I don't think so, Jeff. I'd rather keep photography as just a lovely hobby. Besides, I'd like to go back to my social work. Maybe on a parttime basis—I want some time left over for Timmy. But there are an awful lot of Mrs. Gillespies out there, and if I can help them, I'd like to."

In October, they found an airy, high-ceilinged apartment off Central Park West. It was built on two levels, with a large bay window and a fireplace in the living room. On that level there were also three bedrooms. Upstairs was a bookshelf-lined study and a loft bedroom which Timmy fell in love with immediately. Meg spent the late autumn turning it from a pleasing but barren set of rooms into a real home for the three of them.

She found dark, hand-loomed rugs, keeping them area-sized to let the inlaid parquet floors gleam beneath them. Much of the furniture she chose was oak, with the warm, textured patina and the traditional enduring sturdiness of that wood. The walls they had painted a creamy yellow, and she rummaged in antique and thrift shops for rustic copper and brass accessories. When she had finished, Jeff told her it looked like a weathered old house in New England and she accepted that, correctly, as a compliment.

She had bought a magnificent old brass table lamp one afternoon and was struggling along the street with it in her arms. The boxes were not heavy, but very bulky, and she stopped at a newsstand to set them down and readjust them. The photograph on the front of the afternoon tabloid caught her eye and held it unbelieving.

Johnny Pack's face stared up at her from the smudgy black newsprint. She read the caption beneath it: "Mobster Boss Busted." She fished out a coin and put the paper under her arm. When she got home, she dumped the packages and sat down to read.

Everything fell into place with inarguable logic. The article stated that in the wake of the sweeping reorganization which had taken place in April and May, several disgruntled members of the syndicate were "singing." This inside information had enabled the police to arrest and charge the alleged second-in-command, Johnny Pack, with extortion and income tax evasion.

Meg remembered the late-night meetings, the vaguely answered questions, his refusal to give her his phone number. She felt a deep sorrow, for to her Johnny Pack had been a generous and honorable friend. She sighed, put the paper down and began to assemble the lamp.


They took Timmy out for a festive dinner on Christmas Day. They had been a bit worried that he would feel deserted when they went on their honeymoon, but that fear proved ungrounded. Timmy had met a new girl whose family had invited him to spend the remainder of the holidays with them, and he couldn't have been more excited at the prospect.

The next day, immediately following the simple ceremony held in their own apartment, they left for a week's honeymoon in a small, out-of-the-way ski lodge in Maine. They laughed and agreed people would consider it a peculiar choice, for Jeff still was not up to skiing and Georgia-born Meg had never been on a pair of skis in her life.

But they wanted peace. They wanted solitude together. They loved the clear, cold air; they couldn't breathe it deeply enough on the long walks they took. When they came back inside, they were warmed in body and spirit by the roaring fire in the huge stone fireplace of the lodge's central room. The snow, as it happened, was too soft for ideal skiing, and as a result, they had the place almost entirely to themselves.

They ate ravenously the plain, all-American food prepared superbly by an elderly Pennsylvania Dutch woman who had spent the past thirty winters at the lodge. After dinner, they would talk lazily by the fire, sometimes with a hot rum toddy, and then make their way up the rustic birch-log stairs to the pine-paneled room with the big double bed.

The first night they walked into the room, Meg gasped with pleasure when she saw the patchwork quilt that covered the four-poster. "That's the wedding-ring pattern! My grandmother made one for Aunt Emma, for her hope chest. As it turned out, she never needed a hope chest, but I always loved that design."

"Very apropos, too," said Jeff, and took her in his arms.

Without mentioning it, they had each been somewhat fearful that the long, intervening months might have revived the old difficulties in their sexual relationship. But their first night at the lodge, under the quilt, swept those fears away gloriously and forever.

On their final night there, they went upstairs a little before midnight. Jeff opened the door into their room and let Meg precede him. Once he had closed the door she turned eagerly and walked into his arms.

"So. Tomorrow we rejoin the rest of the world." She sighed wistfully.

He kissed her thoroughly, then held her back to take a long look. "I don't mind rejoining the rest of the world, as long as we do it together. Wait a minute—I'll be right back."

He disappeared into the bath and came back with a bottle of Bollinger champagne and two plastic glasses. "Sorry about these glasses, but we're fresh out of silver goblets."

"Where did you get that?"

"Smuggled it up in my luggage. Left it outside the window to chill." He poured the champagne and brought a glass to her. Seeing her blank stare, he said, "Don't you know what night this is?"

She began to calculate. "We came up on the twenty-sixth, so this would be—" She let out a yelp. "Jeff! This is New Year's Eve!"

"Of course, my oblivious bride. Remember where we were a year ago?"

"Oh, Jeff. It—we were on that cruise. Is it possible that was only a year ago? It seems an eternity."

"Yep. It sure does. But that eternity is behind us now. Let's think of the one ahead of us."

She nodded wordlessly. They did not finish the champagne. He led her to the bed, and together they folded down the wedding-ring quilt.